CLOSE-UP

'There has been no brighter arrival on the shady scene since Graham Greene started entertaining,' said the *New Statesman* of Len Deighton in 1962. His first book, *The Ipcress File*, written at the age of thirty-three, was a phenomenal success – chosen by Ian Fleming as his thriller of the year, it sold more than two million copies throughout the world and was filmed by Harry Saltzman (producer of the James Bond films).

Born in London in 1929, Deighton has been at different times an art student, a railway platelayer and a BOAC steward.

He invented an entirely original formula for the spy thriller, introducing with his tough, sardonic, unnamed anti-hero a new kind of secret agent. Four more best-sellers followed *The Ipcress File*: *Horse Under Water* (1963); *Funeral in Berlin* (1964); *Billion Dollar Brain* (1966), of which the *Sunday Times*, praising Deighton as 'a poet of the spy story', said 'the book puts him, with John Le Carré, so far in front of other writers in the field that they are not even in sight'; and *An Expensive Way to Die* (1967). An expert cook, Deighton has written two cookery books, *Action Cook Book* and *Où Est le Garlic?* as well as editing a guide book, *Len Deighton's London Dossier*. In 1968 he published the comic novel *Only When I Larf*, which was filmed. *Bomber*, an anti-war novel of classic dimensions, was published in 1970, and enjoyed immediate and world-wide success. *Declarations of War* and *Close-up*, published in 1971 and 1972 respectively, are his latest works.

By the same author in Pan Books

BOMBER

CONDITIONS OF SALE

LEN DEIGHTON

CLOSE-UP

PAN BOOKS LTD

LONDON AND SYDNEY

First published 1972 by Jonathan Cape Ltd
This edition published 1974 by Pan Books Ltd,
33 Tothill Street, London SW1

ISBN 0 330 23650 4

2nd Printing 1974

*This edition contains a
few editorial changes approved
by the author*

*Made and printed in Great Britain by
Cox & Wyman Ltd, London, Reading and Fakenham*

In the recent past it has become fashionable for writers to use thinly disguised biographical material about 'show-business' figures, but I have not intended to depict any person, living or dead, or any film, institution or corporation, past or present.

LEN DEIGHTON

1 *Today we spend eighty per cent of our time making deals and twenty per cent making pictures.*

Billy Wilder

The heavy blue notepaper crackled as the man signed his name. The signature was an actor's: a dashing autograph, bigger by far than any of the text. It began well, rushing forward boldly before halting suddenly enough to split the supply of ink. Then it retreated to strangle itself in loops. The surname began gently, but then that too became a complex of arcades so that the whole name was all but deleted by well-considered decorative scrolls. The signature was a diagram of the man.

Marshall Stone. It was easy to recognize the hero of *Last Vaquero*, the film that had made the young English actor famous in 1949. He'd sat at this same desk in the last reel, reflecting upon a wasted life and steeling himself to face the bullets. For that final sequence he'd required two hours' work on his face. Now he would not need it.

A lifetime of heavy make-up had ravaged his complexion so that it needed the expensive facials with which he provided it. Around his eyes the wrinkles were leathery and the skin across his cheeks and under his jaw was unnaturally tightened. The shape of his face and its bone structure would have little appeal to a portraitist, and yet its plainness could be changed by the smallest of pads, tooth clamps or hairpieces, or by a dab of colour over the eyes or a shadow down the bone of the nose. Just the blunt military moustache, grown for his latest role, ensured that some of his dearest fans and nearest friends needed a second look to identify him.

Nor had the ageing process provided Stone with more character. Like many of his contemporaries, he'd grown his hair long enough to cover his ears and make a fringe on his forehead. This hairstyle framing his severe face made it difficult to guess what his occupation might be. His clear blue eyes – as bright as a girl's and as active as a child's – might just be a tribute to the eye drops that he put into them. His raven hair suggested the judicious use of dye. His chesty actor's stride could just as well be that of a seaman or an athlete. Only when he spoke was it possible to label him. The classless over-articulated speech that RADA students assumed so well that few of them ever lost its pattern:

'Jasper, are you there, Jasper?'

Jasper – driver, bodyguard and valet – was seldom out of earshot. He came into the room and closed the curtains. A summer storm had darkened the sky. The study had become dim except for the desk lamp which painted a green mask across Stone's face and chopped his bright hands off at the wrists.

'Yes, sir.'

'A letter to post, a cheque for the club and an open cheque so that you can get me some cash.'

'Very good, sir.'

The bank would remain open for him. Stone had not yet grown blasé about the favours that money could provide. He'd told them six-thirty, but they'd wait: they'd learned that artistes had little sense of time. Through the heavy brocade the London traffic could be heard.

'I waste a lot of money gambling, Jasper.'

'You do have bad luck, sir.'

Stone was not a social reformer and yet his servants made him feel guilty. That's why he was secretive about his after-noon naps and about his shopping sprees. He insisted that they knock before opening the doors so that he could be alert and industrious when they came upon him. It was for this reason, too, that he mentioned to them the worries and problems of his working life. As of the moment he was working on a film called *Stool Pigeon*.

'I'm doing the swamp scenes tomorrow. I hope they've fixed up better heating in the dressing-room. Last week I spent four hours under the lamps before getting rid of that pain in my knee. Roger at the gym says that's the classic way to get arthritis.'

The servant didn't reply. Stone read the letter again.

From the desk of
Marshall Stone   Wednesday evening

Dear Peter,
    The idea of a biography of me has come up from time to time but I have always vetoed it. However, a writer of your talent and reputation could bring a whole new dimension to it. Who better to do a star's biography than the man who wrote the very first script of *Last Vaquero*?
    Now, no show-biz crap, Peter, a real warts-and-all portrait, and damn the publicity boys! And not just a book about an actor! A book about the electricians, the camera assistants, the extras, the backroom boys in production offices. In fact, about the way it all comes together.
    Talk to my private secretary, Mrs Angela Brooks, and arrange our get-together as soon as you like.
    The piece you did for your paper last month was damned good and mightily flattering to boot! I can't wait to see what you will do in a whole book devoted to such a humble thesp as,

                                    MARSHALL STONE

He crossed out damned and inserted bloody, hooking the y of 'you' with the loop of its b. There should always be at least one alteration in a letter. It gave the personal touch. He put his signet ring into the hot bubbling wax and sealed both envelopes.

'Is Mr Weinberger here yet?'

'I showed him into the library, sir.'

'Good.' Stone's vocal cords had tightened enough to distort his voice, and he tasted in his mouth the bile that anxiety created. On such sudden visits his agent always brought bad news.

'He has documents with him. He's working on them. He seems content.'

9

Oh my God: documents. 'You gave him a drink?'

'He declined, sir.'

'People always decline, Jasper. You must persuade them.' Stone cleared his throat.

'Very good, sir.'

'Cut along to the bank, then, and be outside at eight-thirty: the Rolls, and tell Silvio I'll have my usual table. I'll probably sleep here tonight. You can tell the servants at Twin Beeches to expect me for dinner tomorrow.'

'Yes, sir.'

Stone closed the roll-top desk, locked it and went to the bathroom.

He did little more than splash cold water on to his face. Then he dried it carefully, so that the warm yellow towel would not be soiled by eye-black. He selected high boots, a faded shirt, and tied a red kerchief at the throat. After looking in the mirror he retied it and put a crucifix around his neck on a fine gold chain. He tucked it into the front of his shirt. It was almost, but not quite, out of sight.

'Viney!' he said as he entered the library. He spread his hands wide apart in an almost oriental gesture of hospitality. For a moment he stood there without moving. Then he walked to his agent and took the proffered hand in both of his.

Weinberger looked like a gigantic teddy-bear that had survived several generations of unruly children. He was tall, but of such girth that his Savile Row suit did little to flatter him. He had a dozen such suits, all of them equally undistinguished except for the cigarette burns that he inevitably made in the right side of the jackets. His hair was unkempt and his club tie was, as always, askew. Under sadly sagging eyebrows his eyes were black and deep set. His nose was large and so was his mouth, which only smiled to show the world that he would endure without complaint the slings and arrows that were his outrageous lot.

It was his desire to be as unsurprising as possible. He succeeded: except to the people who read the fine print in his contracts. His voice had the gruff melancholy that one would expect from such a man.

'Sorry it had to be tonight, Marshall. No real problem: a

formality, really, but it needs your signature.'

Stone did not release the hand. 'It's good to see you, Viney. Damned good to see you.'

'Epitome Screen Classics – that's Koolman's new subsidiary – want TV rights for resale.'

Stone released the agent's hand. 'Do you realize that we only see each other to talk business, Viney? Couldn't we get together regularly – just for laughs, just for old time's sake?'

'I don't know why they let us have that approval clause in the contract. I'd put it in to sacrifice it for something else.' Viney shook his head sadly, 'They left it in.'

'Business! That's all you think about. Have a drink.' Stone cocked his head and nodded, as if the affirmative gesture would change his guest's mind. Back in the days when ventriloquism was a popular form of entertainment, such physical mannerisms had encouraged wisecracks about the cocky little star being seated upon the knee of the doleful giant who was his agent. But these jokes had only been made by people who hadn't encountered Marshall Stone.

'No thanks, Marshall.' He looked at his notes: ' "Three years after completion of principal photography or by agreement." It's only got six months to go anyway.'

'A small bourbon: Jack Daniels. Remember how we used to drink Jack Daniels in the Polo Lounge at The Beverly Hills?'

Weinberger looked around the huge room to find a suitable space for his papers. Arranged upon an inlaid satinwood table there were ivory boxes, photos in silver frames, instruments to measure pressure, temperature and humidity, a letter-opener and a skeleton clock. Weinberger moved some of the objets d'art and used a small gold pencil to mark a cross on both letters. 'It needs your signature: here and here.' He put the pencil away and produced a fountain-pen which he uncapped and then tested before presenting to his client.

Stone signed the letters carefully, ensuring that his signature was the same precise work that it always was.

'Read it, Marshall, read it!'

'You don't want me interfering with your end of it.' He capped the pen and handed it back. 'What movie are we talking about, anyway?'

11

'Sorry, Marshall. I'm talking about *Last Executioner*. So many shows are losing sponsors that they want to network it in the States to kick off the fall season. It looks like the Vietnam War is going to be the only TV show that will last out till Christmas.' Stone nodded solemnly.

'Except for the scene on the boat, I was terrible.'

'They'll want the sequels too. Leo said you gave a great performance. "Marshall gave a sustained performance – conflict, colour and confrontation." You got all three of Leo's ultimates.'

'What does that schmuck know about acting.'

'I agree with him, Marshall. Think of that first script – you built that character out of nothing.'

'Five writers they used. Six, if you include that kid that they brought in at the end for additional dialogue.'

'On TV they'll be a sensation. Leo would like you to do a couple of appearances.' Weinberger watched the actor's face, wondering how he would react. He did not react.

'And it was the kid that got the screenplay credit. For a week's work!'

Weinberger said, 'Serious stuff: the Film Institute lecture for the BBC and David Frost for the States – taped here if you prefer – and Koolman would put his whole publicity machine to work. We could get it all in writing.'

'They'll sink without a ripple, Viney.'

'No, Marshall. If the TV companies slot them right they could be very big. And Leo is high on the spy bit at the moment.'

'I don't need TV, Viney, I'm not quite that far over the hill: not quite.' Stone chuckled. 'Anyway, they'll die, a successful US TV show must appeal to a mental age of seven.'

'A lot of TV viewers don't have a mental age of seven. I like TV.'

'No, but the men who buy the shows do have a mental age of seven, Viney.' Stone poured himself a glass of Perrier water and sipped it carefully. He knew that the contract was just an excuse. His agent's real purpose was to talk about TV work.

'Now come on, Marshall.'

'Screw TV, Viney. Let's not start that again. All you have to do is nod and then take your ten per cent. I've got just one career but you've got plenty of Marshall Stones in the fire.' He smiled and held the smile in a way that only actors can.

Weinberger was still holding his fountain-pen and now he looked closely at it. The very tips of his knuckles were white. Stone went on, 'Like that blond dwarf Marshall Stone, named Val Somerset! You made sure he got his pic in the paper having dinner with the Leo Koolmans at Cannes. Good publicity, that: national papers, not just the trades. Is that why you didn't want me to go along when *Snap, Crackle, Pop* was shown there?' Stone said the words in a low pleasant voice, but he allowed a trace of his anger to show. He had been bottling up that particular grievance for several months.

'Of course not.'

'Of course not! Have you seen what he does in *Imperial Verdict*? The whole performance is what I did in *Perhaps When I Come Back*. Three people have mentioned it – a straight steal.'

Weinberger went across to the sofa, opened his black leather document-case and put the papers into it.

Stone said, 'Will you please answer me.'

Weinberger turned and spoke very quietly. 'That kid isn't going to take any business from you, Marshall. You are an international star, Val's name's not dry in *Spotlight*. He's getting a tenth of your price.'

Stone walked across to his agent, paused for a moment, shook his head regretfully and then gripped Weinberger's arm. It was a gesture he used to pledge affection. 'Sometimes I wonder how you put up with me, Viney.'

Weinberger didn't answer. He had been close to Stone for a quarter of a century. He'd learned to endure the criticisms and insults that were a part of the job. He knew the sort of doubts and fears that racked any actor and he knew that an agent must be a scapegoat as well as confessor, friend and father.

In human terms Stone might have benefited from a few home truths. He might have become more of a human being, but such tactics could cripple him as an actor.

And for Weinberger, Stone was by no means 'any actor', he was a giant. His Hamlet had been compared with Gielgud's, and his Othello bettered only by Olivier. On the screen he'd tackled everything from Westerns to light comedy. Not even his agent could claim that they all had been successful but some of his performances remained definitive ones. Few young actors would attempt a cowboy role without having *Last Vaquero* screened for them, and yet that was Stone's first major role in films. Weinberger smiled at his client. 'Forget it, Marshall.'

Stone patted his arm again and walked to the fireplace. 'Thanks for sending that *Man From the Palace* script, Viney. You have a fantastic talent for choosing scripts. You should have become a producer. Perhaps I did you no favour in asking you to be an agent.' Again Stone smiled.

'I'm glad you like it.' Weinberger knew that he was being subjected to Stone's calculated charm but that did not protect him from its effects. Just as confidence tricksters and scheming women do nothing to conceal their artifice, so Stone used his charm with the abrupt, ruthless and complacent skill with which a mercenary might wield a flame-thrower.

'Do you know something, Viney: it might be great. There's one scene where I come in from the balcony after the fleet have mutinied. The girl is waiting. I talk to her about the great things I've wanted to do for the country . . . It's got a lot of social awareness. I'm the man in the middle. I can see the logic of the computer party and the trap awaiting the protestors. It's got a lot to say to the kids, that film, Viney. Who's going to play the girl?'

'Nellie Jones can't do it, they won't give her a stop-date on *Wild Men, Wild Women* and they are four weeks over. Now I hear they're testing some American girl.'

'American! Haven't we got any untalented inexperienced stupid actresses here in England, that they have to go to America to find one.' Stone laughed grimly; he had to play opposite these girls.

Weinberger smiled as if he'd not heard Stone say the same thing before. 'I told them how you would feel. You'll only consider it if the rest of the package is right. But I didn't say that a new kid wouldn't be OK. If the billing was right.'

'Only me above title?'

'That's what I had in mind,' admitted Weinberger.

'Perhaps it would be better like that.'

'No rush, Marshall. Let's see what they come up with: we have the final say.'

'It's a good story, Viney.'

'It was a lousy book,' warned Weinberger.

'Eighteen weeks on the best-seller list.'

Weinberger pulled a face.

'You miserable bastard, please have a drink.' Stone held up the stopper of a cut-glass decanter.

'It makes me careless and you fat.'

'A tiny one?'

'OK, Marshall, if you need the reassurance, pour me a pint of your best scotch. But I won't drink it.'

'You're an obstinate old sod.' Stone put the stopper back into the decanter.

'That's why you need me to represent you. I really don't mind being disliked.'

'And I do?'

'Yes, you do.'

Stone chased a block of ice with a swizzle stick. 'It's good, the deal we made for *The Executioner*?'

'It's the most anyone ever got from Leo Koolman for that kind of package.'

'I'll send Leo a little present. Perhaps a first edition, or cuff-links.'

'No.'

Stone looked up in surprise. Weinberger said, 'It will make him wonder if we've put one over on him.'

'You're a devious bastard, Viney.' Stone toasted him before drinking.

Weinberger smiled. 'In Perrier water?'

Stone nodded, and sipped at the water. Then he put the glass down and tightened the knot of his neckerchief before consulting his gold Rolex. Once such a watch had been the prime ambition of every film actor. Now kids like Somerset flaunted Micky Mouse timepieces that anyone could afford. 'Let's go to dinner, Viney.'

Weinberger recognized it as Stone's way of taking his leave.

He said, 'I've got a wife and dinner waiting. Another hour and both will go cold on me.'

'Yes, phone Lucy. She must come too. My God, how long since I last saw Lucy.'

Weinberger smiled.

'No, seriously.'

'Off you go, Marshall. I'll just use the phone and be off. I'll let myself out.'

'Ring for anything you want.' Stone touched some of the tiny roses that he'd brought up from his country garden that morning. He missed the garden when work forced him to stay in his London flat. 'Will you take the roses with you; for Lucy with my love.' Weinberger nodded. Stone was reluctant to leave without being quite sure that his agent did not bear a grudge for his peevish outburst. It was one of his most awful – and most unfounded – fears that Weinberger would refuse to work with him any more. Or, worse, that Weinberger might deliberately go slow on Stone's representation while pushing some other client.

'It was good to see you, Viney, it really was.' He paused long enough in front of a mirror to be sure his hair looked right. Then, still smiling to Weinberger, he let himself out through the carved double-doors that had once been part of a Mexican church.

Weinberger heard Stone greet someone outside in the hallway. A girl's voice replied. Then he heard the front door of the apartment close and soon after that the sound of the doors of the Rolls and then its motor as it accelerated along Mount Street.

Weinberger looked around the room. It had hardly changed since a fashionable decorator had designed it almost ten years before. The colour scheme was pink and blue-grey and even the collection of snuff-boxes had been selected so that those colours predominated. An appearance of spontaneity had been achieved by the big bowls of cut flowers and the casual placing of the footstools and the cushions, and yet these had been ordained by the designer. The three silk-covered sofas were still arranged around the fireplace in the same way. Even the

16

expensive illustrated books and the silver cigarette-box and lighter were the same ones in the same positions.

Weinberger helped himself to a cigarette and lit it before dialling the president of Koolman International Pictures Inc. It was some time before the agent was given a chance to talk, but finally he was able to say, 'Well, I agree, Leo, but an actor must make his own decision about a thing like this. You don't want him blaming you after, and I don't want him blaming me.'

Again there was a speech by Koolman, then Weinberger said, 'All actors are frightened of TV, they think it means they are on the decline. Especially a series – Marshall would certainly do a one-shot for you, or a spectacular, but an option for twenty shows is too many. Let me tell Marshall it's ten. After the first few it will either be such a success that he'll go along, or be such a failure that you won't want more than five.'

Again Weinberger listened. Then he said, 'OK, Leo, and I'd like to show you some girls to play the wife . . .' silence, then, 'Well, yes, and I wouldn't mind that either,' he laughed. 'Goodbye, Leo, and thanks.'

Jasper switched off the tape-recorder and looked at Marshall Stone. The actor got to his feet and smoothed his tight slacks over his thighs. The girl looked up at him, but her face was expressionless.

'Bloody Judas,' said Stone finally. 'He takes ten per cent of my gross income . . .' he turned to the girl, '. . . gross, mark you, not net. It's a bloody fortune.' She nodded. 'And he plots against me in my own home.' He turned to Jasper, 'Pity you couldn't fix it so we could hear the other end.'

'Yes, sir.'

'OK, Jasper. Goodnight. I'll drive Miss Delft home.'

'Goodnight, sir.' Jasper closed the tape-recorder and put it away before going out. As soon as the door closed the girl got to her feet and put her arms round Stone's neck. 'We can't go on meeting like this,' she said, and giggled.

'Seriously,' said Stone, 'you're the only one I have. You're all I live for, darling.'

'I know,' said Suzy Delft.

17

2

*What does [Upton] Sinclair know about anything?
He's just a writer.*

Louis B. Mayer

1949

'All my brother ever wanted to do is make this a better town.'

The taller of the two men fingered the lock of the safe and turned to face the angry young cowhand. 'Wait a minute, boy. Americans built this town with bare hands and know-how: anyone who don't like it here can go back to where they come from.'

The young cowboy leaned across the banker's desk and spoke in the manner of a man trying hard to control his temper, 'Did you ever walk as far your own ranch-house, Mr Sanderson? Did you ever see what kind of shacks those Mexicans live in, did you?'

'Would,' explained the banker, 'but I just can't stand the smell.' He smiled.

They both turned as a sound of gunfire and galloping horses grew louder. Half a dozen horsemen galloped past, firing six-guns into the air. The young cowboy said, 'Seems like you might be taking yourself a long deep sniff.'

Baxter kicked open the doors of the light-trap because he was balancing two thick-shakes and my pastrami on rye: a Hollywood breakfast! I used my thumbnail to prise the lid off the shake carefully, so as not to spill it. Around the cardboard lid, serpentine coils of film spelled out 'San Fernando Valley Drugstore established 1934'. I flicked it as far as the front row of seats. Some days I could hit the screen. I always sat at the very back of the viewing theatre alongside the glass panel of the projection room. The big fans were there, so I could ignore the 'No Smoking' signs without worrying about top brass wandering in to sniff and see why the red light was on. Baxter unwrapped my straws and arranged the hot sandwiches and dill pickle on a paper plate. He was flustered. Normally he would have ducked under the projection beam, but now the mayor of the township was only one inch high as he stamped around on Baxter's forehead.

'You're in the light, Baxter.' He nodded but he hadn't heard me. I wondered why I'd put up with him for five years, but in 1944 only dopes like Baxter and layabouts like me had escaped the Army.

'You're in the light,' I said again.

'They are not renewing your contract, Peter.'

We both knew I didn't have that sort of contract. I was on monthly salary and that's all they had to give me to say goodbye.

I started on the sandwich. 'Every day I tell you, no lettuce. Every day!'

It wasn't really unexpected. I was fighting a desperate rearguard action to protect my script against a 'creative producer'. That's always a mistake, but in 1949 it was a fatal one.

'McCann, the cop on Gate Three, told me. There's an envelope waiting for you when you check out. The girl from accounts told him what was in it.' Things were tough all over: the mayor was being held down on Baxter's chest by three cowboys, and when Baxter moved they rippled.

I ate only the meat out of the sandwich. I put the thickshake under my seat and got up. It was a bright idea to put fascist-style arguments into the mouths of my heavies, but like so many of my ideas it was sadly mistimed.

Baxter said, 'It was a great gesture, Peter. And on your kind of salary an unmarried guy can afford a gesture now and again.' I nodded. He said, 'You could talk to the Guild, but you'll be grabbed by Warner's, or Paramount, you see. You'll maybe double your take-home pay. It's the best thing that's happened to you.' He had a big smile fixed on his face and for a moment I was tempted to see how long he could hold it, but I remembered the good times.

'OK. I'll phone Jim tomorrow and tell him you are some kind

19

of genius. He'll probably find you some other hack.'

'He will if you ask him, Peter. He respects you.'

'Sure.' I didn't turn the lights up. I groped along the seat backs and out of the double-doors of viewing theatre number eight without saying another word. I suppose Baxter told the projectionist to stop showing *Last Vaquero*, or maybe it's still running. Anyway, it was a lousy script. Maybe the first draft I'd written would have made a decent film but the rewrite had got too much stuff about hard work and truth bringing success. That took care of any irony that I'd tried to bring to it. Koolman Studios had a standing order about 'values' and I'd been crazy to try to get by it, let alone to add a few ideas of my own.

I didn't realize that it was going to be the last time I walked through the Koolman Studios for over fifteen years. I blinked in the daylight and went past the big sound stages to the writers' building.

A tractor train with pieces of a Hawaiian village rumbled past. The kid driving it shouted something to me and I waved. A group of men in heavy make-up and silk dressing-gowns were standing outside the door of Number Two stage, smoking desperately. They looked up when the kid shouted and they looked at me. Already I felt a twinge of the paranoia that an investigating subcommittee had brought to Hollywood.

It was still only 8.45 A M on a February morning but the sun was bright enough to burn your eyes out. I called into my office to collect a couple of shirts and a half-completed short story. The typewriter and the ten-dollar fan belonged to the management.

From my window I could see the empty lot where walls and stairs were stored. Beyond it there was the block that housed the accountants and the lawyers. Significantly, theirs was a two-storey brick building with fitted carpets and air conditioning; the writers' 'block' was two timber sheds linked by a dimly lit corridor that was part of film storage.

Around the Koolman layout there was a high white stucco wall surmounted with rows of barbed wire and broken glass, but the executive building faced inwards to bright green lawns above which hovered white sprinkler mist. I took the forbidden short-cut to the main gate. It was time I lived dangerously. I passed Leo Koolman – the Studio's whizz-kid – and my producer Kagan Bookbinder. They were sitting in Bookbinder's brand-new convertible. It was bright red, with a grinning chromium front that people who were still on the waiting-list for new cars called 'Japanese Admirals'. The car radio was singing quietly.

Bookbinder was trying to remember how to look embarrassed, but then decided I'd not had my news yet. He was a tough-looking bastard, like an extra for the desert island set that had been in constant use since Pearl Harbor day.

Leo Koolman was a vain kid with a perfect suntan and a Hawaiian shirt with red and orange flowers on it. In those days he was tipped as the only person with the youth, drive and experience to get the studio out of the jam it was in. As one of his first victims I still find it difficult to admire his judgement.

Koolman said, 'Do you know the nominees?'

'The Academy Awards,' Bookbinder explained. 'They weren't on the early bulletin. We're waiting for the nine o'clock.'

'*Hamlet*,' I said, 'Laurence Olivier.'

'You're guessing,' Koolman accused. He was hoping that I wasn't just guessing. A British winner would automatically mean a rise in the Stone stakes.

'Who else?' I said cockily. 'Dan Dailey, Clifton Webb?'

'You could be right,' admitted Bookbinder, smiling and bull-shitting to the end.

Koolman wasn't so admiring. 'All writers are supposed to use Gate Three.'

I smiled to both of them and kept walking.

'You think Olivier for best actor?' Koolman called.

'And Shakespeare will get "story and screenplay".'

The nine A M newscast gave the nominations as I'd predicted: Dan Dailey, Clifton Webb, Lew Ayres and Montgomery Clift. Seven weeks later Olivier got his Oscar. Leo Koolman was heard to describe me as psychic but he didn't come offering me a seer's job. Perhaps because Shakespeare lost out to John Huston.

Olivier was an easy guess. The previous year – in a tussle

with Colman, Peck, Garfield, Powell and Redgrave – he might have been given a tougher run for his money but there was a growing feeling that Hollywood had been kissing its own backside for too long. *Hamlet* was a fine opportunity to break the tradition that only US productions got the award.

In spite of their accents, at least these limeys spoke some kind of English, and no one could say that the bard was a commie. The 'best actor' was foreign, but at least he was a 'sir' with three previous nominations behind him. It was on this ripple of reckless xenophilia that Leo Koolman launched Marshall Stone to his place in cinema history.

News of neither my genius nor my prescience had spread to script departments of the other studios. Whether I was blacklisted or merely redundant I never found out, but after nearly three months of explaining my screen credits and the ones that got away, I nursed my old Ford back to New York in easy stages.

I hadn't liked New York in 1944 and I didn't like it all over again in 1949. I wrote indifferent advertising in the copy department of a Madison Avenue agency for three months until my air conditioner went out of action in late August. A decision I had been deferring for several weeks was made easier when the agency merged and I was the 'last in' that a management agreement had promised would be 'first out'.

It was only after I got back to London that my luck changed. I wrote a biography – *Stanislavsky: A Man and His Method*. It was a labour of love financed by a job as a bartender. It was a book-club selection. I followed it the following year with a history of Italian opera that was little more than a compendious reference book. Then, after two years hard work, I had a lucky success with my biography of Caruso. Soft-cover rights enabled me to pay off the mortgage on my small house in Islington, and serial rights put something into the bank and got me a contract as entertainment editor on a posh Sunday newspaper.

Many many years ago, my wife had been married to Marshall Stone. We met at a party not long after her divorce. She recognized my face from my days in Hollywood, and three years later a middle-aged author had breakfast in

22

bed with a brunette lawyer before walking round the corner to be married.

So the three articles I did for the paper: 'Cinema tomorrow, overture or finale?' perhaps over-emphasized the importance of Marshall Stone's contribution to the post-war history of the cinema.

Several times I'd mentioned to my publisher the idea of doing a book about the superstar phenomenon. He insisted that only Stone's life had all the ingredients such a book needed: the overnight fame, the ostentatious wealth, the immense talent evident and so sadly squandered. The fact of having done that first Stone script and of being married to his one-time wife gave me all the cards. And yet it also made the task impossible. To write about the other man is difficult enough but when that man is Marshall Stone . . .

There had been times when I wondered if our two daughters – six- and eight-year-olds – would grow up disappointed at a father who had so nearly been Marshall Stone, but one meeting with the grown-up son of Stone and Mary dispensed with that one.

I still would not have gone ahead if Mary hadn't encouraged me. Primarily I was keen on the project because I believed Stone to be a rare talent. It was only after I began work on the book that I discovered other motives within myself. I wanted to revisit the world I'd walked out of, that sunny day on the Koolman lot. And to some extent I wanted to know more about the life that my wife had exchanged for mine.

There was no mistaking the address the film company had given me. Pantechnicons, generators, a couple of limousines with dozing chauffeurs left no doubt that this was where *Stool Pigeon* was being shot. Edgar Nicolson – the producer – had leased this condemned house in Notting Hill Gate for five months at fifty pounds per week. It was a high rent for a derelict London slum but by using the lower half of it as production offices and building his sets floor by floor as they were needed he could save the cost of going into a studio. Offices, projection theatre, workshops, recording facilities and space to do the same film in one of the big studios would have cost him ten times the money. However, the big cars and luxury dressing-rooms were still mandatory. The industry had learned how to tighten its belt, but it still had quite a gut.

These all-location films were more relaxed than studio productions. There was an atmosphere of goodwill and informality among the crews. The big studios had too many elderly technicians watching the clock so that they could rush back to their semi-detached around the corner. These location crews were the industry's Foreign Legion. Most of them had spent their lives travelling from unit to unit. They drank, screwed and gambled like legionnaires too. In the hallway one of them asked me for a light. He was a fuzzy-haired man in denims. I remembered him from a decade ago when I had been on my very first assignment for the newspaper. He'd been a twentieth assistant director then: now perhaps he was eighteenth. I remembered him telling me what was wrong with Godard and Fellini in exact and lucid detail. He was right but it hadn't done him much good. Did he still dream of becoming a director, and did he still believe that this was the way to do it?

He said, 'And next week Richard is going to do the explosions right there in the garden.'

'That should give the neighbours something to talk about.' Two prop men and some grips pushed past us with a plaster section of a battle-scarred Buddha.

We watched them huffing and puffing up the stairs. He said, 'The bangs: yeah, but we've got permission. Dick Preston is quite a character.'

Richard Preston was a director from TV. Someone at Koolman International had decided that, since youngsters made up the bulk of the audience, kids should make the movies. As a business philosophy it would hand Disney to the adolescents and the computer industry to the computers.

'They're shooting on the roof today, Mr Anson. Wait on the top landing if the red light's on.' He took a call-sheet from his pocket. 'You've got Suzy Delft doing shot number 174,' he grinned, 'for the fifteenth time.'

'It's her first day on the set?'

'I think it's her first day anywhere.'

'Is she going to be all right?'

He grinned, 'The greatest little piece in the business, and for half a page and a photo in your rag – she'd do it!'

'Where's the big man?'

'Marshall Stone – he's gone to the Test Match.'

'He's on the call-sheet.'

'Yeah! Fixed it with the director. After the girl's done, there are a couple of pick-up shots with Jap soldiers. We'll finish early. It's a slack day.'

'Where's publicity?'

'Next landing, he's in there, no one with him.'

'Ta.'

The unit publicist had found a nice little office. On a cork board behind him there were a dozen stills pinned up in sequence. On another wall there were the Press clippings that had so far appeared. Mostly they were in the fan mags and trade journals: about one hundred column inches in all. The biggest of the clippings included a photo of Marshall Stone relaxing in a canvas chair. One cowboy boot was flung carelessly over the arm of it and the stills man had angled the shot to include the star's name stencilled on its canvas back. Stone was smiling a wry compulsive grin that made you sure that success had come upon him with the unexpectedness of a traffic accident. I read the final para of the piece.

'The cinema is my life' said Marshall just before I took my leave. He gave the shy smile that tells his friends that he's talking of things that are sacred to him. He said, 'Once I'm involved with a part I just can't leave it, I just can't. If I have a fault it's being too concerned with the craft of acting. Perhaps Larry or Johnny [*Olivier and Gielgud – Ed*] don't need to put in the hours I put in. But we ordinary mortals have to run fast to keep up with such strolling players.' I don't think Marshall Stone need worry as far as a few million movie-goers are concerned.

'Did you write this crap?' I asked the unit publicist. He grinned.

'Can I have a copy?'

'What's the catch?'

'For research.'

'As a bad flack's handiwork?'

'I wouldn't do that to you, Henry,' I said. 'We've both got to live with the industry.'

'In the immortal words of Sam Goldwyn, "Include me out". This is the last picture I'll do as publicity man.'

'Do you know, Henry, you said that to me when you were doing that film at Ealing.'

'I might surprise you.'

'Yes, you might go to Spain and write one of the great novels of the decade: send me a crate of Tio Pepe.'

He passed me a fresh copy of the fan mag containing his phoney interview. I put it into the red folder that I had marked 'Marshall Stone'. It was the only thing in it.

'Where is it all going on?'

'The roof.' He reached for some mimeographed biographies that were stacked near the duplicating machine. Suzy Delft, Edgar Nicolson the producer, Richard Preston the director. 'I've run out of Stone's but I'll send you one. Help yourself to any of the stills you want.'

On the top of the pile was a large shiny photo of the director, dressed like a Red Indian squaw and posed as if screaming directions through a megaphone.

The Prestons in the industry were making so much noise that every magazine and newspaper I opened, and TV too, was talking about the great youth revolution that had taken over the movie industry. Well, youth had taken over the movie industry like Negroes had taken over the electronics industry. There were some, seated near the door and always busy, convincing bystanders that integration was here. But just as the mandatory Negro actors were still only getting feature billing, so the kids who were supposed to be running the film industry were getting their money from the same old big daddies who have been running the movies since movies were old enough to speak.

On this production Koolman had put old Edgar Nicolson around Preston's neck but the kid was giving them quite a run for their money. Whether he'd get a chance to repeat his fun and games was another matter. There had been sixteen re-writes on this script, and that was the official count! The director seldom looked at the latest version and his continuity girl had been told that avant-garde films are fragmented, by which Preston meant that each day's shooting was best invented the previous night. It wasn't a concept his producer found easy to adapt to. Twice Preston had been fired. The major reason for both reinstatements was that only Preston believed that the existing footage could be fitted together to make a coherent whole.

They were filming on the roof amid a jungle of tropical plants. I watched Suzy Delft walk through a shot in which she took a flower from a bush and smelled it. She moved in that stilted way that models do, pausing each time she moved an arm or leg. It was the height of professionalism for a stills photo but in the viewing theatre it could look like Keystone Cops.

Preston talked to his cameraman and they decided to move one of the brutes. Heaving the arc light into its new position took several minutes, and the script girl brought out her portable typewriter and began to hammer at the continuity sheets. Suzy Delft sat down on a prop barrel until the fuzzy-haired assistant came back with a cup of tea and the sort of bacon sandwich that only location caterers can make. Then Preston decided that he could print the last one after all. 'The two-shot,' he called.

Suzy Delft groaned and gulped her tea. Her face was familiar, I'd seen her in bra ads and beer commercials. She was one of a dozen girls that Leo Koolman described as his discoveries. There was a tacit agreement among show-biz writers that the *droit de seigneur* of movie moguls died with the Hollywood czars. But if anyone could give that tradition the kiss of life, Koolman could, and Suzy Delft would not be the first one to get it, even if she was regularly seen at premières and parties with Marshall Stone.

There were several theories about how Suzy Delft broke into films. Journalists liked to believe it was due to the headlines she got from a mangled Marxist quote during the most fashionable of last year's political riots. Girls seemed to prefer the story about her surrendering to Koolman in exchange for a leading role. Romantics had their story about how she starred in dozens of blue movies before coming above ground. These were the sort of stories that the world insists upon attaching to girls like Suzy Delft, for she looked not only as beautiful as an angel but twice as innocent. Without her rumoured depravity her face was a tacit reproach to all of us. Even for the boy who brought her tea she was able to spare more than a brief thank you, and she hung on to every word of his stuttered reply.

Suzy Delft was a montage of her own aspirations. Her half-closed eyes were Dietrich and her half-open mouth Garbo, while the stiff-limbed gaucherie of every movement was Mary Poppins. Her hands were held away from her sides and her fingers stretched like a wooden doll. Her dark hair was pulled tight and fastened in pigtails. Her tomboy toothiness was also part of the role she played both on stage and off. She was a schoolgirl – a stunningly beautiful one – on the verge of sexual awakening; at least, that's how the Koolman people were building the publicity. Her poster was being drawn by the same man who'd done those cuddly Disney animals.

Her agent was on the set watching her. Jacob Weinberger was one of the best-known flesh peddlers in the business but I wouldn't say he was popular; what agent was. I wondered if he had told her not to run back to her dressing-room between each take. Apart from speeding things up, staying here on the floor exchanging shy words with the crew was creating a good impression upon them. It would help her to know that they were all sympathetic towards her, and every actor needed an appreciative audience, even if it was only a crew.

Stool Pigeon was a war film: ten soldiers in the jungle trying to get through the enemy lines. It was an opportunity for miscegenation, full frontal nudity, cannibalism, sodomy at gunpoint, blasphemy and incest in a story that would otherwise have had to rely upon killing as its sole entertainment. They had shot the previous scene with the sunlight full on Suzy Delft's face. Now they had to do a reverse of the two Negroes against the light. Understandably they were running into lighting trouble.

I was standing near the water tank. With tropical plants

28

concealing its edges the Japanese soldiers were going to wade through it pretending it was swamp. They would have to keep the cameras low to avoid the London skyline but they would have real sky instead of black projection or a painted set.

'Real sky is more important than matching,' Preston told me. I nodded. Preston looked back to watch his lighting cameraman take a reading from the Negro's face. He shook his head. There was still not enough light there. Preston said, 'The stupid bastard. If he'd told me we were heading into problems, we could have shot the girl against the light and had the spades looking into it.'

When they had positioned another brute they couldn't find the slate or the slate-boy. Finally he emerged, bringing a second cup of tea for Suzy Delft.

'Turn over,' said Preston.

'Running.'

'Scene: one eight one, take one,' said the slate-boy.

The first Negro stared into the camera, shielding his eyes from the brute as if it was the sun. 'Cut,' yelled Preston. 'That was good,' he said. 'Let's print that.'

'There was a hair in the gate, Richard,' said the operator, his voice muffled as he examined the inside of the camera.

'What is this: amateur night?'

'Sorry, Richard,' said the lighting cameraman.

'Sorry, Richard,' said Preston sarcastically.

He walked over to the continuity girl and grabbed at her hair in mock anger. She winced with pain. He said, 'If we don't get it by quarter past we'll let the Japs go.'

The four Japanese soldiers were playing bridge on a prop horse carcase. One of them, a fat fellow with a long false moustache, smiled briefly at Preston before bidding.

The producer walked over to me. He said, 'We'll never get to the Jap soldiers today.' Edgar Nicolson was an old crony of Marshall Stone's. Some rumours said that their friendship was the only reason that Stone was doing this low-budget undistinguished production.

There were other opinions. Preston said that Stone had approached him personally and asked to be in it. Stone said that old friends come before a man's career. My information was that Stone had had a two-picture obligation to Koolman International after backing out of the Civil War epic they did last year. He'd already done *Silent Paradise* with Edgar Nicolson and that was in rough assembly. This would fulfil his obligation.

Edgar Nicolson was forty-eight. A short Englishman with a complexion like a raw pork chop. His eyes were bright blue and he had a habit of opening them wide and staring to emphasize the many important things he said. He contrived to dress like a country squire but the cut of his lightweight tweeds, Cardin shirt and Garrick Club tie suggested a successful character actor. His voice was pitched artificially low and it was the voice of an actor. His classless speech was studded with the Americanisms that everyone in the film business picked up, but his clipped articulation would have suited a guards officer briefing his troops for a dawn attack.

'How are you doing, Edgar?' He twitched his nose. To say he always looked as if he'd detected a bad smell was a slander: his nose was as inscrutable as his eyes. It was Edgar Nicolson's tiny mouth that revealed the slightly sour taste that the world had left there. Or perhaps it was only me who saw his mouth like that.

'If producers worked a forty-hour week, I'd finish work every Tuesday evening.' He waved his progress sheets in front of me.

'Your Japs are a bit plump.'

'They usually play tycoons these days.' He used his ivory-handled walking-stick to flick a plastic cup out of his path. 'You know the worst thing about my job?' He didn't pause in case I did know. 'It's like running up a down-escalator. At the end of any given week which I've spent arguing with catering companies about the temperature of the location soup, apologizing to an agent that it should be a Ford – and not a Rolls – that collected his client one morning last week, persuading a shop steward that one muddy field doesn't justify a protective clothing allowance and pleading with New York to give me an extra ten days on their delivery date without changing their release arrangements – after that kind of week, all anyone on the production knows is that nothing happened: it's a negative

30

sort of process being a producer.' He stared at me until I replied.

'Like running up a down-escalator.'

'At least like walking up. This industry likes to pretend the producer is some sort of blimpish general dozing in his HQ while the crews fight the battle. In practice it's the producer taking all the shit so that the crew can work undisturbed.'

'So Stone's watching cricket today.'

He smiled. He wasn't going to be drawn as easily as that. He looked around the roof: they were changing the lighting set up for the third time in half an hour. He called to the runner, 'I'm going for coffee with Mr Anson, tell me when my rushes are ready.'

On our way to the canteen he showed me his mountain shrine. They had assembled the Buddha there; its nose was taller than the painters and property men who swarmed all over it. There was a smell of freshly sawn wood and quick-drying paint as the chipped edges of the plaster mouldings were covered with gold. The room was hot with the rows of bare bulbs, installed so that the carpenters could work through the night. A set dresser experimenting with joss sticks made a thin plume of sweet-smelling smoke. Already it was convincing enough for the hammering to seem like blasphemy and to make the set dressers whisper as they arranged the flowers and offerings before the enlightened one.

'All OK, Percy?' said Nicolson.

The construction manager said, 'It'll be ready by morning but I'll need an extra painter or two on my overtime crew.'

'Let's try and make it one,' said Nicolson. He closed the big mahogany door to muffle the sound of the construction gang. The canteen had once been beautiful but now its moulded ceiling had a pox of damp marks and its paper was torn. With lunch over, the room had been used to park scaffolding and sandbags and pieces of a machine-gun nest.

At the far end of it, the caterers had left urns of coffee, tea and milk, a stack of plastic cups and a tin of biscuits from which all the chocolate ones had been removed. Lunch had been cleared away, apart from a fleet of plastic spoons that had been obsessionally arranged to sail the length of one table, and a steamed potato that had been trodden into the parquet.

'White?'

I nodded. It was an unusual concession to my taste; Edgar usually knew exactly what was best for everyone. He poured coffee for both of us and we sat down. A youth in a dirty apron appeared from the room beyond. He brandished a plate of biscuits: all of them were chocolate.

Nicolson nodded his thanks to the boy. 'How's Mary?'

'She works too hard.'

He nodded. He sorted through the chocolate biscuits. 'My wife thinks I have endless lines of big-titted girls trying to get me on to the couch.'

'I'll tell her about the chocolate biscuits,' I warned him.

'That's all it needs,' he devoured a biscuit hungrily. He took a second one, bit into it and then studied the edge as if trying to understand the secret of its manufacture. 'It's a great life,' he said.

The runner returned. 'There's a lady,' he said to Nicolson.

'A lady!' He did a piece of comedy.

'To see you about casting, she said. She's with Mr Weinberger.'

'I know,' said Nicolson. To me he said, 'An actress: it won't take a couple of minutes.' I nodded. 'Tell her to come down here,' Nicolson told the boy.

'I'm doing a picture called *The Farmer's Wife*, after this one: Gothic horror. I'm looking for people. It's bloody difficult finding a convincing Wisconsin farmer's wife of about thirty-five. Here in London.'

When the woman came in I recognized her. I'd seen her with Richardson and Olivier at the Old Vic at the end of the war. She had that glazed look that actors get when they have to look for work instead of work looking for them. Goodness knows how many auditions she'd been to in her time. I saw her switch herself on as she came through the door. Nicolson changed too, he used a voice that was not his own, as if it was a plastic overall he put on to stop the blood splashing.

'I can't quite remember the name . . .'

'Graham.'

Nicolson laughed. 'Oh, I know your last name, it's your first name I can't remember.' I had the feeling that he would have known her first name if she'd told him that.

'Dorothy,' said the woman.

'Dorothy Graham, of course. I've seen you so many times on the stage, Dorothy. It's wonderful to meet you.'

'We've met before: at a party at Mr Weinberger's last year.'

'Oh, sure, I remember. Smoke?'

'Thank you.' She declined with a movement of an uncared-for hand.

'What have you been doing lately, Dorothy?'

'I did the Albanian secret agent in the TV series "Mayday".'

'I remember it.'

'It wasn't very good but the money was good. Very good, in fact.'

'That was the winter before last, wasn't it. What have you done since then?'

'I'd worked so hard the previous year that I decided to have a bit of a holiday after the series ended.' She said it in a rush, as if she'd said it many times.

'Now, I'm not casting this picture,' said Nicolson, 'because I haven't yet settled the deal. I'm just taking a look at a few people.'

'When would you be shooting, because I do have a few things planned for the coming year.'

'October, November. Probably at Pinewood, no location work or anything. From where you live could you get out to Pinewood each morning?'

'Dear old Pinewood.'

'I'd send a car, of course.'

'Of course.' They left it there for a moment or so, each relishing their role of successful producer and glamorous star.

Nicolson, said, 'It's the story of a woman who is haunted. She sees the past, the things that have happened in this strange old farmhouse, the things that are going to happen. Her husband and the grown-up sons think she's going nuts and then one night this kind of crazy monster turns up. It's a pretty scary movie; hokum, lots of special effects.' He nodded to himself and added, 'And a great part for you, quite different to anything you've done before.'

She tried to think of something appropriate to say. 'It sounds fun. I've never done a horror film. Who will be directing?'

'This is something that still has to be sorted out, Dorothy. I'm just taking a look round, you know.'

She smiled. I remembered her more clearly when she smiled. New York: a wonderful St Joan. And a *Lear* that had nothing except her superb Goneril. 'I will have that cigarette,' she said.

'Sure,' said Nicolson. He got to his feet, grateful to her for lessening the guilt he felt at knowing she was not suitable. She opened her handbag to look for a lighter. It was real leather, a treasure from the days when she was rich and had every prospect of getting richer. Now the leather was scuffed and one corner had been carefully repaired. Nicolson lit her cigarette for her. She had an envelope alongside her in the chair and now she put it on the canteen table. 'I brought these,' she said.

Nicolson tipped the contents of the envelope out on to the table. There were a dozen large glossy photographs. Some were the dreary stills of British films of the 'forties and others were stagey publicity pictures, the definition softened to a point where her face was like a black-lit bowl of rice pudding. The only thing they had in common was that in every one she was very young and very beautiful. We found it impossible not to look at her to compare the reality. Whatever she read in our faces it was enough to make her flinch.

'You take these with you,' said Nicolson. 'As I say, we're not casting yet.'

'I had to come this way,' said the actress. 'I was visiting some friends who live just round the corner.'

'That's swell,' said Nicolson. 'It's lovely to see you again.'

'I like to keep in touch.'

Neither of us spoke until a couple of minutes after she had gone. 'I'll have to see a lot of people before I decide,' he said.

'Yes.'

'It's a special kind of technique, horror films. And anyway, the director is going to want a say in who we use. The wife: that's a feature role we're talking about.'

The unit runner came into the canteen. 'Mr Benjamin says

your rushes will be on the projector in ten minutes, sir. Will you be coming down or will you see them with Mr Preston this evening?'

'I'll be down.'

'And your secretary says to remind you that they are screening the rough assembly of *Silent Paradise* at Koolman International tonight. There was a message from them saying that if Mr Koolman comes on the early plane, he will be at the screening too.'

'OK,' said Nicolson without enthusiasm. 'And Mr Stone?'

'His secretary says he'll be there.'

To me Nicolson said, 'Did either of us think we'd ever be pleading with Eddie to come and see himself starring in a movie?' He sighed. Only Stone's intimates called him Eddie. Often it had a disparaging tone, as if by knowing him before he was rich and famous, the speaker was in a privileged position to criticize him. Even Mary was able to imply that 'poor Eddie' or 'little Eddie' was what she meant when she used his first name.

'Bookbinder must have seen something in him.'

'Sure: Olivier's head on Brando's body. That's what every actor was in 1948.'

'But you don't think so?'

'Wait a minute, Peter. Eddie is bloody good. He has some of Olivier's economy . . .'

'But?'

'Gielgud has perception, Peter. That's why actors envy him.'

'I screened *Last Vaquero* twice last week. Stone is very stiff. Did you ever notice that?'

'He wanted that. He worked on it. Maybe he's not very intellectual, but he's not an instinctive actor: he uses his brains. I saw him acting with some old fellow once and this guy had thought up the business of pulling his ear lobe – he was Italian or something. Eddie said, look like you might pull your ear lobe, even touch your ear, but best of all be a man who is ashamed of this awful ear-pulling and is trying to break the habit. Now that's what I mean by economy. Use that for your book, if you like.'

'Thanks,' I said, although I had the feeling that Edgar Nicolson's anecdote had been related many times to many reporters.

'Ellen Terry said it: act in your pauses.' He arranged the empty plastic cups in front of us. The fleet of spoons was probably a Nicolson. He said, 'The trouble that Preston is having with the girl is the thing you have with all young actors. They only act when they are speaking their lines. But acting is using your mind so that when you do speak, the lines come as a natural sequence of thought and emotion.'

'Getting the lead in *Last Vaquero* made him,' I said. 'Without that, he'd still be hanging around Chasens hoping for a walk-on.'

'And would you believe me if I told you that I nearly got that role, Peter.' He took a pipe from his pocket and filled it. He closed his eyes while he did it and his face and his body gave those little twitches that dreamers show in heavy sleep.

There was electricity in the air that almost forgotten night in 1948. There was no rain or thunder, nor even the silent erratic lightning that so often presages a storm in southern California. Yet Nicolson remembered feeling that the air was charged. He might have ascribed this to his anxiety or to the special tensions of the night, except that the radio reacted to the same disturbance in the air. The San Jorge station had an hour of big-band jazz every night at the same time. That night it was Jimmie Lunceford, and Nicolson remembered how the static had eaten most of the vocal, 'When you wish upon a star.' He could never again hear that melody without going back to that night.

Even today that interstate highway out of San Diego isn't complete. In 1948 there was not even talk of it. The road past the Sunnyside was dark except for the tourist court itself: a yellow floodlight on two moth-eaten palms and a jacaranda tree. The broken vacancy sign was flickering.

It was only after the car lights were off that the mountains could be seen, like huge thunderclouds that never moved on. San Jorge was on the far side of them, ten miles or more along the valley road. When the cops came – just county cops from

San Jorge – the red lights of the two cars could be seen moving down those foothills like the bloodshot eyes of some pre-historic monster slithering across to the Pacific Ocean to slake its thirst. But it was much later that the cops came. When Nicolson arrived no one had even phoned them.

He locked the doors of his car. By the uncertain light of the sign he could see a grey Ford sedan from the Koolman Studios car pool. Beyond it, carelessly parked, was Eddie Stone's new MG. Nicolson wanted to enter the coffee shop as quietly as possible. It was a neurotic desire that could make no difference to the outcome. He tiptoed across the porch but a broken board creaked and the fly screen slapped closed with a sound like a pistol shot. Nicolson had never felt more clumsy both physically and mentally. Stone would have done it all quite differently. A bell pinged as he opened the door. Neon strips lit the place with a harsh blue light. In the centre there was a U-shaped counter with stools. On each side of it there were half a dozen scrubbed wooden tables. One table, near the juke box, was covered with a red cloth and set with ice water, tableware and a menu. Kagan Bookbinder – the producer of *Last Vaquero* – and Eddie Stone were sitting at the table.

A Mexican woman with a stained overall looked out of the service door when she heard the bell. She waited only long enough to make sure that Edgar Nicolson was the man that the others had been expecting.

Bookbinder said, 'Sit down, Edgar.' He got up and reached over the counter to the shelf under it, and he groped to find a clean cup. He poured Edgar Nicolson a cup of coffee and put it on the table in front of him.

Seen through Edgar Nicolson's eyes the scene was static, as memories always are. The air is blue with cigar smoke in a way that it seldom becomes in these tar-conscious days. The men's haircuts are so short as to be almost military and their California sports clothes now seem freakish. Eddie Stone and Nic-olson are wide-eyed kids with long necks and slim hips. Stone has a kiss curl that falls forward across his forehead. Book-binder seems elderly to the two young English actors but in fact he is only four or five years their senior.

Kagan Bookbinder was wearing one of his old Army shirts,

Still visible on it were the dark green patches where he'd recently worn major's rank and a slab of medal ribbons. His war decorations were not all of coloured ribbon, though. His cheek was scarred and his nose had suffered a multiple fracture which proved impossible to reset. On some men a scarred cheek can evoke thoughts of university duels. On the barrel-chested Bookbinder it was easier to imagine that he had fallen down a staircase while drunk on cheap wine.

Bookbinder's voice was similarly unattractive. Among the soft California drawls that even the Hungarians managed to assume after a few weeks, Bookbinder's Eighty-First Street accent was hard and aggressive. Perhaps with a less notable war record he might have chosen to conceal his German origins. Perhaps he was just lazy, perhaps it was his way of being provocative. Perhaps he just didn't know he had any accent.

'Sit down,' repeated Bookbinder. 'We haven't got a lot of time.'

'I must see her.'

'Not yet.'

Stone said, 'Why didn't you tell us?'

'How is she?' said Nicolson again. So Stone was going to play it like that – why didn't you tell *us* – oh well, espionage and show business have in common the tradition that everyone abandons you when you are in trouble. Again Nicolson said, 'How is she?'

Bookbinder didn't answer. He pulled the blind a little to one side and looked out of the window. He waited to see another grey Ford sedan park alongside the one he had brought. The studio drivers ignored each other.

The Studio had three doctors on the payroll. This one was the senior, a man of about fifty with grey wavy hair and a dark suit. Bookbinder excused himself with no more than a grunt before going out to talk with him. Edgar Nicolson and Stone looked at each other covertly but did not speak. Stone drank coffee and Nicolson read the menu to divert his eyes.

Hamburger with all the trimmings. Roll. Butter. Jello. All the coffee you can drink. 85 cents. Today's special. Thank you for your custom. Come again.

Clipped to the menu there was a white card distributed by the local radio station.

The headlines from the four corners of the world by courtesy of YOUR local radio station, San Jorge, California. Hollywood, Tuesday: new evidence of commie subversion in movie colony will bring famous stars to hearing. Washington, Tuesday: State Department official predicts indictment of Hiss on perjury charges. Nanking, Sunday: Chinese government army mauls reds in struggle for coastal cities. Weather: more floods feared for north of state. Low today: 71°. Downtown San Jorge 77°. Humidity 87 per cent. Pressure 29·6. Pollen count 40. Wind from south-west at 15 mph.

'Stone. Eddie Stone.'

Nicolson looked at the bronzed man sitting opposite him. 'That's my name,' explained Stone.

Nicolson awoke from his reverie with a convulsive start. 'Yes, I know you. I'm Edgar Nicolson. And I've seen you around in London: Legrains, the French, Gerry's.'

'That's it,' said Stone. There was a long silence. 'This is bad luck for you,' said Stone.

'Yes, you'll get the part now,' said Nicolson.

'I wouldn't be too sure. He seems pretty keen on your test. He showed it to me as an example: the first one I did was so terrible.'

Nicolson did not believe him but it was a friendly fiction. They looked at each other, assessing the competition that each faced from his rival. They had both invested in steam baths, facial treatments and had had their hair conditioned, waved and set. Stone's brows had been trimmed and his lashes darkened. Nicolson couldn't decide whether Stone's tan was genuine or not but it made him look very fit and made his teeth seem very white. Nicolson tried to decide if any of Stone's teeth were capped. Whichever of them got the role in his film, Bookbinder had already arranged for extensive recapping of the teeth. Many stars began their movie career with a week in the dental chair. It was one part of the contract that Nicolson did not relish.

'Yes, you'll get the part,' said Nicolson. 'This business with the girl will terrify the front office. And, let's face it: the final decision is going to be made by some bastard in publicity.'

'These bloody film people . . .' said Stone. It was almost an agreement with Nicolson's despair. Stone reached forward and gripped his arm. 'I won't do it.'

'What?'

'Take it from you. Winning the role fair and square: yes. I'll fight you tooth and nail for the part, but I don't want the part as a last resort of a nervous flack.'

'Don't be so stupid. If I don't get it and then you turn it down they'll give to to some other actor. Where does that get me.'

'I'll not take it, Edgar. You'll see. These Hollywood bastards behave like Lorenzo the Magnificent, it will do them a power of good to hear an actor telling them to stuff a contract. Screw Hollywood!'

'I could never live here,' said Nicolson.

'The stage,' said Stone. 'An actor needs the stage and an audience. The juices drain out of a man who spends his days transfixed by a bloody one-eyed machine.'

'I like films—' said Nicolson.

'*Films*,' said Stone. 'Yes, we all like films. If you are talking about De Sica and Visconti. If you're talking about *Bicycle Thieves* or *Open City*: everyone likes real films about real people in true life conditions.'

'But there's a new realism here in films—'

'Hollywood films are about murderers, psychopaths, gunmen. What I'm talking about is the starkness of *Bataille du Rail*, the poetry of *Belle et la Bête*. No, Hollywood is a fine place to earn some money and to see some great professionals at work, but Englishmen like us are rooted in European culture. We die if we stay out here. Look around you, look at the limeys who live here.'

'You think so?'

'Sure of it. You charge your batteries in the theatre – here you just flash the headlights.' He nodded. 'What are you drinking, Edgar. It is Edgar?'

'Diet soda. Yes, Edgar Nicolson.'

'What you want is strong black coffee with a slug of something in it.' He took a hip flask from his jacket and poured both coffee and brandy. 'And stop looking so bloody worried, Edgar. We English have got to stick together. Am I right? Stick together and we can beat the bastards.'

Until that moment Nicolson had still been confident that the part he wanted would be his. Nicolson had the right build for a cowboy, a better walk and his voice was far far better than this fellow's. But now he knew that Stone would stop at nothing to wrest the part from him. He'd been in the profession long enough to know the desperation with which actors fight to secure work but usually they had been crude oafs who could not stand up to Nicolson or measure up to his skills. Stone was not just another stupid actor. He was as smooth and as hard as an aerial torpedo and just as dangerous, but not perhaps as self-destructive. Stone surely didn't expect Nicolson to believe that soft soap about turning the offer down, it was his way of declaring that he was going to do battle. Stone smiled a silky smile.

Nicolson said, 'Yes, we must all stick together,' and then he pushed the coffee to the far side of the table. If Bookbinder smelled the alcohol he would be marked down as a lush, and that was enough to lose him the part without this stupid girl going dramatic on him. Stone noticed him move the coffee. 'Don't feel like it, eh?'

'I get tense,' said Nicolson, 'and then my stomach just rejects everything.'

'I understand,' said Stone. He understood.

A dish broke in the kitchen and there was a brief snatch of Spanish. The swearing was quiet and ritualistic as if there were too many breakages for a man to waste much energy on any one of them.

Bookbinder came back to the car with the doctor. They stood outside talking, and then the doctor went away. When Bookbinder came back inside, he poured himself coffee from the Silex on the burner and drank a lot of it before he spoke. 'It's happened before, Edgar, and it will happen again. The studio publicity guys spend more time keeping news out of the papers than getting it in.'

Nicolson said, 'She took an overdose, you said?'

'The whole bottle. The label of the studio pharmacy on it.'

Stone, said, 'Are you going to remove the bottle?'

'That's another department.' Bookbinder pulled the curtain aside as another Ford arrived. The door pinged and a young curly-haired man entered. He wore a dark-blue windcheater, flannel trousers and white sneakers. He looked like a young stockbroker on vacation, or a half-back who'd broken training. Already he was showing the plumpness about the face and arms that predicted the huge middle-aged man he was to become.

'Weinberger! Am I glad to see you,' said Bookbinder.

'Wie gehts?' said the young man. Bookbinder nodded but was not amused. 'You really screwed up a heavy date.'

'Complain to Nicolson,' said Bookbinder, 'it's his party.'

'I want to see her,' said Nicolson.

'Sit down and shut up,' said Weinberger. He put his hand on Nicolson's shoulder and pushed him down on to his seat. 'You do exactly what you are told and you might come out of this unscarred. First, her real name.'

'Rainbow,' said Nicolson, 'Ingrid Rainbow.'

'So why did she check in as Petersen?' asked Weinberger harshly. It was a new side of Weinberger that Stone and Nicolson were seeing: he frightened them.

'I don't know. Perhaps that's—'

'You stick to not knowing. I don't want you doing any guessing.'

'Can I see her?' said Nicolson.

Weinberger shook his head.

Edgar didn't protest. He wanted to see the poor child. He wanted to talk to her, reassure her and tell her that he was worried. But he didn't want to do it right now. The atmosphere was not sympathetic; even if Stone and Bookbinder remained here he would still be inhibited by them.

'The doc's been?' said Weinberger.

'That will be OK,' said Bookbinder.

Bookbinder turned in his seat, stubbed out his cigar and bit his lower lip. Weinberger said to Nicolson, 'You've visited her here? Here at the motel? The receptionist would recognize you?'

Nicolson nodded.

'Oh well,' sighed Weinberger, 'we'll sort that one out too.' He nodded to Bookbinder.

Weinberger got up and steered him across the room to the service door. As they went through it there was a smell of burned fat and the strangled scream of a mixer. Just inside the kitchen Weinberger leaned close to the producer and gestured angrily. The service doors flapped, each swing providing a frame of a jerky old film. Nicolson knew they were deciding.

Eddie Stone was sitting well back from the table on the far side from Nicolson. He caught his eye and Stone smiled. As a child, Stone's smiles had been nervous ones, but he'd soon learned the advantage of preceding all his remarks with an unhurried smile. 'I didn't know about it, Edgar. I was with Kagan when you phoned.' He moved his chair back even more. Nicolson felt like telling him that whatever the trouble was, it wasn't contagious. But they both knew it was. Nicolson looked at the service door. He could see the feet of the gods.

Weinberger said, 'It's not impossible to do it the other way: it's tricky but not impossible, Kagan.'

'What the Nicolson kid does once, he'll do again. If Stone fouls up we can both say we're surprised. But if Nicolson even gets a parking ticket, front office will want our balls.'

'I'll try to keep them both out of it.'

'I know you will. You talked to New York?'

'I can't get New York for a couple of hours. But if you say Stone, he'll stay as clean as a whistle. I promise.'

'Stone,' said Bookbinder and nodded.

'Whatever you say,' said Weinberger. Bookbinder grabbed him as he began to turn away. He reached for the top of the half-door and pulled it closed. 'Don't give me that, you bastard!'

Weinberger looked at the producer but said nothing. Bookbinder finally said, 'I carried this idea for nearly three years: lunches for story editors, presents for production guys and ten thousand bucks for a lousy story treatment. I'll never recoup that dough. Why shouldn't I have five per cent of Stone's contract? Two pictures from now he'll be earning ten times my salary.'

'And Nicolson's agent wouldn't play?'

'Stick to publicity, kid. You don't know when you're well off.'

'Stone, then?'

Bookbinder just looked at him.

They came back from their conference with grim determination on their faces. So must Bookbinder have looked when shooting down his Jap bombers. When they got to the table they halted like a firing squad. Then they exchanged the briefest of glances to decide who should say the next bit. Everyone knew it was the producer's decision but Weinberger was paid his salary to handle trouble. Finally Bookbinder said, 'Weinberger can cool the local Press and handle the cops but this means that I can't use you to star. I'm sorry, Edgar, I can give you the role of the thief if it all blows over, but even that. . .'

Edgar Nicolson said, 'What do you get for attempted suicide in this state?' His voice was only a whisper.

'Don't worry about that end of it,' said Weinberger.

Bookbinder made a gesture towards Stone. 'Eddie will go back to your place with you. You've been together all day. The cops will probably want you, so stay off the juice.'

'I never drink.'

'Good. Weinberger will do what he can. It might happen that the cops won't phone you.'

Weinberger was sealing large-denomination bills into plain envelopes and pencilling the corners to show how much they contained. Bookbinder said, 'I'm sorry about all this, Edgar . . .' He looked at Stone and Weinberger. 'We're all sorry about it. You would have made a swell cowboy.'

Edgar stood up and Stone did too. 'Get going,' said Bookbinder, 'I'm going to phone the cops now.'

'What about the waitress?'

'Manageress,' said Bookbinder. 'Weinberger will see to that. You haven't been here tonight.'

When they were outside in the dark, Edgar said, 'I'll lead the way, you follow. Flash me if you want to stop.' Stone didn't answer. He turned away. Edgar Nicolson touched his sleeve.

'Did you hear anything about Ingrid? Will she be OK?'

Stone kicked an empty beer can. The entrance to the tourist court was littered with them. 'Edgar,' said Stone gently, 'she's dead. That's what everyone is so worried about.'

44

3

I have a washbasin but no shower in my office. Dory [Schary] has a shower but no bathtub. L.B. [Mayer] has a shower and a bathtub. The kind of bath facilities you have in your office is another measure of the worth of your position.

Gottfried Reinhardt

No oriental potentate had a more attentive retinue than followed Leo Koolman through the London offices of Koolman International Pictures Inc that Wednesday afternoon. And, like the entourage of an Eastern ruler, this following was entirely male. Koolman lived in Santa Monica, but he also lived in London. Because so many KI films had been shot in Spain he used some of the tied-up money to buy a house in Marbella too. Each of his houses provided cars, horses, paintings, servants, food and love. And such was the style of Koolman's life that for three or four years at a time, all of these elements would remain unchanged.

However, most of his year was spent in New York. For that was where he found the computers and the accountants and the men from the banks and investment companies, and that therefore was the centre of power. Call him president, chairman or production chief, in the Koolman company it was the man who sat in New York who called the tune. So his European executives kept close to Leo Koolman that afternoon. They made sure that no possible whim might be frustrated or allowed to cool. Cigarettes – always Parliaments – and cigars – Monte Cristo – appeared and were lit by steady hands almost before they reached his mouth. Stiff Martinis were delivered in heavy cut-glass goblets, tinkling with ice. Inside each was a row of olives transfixed by a plastic spear with *The Long Tornado* embossed upon its stem. *The Long Tornado* was KI's latest film; Leo Koolman liked to be reminded of what his advertising men were doing for it. He used the spears to emphasize

45

his words, and he punctuated his theories by biting into the olives with strong white teeth.

The men in the room were curiously alike. They were slim and healthy: tanned by lamps and exercised by machines. They wore expensive suits of dark wool or tailor-made blue-flannel blazers. White shirts set off club ties both real and ornamental. Their hair was short, and more than half of them were wearing tortoiseshell-rimmed spectacles. Their fingernails were manicured, their faces showed a trace of talc and their voices were soft and sincere and, because the Englishmen tried to speak like the Americans and vice versa, it was difficult to tell which were which. They moved constantly, turning so as to keep Koolman in sight. None sat down. They conversed and laughed and drank and patted shoulders, but it was all done in a rehearsed and subdued manner, being little more than displacement activity for men who knew that their livelihoods could depend upon a murmur or a gesture from Leo Koolman. So only Koolman could look where he liked, and he moved among them talking in the soft sympathetic tones of a Schweitzer among incurables.

Leo Koolman was a tall man in his late forties. He wore a dark-grey silk suit and a cream shirt with a Palm Springs Raquet Club tie. He had a thin bony nose and a large generous mouth which a small scar caused to pucker on one side. His eyelids were heavy, which prevented any but the lowest-placed lights reflecting from his eyeballs. It gave him a dead-eye appearance. Photographers used eye-lights to avoid such a look, and thus portraits of Leo Koolman made him look younger and more active than he looked in life. But those unlit eyes were not dead; they studied the men in the room. He looked at their ears and their shoes and their spectacles and the knot of their tie and all the time he judged their capability and remembered their salaries. Koolman was an attractive man: few men and even fewer women resisted the spell of the energy he generated and wasted with profligate disregard. He slept less than four hours a night, and could get off a transatlantic plane looking as neat and tidy as ever he did, and be ready to confute teams of lawyers single-handed. He played tennis like a pro, swam, danced and rode a horse with far above average skill. What he could never get from reading books, he got from reading accounts, and he'd add up columns while talking. His memory was a widely discussed phenomenon. By any standards Koolman was a remarkable man. If he had failings – and few of his associates believed that – they were an indifference to books, a hostility to serious music and no discernible sense of humour. Koolman laughed only at disasters; particularly those of his rivals.

If the last of the Hollywood czars has gone, then Koolman was one of the first Stalins. Perhaps by the turn of the century even journalists will be suspecting that such men are with us to stay. Stalins don't live by movies alone. Koolman's contemporaries governed conglomerates and were as interested in car rentals, airlines, frozen food and computers as they were in movie-making. Koolman International also owned subsidiaries, but Leo Koolman had grown up in Hollywood and he never forgot his childhood, and never ceased to implement his dreams.

All the executives in the room had once been agents, lawyers or actors. Koolman had found another way of calling the tune in the movie business: he'd inherited the president's chair from his Uncle Max, who'd formed the company when both the movies and the accountants were silent.

These men were Koolman's janissaries: men he'd brought from New York and California, the dukes of distribution and the princes of publicity. Perhaps they too lit Koolman's cigars back there on Fifth Avenue but here in London they enjoyed a different, vicarious power. They were praised and pandered to. For they would have Koolman's ear in the days to come, when he was deciding what he really thought about his European offices and the men who manned them.

At five-thirty Koolman retreated beyond the ramparts of the outer office, through the anteroom where Minnie guarded the sofa worn shiny by nervous behinds, and to the extraordinary art-encrusted office which was kept for his exclusive use. He spoke to New York and California, as he did every day from wherever he was. He retired to his private bathroom, took a shower and changed his clothes. By six o'clock he was ready for the audience.

An agent brought a director who wanted to do a musical about Marx and Engels and a girl who'd spent all afternoon painting her eyes. A Cockney actor was modelling his Biafra hairdo. A producer showed everyone a photo of his new house in Palm Springs and a scriptwriter in a studded leather jacket brought the eighth rewrite of *Copkiller — Anarchy Rules in Youth's New State.*

'There's a frisson or two there,' said the scriptwriter modestly. He took off his dark glasses and scowled. Koolman flipped it carelessly and read a line. 'It's good,' said Koolman, although the line he read had remained unchanged in all eight versions. In fact Koolman had read none of them: his script department took those sort of chores off his back. He looked around the room. A girl in a see-through dress embraced the European head of publicity enthusiastically enough to break a shoulder strap. Suzy Delft brought a friend named Penelope and they both kissed Leo Koolman, who blushed.

The gathering continued for two hours, although few visitors stayed that long. Agents paraded their clients and cued their exits. One of the first people to leave was a pretty young girl named Josephine Stewart. She was one of the few people in the room to address her host as Mr Koolman and yet the very formality of that might have indicated the influence she wielded. Not only was she a beautiful young wife with a wealthy family and a brilliant Oxford degree not so very far behind her, she was also an active campaigner against the bomb, apartheid and censorship. She was in addition one of the most influential London film critics.

She gave her readers sociology, history and art for the price of a film review. She could recall shot by shot a Jean Vigo masterpiece, relate it to the abortion rate in pre-war California and explain how Vigo took the idea from a Kurt Schwitters collage before excoriating a director for its misuse in the film she was reviewing.

To Koolman she said, 'I loved *The Sound of Music*. Don't quote me, but I loved it. Three times I've taken my little daughter back to see it.'

'Did you pan it?' Koolman asked.

'Nowadays directors think only of foreground action —

television directing – they can't handle big scenes.'

'You panned *Sound of Music*, didn't you?'

'Beautifully photographed, superbly edited, with jump-cutting at least ten years ahead of its time.'

'Did you pan it?'

'I can't afford to tell my readers to go and see schmaltz.'

'Do you think they haven't taken their kids three times, too?'

'They probably have. But that doesn't mean they want me to tell them to.'

Phil Sanchez brought drinks for them: whisky and soda for Jo Stewart and tonic water for Koolman. 'Thanks, Phil.' Koolman grasped the girl's arm and turned her so that he was looking directly into her eyes. In some other environment such passion might have attracted comment, but here it was strictly professional. Koolman said, 'One of our companies did a market survey about the way people borrow money. People preferred to go to a money-lender than to a bank, even if the bank gave them easier terms. They felt inferior in a bank, they felt out of place there. But in the money-lender's office they felt morally superior.'

Jo Stewart said, 'That's fascinating.'

'You critics go to your Press shows at the nice comfortable hour of ten-thirty A M. Champagne, lobster sandwiches . . .'

'When was that?'

'OK, but you do get a carefully matched print, a chosen track. No adverts or people coming in halfway through.'

'Going out halfway through sometimes.'

'You are confident and at ease. Right? You had a nice printed invite to go and you're being paid to be there. You welcome a stimulating film and you'll judge it in intellectual terms. You're looking for talent. You'll respect a film that you have difficulty in understanding and maybe you'll give it the benefit of the doubt. Right?'

Koolman raised an admonitory finger alongside his ear. No imitation of him omitted this hand movement. With the right timing any wag could use it to raise a smile or a shudder. For Koolman's finger jabbed at heaven suggesting that he was in close collusion with God. 'Right?'

Koolman said, 'But my audiences are in their neighbourhood movie houses, sitting in wet coats, after a day's work, maybe tough manual work. They don't need mental challenge by some smart little movie-maker. They don't want to feel inferior to a film's intellectual content. They want a laugh and a bit of excitement. They'll forgive a movie that is predictable, slick and superficial because those very faults will make them feel superior.'

'That's a gloomy policy for a movie-maker.'

'It's a realistic policy,' said Koolman.

'I never know when you are teasing,' said Josephine Stewart.

'I'm never teasing,' said Koolman.

Weinberger came into the room warily. He reached inside a fake bookcase and opened the refrigerator. He poured himself a bitter lemon and sat down in the corner. Koolman squeezed Jo Stewart's arm as she said goodbye and waved hello at Weinberger. He looked around the room to see if there was any unfinished business. Having decided there was not, he looked at his watch. He used a fob watch so that he could look at it without any danger of the gesture passing unnoticed. Dennis Lightfoot noticed and took it as his cue. 'It's about time, Leo,' he said loudly. Lightfoot was the executive in charge of European production. He could OK anything with a budget under two million dollars. Leo Koolman was here to see how Dennis Lightfoot's guesses were making out.

Koolman put his arm around Lightfoot. 'Let's go, everyone,' he said softly. The roomful of people began to move. The lift gates were open and the canned music was moaning softly. The men who travelled in the elevator were relaxed and smiling and yet they were as alert as the Secret Service men who guard their president. Only Weinberger and six chosen executives took the lift to the basement where the viewing theatre was situated. The others wandered down to the lobby where they chatted and laughed, sub-divided and re-formed several times until they were in three mutually agreed groups. Only then did they make their separate ways to three very different restaurants.

The viewing theatre had thirty seats. Two of them were

already occupied by Edgar Nicolson and the director of *Silent Paradise*, the film they were about to see. Nicolson was sitting at the console tapping his fingers on the projection room phone. Koolman guided Lightfoot to a chair and then sat between him and Nicolson. The rest of the men seated themselves in the four corners of the theatre, knowing that whether the film was good or bad it was just as well to have a row of seats between oneself and Koolman.

'Everyone here?' said Koolman. *Silent Paradise* had finished shooting over three months before and still was not ready. His voice clearly implied that no one was going to leave the room until he knew why.

'Everyone is here,' said Lightfoot.

'Where's Marshall Stone?' said Leo Koolman.

'He's coming straight from the location, Leo,' said Weinberger. 'He said to start.'

'He said to start,' said Koolman. He nodded. Weinberger realized that that had been a tactless way of putting it. 'Then let's start.'

Nicolson picked up the red phone and pressed the button. 'OK, Billy, let's go.'

The room lights dimmed slowly and a beam of light cut a bright rectangle from the whorls of cigar smoke. The KI trademark came into focus and Nicolson pressed the buttons to make the curtains divide. He was a little late. By the time they were fully open, the trademark – a large tome with 'Koolman International IncPresents'written on it in Gothic lettering – had cut to some second unit footage of a street in Anchorage.

'No titles?' said Koolman in a loud whisper.

'They come at the end,' explained Nicolson.

'At the end,' said Koolman affably. 'Is this for the Chinese market, this movie?'

'No, Leo,' said Nicolson and then he laughed. 'Ha, ha, ha.'

'Chinese market,' said Lightfoot, his words ending in the sibilant hiss of a man desperately trying to suppress his merriment.

'Titles go in the front of a movie,' said Koolman patiently.

'I think you're right, Leo,' said Nicolson. 'It was just an experiment.'

'Tell them you're going to tell them. Tell them. Then tell them you told them,' said Koolman. 'Don't say you don't know that basic rule about the movie business.'

Nicolson didn't answer but Lightfoot gave a hint of a chuckle.

On the screen there was a helicopter shot of an Arctic wasteland. 'Great camerawork, Nic,' said one of the Americans.

'Did it in Yorkshire,' said Nicolson.

'No kidding,' said the American.

'Had to remove four hundred telephone poles,' said Nicolson.

'Don't you have a music track?' said Koolman.

'We have a wonderful track but we thought we'd try and get a feeling of emptiness and loneliness right here.'

'That's the feeling we'll get all right,' agreed Koolman, 'emptiness and loneliness – right there in the movie theatres,' he gave a grim mirthless chuckle.

'It's a great soundtrack, Leo,' said Nicolson. He turned up the volume control and hoped it would start. It did. There was an eerie sound as massed trumpets began the musical theme.

'It's not bad, that tune,' said Koolman.

'It's just running wild at present,' said Nicolson.

'It's great,' said the same American as before.

'It's a catchy tune,' said Lightfoot modestly.

'I'll tell you what to do with that . . .' said Koolman. He leaned aside to Lightfoot.

'Edgar,' supplied Lightfoot, and Koolman leaned back to Nicolson again.

'I'll tell you what to do with that, Edgar,' said Koolman.

'Yes, Leo?' said Nicolson as if he really wanted to know.

'Lyrics: get some kid singing it. Look what that tune did for *Dr Zhivago*.'

'Great idea,' said Lightfoot.

'We'll give it a try,' said Nicolson.

'Don't give it a try,' sighed Koolman, 'just do it.'

'It could be great,' said Nicolson doubtfully.

'Da, da, di, da, da, daaa, daaa, daaaaaa I could be a lonely man.' Koolman tried to improvise words to the theme which was now being repeated for the tenth time.

'This is just the rough track,' said Nicolson. 'It will have a big orchestra when we do the real one.'

'Get that lonely feeling in the words,' said Koolman. 'All these kids love to feel sorry for themselves.'

One of the Americans was head of the KI Music, Koolman's sheet music and recording company. He said to Nicholson, 'You give me your wild track, I'll talk to my people in New York.'

'Thanks a lot,' said Nicolson. 'A tape will be on your desk tomorrow, that's a promise.'

The film cut to a studio interior. Four actors in fur clothing were seated around a table. The door opened and a fifth man came in along with a handful of effects snow from a wind machine. Through the door there was a glimpse of a polystyrene ice-face and a painted backcloth that wasn't sufficiently out of focus. The fifth man pushed his snow glasses off his face and pulled back his fur hood. It was Marshall Stone. He'd just returned from a vacation in Nice when they shot the sequence: one of the first they did. Stone looked tanned and lean and very fit. He'd had a small hairpiece fitted for the role and he looked as handsome as he'd ever been.

'That's Marshall Stone, isn't it, Nic?'

'He looks wonderful, Jacob,' Koolman said to Weinberger.

Weinberger said nothing. Koolman said to Nicolson, 'Do you want to make that music a little quieter? I can't hear myself speak.'

Nicolson twisted the offending control viciously.

On the screen Marshall Stone said, 'Why couldn't they find oil in Maidenhead or Cowes or somewhere decent?'

'Now I can hardly hear the track,' said Koolman.

'This is just a guide track,' explained Nicolson.

'Maidenhead,' said Koolman, 'was that in the script?'

'It's a place near London,' explained Lightfoot.

'I know it's a place near London,' said Koolman irritably. 'I've got one of my boys at Eton, haven't I? But what about the audiences in Omaha?'

Nicolson said, 'When we loop it, we'll change it. Stone can say London.'

The director spoke for the first time. He was seated at the back. They were all surprised to hear his voice emerge from the gloom under the projection light. He stuttered slightly, 'It will show. You can't loop London into a close-up like that and have it lip-synch.'

Koolman turned around slowly. The director was a white haired old man who had promised Nicolson that he wouldn't say a word throughout the screening.

Koolman looked at him. Koolman didn't know much about the technical side of movie-making but he knew sufficient of the basic principles to win arguments with directors. 'You mean you haven't got any cover?'

'I don't cover everything. It would be too expensive.'

'We got cover, Tony,' shouted Nicolson, leaning back to grab his director's arm in a warning hug. 'We got cover: a tracking shot, a two-shot, lots of stuff. We can loop it for London OK. We are still doing the loops.' He bound his left hand tightly with a silk handkerchief.

'Shoot it again if you have to,' said Koolman slightly mollified by Nicolson's anxiety. 'Basic rule in movies: plenty of cover.'

'This is a great sequence, Leo,' promised Lightfoot believing the sequence was Marshall Stone punching an Eskimo stunt man in the head. They all watched attentively while Marshall Stone and two extras plodded over a hillock of special effects snow. Now it was Lightfoot who twisted his hands in silent prayer.

'Yeah, great,' said Koolman. 'Really terrific: it builds.' He'd hardly spoken when the film cut to a two-shot of the men, to a close-up of Stone, then the long-shot in which stunt men substituted for the actors. There was a brief exchange of blows after which a man wearing Marshall Stone's distinctive red gloves somersaulted to the bottom of a snow drift. Lightfoot slowly released the breath that had almost exploded his lungs.

'You'll have to get rid of that,' said Koolman. He flung the words over his shoulder. He sensed that the old director was his only vocal opposition in the theatre.

'I thought it was pretty good,' said the director.

'Corny,' said Koolman, 'acrobatics.'

'I think it should . . . stay in,' said the director.

Koolman turned to Lightfoot. 'Who have you got editing this

picture?' They both knew that it wasn't the sort of information that Lightfoot was likely to have in his mind, so they waited until Nicolson said, 'Sam Parnell, an old-timer, a really great editor.'

Koolman made a whirling movement of his finger as a signal to Phil Sanchez, his personal assistant. 'I'll talk to Parnell before we go back.' He turned to Nicolson. 'That be OK with you, Edgar?'

'Sure thing, Leo,' said Nicholson. 'Anything you've got to say, we can always use advice.' Phil Sanchez made a note in his little book. Nicolson unbound his bloodless hand.

'I think we can do something with this movie. We can shape it into something,' said Koolman. No one spoke.

On the screen Marshall Stone had lost his goggles and was feeling around in the snow between brief cuts of lens flare to show that the reflections were blinding him.

'Great performance from Stone,' said Koolman. 'Now there's a man who's really learned his trade, eh, Edgar?'

'Great performance, Leo,' said Nicolson. 'He gives gives gives all the time. This could be one for a nomination.'

'Best actor,' mused Koolman.

Weinberger said, 'He's had three nominations. This one could do it for him.'

'What do you think, Arty?' asked Koolman of one of his publicity men.

'If we play it like that, then this movie is going to need some special nursing, Leo. We'll need serious interviews, woo the egg-heads a bit. Even then I'd say this movie doesn't stand a prayer for a "best picture" award – the whole membership . . .' he wiggled his outstretched hand. 'A "best actor" for Stone . . . maybe. But it will cost us, Leo.'

Nicholson said, 'If we were going to go for an Oscar, that will control our release.' He rubbed his hand to help the circulation. It began to tingle.

'Sure,' said Lightfoot. 'Thirty days of exhibition in Los Angeles before the end of December. That would be quite a rush.'

'We could do it,' said Nicolson. 'We're close to dubbing.'

'It wouldn't stand a chance the following year unless we held it until fall.'

'You guys work it out,' said Koolman.

The music man said, 'With great music like this maybe I'll talk to Barbra or Andy.'

'Or Sammy,' said another voice. 'Sammy's a very good friend of mine: he comes to the house.'

'Sure,' said the music man, 'Sammy, or better still Tom Jones might like to do an album, or Johnny Cash.'

'Tom Jones is a wonderful person,' said Nicolson, 'and he would be great for the main title, we could use a vocal opening.'

'Tapes or disc,' said the music man, 'but I'll need them yesterday.'

They all laughed.

'Great camerawork, Nic,' said the only person still watching the screen. Marshall Stone had not found his goggles because they were caught on a crag which was kept in frame centre while Stone scrambled pitifully on the ground. Stone buried his head in his hands and gave a manly sob. The camera zoomed in to show the make-up department's frostbite.

'Do you want to turn that music down a little, Edgar?'

'This is just a wild track. It's not balanced or anything.'

'Best actor,' said Koolman softly. He leaned close to Lightfoot. 'If we can get an Oscar for Stone it will make a great launch for the TV series, Dennis.'

'Right, Leo, right.' They both smiled at each other as though this idea had only just come to them.

There were eight motor-cars waiting outside KI Pictures in Wardour Street. Nine, if you count Jacob Weinberger's chauffeur-driven Jaguar, although no one did count it because Weinberger said he had no car. This gave him a chance to ride with Leo Koolman in the Rolls limousine. Also in the car there were Suzy Delft, her friend Penelope, Leo and Phil Sanchez his assistant. The girls had been waiting upstairs in Leo's office.

When the convoy of cars arrived at Jamie's Club, Leo was shown the big circular table set for ten. The two girls hurried away to repaint their faces. Koolman arranged the seating around the table. Nicolson and his director were across the table and Weinberger was two seats away, leaving an empty seat on each side of Koolman. When the girls returned Penelope was wearing a different dress. Koolman noticed this and remarked on it. The girl smiled. Koolman looked at the menu and patted the seat of the chair next to him without looking up. Obediently Penelope slid into it and gratefully took a menu from the waiter.

The New York executives alternated with their London equivalents. The seat between Weinberger and Koolman was held for Marshall Stone, who arrived with the wine waiter. Stone was in a dark suit with a stiff cutaway collar and a Travellers Club tie. A gold watch-chain on his waistcoat carried a gold nuclear disarmament medallion. He made a fine entrance. He walked up to Leo Koolman and stood with his hands stretched forward. He searched for words that might convey his sincere good wishes. When he did speak his voice was husky. 'Leo. It's good to see you. It's damned good to see you.'

Koolman jumped to his feet like a bantamweight boxer coming out of his corner. 'We saw a great performance tonight, Marsh. A truly great performance.'

Marshall Stone looked around the table with a quizzical smile on his face. 'You've screened the new Richard and Liz film?'

'We saw *Silent Paradise*, Marshall.'

'You old bastard, Edgar,' said Stone to Nicolson. 'You might have told me.'

Nicolson said, 'You were great, Marshall, we all thought so.'

'It's a great performance, Marshall,' said Koolman. 'Dennis thinks we should go after a best actor nomination and I agree.' Dennis Lightfoot made a mental note of the fact that if anything went wrong with Koolman's latest idea, it was going to become a Lightfoot idea.

Stone shook his head. 'I was just part of a fine team, Leo,' he said.

'It's time we got you one of those metal dolls, Marshall,' said Koolman.

Stone sat down and blew his nose loudly.

The waiter asked Stone what he would have to drink. 'Perrier water,' said Stone. To Koolman he said, 'I never drink when I'm making a picture.' Stone looked around the table. 'Darling,' he called to Suzy. 'That dress: sensational!' He pretended to look around the room for the camera. 'Are we doing the orgy scene?'

'How is *Stool Pigeon* coming along, Marshall?' said Koolman. The others went on with their conversations while keeping their eyes and ears on Koolman. Koolman said, 'I like that moustache. That's for the role, eh?'

Marshall smiled at the other guests before he answered. 'It's not a film for over-sensitive people, Leo. It's a tough, no-holds-barred story of what war is really like.' He touched his moustache. 'Yes, for the film.'

'But are the kids going to like the film, Marshall?'

'The kids will love it, Leo, because there is lots of fun in it too. And a challenge to authority.'

'A film has got to have confrontation, colour and conflict,' said Leo who had got that cinematographic philosophy from a film about a producer.

'This has got it,' said Marshall Stone.

'Who's directing?'

'A new director: Richard Preston. It's his first feature.'

'A TV kid,' said Koolman. 'I hope we're not getting too many flick zooms, whip pans and all that psychedelic crap. Are you watching that, Dennis?'

Lightfoot said, 'You bet, Leo. I saw the rushes last week and it's good solid footage and Suzy is going to be really great.' His voice betrayed the doubts he shared about the picture.

'Aren't they three weeks over?' He tried to recall the paper-work.

'Weather trouble,' said Lightfoot.

'Don't these guys who prepare your budgets know that it rains in England, Dennis?' Lightfoot didn't answer, so Koolman said, 'I think it rains here now and again. I think I've heard rumours to that effect.' He looked around the table and everyone smiled.

Lightfoot smiled too. He said, 'We scheduled it so that we could go inside when it rains but we only have Marshall for three more weeks so we have to do his shots whenever we possibly can. That means holding the crew ready instead of doing the cover shots.'

Koolman nodded. 'Location films, who needs them. We have the same trouble in New York. They tell me how much we save by not going into the studio and then they stand scratching their arses waiting for the rain to stop. So that's saving money? If we must have location shooting, what's wrong with California. At least you can bet on the sunshine.'

Stone said, 'I'm so pleased that you liked *Silent Paradise*. Did you notice that wonderful performance by Bertie Anderson?'

'Which one was he?' said Koolman.

'The truck driver in the first reel,' said Stone. 'A fantastic performance. Jesus, if I could act like that man . . .'

'I don't even remember it,' said Weinberger, as soon as he was certain that Anderson wasn't one of his clients.

Nicolson said, 'It was the very old man who throws the mailbag on the ground.'

'Oh, him,' said Koolman. The part had only had about fifty seconds of screen time.

'Almost eighty,' said Stone, 'a wonderful old man. I made Edgar give him the part.' Stone took a bread roll from the waiter, broke it into three parts and spread some butter upon it. A careful observer would have noticed the care with which he did this, as if he had no other thought in his mind. And a careful observer would also have noticed how, in spite of all the activity, very little food ever got as far as Stone's mouth. The little that did was bitten cautiously and probed with the tongue as if he expected to find some tiny piece of foreign matter there. Yet many times during the meal he remarked how fine the food was and how much he was enjoying himself and how little self-control he had when it came to watching his waistline.

'A wonderful old man,' said Stone again.

'Do you know something, Marshall,' said Koolman, 'you're a damned sight too modest, that's your trouble.' Koolman turned to Suzy Delft. 'Only a real artist can talk that way: that's what I love about this business.'

'Artiste,' she corrected him.

'Is there something wrong with that drink?'

'No,' she said.

'Then why aren't you drinking it?' He didn't wait for a reply.

He turned to Stone. 'You'll get the best actor nomination or I'll know the reason why.'

All round the table there was the friendly buzz of people in agreement. Patiently the head waiter stood near to Koolman with pencil poised. Koolman said, 'You know what they do very well here: chicken Kiev. Is there anyone who can't eat a chicken Kiev?'

No one spoke. 'And the borsht,' said Koolman, 'with the sour cream and the pastry things. OK, there you go.'

'Thank you, Mr Koolman,' said the head waiter.

'I'll be cutting away early,' announced Koolman. To reinforce this decision he reached under the tablecloth and grasped at Penelope's thigh.

4

Of course he romances, but an impressionable person of his sort really believes in his fabrications. We actors are so accustomed to embroider facts with details drawn from our own imaginations, that the habit is carried over into ordinary life. There, of course, the imagined details are as superfluous as they are necessary in the theatre.

C. Stanislavsky, An Actor Prepares

The unit publicist on *Stool Pigeon* sent me the biography they were using for Marshall Stone. It was printed on duplicating paper. Most of the first sheet was taken up by a letterhead design in which three soldiers and a girl fought their way through an Aubrey Beardsley jungle that had already overgrown the address and telephone number. Although a small clearing had been chopped for Edgar Nicolson's name.

Edgar Nicolson Productions for Koolman International presents
Stool Pigeon starring Marshall Stone
Director: Richard Preston
Introducing: Suzy Delft.

MARSHALL STONE. A brief biography

Marshall Stone was born in London. In a family that traditionally supplied its sons to the theatre and to the Army, Stone's dilemma as an only child was resolved when war interrupted his studies at the Royal Academy of Dramatic Art.

After the war he auditioned for Robert Atkins at Stratford and was so disappointed at being turned down that he toured South Africa with a company that did light comedy with music in its repertory, as well as a detective play and a farce. 'It was a lunatic asylum,' said Stone afterwards, 'but we never stopped laughing in spite of the miseries and the hard work of it all.' When he returned to England he joined the

Birmingham Rep. His performance as Fortinbras in *Hamlet* was singled out for critical praise but apart from this his season went unmarked. 'I spent my whole time there in open-mouthed awe. Perhaps I took direction too slavishly, for I never recognized anything of myself in the roles I played.

'After getting into Birmingham – which had long been my ambition – I believed that the world was at my feet. I was wrong. After Birmingham I was turned down for three London parts. For a year I took anything I could get, including some TV work.'

In 1948 he was offered Lysander in a production of *A Midsummer Night's Dream* that was to be staged in New York. They were actually in rehearsals when a network cut-back caused the whole production to be scrapped. He stayed in New York and got a small part in an experimental group's production of Brecht and eked out his finances with odd jobs on TV. He was in a restaurant in New York when he was seen by a Hollywood producer who screen-tested him for *Last Vaquero*, the film that brought him world-wide acclaim and broke box-office records in many countries from Japan to Italy.

In the following two years he starred in three Hollywood films, as well as creating his memorable *Master Builder* on the London stage and the exciting *Tristram Shandy, Gent* that was written for him to do at the Edinburgh Festival. No theatrical event of the nineteen-fifties was more important than Marshall Stone's Hamlet. Gielgud himself called it 'a miracle of discovery'.

Since that time Marshall Stone has divided his work between the stage and screen, as well as financing some avant-garde productions in Paris and doing a series of poetry readings for the BBC Third programme.

If there is one certain thing about the career of Marshall Stone, it is that no one can be certain what he will do next, except that it will be important, highly professional and never, never boring.

It was a good piece of publicity. But for those of us in never-

never-boring-land who had learned to interpret avant-garde as disastrous, and exciting as unrehearsed, it left only the radio poetry, an assorted collection of forgettable films, *Hamlet* and *The Master Builder*.

The fact that the Ibsen performance had been superb and his Hamlet even better made the whole thing more, not less, depressing for me.

Listed under the biography were his films. *Las Vaquero* was at the top, but the compilation had omitted some of his worst flops including *Tigertrap* which, after its panning in New York, had been shelved until this week.

Even so, the achievements of Stone were remarkable and it would be a foolish historian who wrote of the post-war theatre without acknowledging his contribution. That he'd neglected the stage since *Hamlet* and contented himself with countless disappointing films didn't obscure the dazzling talent that could be discerned in every performance he gave. As Scofield followed in the steps of Gielgud, so could Stone have followed Olivier. It still wasn't too late; it was simply very unlikely.

In the same envelope there was the call-sheet for *Stool Pigeon*. The unit was on location outside Wellington Barracks.

Dear Peter Anson,

For the next three days Mr Marshall Stone will be working at Tiktok Sound Recording Studios in Wardour Street. He will be pleased to see you at any time you care to drop in.

Yours sincerely,

BRENDA STAPLES,
Publicity Secretary

No wonder schizophrenia was an occupational hazard among actors. At any time an actor might be doing publicity for a film that was being premièred, recording for one in post-production, acting in a third, fitting costumes for a fourth while reading scripts to decide what will come next.

In the competitive spirit of all flacks the note didn't say which film Stone was looping, but I guessed it was one about the Alaskan oil pipeline that had been recut half a dozen times due to arguments between Nicolson, the director and some of Koolman's people.

I saw Stone's Rolls outside Tiktok, parked with the impunity that only chauffeurs manage. Its dark glass concealed the interior, which made one wonder why Stone had gone to the trouble of getting a registration plate that contained his initials.

Usually the door of Tiktok was ajar but today it was locked, with a suspicious guardian who grudgingly permitted me inside. Only fifty yards of corridor separated Studio D from the door but I passed through a screen of secretaries, bodyguards, tea-bringers, overcoat holders, messengers, advisers and a bald man whose sole job it was to pay for refreshments for the whole ensemble and note each item in his tiny notebook. Even the man who answered the phone that Stone had commandeered was not the one who made calls on Stone's behalf.

They were a curious assembly of shapes, sizes and ages, dressed as variously as a random crowd in a bus queue. Their only bond was the fealty they demonstrated to Stone, for homage must not only be paid but also be seen to be paid. In common they had the same expression of bored indifference that all servants hide behind. They used it to admit me and to reply to my 'good mornings'. They would use it to take my coat and bring me coffee and politely acknowledge any joke I cared to make. And, if necessary, they would use it when they tossed me out of the door or repeated for the umpteenth time that Stone was not at home.

Stone had hired them under many different circumstances, and in some cases their employment was little more than an excuse for Stone's charity. Valuable though they were as retainers, they were even more vital as an audience. They travelled with Stone providing the affection, scandals, jokes, flattery and feuds – arbitrated by Stone – that an Italian padrone exacted from his family. This was the world of Stone and, like the world which he portrayed on the screen, it was contrived.

When I finally penetrated Studio D, Marshall Stone was sitting in an Eames armchair alongside an antique occasional table, on which was set coffee and cakes with Copenhagen china and silver pots. Later I was to hear that the chair and all the trimmings were brought there in advance by his employees, whose job it was to scout all such places and furnish them tastefully.

I recognized Sam Parnell and his usual assistants. They were sitting in a glass booth surrounded by the controls of the recording equipment. They were drinking machine-made coffee from paper cups. The booth was lighted by three spotlights over the swivel chairs. Enough light spilled from them to see the six rows of cinema seats and Stone sitting at the front. Parnell's voice came over the loudspeaker as I entered. 'OK, Marshall. Ready when you are.'

Stone gave him the thumbs-up sign and handed his copy of *Playboy* to a man who would hold it open at the right place until it was needed again. On the screen of the dimmed room there appeared a scratched piece of film. It was a black and white dupe print of *Silent Paradise*. Carelessly processed, its definition was fuzzy and the highlights burned out. A blobby man in glaring white furs said, 'It should be me that goes, the other men have wives and families. I have no one.'

Marshall Stone watched himself and listened to the guide tracks so that as the loop of picture came round again he could record the words in synchronization with his lips. The trouble with looping was that men on the tundra were likely to sound as if they had their heads inside biscuit tins. This film was not going to be an exception. Edgar Nicolson productions seldom were.

The picture began again, Stone said, 'It should be me that goes, the other – no, sod. Sorry, boys, we'll have to do it again.' The screen flashed white, and by its reflected light Stone saw me standing in the doorway. Although one of his servants had announced my arrival he preferred to act as though it was a chance meeting.

We had exchanged banalities at parties and he'd given me a brief interview for the newspaper articles, but this was a meeting between virtual strangers. That however was not evident from the warmth of his welcome.

He came towards me smiling broadly as he took my hands in

his. He delivered a salvo of one-word sentences, 'Wonderful. Marvellous. Great. Super.' Narrow-eyed, he watched the effect of them like an artillery observer. Then he adjusted the range and the fuse setting to hit instead of straddling. 'Damned fit. And a superb suit. Where did you get that wonderful tan: I'm jealous.' Perhaps because he told me the things he wanted to tell himself there was an artless sincerity in his voice.

'You're looking well yourself, Marshall,' I responded. He gripped my hand. He was smaller, more wrinkled and more tanned than I remembered, but his voice had the same tough reedy tone that I'd heard in his films.

'Are you having problems?' I asked.

'It's the stutter, darling.' He could say 'darling' with such virile aplomb that it became the most sincere and effective greeting that one man could use to another.

'I see.'

'I would never have used a hesitation if I'd guessed I'd be looping it.' The joke was on him but he laughed.

'The sound crew thought they could use the original track?'

'They swore that they'd be able to, but I could hear the genny and so could everyone else. If we could hear it, then the mike could pick it up. I should have put my foot down. God knows, I've been in the business long enough to know about recordings. But a bloody actor must know his place, eh, Peter?' He pulled a slightly anguished face — hollow cheeks and half-closed eyes — before letting it soften into a broad smile. Just as his speech was articulated with an actor's care, so did all his gestures have a beginning, middle and an end. He shook his head to remove the smile. 'Get Mr Anson a fresh pot of coffee and some of those flaky pastries, will you, Johnny.'

Another man helped me off with my coat. I said, 'The publicity secretary said . . .'

'Sure, Peter, she said you might look in. Sandy, take Peter's coat.' Yet a third man put my coat on a hanger and carried it away with either reverence or disgust, I could not be sure which. 'Glad of someone to talk to,' said Stone. 'Bloody boring, doing these loops. Will it be a full-length book?'

'Yes. About eighty thousand words and lots of photos. By

the way, the publicity people will let me have plenty of film stills but I was wondering if you have any personal snapshots you could lend me. You know: school groups, holiday snaps, mother, father or wartime photos.' He looked up and stared at me.

'I was in the war,' he said.

'What did you do?'

He stared at me until I shifted uncomfortably. 'What did *you* do in the war, Daddy?'

I laughed nervously. 'You know what I did, Marshall. I sat on my arse in Hollywood.'

He sensed my discomfort. 'Yes, I know. Why?'

I'd rehearsed the answer to that a million times, so I had it pat. 'I'd saved thirty shillings a week to pay my fare to California. It wasn't so easy to chuck it up when war was declared. It was May 1940 when finally I went up to Canada and volunteered.'

'And?'

'When that Army radiographer found an ankle fracture from schooldays had mended badly . . . I wasn't exactly heartbroken. But I volunteered every six months for the rest of the war just to appease my conscience. The nearest I got to active duty was working with John Ford and Darryl Zanuck making a US Army film about venereal disease. That was my war, Marshall, how did yours go?'

'I worked with a chap named Millington-Ash, a brigadier. He ended the war a major-general. On paper I think I was probably a lance-corporal.'

'What kind of outfit was that?'

He smiled at me as if I'd made a social gaffe. 'Put infantry.'

'I'll forget the whole thing if you like.'

'Office work for the most part but they quoted the Official Secrets Act at me a couple of times – you know.'

'You mean you were some sort of agent?'

He moved his head in the direction of the man bringing the silver pot of coffee and the cream pastries. He didn't answer until the man had gone again. Even then he took the precaution of covering the microphone with his hand, in case it was alive. 'Not for publication, Pete, my boy. We could both get into hot water.'

'Subject closed.'

'That's the best. Now, tell me what your readers will want to know about me.'

It was a practical if unorthodox attitude to biography. For a moment I was unable to think of an answer. I knew what I believed to be the job of the biographer. I knew it to be a process of selection, of emphasis and the relationship between events and attitudes. Just as Toynbee had once dismissed the 'one damn thing after another' school of historians, so I believed that a man's activities were only a means to an end. A biography must show what a man is, rather than what he does. But to emphasize the influence that a writer had upon a finished life story was a dangerous thing to explain to Stone. Tactfully, I said, 'They'd probably like to know what your life is like. They'd like to share your pleasures and your disappointments and learn something of your craft. They'd like to know how much of your success was luck and to what extent you created your own opportunity.'

'Yes, yes, yes, and how much I earn and what I spend it on, what my house is like and who am I screwing.'

'Not exactly,' I said primly.

'Listen, Peter. If you are going to have a go at me, you'd better be frank right from the start.'

'Why would I want to do that?'

'And why would some little creep grab me when I'm getting out of the Rolls this morning and tell me my last film was shit?' He laughed to smother the spark of temper.

'Did that happen?'

'You get used to it.' He sighed and smiled. 'We all get them. Even the ones who are not actually insulting feel free to criticize your voice, your face, walk, dress, car, acting ability, et cetera. And they are amazed if you're not grateful for it! There is a widespread illusion, Peter, that film stars lead protected lives and urgently need members of the public to stride up uninvited and start being frank with them.'

I nodded sympathetically.

'Well, I don't need it, darling. No one needs it. No one needs insults. You don't need insults to your writing and I don't need it for my acting.'

I guessed he was still smarting from the US reviews of *Tigertrap*. Too, he was girding his loins for the London showing. 'That's how it goes,' I said.

'We have enough doubts and fears already. God knows I'm my own most bitter critic . . .' He laughed. He got up to do the next recording. During our talk he was always ready to do each recording as the technicians had the loop ready. Post-recording can kill an actor's performance. Alone in a dark recording studio it's not easy to reproduce the power and spontaneity of a performance created under the lights with other actors, and with a director to prod and interpret and stand ready with a vital potion of praise. But Stone was able to improve upon his guide track: he was able to make the words carry the emotion a step further. On the other hand I noticed the way he corrected the too forceful gestures in his performance by flattening the phrasing of the words. Stone was a pro and he completed each loop expertly and quickly.

'I'm a professional too, Marshall,' I warned him. 'I'm not going to attack you but I'm not going to omit whole sections of your life to leave just a history of your successes. For instance, I don't want to dwell upon your divorce but I can't just forget that you were ever married. Neither of us can forget it.'

He looked relieved, if anything. 'Poor Mary,' he said. 'How could you imagine I'd want to forget our life together. I owe her a lot, Peter, more than I can tell you. The divorce affected her more than she will ever admit, even to you. Rejection can make any of us say bitter things that we don't really mean. You must remember that when you talk with her.' He stopped, and I saw in him a cruelty that I'd never suspected and at which Mary never did hint.

'She's a truly wonderful person,' he added.

I said nothing. The masterful inactivity that is the working method of doctors, interrogators and journalists did not fail me.

He continued, 'When a woman marries a man who is dedicated to an art, her first object is to find out how dedicated.' He smiled as he remembered. 'Mary saw my acting as a direct rival. She wanted me to be home early, only take jobs where we could be together and not talk too much about my work. Can you imagine? I was a struggling young actor. I would have signed a ten-year contract for a repertory company in Greenland. I was desperate to act.' He laughed, mocking his foolishness.

'I tried with Mary. I really tried. But when a woman wants to find out if she's married a hen-pecked type of man she starts to peck. Jesus, the rows we had! Sometimes we threw things. Once we smashed every piece of china in the house and then she cut my face by throwing an egg beater at me. It was only this marvellous man I've got in Harley Street who saved me from being scarred for life. As it was, when Mary saw his bill she started another row.' He poured more coffee for me. At first I had been angry with the way he talked of Mary, but then I realized that he was trying to disregard the fact that she was now my wife.

'When I had this chance of going to Hollywood, I sent for Mary as soon as it was practical. I thought a new country would give us a chance of starting again. You know.' He pinched the bridge of his nose and looked away. When he turned back to me I saw that a tear had formed in the corner of his eye. It was a jet-black teardrop coloured by the mascara that he used on his lashes.

I said, 'I saw your Hamlet twice. I've never seen its match.'

He brightened. 'Schtik,' he said modestly.

'Skill! Your Yorick speech: the second time I was waiting for it, but it was still as natural as an ad lib.'

'I delivered the previous lines tight on cue. But just after starting the Yorick speech I let them think I'd dried.'

He picked up the milk jug and twisted it in his hands. ' "Let me see. Alas, poor Yorick." ' He stared at the jug as if trying to read his lines there. He turned his eyes to me, hesitated, and then spoke in the lightest of conversational tones, ' "I knew him, Horatio; a fellow of infinite jest, of most excellent fancy; he hath borne me on his back a thousand times." ' Stone smiled, as if he'd performed some puzzling party trick for an appreciative small child. He was happy to amuse me further. ' "Where be your gibes now? your gambols? your songs? your

70

flashes of merriment that were wont to set the table on a roar?" '

Stone put the jug down. 'Schtik,' he said, but he could not conceal his pleasure. I remembered the wonderful notices he'd got and the predictions that had been made about him. Few doubted that he'd turn his back on movies and the rewards of Hollywood. The London theatre cleared a space for him, the electricians readied his name in neon and theatre critics sharpened their superlatives, delighted that an errant player should discover the London stage to be the only true Mecca.

But the 'fresh young genius', the 'modern Irving', this 'giant in a land of giants' soon caught the plane back to California.

Stone caught my eye. 'My prince was a fine fellow.'

I nodded. 'It wasn't schtik.'

'No, it wasn't.'

Marshall Stone did not go to lunch. He'd eaten none of the cream pastries, although after I'd eaten both of them he sent out for more, as if having them there to resist was important to him: but perhaps it was just hospitality. At lunchtime one of his men brought him a polished apple wrapped in starched linen, a piece of processed cheese from Fortnum's and three starch-free biscuits. The recording boys took their allotted lunchtime and Stone sent his men away, so we were alone in the dim studio. It was then that he gave me a demonstration of his skill.

He had been talking about speech training and how poor his voice had been when he was a young actor. He quoted his piece from the Bible making the sort of mistakes he made then, and after that he gave it to me with everything he'd got. It was an impressive demonstration of speech training. His voice was held low and resonant, and his articulation was precise and clipped so that even his whispers could have been projected a hundred yards or more. There were no tricks to it: no lilting Welsh vowels or hard Olivier consonants. He didn't point any lines or throw any away. He didn't pause too long or try to surprise me with the use of the thorax. He just did everything he could to make the words themselves transcend the fact that they were too well known.

' "To everything there is a season, and a time to every purpose under the heaven:

' "A time to be born, and a time to die; a time to plant, and a time to pluck up that which is planted;

' "A time to kill, and a time to heal; a time to break down, and a time to build up;

' "A time to weep, and a time to laugh; a time to mourn, and a time to dance;

' "A time to cast away stones, and a time to gather stones together; a time to embrace, and a time to refrain from embracing;

' "A time to get, and a time to lose; a time to keep, and a time to cast away;

' "A time to rend, and a time to sew; a time to keep silence, and a time to speak;

' "A time to love, and a time to hate; a time of war, and a time of peace." '

It was very good, and Stone was smart enough to follow it with a moment's silence while he searched his pockets for a cigarette.

'You've talked with Edgar?' Stone offered me a cigarette.

'Yesterday.'

'He was with me when I did *Last Vaquero*.'

'So he said.'

'He had that business with the girl ... did he tell you?'

'Yes.'

'It was rotten luck. And Edgar is a sweet man.'

'He said it spoiled his chance in *Last Vaquero*.'

'He played the thief.'

'Was he in the running for the lead?'

Stone gave a good-natured chuckle. 'Did he say that?'

'He told me he had a chance at the lead, except that Bookbinder was frightened of the scandal when the girl committed suicide.'

'He's wonderful, that Edgar,' Stone shook his head. 'By the way, the girl didn't die. I mean, she did die some years later in a traffic accident, but she didn't die because of the abortion.'

'Who was she?'

Stone lit his cigarette. 'Some actress or other – starlet, I should say – she'd never had a part in a film or anything.'

'Did Edgar meet her in Hollywood?'

Stone inhaled and blew smoke before replying. When he did, his voice was icy and almost menacing. For the first time I saw the dangerous quality that all actors must have if they are to be really good. This coilspring of repressed violence had seen many a bad film through reels of dull dialogue. 'Don't let's pry into Edgar's life,' he said.

I turned the page of my notebook and decided to press on with the nuts and bolts. I said, 'In a TV interview some years ago you said that a star should stop acting altogether rather than do character roles as he gets older. Do you still think that?'

'A star has the vehicle built round him. He faces very different problems if he becomes part of building a film around another actor. Is that terribly vain?' He gripped my arm tight enough to hurt. There was nothing homosexual about such Hollywood caresses; they were intended to get undivided attention, and Stone used them expertly.

'No,' I said.

'If I was no longer playing leads – and luckily I'm having as many offers today as I ever had – but if I wasn't getting leads, yes, I would stop acting.'

'What would you do?'

'Sail. I'd sail around the world, like Chichester or Knox-Johnson. A man only discovers himself when he's alone with the elements.'

'I didn't know you were a sailor.' I knew he had a motor-cruiser – that was mandatory equipment for all superstars; I'd seen it at Cannes during the festivals – but his enthusiasm for sailing was a new aspect of Marshall Stone.

'I sailed alone across the Atlantic,' he said indignantly. 'I'm prouder of that than of any film I've made.'

'Which route did you take?'

'Shannon to Port of Spain, except that I got lost and had to swim ashore to ask where I was.'

'And where were you?'

'St Kitts.'

'Not bad.'

'Seven degrees error.'

'When was this?'

'Nineteen forty-six. A couple of years later I went to the States. It was 'forty-eight that Kagan Bookbinder gave me the part in *Last Vaquero*.'

'I've never seen the voyage used in your publicity.'

'It means too much to me, to have it used like that. You know what sort of biogs these publicity chaps dream up.'

'They sent me yours this morning.'

He laughed. 'Well, there you are.'

'You won't mind if I use the sailing story?'

'I don't know, Peter, it's a very personal thing.'

'So is a biography, Marshall.'

'You're right! OK, but use it soberly. I mean, don't make it sound as though I've scaled Everest alone or something.'

Stone told Sam Parnell that looping would end for the day and one of Stone's men helped him into his jacket, adjusted his handkerchief and held a comb and mirror for him. Stone nodded to tell me to go.

The biography could begin with the yacht. Far from the shipping routes a young actor, fresh from minor roles on the London stage, reviews his life so far.

The mountaineer, explorer and the lone sailor show a dogged indifference to hardship and privation. They also persevere in the face of a high probability of failure. These qualities they share with the actor. There were other things I liked about the lone yachtsman beginning: the sea and the stars, the nautical analogies and the man navigating through the dangerous shoals (of Hollywood?). Well, that might be too corny even for an actor's biography.

I put away my notebook and thanked Marshall. His eyes were his most powerful asset, he could momentarily hypnotize a person he faced. He must have known this, for I suspect now that he held my hands in that vice-like grip of his only in order that I should not escape his gaze. For, at the moment when Stone took your hand, there was nothing in the world for him except you. A million volts of superstar surged through you and even the most hardened cynic could become a fluttering fan.

* * *

Most of the people working in the industry are fans. Not only directors, producers and actors, but the wardrobe workers, grips and sparks are all under the spell of the golden screen. Perhaps films would be better if more of the crew were the hard-nosed cynics that the audience have become, but they are not. At any première you will see the crews, dolled up in their best suits and sequined dresses, gawking at the celebrities as pop-eyed as school kids.

That was the way it was at the European première of *Tigertrap*. They all knew that it hadn't impressed the Americans. The New York Press gave it a terrible roasting. Yet in Leicester Square the policemen were holding back the crowds as the Rolls-Royce cars arrived.

Some of the people there could remember Hollywood premières of the 'thirties, with the gigantic searchlights, jazz bands and crowds enough to back up the traffic as far as Laurel Canyon. This wasn't quite the same, but the *Tigertrap* première was as good as they got in the London of the 'seventies. The publicity boys had supplied three dozen gift-wrapped starlets, the Queen had supplied one of her relations, and the box-office money was going to charity.

I wore my dinner suit and Mary wore her pink woollen Dior. We talked to Suzy Delft, exchanged weather predictions with Stone, got a quote from Koolman, gave the photographer a caption before he left and had my own piece ready for the Ulster edition. What editor could complain about that?

Royal Première brings West End to Standstill
by our Entertainment Editor Peter Anson

A glittering array of film and TV personalities graced the Empire Cinema tonight to greet Princess Beatrice. Marshall Stone's new film *Tigertrap* was shown in aid of the Cripples Fight Back fund, of which the famous film star is the patron. Showbusiness folk turned out in their hundreds and the foyer had seldom known a more dazzling spectacle of mink and diamonds as the hard-working men and women who spend their lives entertaining us took an evening off. Before the film was shown, a number of famous personalities were presented to the Princess by Mr Marshall Stone.

Among the most important of the show-business men and women presented to Her Royal Highness was Mr Leo Koolman, the energetic president of Koolman International Pictures, the company that financed *Tigertrap*. I asked him if he thought that American companies were now reluctant to invest in British films. He said, '*Tigertrap* is a great movie, and it's British through and through. As long as your actors, producers, directors and writers remain the finest, then movie men who want the best will come here to buy.'

Among the other personalities present was Val Somerset, the young English actor whose success in *Imperial Verdict* has won him comparisons with Scofield, Guinness and Stone. Somerset said, 'I'm still learning my business and I've come along tonight because Marshall Stone is not only one of the world's great actors but also a very good friend. And Cripples Fight Back – for which Marshall has given so much of his time and energy – is a cause very dear to me.'

West End traffic was held up as far as Hyde Park Corner and Baker Street. A Metropolitan Police spokesman said, 'The worst traffic jam since the Christmas shopping last year.'

I typed it in the office and took it to the sub. He read it and said, 'You'll go too far one day, you sarcastic bastard.'

I said, 'I don't know what you're talking about, Billy.'

The photos arrived while I was talking to him. They were good photos and I wondered how much of my space they would take up. I sent one of the kids for a cup of canteen tea and then I went through the sub's tray to find a review of *Tigertrap*. The film critic had gone to the trade show three days earlier and must have turned in the copy by now, but I couldn't find a pull of it anywhere. I didn't ask for it, in case they thought I wanted the reviewer's job.

I smoked a couple of cigarettes with the sub and we talked office politics. It was too late to go back to the film so I decided that I would meet Mary when she came out.

Jack Quarrel came back from the pub looking miserable.

Jack had been on the main desk with me when we were kids at the news agency. We used to produce fillers, which is what the papers use to cement the real news to the adverts: 'Sacked stripper organizes strike', you know the sort of thing.

'Return of the reluctant hero,' said Jack. 'How are your wounds, soldier?'

'I'm expected to live.'

'Yes, I heard the prognosis was poor. How do you like being in the land of the midgets?'

'I'll get used to it.'

'I never got used to it. I'd rather be back in the bloody news agency than listening to those wonderful human beings whining for publicity.'

'They confess readily,' I agreed.

'Don't they just. Actors will confess to murder if they are guaranteed a front page.' He grinned. 'Did I just strike a nerve, Peter boy?'

'No,' I said, but it was difficult to conceal one's thoughts from Jack. His cynicism made me think that perhaps I was getting soft in my old age. And it made me think of Edgar's story about the girl and the coincidence of Stone remarking upon it too. You'd think they'd both want to hush it up.

'Look at this one the old man's thought up,' said Jack. He passed me one of the editor's long memos: 'The Senior Officer of the 'Seventies: Tyrant or Technician?'

I said, 'Judging by the amount of advertising space the Army has been buying lately, my guess is technician.'

'Clever you,' said Jack without admiration. 'They've just taken six pages of colour magazine. Why do these generals live so far out in the sticks? There's two thousand miles of driving there, and I'm not sure my old Hillman has it in her.'

I marked the name of General Millington-Ash with my thumbnail. 'Ask him if he remembers a young officer named Edward Brummage during the war, will you, Jack?'

'Marshall Stone. OK.'

'The memory box is still ticking over.'

'You book-writers haven't got it all,' said Jack, and winked at the sub.

THE BIOGRAPHY OF MARSHALL STONE

CHAPTER ONE

It was moonlight. The small ketch – *Band of Hope* – was tossed upon the grey mountainous seas like a cork along a gutter. The pump was set to full speed, and it gulped air and gasped each time the boat rolled. To the tired man who sat at the tiller there was only a glimpse of the dark sky when his cabin tilted enough to see it, the armour-glass windows ran with sea-water, making the world into a wobbling grey jelly.

The man eased his body to move the soaking clothes that hugged him like wet plaster and had already begun to make the skin of his elbows and buttocks red and raw. To the north the storm clouds had cleared enough to reveal a few stars. One, brighter than the rest, interested the lone mariner. He pulled the tiller against the fierce, throbbing sea. The bow heaved and then moved through the wind. The sailor released the lee jib sheet as she came about. He moved painfully: winching in the new lee jib and letting the main take the wind. There was a mighty thump as the sail took the blow and the boat staggered drunkenly before it filled tight with roaring wind.

Moving with the slow articulation of a robot, the sailor unlocked the door of the cabin and stepped down into it. A wave hit the deck and sprayed him with enough force to sting his face. The floor tilted unusually steeply as the ketch raced up a mountain of spume-flecked water. It came down the far side faster than the wind so that the sail gave a limp shudder. At the bottom of the trough the air renewed its grip, levering the keel against the press of the ocean.

From the shelf over the unlit stove, his last dozen tins of food shunted along the retaining rod. He struggled with the teak box that was mounted upon the bulkhead. His finger-tips were soft, white and without feeling as he tried to undo the sickle-like clip. After a few wasted moments he succeeded, and locked away the instrument that had cost him so many weeks of wages. Even that small effort caused him to sigh with exhaustion. Working in the almost impossible conditions of the small boat he had taken a sight upon the star. It was Polaris, the most important one in the heavens.

He adjusted the battery-powered lamp on the chart-table. Its beam centred upon the blank white space of the Atlantic. The ruled pencil lines bent as *Band of Hope* lurched over another wave and into its trough. There was a crash of sea-water pounding upon the cabin roof, and a long low hiss as it ran across the deck and into the scuppers. He leaned closer to watch the converging point of the pencilled bearings. 'Not bad, Eddie,' he whispered to himself. 'Not bad at all.'

Twenty-eight days from Shannon River, Eddie Brummage, today known throughout the world as Marshall Stone, had pitted himself against the odds, and won!

I would have a photo of a boat, a tiny speck in a vast ocean. There wasn't a picture of the *Band of Hope,* but any boat would do if it was too small to recognize. I clipped the rough draft together and went downstairs to breakfast. On Sundays my elder daughter cooks it and the younger sets the table. I beat in the top of my plastic egg while Mary scanned the draft. She gave it back to me without a word and continued with her coffee. She doesn't like eggs. I swallowed mine with enthusiasm and said, 'Well?'

'It's better than show-business folk turned out in their glittering array, isn't it.' I looked pained enough for her to kiss me and say, 'You're so clever, darling. It will be a wonderful book.'

'There are a few technicalities. I don't know if you do take pencil bearings from a star-shot. I've got a nasty idea that you look them up in a book, or something.'

'Why don't you ask Marshall?'

I looked to see if she was being sarcastic. I couldn't be sure. 'It's an idea,' I said.

We heard the papers arrive, and the kids rushed downstairs to get them and there was an argument about who pushed who on the way back. I kissed them better and Mary gave them a whole lettuce to feed Che.

I looked for my story but it had been spiked. They had raided my piece to make a caption for the photo of Koolman, Somerset, Stone and the Princess talking together.

> Marshall Stone with his new young colleague, Val Somerset (star of *Imperial Verdict*), talking to Princess Beatrice at the Cripples Fight Back benefit of which Mr Marshall Stone is the patron. Mr Koolman (far right), President of Koolman International who made *Tigertrap*, told our correspondent that he thought the British film industry will always remain the world's most expert.

That's the sort of thing our readers like to read with their Blue Mountain and croissants on a Sunday morning. I turned to the entertainment section and found the film reviews. Marshall Stone was important enough to get the photo and the lead review, even if it was Godard who got the rave.

FILMS

STAY OF EXECUTION
by Josephine Stewart

At one time sequels were unusual in the cinema. Now it is becoming quite common for an actor to play the same role in three or four films. Unfortunately it is seldom that such sequels excel the original. Marshall Stone's new film (*Tigertrap* – Empire Cinema) is no exception to the rule.

Is there by now anyone not bored with *Execution Man*, the ex-guards-officer secret agent who is employed by an ultra-secret department of Whitehall to eliminate those anti-social elements who are impervious to the normal processes of the judiciary. Is this why *Tigertrap's* producers feel it necessary to devote so much of their hero's energy to the gratuitous use of meretricious violence.

Undoubtedly the suggestion that inconvenient members of our society can be made to disappear found welcome audiences in both the riot-torn cities of America and the strike-bound economies of Europe. Thus the previous films featuring Marshall Stone in this role were well received by the international blue-rinse set. *Tigertrap's* emphasis upon violence will however have no appeal to the last remaining supporters of the *Execution* ethic, who prefer their ills to disappear in a puff of dust, not a sea of blood.

The self-conscious photography does nothing to hide the inadequacy of a script that is credited to no less than four writers (usually a sign of a basic weakness). Marshall Stone, with strong support from a selection of Britain's best character actors, finds no motivation or definition in his role. He vacillates between his own rangy cowboy style to the curiously tentative whisper that so ill suited his stage Hamlet.

If *Tigertrap* is a lesson in how to waste four million dollars then *Emergency Plans* shows how to make an intelligent, all-location film for less than one million. Val Somerset, who found fame overnight as the young centurion in *Imperial Verdict* now returns to the screen only five weeks later with a brilliant performance as a young doctor in a drug clinic . . .

I didn't read on. *Tigertrap* had been given the elbow by all the papers, and some of them hadn't wrapped it up as Josephine had done. Perhaps the failure in New York had already decided its fate, but I didn't think so. *Tigertrap* was a bad film. There's some kind of inverse square law that ensures that the richer, more powerful and more independent an actor becomes, so will the scripts he chooses be more feeble. Anyone who says you can't generalize about actors should add that one up some time. It must be a great temptation when you're reached the top of the acting profession to believe that you know a thing or two about scripts. Undoubtedly it was a temptation that Marshall Stone had been unable to resist, for I knew that several of *Tigertrap*'s more violent scenes had been added at his insistence.

I passed the paper to Mary. It was folded at the review. 'Josephine's given poor old Marshall a beating,' I said.

Mary read it very slowly. 'She's a spiteful little cow.'

I am always ready to play devil's advocate. 'It's a typical Jo Stewart egg-head hatchet-job, and it's exactly right for the paper. She's writing for salesmen who think they are tycoons and school teachers who think they'll become Bertrand Russell. Only one in a hundred will actually go to see the film. Only one in a thousand will see it and remember Jo's opinion.'

Mary stacked the plates. 'For the people who make the films, who devote perhaps a year to doing it . . . then it's dismissed in a couple of paragraphs. It must be very depressing.'

Mary knew that, long before our marriage, I'd had a short affair with Josephine, so we weren't really talking about film reviews but I continued as if we were. 'It's an entertainment piece: she'll keep her job according to how many readers like to read her, not according to how acute she is.'

'She likes being nasty.'

'Nasty reviews are more amusing to read than kind ones. And everyone is busy nowadays. It's a relief to hear about films, plays and books that you should miss.'

'Sometimes I wish you didn't work on the paper.'

'I know.'

'We don't need the money, darling.'

'But I've got used to the paper. One gets hooked on being close to the news. There's an atmosphere in the office . . . I can't explain.'

Mary put all the dishes on the tray and separated the knives from the spoons. 'There are times, darling, when you sound exactly like Marshall.'

That Marshall Stone smile! Here it's being aimed at pretty screen newcomer Suzy Delft while Marshall holds her make-up box. This picture answers the questions about why so many beautiful young actresses like to work on the Koolman lot. Marshall Stone is dressed as the fighter pilot for his new film *Where the Clouds Divide*.

5

Those of us who became film producers hailed from all sorts of occupations — furriers, magicians, butchers, boilermakers — and for this reason highbrows have often poked fun at us.

Adolph Zukor

The phone at Weinberger's bedside had the quietest ringing tone of any in the world: Mrs Weinberger had removed the bell. And yet after only one buzz Weinberger would always have the phone at his ear and be talking into it like a man wide awake, with a thousand contracts and letters of agreement flowing through his mind. New York was five hours behind London and calls from the West Coast were even more inconvenient. When there was a complicated deal going through, Weinberger slept late, knowing that his working day would start in the afternoon and go on into the small hours of the night.

'Weinberger.' He looked at the clock by his bed. It was ten o'clock Sunday morning. He slapped the bed beside him sleepily but Lucy was not there. She was a good wife. Soon she would bring him coffee and freshly pressed orange juice, the airmailed *Variety* and *Daily Cinema* that he liked to read in bed on Sunday while she read the newspapers.

'Putting you through now: here's Mr Weinberger.' Someone even had his office staff working on Sunday. There was only one person it could be, thought Weinberger.

'Jacob? Leo here. Leo Koolman.' To offer his surname was as near to modesty as Koolman ever came.

'What is it, Leo?'

'I'm in the office, Jacob. I've had a telex from the Coast. They want an OK on the TV series for Stone. They are running out of time on their option for the sequel rights. It will cost us another hundred thousand to renew it. I want Stone signed. Bring me the contract today, Jacob, and then I can call them back.'

'I haven't talked to Marshall yet, Leo. I need to have him in the right mood.'

'The right mood! I'm paying that dummy four million dollars and for this you need him in a good mood?'

'That's if it goes very big, Leo. That's if it's the greatest TV serial since "Peyton Place", he might get three point seven for eight seasons. But when you read the small print you'll find it's also possible to unload him with fifty thousand and a thank you.'

'Jacob. In the States, Marshall is represented by that little woman Sandra Behring, isn't he? She's a good little soul.'

Weinberger smiled to himself. He'd wondered how long it would be before Koolman threatened to shift the deal across the Atlantic so that Weinberger would have to split his ten per cent. 'You'd worry Marshall if you did that, Leo. Do it, but you'll worry him.'

Leo Koolman grunted and abandoned his threat. His voice changed. 'Jacob, old friend, I'm just trying to make fine films. That's what we all want, isn't it. The cinema is an art, Jacob, and Marshall is an artist – or rather an artiste – a great artiste. On TV a work of art becomes available to millions, am I right?' There was a long silence until Koolman said, 'Are you still there, Jacob?'

'The trouble is, Leo, all you ever think about is art, and all the artistes ever think about is money.'

'What are you trying to do to me?' said Koolman. 'Are you going to stall until a few minutes before my option ends and then screw me for more money?'

'Have I ever done that, Leo?'

'Of course you have,' said Koolman. 'You screwed a stop-date and eleven days of dubbing out of me after Marshall had signed for *Silent Paradise*.'

'Let's not open that can of works, Leo.'

'OK, OK, OK, what you do is to see Stone today and talk to him, right? Tell him to crap or get off the pot, Jacob. If he doesn't want the TV deal, we'll give it to someone who does. Already I'm talking to other people – and other agents – talk to him today.'

'Marshall might be recording.'

'He's not recording. They are on a five-day schedule; they record on Saturdays.' Weinberger nodded. Trust Koolman to know the day-to-day schedule of his productions.

'Then he's probably at Twin Beeches,' said Weinberger.

'Sure, he's down at that big country place where he gets himself photographed with the horses. His director has a meeting with him there. Somerset will be lunching there too. Just drop in and talk some sense into your client.'

Lucy Weinberger entered the bedroom quietly. She put the tray on the bed and put saccharin into her husband's coffee. He scowled in mock anger. He preferred sugar.

'We're businessmen, Jacob. If we ever started to make things difficult for each other, our lives would become unbearable. There are probably all sorts of odds and ends of paperwork which I'm in no hurry to complete and you are. With the Stone contract it's the other way round. I know I can rely on you, Jacob, my old friend. You've never let me down.'

'I'll try, Leo,' said Weinberger, ignoring a threat about Suzy Delft's contract, which Weinberger needed soon if he was to help her tax spread. Weinberger took his coffee and smelled the strong black brew with its faint aroma of figs. It took him back to his childhood.

'That's it,' said Koolman. 'You try. Have you got the contracts at home with you?'

'Yes, I've got them.'

'If you've left them in your office, I'll send you another set by cab.'

'I've got them here, Leo. But there's no chance of my letting Marshall sign them without a change in that deferment clause. If he had to wait for profits to arise before getting the second-stage payment he might find himself working for a thousand dollars a day.'

'That would be tragic,' said Koolman sarcastically. 'Imagine him only getting one thousand dollars a day. Let me tell you something, Jacob. Some of the men who teach my son at Eton College get less than twenty dollars a day and Marshall God-damned Stone isn't fit to wipe their arses.'

'You could be right,' said Weinberger calmly. 'But Marshall's rate for the last three pictures has been a million straight, or

85

sixteen thousand a day. We must delete the whole deferment clause.'

'How many days?'

'For what?'

'How many days has he had on each picture? You're talking about guest-star fees. You're talking about a few days as a guest star on films that need a name on the marquee. I'm talking about full-length star parts.'

'You know what his fee is, Leo.'

'On *Silent Paradise* he got eight hundred.'

'Plus ten thousand a day for the three weeks over, and the same for the recording days.'

'So we are talking ten now? Well, that's better than sixteen.'

Weinberger realized that he had been tricked into bargaining. 'Anyway, that's history, Leo. Until I talk to Marshall I can't be sure he'll agree to do the TV series whatever kind of money you offer.'

'What's wrong with this guy's mind?'

'There's nothing wrong with his mind, Leo. All actors are careful about going into a TV series. The over-exposure could ruin him.'

'This is not a TV series: there are ninety-minute specials going out once a month. I've got the finest writers and the finest directors in the business working on these stories: people he should be proud to associate with. Already I'm selling this in Germany and France and Italy. For some territories it will go for regular movie theatre distribution. Only the US will put it straight on to television.'

'Then let me put that in the contract.'

'Put what?'

'Outside the US it will be for normal theatre distribution.'

'What are you trying to do, Jacob? You want to take over my office? You want to do my job for me?'

Patiently Weinberger started all over again. 'It will help me persuade Marshall if I can tell him that. I'll put it to him like that, Leo, but I will need it in writing.'

'You tell Marshall Stone that if there's anything he wants to know he can call me, at home or the office.' It was a regal dismissal. Weinberger had learned to recognize them in many forms.

'Right, Leo.' The phone went dead even before he said it. Koolman never said goodbye. At one time Weinberger had persistently phoned him back and pretended to believe that they had been cut off. Now he no longer had the energy for such jokes and the humour had worn thin.

Weinberger turned to his breakfast. *Variety* remained unopened while he ate Harrods croissants and his wife's apricot jam. Sunday morning was an unreal time, and Weinberger cherished it. He read and listened to the radio, dozed a little and sometimes made love. One day he would retire, and the remainder of his life would be one long Sunday morning.

Weinberger yawned and climbed out of bed. He looked at himself in the mirror. With his rumpled pyjamas and disarranged hair he looked like a clown and yet he performed his morning exercises with ease. If his wife was surprised to see him bending and stretching she gave no sign of it. She poured herself a cup of coffee and said, 'Have you got to go out, my love?'

'Twin Beeches.'

'Take your coat. It's sunny but it's cold. There will be all sorts of famous people there.'

'How do you know, darling?'

' "Sunday is a special event at Twin Beeches. Marshall Stone has all the notables of show business to wine and dine with him on Sunday. After lunch he shows a film in his private cinema. Every friend he has in show business feels free to go along." '

'It won't be crowded,' said Weinberger. His wife was a good woman, but he wished she wouldn't quote the fan magazines to him.

It's a funny thing, these kids get out here from New York, stage directors, and the first thing they do when they

*get here, they forget the story, forget the people, forget
the characters, forget the dialogue and they con-
centrate on this new, wonderful toy, the camera.*

John Ford

Stone got up from the sofa and walked to the window. Richard
Preston – his director – was uneasy, wondering if he had
offended him. He looked the way Stone was looking. The sky
was dark and cloudy. It was darker than the fields of corn
which the sun lit bright gold. Now that the rain had passed, the
air was unnaturally clear and they could see the whitewashed
cottages on the London road.

A groom and a stable boy had been caught in the shower.
They cantered through the lower meadow. Stone watched
them as the boy opened the gate and remounted to take the
copse path back to the stables. These new yearlings were going
to be very special, but it was absurd that he had so little time to
enjoy himself. He'd heard people say that the public used
film stars to do their living for them: to make love and money,
brawl, drink and die on behalf of the man in the street who
regarded life as a spectator sport. But in his life it seemed just
the reverse: the crew of his boat, his pilot and even his stable
boys enjoyed more of the luxury of life than he ever did.
Perhaps it was a self-inflicted deprivation.

It was ironic: he was at the peak of his career, a million
dollars per film with a couple of good performances not yet
screened, and yet he was grappling with his latest role like an
amateur. Ever since Leo had mentioned the possibility of an
Oscar he had been unable to do anything right. Such lavish
compliments, and the interest shown by the fellow writing the
biography, made him feel guilty. There were moments when he
wanted to jump for joy or do a film for nothing just to show
Leo – and all the world – how much he appreciated such recognition.

He turned again to the script of *Stool Pigeon*. He didn't like
Captain Holloway – the part he was playing – he was a cynical,
devious man, indifferent to the pains and anguish of his fellow
men. He couldn't find such a man within himself.

'He's wrong, he's wrong, he's wrong,' said Stone.

'If he goes back to save the injured sergeant, it will be contradicting everything we've said about him,' said Preston.

'But that's just why it's more truthful,' said Stone. 'Sometimes a man does change like that.'

'Are you sure it's not because you want the audience to like you better?'

'No, no, no,' said Stone. He wondered why he had agreed to do this film. He'd never liked the script and he'd never really had confidence in this twenty-one-year-old director, and yet the director's youth had made Stone hope that in this film he'd again find the enthusiasm and energy that he'd once known. The crew were quite good: he knew all of them, from the art director to the wardrobe master. He'd been confident that those old-timers, with Edgar running things, would be enough to control the crazy enthusiasm of the boy: now he wondered. He looked again at the script.

197 INT. JUNGLE HUT. DAY

CAPT HOLLOWAY *is counting ammunition on to the table.*

SGT BOX *is standing beside him, dividing the bullets into seven separate heaps.* PTE FORTESCUE, *almost dead, is groaning as he moves restlessly on the native bed in the background.*

CAPT HOLLOWAY: Make it six heaps, Sergeant. Private Harmsworth will be armed only with a bayonet.

SGT BOX (*looking up in surprise*): But Harmsworth is the best shot in the regiment, sir. We'll need him if we are going to get through the Jap lines.

CAPT HOLLOWAY (*quietly*): Harmsworth is an insubordinate bastard, and when we get back to base, I'll have him serving a couple of years in the glasshouse.

SGT BOX (*meaningfully*): You mean, if we get back (*pause*), sir.

CAPT HOLLOWAY (*parade-ground voice*) Get the men on parade.

SGT BOX: Sir!

*   *   *

There was a long pause during which they both stared at their copies of the script. Finally Preston read a line aloud: 'Get the men on parade.'

'Please don't do that, Richard.'

'What?'

'Speak a line before you've heard me say it. It screws an actor up to hear a line before he's created it.'

'But I've been doing that since we started.'

'Yes, I know.'

'You should have told me.' Preston was ruffled and Stone did not want that.

'It's a good tip when working with actors, Rich.'

'You just want me to talk motivation?'

Stone smiled. He thought he'd say motivation before eleven AM. It was a wonder that it had taken so long. He wondered if he would ever meet a director who had as little faith in motivation as he had. If motivation was the secret of a performance, then why weren't these bloody directors – and writers – the most famous actors in the world. 'We can spend all day talking about motivation, but the audience are concerned with the credibility of my actions, not the profundity of my thoughts. It's my face, my manner, my bits of business that create this man Holloway. Motivation is just the perspective.'

'I want you to be happy,' said Preston. It was a meaningless interjection that he'd learned from Edgar Nicolson.

When he had first read the script, Stone had thought it rather slick. There had been many films like this before and they had usually done well at the box office. The role of Captain Holloway had been an exciting prospect. Stone had even taken lessons in driving a motor-cycle with a view to a touch of the Easy Riders in the sort of close-ups that stunt men couldn't do for anyone. He'd gone on the pistol range, too, and Jasper had given him some military drill – saluting, marching and yelling orders – but Holloway had never come to life. There was no tension within the role, no contradiction, no paradox that made the part worth tackling.

Of everything learned in a lifetime of acting, nothing was more vital than to bring sympathy and understanding to the role. Child-murderer or dictator, they must be portrayed with enough skill to persuade the audience that here, but for the grace of God, goes them: every man jack of them! For Captain Holloway, Stone could not do it, and Preston was not likely to show him the way.

The rewrites had done nothing to improve things. Each had been printed on a different-coloured paper so that the edges of the script were a rainbow of renewals. There had been other alterations, too. This version had the word 'Nip' deleted in Pentel and rewritten 'Japanese'. Someone from head office had warned them that such slips could ruin the chances of this film in the Far East.

Stone stroked the blunt moustache. He liked to change his appearance for a new role. The physical change helped him maintain the new mental attitude that each part demanded of him. He read the scene again. 'It's a bloody awful script, darling,' he said to the director.

'You're telling me.' Preston produced a small tin and some cigarette papers. Carefully he rolled a joint, looking up from time to time to see if Stone was watching, but Stone was examining his fingernails.

'Got a light, Marshall?'

Without looking up, Stone passed him a silver table-lighter. The boy lit the warped cigarette, holding it between all his fingertips and his thumb in an ostentatious way. He inhaled and then offered it to Stone.

'Have a drag?'

Stone took his time in examining the stained cigarette before shaking his head.

'Nervous?' said Preston. He smiled and winked.

'Yes,' said Stone, 'but not of mary-jew-arna – of your germs.'

'Come on, Marshall. It'll relax you.'

'Doesn't seem to be relaxing you, Richard. No, if I want a joint I can afford one all to myself, thanks. I don't care for the communal life bit.'

Preston smiled awkwardly, not knowing if he should re-taliate, or how to. This was his first visit to Stone's house, and he was suitably over-awed by the wood carvings, the antiques and the white-coated servants who moved quietly and spoke like bank managers. Preston felt out of place in his beaded headband and embroidered Afghan waistcoat. He looked at Stone.

Stone closed the red leather script cover that he'd bought in Gucci. He remembered how excited the salesgirls had been: they'd made him sign the backs of their hands in lipstick. They'd followed him out on to the via Condotti and called after him. Stone put the script aside and patted the cover. 'Can't understand a word of it, darling. I'm only a bloody actor, you know. I'm not an intellectual, I mean . . . Richard . . .' He patted the director's knee. 'What does the beginning mean? Why am I stabbing the pillow? And that explosion at the end . . .' he shrugged.

'Every movie should have a beginning a middle and an end,' said Preston with the gentle smile of a conjuror about to perform a particularly baffling trick. 'But not necessarily in that order. Godard said that, and I believe it.'

'But does the audience believe it? That's what I want to know, Richard.'

'Jesus, Marshall, you keep on about the audience, just like those bastards in Wardour Street.'

Stone smiled, and that irritated Preston. Stone said, 'It's the audience who pay to come in.'

'Screw the audience. Just for one moment will you try and understand that we are trying to create a work of art. Rod Steiger said, "A film is the most expensive art form in the world." '

Stone nodded glumly. The boy had read every film book and magazine ever published and he could remember every word of them, when it suited him. Preston had a thousand theories about movies and he was determined to try them all out in his first film.

'But this scene with the wife,' said Stone. 'I'm never going to see her again. I must kiss her goodbye. That must be the climax of that whole sequence.'

'What we are seeing is a subconscious fantasy. He's not going to the war at all – at least, not in his mind.'

'No imagination,' nodded Stone. 'Well, perhaps I've got too much imagination.' Preston said nothing. Stone said, 'I can imagine myself getting a big laugh in that scene, for instance.'

'Don't worry, Marshall. We will have cut from the boat when your adjutant is fished out of the water dead. No danger of a laugh on that cut.'

'I'm not so sure.' Stone had a nasty suspicion that the scene on the rowing-boat with Percy Hampton soaking wet and flying through the air on the end of a crane hook could be highly risible. He turned his script back to the bedroom scene. 'I want to talk to you about the bedroom scene, from ninety-three to one hundred and eight. There's too much of me in voice-over. I think I should come on camera much earlier. What will the girl be doing in shot ninety-five, for instance?'

'This will blow your mind, Marshall baby. A great sequence: a wind machine blowing her hair, but over-cranked. Get it? The hair in slow motion, symbolizing the torment in her mind.'

'Suppose I lean into the frame and kiss her before I speak? Just to give the audience the geography.'

The boy's voice had pain and reproof in it. 'No can do, Marshall love! She's in bed; you're in the dressing-room. You stay apart: no two-shot. We did the girl's scene – except for the over-cranked close-up – last week.'

'You didn't?'

'It was scheduled, Marshall. And let's face it, could you handle that sort of close-up with the girl? She's only a kid, you know, and you are getting a bit wrinkled.' Preston rubbed his face and tried to focus on Stone. His shoulder-length hair was getting into his eyes and he pulled it into a pony tail and snapped an elastic band over it. 'It was scheduled.'

'I don't care if it was ordained by the Archbishop of Canterbury,' said Stone. 'That's a key scene, we must do it together, me and Suzy.'

'It *was* ordained by the Archbishop of Canterbury,' said Preston. 'Leo Koolman made us give a stop-date on Suzy so that she can do a skin-flick they are shooting in Stockholm. In Stockholm they really need the daylight.'

'Never mind what they need in Stockholm,' said Stone. 'You should have put your foot down. Why give a stop-date? You tell Leo Koolman to get screwed.'

'You can do that and get away with your life, Marshall. I'd never be heard of again.' He shook his head sorrowfully.

Stone got up and walked across to the fireplace. He stood looking at the flames for a moment. He liked an open fire. One of the reasons he'd moved to England was that he could have an open fire even in summer. He pressed the service button. The butler entered. 'Yes, sir?'

'Let's have another bottle of champagne, Patterson. And some coffee and that cream gâteau that we had before.'

'No gâteau for me,' said the boy. He held up his hands as if shielding his eyes against celestial light. 'I'm trying to cut my weight down.'

'Bring some,' said Stone. 'He might succumb.'

Stone stood in silence at the window, watching the cows move along the lower field. Preston remained where he was. Neither spoke. They still hadn't moved when the butler returned to set china, silver and linen upon the coffee table in front of the fire. They heard him open the champagne and pour the coffee. Preston tried to think of some appropriate remark about the champagne being opened but Stone seemed not to have heard it. It was a more sophisticated attitude, and Preston noted it.

'It's cold for August,' said Stone.

'Damned cold,' said Preston.

'You're too young to remember the war,' said Stone.

'Wasn't born.' Preston would have liked to have kept the conversation going but he could think of nothing to add. Stone offered him the coffee and champagne and forced a piece of cream cake upon him. As soon as the boy took the large piece of cream cake Stone felt much happier. It reassured him to see that the boy was unable to keep his resolve. Stone could resist temptation and that made him stronger than all the Prestons in the film world, and as far as Stone could see, the film world was becoming all Prestons.

The boy swallowed a large portion of cake and said, 'Have you ever thought of directing, Marshall?'

'I've directed a stage performance: Richard Three, Harrogate Festival, about twelve years ago.'

'What about a feature film?'

'It's a disease that actors past their prime fall prey to.'

'Seriously?'

'Look,' said Stone, walking across the room and glancing at his reflection in the ornate mirror over the fireplace. 'The only way I could talk a distribution company into letting me direct would be to give them my own performance at bargain price. That film would have an amateur director and a twit as the star. What chance would it stand?'

They both laughed. 'If the script was right . . .?'

Stone shook his head.

Preston rubbed his face again. 'Jesus, I was smashed last night. Some of the guys at this party were on methedrine with their acid. I mean it. They were speeding and tripping at the same time. That's too much, man, too much.'

Stone took a sip of champagne and then some coffee. He said nothing.

'I was on LSD. It expands the frontiers of perception. All creative people need it. Can you imagine what great stuff Michelangelo would have been able to paint if he'd had some really great trips?'

'Michelangelo Antonioni?'

'Don't kid around, Marshall; the painter.'

'Some of his things are not bad anyway.'

'Are you putting me on, Marshall?'

'Of course I am,' said Stone. He put his black coffee, no sugar, down on the grand piano. He leaned across the framed photos and inhaled the perfume of four dozen roses that were in a Chinese vase. 'That's my trip,' said Stone, Preston watched Stone. There was a long silence. The boy never knew when he was saying the right thing or the wrong thing. He felt that Stone was judging him all the time.

'You were in the war, Marshall?'

'I was,' said Stone. 'I killed a few chaps, too, if that's what you're leading up to.'

The boy said nothing. That was what he had been leading up to.

'It was ghastly,' said Stone.

'Perhaps that's why you're having trouble with Holloway.'

'Sure of it,' he nodded.

'You should have said.'

'The show must go on,' said Stone. He smiled. 'It's just that this business with the knife . . .'

Preston waited. Stone said, 'Well . . . it was just like that . . . that time . . . bloody, sodding awful, Richard.' He smacked a fist into his open hand. 'German diesel fuel had a strange smell. The three Huns I'd put paid to floated with me all night. Kept shoving them away but they floated back. Years after I could still smell that diesel oil.'

'Could you?'

'Not really, of course – head-shrinker jaw-jaw – *Macbeth*, and all that.'

'I'm sorry, Marshall.'

Stone came and sat down near to Preston. He poured more champagne for the boy and helped him to cake. For himself he poured coffee. His voice was almost a whisper. 'I'll be all right, Rich. Catharsis, eh? I'll give you your Captain Holloway with knobs on. Only you and I need know that this will really be Captain bloody Brummage doing his little bit of blood-letting for England, home and beauty.'

Preston finished the cake and two glasses of champagne. Then he said, 'Marshall, you haven't got a joint anywhere around the place, have you?'

'No,' said Stone, 'I don't use them.' He said it in the same stern voice that he used for Captain Holloway.

Sunday lunch at Twin Beeches was a ritual. Jealous voices made fun of Stone's lavish hospitality. They said that the vocal accompaniment of so many show-business personalities prevented it being compared with a ballet, so they called these lunches 'operas'. Three servants brought each dish to the table and paraded it past the guests before putting it upon the heated serving table that was built into a seventeenth-century sideboard. Silver lids were drawn aside with no more sound than might be produced by the most discreet Chinese gong. The platters were precious metal, the garnishes were flamboyant and anything that could be flambé was flambé. Weinberger said the only time he'd ever tasted gefillte fish flambé was at Twin Beeches, and only people who had never been there laughed.

There were seven people at lunch that Sunday. Stone didn't invite Preston to stay. Stone believed that the whole art of entertaining was to reject people who brought neither wit nor beauty nor prestige to the gathering, although it would be hard to define which of those vital elements the two PR men from Hollywood represented.

Weinberger had a drink with Suzy Delft – a weekend guest – while Stone said goodbye to Preston. Then Val Somerset arrived with his girlfriend, Joan Forrest.

It was easy to see why Stone regarded Val Somerset as a serious rival. He had the same bony face and hard eyes that Stone had made famous. His hair was long and wavy, as one could see Stone's in old movie annuals. He had the same tight-lipped smile that made the broad teeth-flashing radiance so welcome when it did finally come. To what extent Val Somerset had based his technique upon Stone was difficult to say. Even Somerset himself was not too sure. But he certainly knew at what point to depart from Stone's style. At lunch Somerset was dressed in a lightweight suit that was the colour of plain chocolate. His white shirt was slightly open at the neck, which made his deep tan more apparent. The modest simplicity of his appearance made Stone seem conspicuously over-adorned.

Inspired by Preston, Stone came to lunch in pale-blue cotton trousers and a floral silk shirt that fastened along the shoulder. A golden chain and a medallion dangled upon his chest. From time to time Stone fingered the medallion.

Somerset had used against him the weapon to which he was most vulnerable: youth. Never had Stone felt his age weigh so heavily upon him. Almost half a century: it suffocated him so that he spoke in a whisper, and disgusted him so that he could not bear to look at the liver-spots on the backs of his wrinkled hands. Even the careless way in which Somerset had parked his second-hand, souped-up Mini – filthy and dented and one door ajar – alongside Stone's immaculate Rolls-Royce was a way of saying that the cinema had entered a new youth-worshipping phase of its history: a phase without superstars.

Weinberger knew what was troubling Stone. He knew from the way in which he treated Somerset. Stone surprised the young actor with his attention. He refilled the boy's glass instead of letting a servant do it. He admired his appearance, asked who his tailor was, delighted in his dark tan, guffawed at the boy's jokes and found for him the oldest brandies and finest cigars.

'When I saw *Imperial Verdict*, I knew it was one of the finest performances that I have ever seen on the screen.' He shook his head as he remembered it. 'I went back the next day in case I had been mistaken: I hadn't been.'

'The funeral scene was good,' admitted Somerset.

'The funeral scene was good?' repeated Stone in amazement. 'The funeral scene was good?' He laughed briefly. 'The funeral scene, my dear boy, was bloody marvellous. A masterpiece.'

'Old Tommy is still the guv'nor with a historical film.'

'He's a good director when he's handling a crowd, but what he knows about actors you could write on the head of a pin . . . and still have room for the Lord's Prayer.' Stone laughed. 'That sequence where you are in the barge trying to persuade the empress to reprieve the slave. That was great, Val, and don't tell me old Tommy could give you any help with a scene like that.'

'I'm glad you liked it, Marshall. Coming from you, it's a really wonderful compliment.'

Joan Forrest had played minor parts in TV films with Somerset when he too was playing those sort of roles. She was a thin edgy creature, with a shrill London accent and a wailing laugh that she used in fashionable restaurants and interviews.

'What do you think about acting with Val, Marshall?' she asked.

'It would be wonderful,' said Stone, 'really wonderful.'

Weinberger shot Somerset a warning glance, but they both knew it was too late. The only way to handle it was to rush right in. Weinberger said, 'Leo Koolman was toying with the idea of asking Val to play the part of the American general in *Stool Pigeon*.'

Stone said, 'He's already signed that German actor – Max Georg – for the part.'

'He's released him to star in some German film that Koolman's got an interest in,' explained Somerset. 'I can have the part if I want it.'

Stone had always used his smiles as a mask behind which he

could arrange his thoughts and his attitudes. The broader the smile; the greater his disquiet.

'And if you want me,' Somerset added.

'Want you, darling,' said Stone. 'That would be absolutely fantastic. You, me and Suzy . . . that would be superb fun. Can't we persuade old Leo to find a part for Joan too? How about that, Viney, she's also a client, isn't she?' Weinberger's face tightened as he registered the implication.

'Joan's retired,' said Somerset.

'Retired?' said Stone.

'Val has bought me a boutique.'

'Then perhaps we could find something more for you, Val. Perhaps the Japanese sergeant could be the American general's twin brother. You could play both parts, like in *The Corsican Brothers*.' Stone smiled and punched Somerset playfully, to show that it was all in fun. The young actor smiled and nodded his forgiveness.

Joan Forrest said. 'You are a shit, Marshall Stone.'

There was a silence, broken by Weinberger pouring himself a glass of iced water. An ice cube tumbled into his glass with a loud splash.

'Thank you and goodnight, Miss Joan Forrest,' said Stone, trying to make a joke of it.

'That's the dignity that aristocrats show in the face of ungrateful peasants, I suppose,' she said. 'Well, Val didn't write your reviews today, so don't take it out on us.'

Stone said nothing. He believed that Weinberger would do something immediately to relieve the distress and humiliation. After all, Weinberger took ten per cent of his gross – gross, not net, mark you – and that's a bloody fortune. But Weinberger did nothing except fold his table napkin into complex accordion pleats and press it down on the table while examining it closely.

'We must be going, Marshall,' said Val Somerset. 'My God, is that the right time?' He looked at the clock on the mantelpiece. It wasn't the sort of clock that ever told the wrong time. 'A really great lunch, Marshall, and don't take any notice of Joan's ribbing. That's what I have to put up with all the time.'

'I thought you'd stay for the movie: *The Red Desert*. Anyway, let's crack another bottle of champagne.'

Somerset said, 'I'd love to, but it's the *Imperial Verdict* première in Paris. I must be there.'

'Good grief!' said Stone. 'You could have used the Friendship.' Stone's one-third share in the Fokker turboprop remained one of his most cherished possessions. A Lear Jet like Sinatra's might have double the speed and far greater range but it could take only eight or nine people. Stone could throw a party in his aeroplane, and had done. It was a pity that the fifteen-year-old plane had to spend so much time in the maintenance hanger, but Stone feigned an interest in the technical decisions. 'Why didn't you say, Val? The starboard motor had to go to the bench for a new fan but it could easily have waited a week. She wasn't overheating or anything.'

'Next time, Marshall.'

'We could have all packed into it – it seats forty passengers.'

'That would be great, Marshall.'

'Any time, Val, any time.'

Laughing, shouting and hugging Stone, his guests went away. He responded joyously, joking about the rust on the Mini, and half closing the big white gate so that they could not get away. But when they had gone his energy had gone too. He waved away a servant's query about screening the film, and picked up a napkin to rub his face hard and be rid of the perfume of the kisses that Joan Forrest had left there. The memory of Suzy being a witness to the scene made him flush with shame and anger.

Weinberger had not moved from the dining table, but when Stone came back he stood up. Stone put an arm around his agent and guided him into the drawing-room. It was a big room and, in spite of the wide windows that looked out to a gigantic lawn, dark. It had become another chilly August day and the log fire flickered as convincingly as the electric fake in his London flat. Everything in the room was expensive and that, together with the stillness and the gloom, produced a forbidding atmosphere, like a museum. There was nothing cheap or vulgar here, nothing that its owner might have bought when he was young and poor. Just as there was no photograph or memento that dated from that period. His family, his schooldays, his courtship, his marriage, the years of the war and his time as a struggling young actor were unrecorded as if they had never been.

Stone went to the sideboard and poured two stiff brandies with soda. He seldom drank alcohol, but today he needed one. Weinberger arranged a big pile of documents on the carpet.

'Marshall, I want to talk to you about your whole career.' Stone felt a wave of nausea. He always did when he had to talk about money, or business, or insurance, or health, or any other aspect of life where fate could attack him. He gave Weinberger the drink in the hope that he could defer the moment, but Weinberger put it aside without looking at it.

'Looking over the last decade, you've achieved miracles,' said Weinberger. Stone didn't answer. 'No actor grossed much more than you did last year. Mind you, it was hard work, but I think you'll agree it was worth it.' He leaned down over his papers so that his forehead almost touched the floor, as if he was praying. He turned over a neat page of notes and figures.

'Thanks to you, Viney,' said Stone. He knew that this was only the sweetening on the pill.

Weinberger shrugged. Stone prepared himself for the next part of Weinberger's talk. 'The industry is changing, Marshall.' He was still bending close to his papers.

'It's been changing every year for the last fifty years, Viney. They'd all like to get rid of the stars. They hate us: the renters, directors, writers and producers, they all hate us. They'd all be happier if there were no stars.'

'Perhaps,' said Weinberger cautiously. He sat back and looked at Stone. 'But until now the whole industry has remained convinced that it is big names who bring the public into the theatres. Now, everywhere I go, I detect a tendency to think otherwise.'

Stone got to his feet. 'Look, Viney, this industry is always looking for the philosopher's stone. When *Gone with the Wind* broke all records they couldn't get enough costume dramas — *Sound of Music* put the smart money on musicals. *Love Story* had them making weepies again. And what happens: all the imitations sank without a ripple.'

'Imitations are always dangerous.'

'Certainly they are. How many times have they told us that they were going to do another *Easy Rider* or another *Graduate*, when all they meant was they didn't have a story or a script.'

'Or another *Dirty Dozen*,' said Weinberger archly.

'I was wrong about *Stool Pigeon* and I admit it. I just wanted to do poor old Edgar a favour.'

'Now, that's not quite true, Marshall. You wanted Leo to buy *Stool Pigeon* from Edgar in order to have another producer do it for you.'

'I can't remember the exact details,' said Stone. 'But I remember saying that we must be sure that Edgar comes out of it financially OK.'

'Well, he is financially OK: he's getting his producers' money up front and he didn't get stuck with the property. If that kid can't put the footage together it will be Leo Koolman's headache, not Edgar's.'

'Leo is no fool,' said Stone. 'He knows what's what. You heard what he said to me at dinner the other night. He knows that stars still sell tickets.'

Weinberger hedged. 'Leo has a well-developed sense of self-preservation. He'll make a dollar in the industry as long as there is a dollar to be made there.'

'There will be big money there for a long time, Viney. Three billion dollars world-wide in admissions last year. Slice it up any way you like, there are still big crumbs spilling from that plate.'

'We've got to get into the TV and the cassette business, Marshall. The movie house is a dying institution.'

'The six-hundred or seven-hundred-seat theatre is doing all right. It's the huge fifteen-hundred-seaters that are closing.'

'And then it will be the two-hundred-seaters that are doing all right. And then the fifty-seaters. And then it will be only the two people on a sofa that are doing all right. You've got to face it, Marshall, TV is here to stay.'

'You're not going to start that all over again.' He smiled. 'Viney, have you ever had your hair done at André: my barber?

He'd razor-shape the sides for you. You'd be surprised what a difference it could make.'

Weinberger looked at Stone, smiled, but didn't reply.

'You wouldn't have to leave your regular barber, Viney. You'd just need André to shape it once a month.'

'I don't have any overdeveloped feelings of loyalty to my barber, Marshall. But I don't have enough time, enough money or enough hair to go to André.'

'That's a good one, Viney.' Stone laughed. Weinberger laughed just long enough to get Stone's full attention. Then he said, 'You'd better listen to this, Marshall, because it's a very serious decision you are going to make, and I can't make it for you.'

Stone nodded and sat down.

'The cassette TV market is going to be big. We both believe that.'

'Right, right, right.'

Weinberger continued his argument without pausing, 'And that market is going to be influenced by day-by-day TV programming.'

'Perhaps.'

'No one can be sure, Marshall, but I believe that to be seen only in movie houses will mean a slow death. Koolman has sold your three *Execution Man* films to the networks. Now he wants to prepare a pilot to show how the same serial character could run as TV specials: one a month.'

'With me in the lead?'

'Leo knows he can't get anyone to take over from you without the bottom falling out of the characterization.'

'Don't snow me, Viney.'

'I'm just repeating what Leo said.'

'How many would he want?'

'Ten episodes.'

'Not twenty?'

'Leo wants twenty, but I think I can convince him that ten, and a chance for either side to break, would be better business. He knows you can always be sick or something.'

'I don't like it, Viney.'

'Marshall, I don't think we are in a position to argue. *The*

Folksinger and *Snap, Crackle, Pop* have both lost money. *Tigertrap* is not doing so well. We might have trouble getting your price on the next movie.'

Stone shivered. Weinberger wouldn't say such things if he knew the terrible effect his words could have upon an actor's metabolism. His stomach rebelled. He'd be unable to face solid food for at least twenty-four hours. '*Tigertrap* is picking up. Did you see this week's *Variety*? The Philadelphia figures had the headline "Trap is Sprung" and Seattle had "Trap Warms". It could turn out to be a sleeper.'

'Did you read the grosses in those headlines? Did you look at the computerized chart? The trouble is, the few places where it's picked up have been hard-top theatres. In the drive-ins and in the college circuit it's died everywhere.'

'The drive-ins,' scoffed Stone. 'They were running it with two other features in the same bill. *Two* others, Viney: *Girl Time* and an old Doris Day. What chance does it stand with that kind of programming? And who cares about the college circuit.'

'The kids are in the college circuit, Marshall. Too many of your fans are over forty. They stay at home with their TV, and that's why we are stuck with this deal of Leo's.'

'Where have you been lately, Viney? The kids go for me. There's a lot of protest in that *Tigertrap* film and the kids just have to find what sort of film it is to make it into a smash. Did you hear about the army of kids that mobbed me outside the Tiktok the other afternoon?'

'I was there, Marshall, I collected you from Tiktok, remember? But Marshall, you *know* those kids were waiting to see The Counting House Silver.'

'The what?'

'A pop group, recording in Tiktok's big recording studio upstairs. The kids were waiting for them. You were a bonus. You knew that.'

'Jesus, Viney. You hit below the belt.'

'Did you read the reviews today, Marshall?'

Stone shook his head. 'Please, Weinberger, stop, please stop. I've been on the go all day. The horses . . . the mare might be in foal . . . I've been trying to contact the vet. And there was my meeting with Preston.'

'Marshall!'

'Are they that bad, Viney?'

'They don't exactly put us in a position to give Leo Koolman a tough time.'

'Oh, Lord.'

'I don't want to hurt you, Marshall.' Weinberger wished that for just one moment he could muster some of the schmaltz of show business. He wanted to hug Stone, to comfort him in the sort of embrace that came so naturally to the actors that Weinberger represented. He wanted to tell Stone what a superb actor he was, and of the pleasure and understanding that he brought to millions of people. He wanted to tell him that his Hamlet had given Weinberger a new insight into a play that he could almost recite by heart. He wanted to tell him of the coilspring energy that had been *Tigertrap*'s one and only saving grace. He wanted to tell Stone that in spite of his paranoia, rudeness, lies and egomania, representing such a great talent gave Weinberger a satisfaction that no other client could possibly give him. He wanted to tell Stone that he loved him like a brother, but Weinberger would rather be dead than display his feelings thus.

Weinberger rubbed a big hand over his face, squashing it mercilessly as if in self-punishment. He blinked, and then said, 'Leo expects a bit of foreplay on any contract. It would probably make him nervous if we didn't act the frightened virgin. But he knows us well enough to recognize a real "no". I want you to understand that if we nix Leo we haven't got a queue of people waiting to sign you after *Stool Pigeon*.'

'By the time *Stool Pigeon* is in rough-cut I might have a nomination for *Silent Paradise*.'

'Not if you haven't signed for Leo, you won't. He'll let *Silent Paradise* sink without a lifebelt unless he's got you as a future investment.'

'A renter's mind doesn't work like that, Viney. They are set on getting a nomination, they are talking about a new title . . .'

'*Polystyrene Paradise?*'

'OK, Viney, I know you hate the movie . . .'

'Your performance is lost in the gimmicks. It's the kind of

movie where the special effects man gets his name above title.' Weinberger laughed at his own joke, but Stone nodded dolefully and said, 'Yes, it's a man's picture.'

'It's a family picture. Koolman should put it out in the school holidays: sixty prints nationwide while the reviews are still warm.'

Stone hissed through his teeth. 'Advertise it as a kids' movie and we can forget any nomination ideas.'

'Sure, and now can you see why Koolman will only nurse it for a nomination if he's going to get our TV sales.'

'Let's just see what the films do on the box,' said Stone.

'Marshall, we must make Leo slot those films for high ratings. At eight in the evening they'll do treble what they can get two hours later. Put them behind a popular show and they'll inherit its audience. Make sure there is nothing fancy on the rival channels and they will double again. But all these things cost money, Marshall.'

'TV's a racket.'

'Why stop at TV? These guys have got a whole bag: radio, records, sheet music and chunks of the media that they can plug you into. You'd be in their fan mags, programme guides, and syndicated like you'd never believe. Look what they did for Val: a year ago I was lunching guys, trying to get him one-liners in "Coronation Street". Believe me, Marshall, considering the way these guys can invent a star, Leo's offer is generous.' Weinberger watched his client carefully. 'Generous.'

Stone nodded. He wanted to believe that he could come out of such a TV series unscathed, but one had only to switch on to see the sort of shows the networks demanded. Superficial plots that would not distract from the commercials, scripts produced by the yard by teams of hacks. Cheap sets, crudely lit; unrehearsed sequences hastily shot by quickie crews. And carrying the burden of that mess would be Marshall Stone. Millions would see it and he'd be condemned to repeat the same fiasco week after week. His friends would shudder, his enemies would snigger and all would agree that Marshall Stone had finally found his true level. What was worse, they'd option him to eternity. If it was successful he'd be on TV for years. And then who'd pay to see him in cinemas.

'It's not just the money I'm thinking of.'

'And it's not the money I'm thinking of, Marshall. But Leo mustn't let those three movies die the death on TV. If he does – out of spite, or neglect – then getting you your price is going to become impossible.'

'Leo's not like that.'

'Leo is exactly like that, Marshall, and the sooner you realize it the better.' For a moment or two they stared at each other.

Stone shrugged. 'I'm just a bloody actor, Viney. I can't handle this high-powered business stuff.'

'Then let me handle it for you. Do the TV deal. I'll get the pilot money up and the option down to ten, but sign it, Marshall.'

Stone desperately wanted to put the whole matter into Weinberger's hands and let him decide every part of it, but he couldn't forget the phone call to Leo that Jasper had recorded. He no longer completely trusted Weinberger. Who could tell what devious schemes he might be hatching with Koolman. His warnings about Koolman could be part of a devious plan. He had seen a movie where such a thing had happened.

Val Somerset was Weinberger's client. He was young. There was a lifetime of earnings – and ten percent of them – stretching ahead. If Weinberger had to choose between them, whom was he likely to sacrifice. And why had he made no remark about the scene at the lunch table. Weinberger was acutely distressed at such things – as Stone had discovered when complaining in restaurants – so his silence might well be due to the guilt of betrayal.

'No,' said Stone. 'No TV deal. You tell Leo, I'm a feature film man and that's what I'm going to stay.' He watched Weinberger's face to see the reaction.

Weinberger didn't look up. He leaned even closer to the documents on the floor and put them in some sort of order, as a card-sharp might arrange a deck. 'You can do both, Marshall.'

'Get me *Man From the Palace*, Viney. I'll do it for three hundred thousand, flat fee, dollars.'

'They offered one hundred, plus fifty deferred and five per cent of the producer's profit.'

'Jesus H. Christ! Five per cent of nothing is nothing. Screw them! You get me another feature – a good one – Viney.'

'I'll try, Marshall, but think everything over meanwhile. Let's talk about the TV tomorrow.'

'Not tomorrow. Not ever, Viney. You get out on the road and get me a feature. If you mention TV again, we might part company.'

'Whatever you say, Marshall. The client is always right.'

'There comes a time in a man's life, Viney, when he must make a stand. A time when he follows some inner conviction.'

He watched his agent, waiting to be angry if Weinberger should sigh or grin to himself, but he didn't.

Weinberger replaced all the documents in the slim black case. He spared a brief glance at the TV contract as if trying to visualize what it would look like with his client's signature on the end of it. Then he put that away into a separate red-lined pocket of the case. He closed the lid, and the latches snapped with a terrible click of finality.

Once alone, Marshall Stone walked around his study, touching the fine furnishings and looking at the valuable pictures and ornaments. Just as his collection of snaps and cuttings was part of an attempt to erase his birth, schooling and youth, so was this house an attempt to acquire a different background. Its worn stones, creaking stairs and crippled chimneys made a setting of which he'd never tire. He'd always wanted such a home. And yet it remained a foreign land – however friendly – and he was an exile in it. No ancestor of his had left the sword-marks on the library panelling, or added the great hall when the stockmarket reflected Wellington's glory, or played host to the sovereigns who'd slept in the great four-poster bed.

This drawing-room – or withdrawing-room, as he preferred to call it – was his favourite: it contained six elegant mirrors, but no clocks. He had never noticed that before; perhaps it was significant. Many of the items had his initials on them. (Not E.B., of course, for that would have been puzzling for the people who only knew him as Marshall Stone.) It gave him a sense of permanence and reassurance to see and touch the rewards of his success.

At the far end of the room there was a bar, complete with beer engines and stools. Behind the bar was the ornamental dagger he'd used in *Hamlet*. Around it were photos, and a golden-coloured diploma that an association of clothing firms had given him for being the best-dressed man of 1965. There was a photo of Stone on a poster for Cripples Fight Back, and a Lasserre menu which Bette Davis had autographed in lipstick. Some of his best reviews had been framed in teak, and so had a Jak cartoon from the *Evening Standard*, depicting Stone leading an actors' demonstration against the war in Vietnam. There was a plaque from an amateur theatre group in New Jersey who had called themselves the Marshall Stone Company. There was a soiled pocket handkerchief that Stone had borrowed from Bogart and never had laundered. There were many photos, signed with the most illustrious names of show business. Stone was in all of them: linking arms with Olivier and Richardson at a festival; kissing a starlet in Venice; embracing a 150-pound marlin with Catalina Island in the background; grinning fit to burst at the Duke of Edinburgh; and flexing his muscles with the Burtons at some sun-drenched beach in the West Indies. None of the doubts and dislikes that he sometimes felt about his fellow actors assailed Stone now. This was 'the profession'; a coterie of fun-loving friends who had created for themselves a soft world of warmth and love and wealth. False it might be, but it was better than the cruel grey world of which Weinberger spoke. It was better than the world he saw through the blue-tinted windows of his Rolls or the capricious and aggressive world of which he read in his newspapers.

Stone found solace in his collection of souvenirs, as he had found it on previous occasions. Here were his credentials, his articles, his passport to the world he loved so much. Thus reassured, he picked up the telephone and put in a call to Paris. He looked at his watch and worried in case Suzy Delft was not there. It was a relief to hear her voice.

'Suzy Delft speaking.'

'Suzy? I've just had an amusing idea. Why don't I pop over to Paris and spend tomorrow with you.'

'Darling, you're filming tomorrow.'

'No, they have changed the schedule again, darling. They

don't know what they're doing from day to day.'

'What a nuisance for you, my poor darling.'

'I'm getting a bit bored with it, I must say. I could have arranged my other commitments: dubbing, fittings and so on. And I've got a pile of scripts a mile high. I'll bring some and read them there. If I return them without reading them . . . well, you never know . . . there might be something really fabulous there.'

'Like *Man From the Palace*.'

'Weinberger and I are having second thoughts about *Man From the Palace*.'

'But you were so keen.'

'I'd like to do something more challenging, Suzy. *Man From the Palace* is all right in its way, but it's a part I can play so easily.'

'An actor needs challenge. I told Leo I'd like to do a costume drama.'

'What did he say?'

'He's going to have one written for me.'

'He's a wonderful person,' said Stone. There was a long silence.

'I must be going, darling. The traffic on the Champs is beastly tonight. It will take hours to get there so Val has ordered the car extra early. It's a ten-seat Mercedes, so we'll all be together. It's going to be fun. Everyone will be there, Val says.'

'What do you say to me dashing over? I could be there by the time the film is over – I've seen it before – and I could join you for dinner.'

'But the plane is out of action.'

'I'll go to London Airport.'

'It'll be a rush, darling. And London Airport is a ghastly slum at this time of year.'

'I don't want to spoil your arrangements.'

'Just as long as you're not going to get bored when I go for my facial and have my hair fixed tomorrow, and do some shopping.'

'No, it will be fun. Where is dinner tonight?'

'Fouquet's. It's so convenient, just a few steps away from the movie. Darling, I must fly, the others are waiting.'

'With the speed of an arrow I will come over the deep waters in machine like mighty bird.' She laughed.

'Marshall, darling, it was so wonderful of you to phone me. I shall be thinking of you all through this tiresome film – hurry, precious.'

'Au revoir,' said Marshall Stone. He hung up.

Well, he might be bored following her around shopping the next day. He wondered if she had a lover there. Somerset had his own girl there, so that was all right. But there was a little French director who'd been chasing Suzy last year at Cannes. He wondered if he would be in evidence tonight. It didn't worry him. He knew how to take care of young film directors.

Again he dialled the phone. Richard Preston answered.

'Rich?'

'Oh, hello, Marshall. I've just come in. Feeling better now – about tomorrow's sequence?'

'Well, that's what I want to talk about, Rich. After our talk today, I was pretty . . . what shall I say . . . well, traumatized.'

'Sorry to hear that, Marshall.'

'Don't be, love. I've a lot to thank you for. You cleared me when I was completely blocked. It was the worst time I've ever known – careerwise. You unlocked me. That was a wonderful thing to do for an actor, Rich. If you can do that for me, you can do it for other actors. That's something that only truly great directors can do: Huston, Ford, Fellini, Hitchcock – the greats. I'm going to tell you this to your face, just as I have been telling Weinberger all the afternoon: Richard: you are going to be a director of international status. And soon.'

'I was glad to be able to help, Marshall. At first I thought I was making things worse.'

'That's exactly what I'm phoning about, Rich. I need a day or two to get it through my system. I need breathing space to absorb the role you've shown me.'

'I did nothing, Marshall.'

'You pulled the curtain aside, Rich.' Stone laughed. 'You don't know what you did for me. If you could just reschedule tomorrow and shoot around me, I'd be eternally grateful. I really would.'

'I'll phone Edgar and have him ask the production manager. We'll see what they can give me to keep me going.'

'Don't let those people push you around, Rich. I hate to see old dead-beats taking advantage of youngsters just because they are new to the game. Old-timers always hang together, have you noticed that? No, Rich, you decide about tomorrow, that will be good enough for me.'

'Hang on, Marshall. I'll look at the cross-plot and see what I could rejig. I'll ring back in five minutes.'

'Take your time, Richard. I'll hang on.'

Preston fumbled with a deskful of papers. He found the budget, the breakdown, the unit list and the recording schedule. The cross-plot was folded into four and he needed both hands to spread it across the table-top. This was a photocopy and he couldn't quite read it. He had almost given up when he heard Marshall Stone talking. Preston picked up the phone to confess that a rearrangement of the schedule was beyond his ability. He heard Stone say, 'The way you chaps handle that cross-plot never ceases to amaze me, but you're all the same: Godard, Kubrick, Antonioni. If there's one thing you all have in common, it's complete mastery of that damned paperwork.'

'I'm trying to fix it, Marshall,' said the boy. He ran his finger down one side of the graph noting the list of actors and moving across the sheet to see which days they were called. There were always ways of shooting around an actor, but it could make a film look cheap. Tomorrow he was going to do the sequence in which Stone and his two sergeants were hiding under a cargo stacked at a dockside. The script fell open at the page. He could do scene 143, the long-shot of the lorry coming through the dockyard gates. Then he could go on with 148–153: the Japanese searching for Stone. On Wednesday he could do Stone's sequence: 144–147.

'OK, Marshall. I'll find a way around it tomorrow and Tuesday but be sure you are there on Wednesday or we won't be out of the docks by Friday. And that will mean weekend working for our Security on the set and God knows whether the Port Authority will let us go back.'

Stone wanted to thank him warmly, but he knew instinctively that brusque efficiency should be the tone. 'Wednesday will do, 'bye for now.'

Female hearts flutter at the name of Briton Marshall Stone. But now I can reveal in the strictest of confidences that sitting on his lap can make for a tiring day. Take the word of singing star Marcia Morgan. For one scene in their new film *Glory Street* she spent eight hours perched on Marshall's knee. It was uncomfortable, she complained, and at lunchtime she was supplied with a soft down cushion.

Syndication Service

6

*The best of all screenwriters, William Shakespeare,
whose Lear story has all the ingredients of a popular
movie – action, suspense, sex, heroism and humour, all
the essence of drama.*

Film publicity (King Lear)

Ooo! I didn't know Comanches kissed like this.
Film script (The Last Wagon)

Marshall Stone had almost forgotten the miseries that airline
companies heap upon their clients. Usually Stone waved to the
immigration men before the Rolls took him to the door of his
private aeroplane. Even when he travelled on scheduled services a man from the travel company waited with an airport
policeman at a space marked 'No Parking' a few yards from the
VIP room. While Stone had a complimentary drink with the
station manager, his baggage was checked through so that he
could be preboarded into a seat of his choice. At the foot of the
steps there would be an airline photographer, and at the top of
it a steward chilling champagne.

This trip might have been like that, except that the travel
company closed on Sundays. The airline phone seemed to be
permanently engaged and Stone thought the best way to the
airport was via London and the motorway. As they neared
central London the weekend traffic was so thick that Jasper
suggested it might be quicker to use the underground railway.
For the first time in many years Stone discovered what it was
like to be a member of the public.

The underground railway was a nightmare: the escalators
and the peeling posters, the humming generators, and the
sweet warm stale air, and the way it stirred the waste paper to
herald the arriving train. He'd forgotten how dimly lit it was.
He had changed, but these things had not changed in the slightest detail since he'd last been down in these bloodless arteries
nearly a quarter of a century before. It was amazing to be
returned with such fidelity to the décor of his youth.

At the booking office the ticket clerk looked at him suspiciously before handing over the ticket. 'Here,' he said accusingly. 'I know you. You used to be Marshall Stone.'

'No,' said Stone. The new moustache helped to convince the clerk that he was mistaken and Stone hurried away before he was trapped by some other busybody.

At the airport ticket counter he tried again. 'First Class! First Class to Paris!' but three people in front closed ranks against him.

He wanted to say, 'I'm Marshall Stone,' but the ticket and passport belonged to a nobody named Brummage. He considered asking for the manager, who knew him, but there was no time to spare. A man fell over his matching Hermès baggage and swore softly at whoever had left them there.

'Don't you dare swear at me,' said Stone. He looked around him and told the world, 'I just won't tolerate people swearing at me' but the world hurried past and the angry man kicked the side of Stone's overnight bag and walked away, without even hurrying. Stone was pleased now that he hadn't yet been recognized. He grinned to himself: 'Marshall Stone in ugly scene at airport.'

'You can't take all that baggage,' said the girl at the ticket counter.

'I'll pay for it,' said Stone.

'Too late. This one's finished loading. Hand baggage only. If you want to take that stuff you'll have to wait for Air France.'

'I must have it,' said Stone.

The girl shrugged. She turned to the girl at the next counter and said, 'And she's had it done with those side curls and swept up at one side. She looks a proper sight.'

Stone said, 'I need this baggage for my work.'

The girl chewed the last trace of lipstick off her lower lip and looked at him under lowered eyelids to indicate that it was within her power to get the luggage on to the plane. Regally, she awaited his supplication.

'It's special clothing,' said Stone. 'For refugees. It's going to Africa tonight.'

The girl didn't believe him and she made no secret of her disbelief, but even that feeble lie was a pleasant variation on the dull routine of her job. She accepted the fiction readily. By the time he had picked up the phone, she was rehearsed and perfect in her new role. Her voice was slightly lower and urgently vibrant. 'Hello, Jimmy. Ticket counter here. There's a special consignment of clothes for African refugees. It must be on the Paris plane, it's connecting with a special flight out of there. Yes, special priority.' She looked up at Stone and nodded soberly.

'Thank you,' said Stone.

'With things like that,' said the girl, 'we'll do anything to help.'

'I appreciate it,' said Stone. He wondered whether she expected a tip; Jasper would have known what to do. Sometimes Stone envied the self-sufficiency of Jasper.

'Don't I recognize your face?' said the girl.

'Perhaps,' admitted Stone.

'You used to read the news on TV, didn't you? About five years ago, or more.'

'Yes,' said Stone. It was the easiest way.

The girl nodded. Already she was preparing the story she would tell her family when she got home. They were always curious about what went on at the airport. Stone smiled too: there's no business *but* show business. Everyone liked playacting if they were given a chance.

The aeroplane climbed steeply into the sunset. He closed the curtain and opened his news magazine to the show business section. They had hacked *Tigertrap* into shavings some weeks before. Now Stone got perverse satisfaction from the unenthusiastic way they wrote of Val Somerset's performance in *Imperial Verdict*. The reviewer called him a 'trendy centurion' and 'camp Roman in the Roman camp'. Stone read it three times. Guiltily, he admitted to himself that the savaging of Val Somerset made him feel good. He supposed it made all the readers feel good.

Fouquet's was still open by the time he got there, but the *Imperial Verdict* party – eighty-five five-course dinners – had moved on. Some outdoor tables were occupied but inside it was almost empty. Two English couriers were drinking Carlsberg and comparing a typewritten passenger list with stacks of airline tickets. They looked up when Stone entered, and whispered together. They had recognized him, but Stone could not hear what they said. He felt a great temptation to speak to them just in order to hear them call him Marshall Stone. But he didn't.

The Georges Cinq was only across the road. He remembered how, as a young actor in rep, they'd revered it as the ultimate temple of the show-biz life style. It was preferable to Suzy's cramped apartment – a long taxi ride out at St Cloud – but it was Suzy he wanted to see, and no one else would do.

Once inside the tiny apartment the journey almost seemed worthwhile. He put an old Hardy record on the hi-fi and turned the volume low. He took a cold shower and changed into linen slacks and a cashmere polo-neck shirt. Soon Suzy would be back.

He looked across Paris from the tall block. It was a tangle of coloured lights with a glimpse of the river far below him. The trip had been a nightmare. It had been an opportunity to discover how the world would treat Edward Brummage if it got the chance. He must never, never become Edward Brummage again. He went to the kitchen and poured himself a glass of Perrier water. A year ago it had been great fun to transform Suzy's austere little apartment into their make-believe cottage. But now antique furniture from exclusive shops on the St Honoré, old engravings from Twin Beeches and enamel signs from the Flea Market contrived to make the place like some sort of dealer's storeroom. As always, Suzy had left the bathroom in chaos. Grey dribbles of eye-black made the washbasin like zebra skin. Four coloured towels were strewn across the floor and the phone was standing in a puddle of water.

Stone sat down at the white baby grand piano and played the opening bars of a Brahms intermezzo that he'd learned for *Sables with Love*. The camera had opened on his hands and then pulled back to a medium-shot. He'd learned only the first thirty-two bars – it had cut to a close-up after that – but he could play those with the skill of a concert pianist.

As he played he looked at Suzy's photo on the piano top. She was very beautiful. There were so many photos of her here in the apartment. Everyone liked to have their photo taken with the famous face of Suzy Delft, even Leo Koolman. Suzy could get anything out of Koolman. Stone wondered how she did it. Then he made himself not wonder about it.

He finished playing the Brahms as far as he knew, faltered on some discords and got up and walked around the room. He strummed the antique guitar he'd bought for Suzy's birthday, and examined the canvases completed when fate seemed intent on making her a great painter. The canvases were easy to date: Soutine, Seurat, a touch of Modigliani and the inevitable Van Gogh. That was a family weakness, for he himself acknowledged sadly the influences of Brando, Olivier, Paul Muni and a walk he'd stolen from Coop. Every new enthusiasm had been swallowed whole, driving directors to rages and despair. If only he'd lost a few more of those arguments, the resulting films might have been masterpieces.

Suzy allowed all manner of kids to use this place as they passed through Paris. He disapproved, but his sympathy for her youthful friends, their far-reaching political theories, sartorial enthusiasm and septic neglect, was an important factor in his relationship with Suzy. Together they condemned fastidious, reactionary old fogies, one of which he secretly knew himself to be.

At 2.30 AM he abandoned the speech he'd rehearsed to persuade Suzy to New Jimmy's or Castel's, and looked again at the unmade bed. He could not guess what spotty hippy might have slept there, but it had been a long day. He put a tentative foot between the sheets. Hiding there like a dead toad was a damp green towel. He tossed it aside, angry at the way it had made him jump. He laughed at himself and then he laughed at the extraordinary way his life had changed from the days when he could not afford sheets, not even dirty ones. Balanced on the bed-head there was the teddy-bear that Suzy took everywhere with her. It stared back at Stone with the same blank look that he had seen on Val Somerset's face at lunchtime.

'You too, you bastard,' said Stone. He grabbed it by the foot and threw it across the room. 'Bear-faced effrontery,' called Stone after it, and laughed again.

It had been quite a day: Preston, the kids, Weinberger, all that nonsense at the airport. Like a French farce. He'd played

Feydeau once and he remembered the deliberate shrillness that he'd inserted into it, the edge of hysteria and the tempo. It was like two hours of squash each night. And like a squash game, it all depended upon footwork. Those were the days. He'd never do Feydeau again: the sheer stamina it required would defeat him now. That was the trouble with film work; one lost the capacity to act for two or three hours at a time, wooing the audience, softening them, building and holding a mighty climax and then going back next day and doing the whole damn thing again.

He still remembered long chunks of the farce. He laughed as he recalled some of the funniest bits. As he dozed he was murmuring his explanation on being found trouserless in a cupboard. It had been that sort of day.

My toughest role was learning to grow up.
Elizabeth Taylor

There must be finishing schools near St Trop, but almost every girl that Suzy Delft knew had been to school in the suburbs of Geneva or the hinterland of the Marne where she had spent five long boring years learning how to paint bad pictures, speak perfect French and climb over a nine-foot wall without waking the night watchman.

Compared with other girls, she'd been lucky. Her pocket-money was never delayed, and her dress allowance could be loaned out at fifteen per cent during the last month of every term. Her trustees were two humourless bank officials, easily gulled into a few extra travel expenses, and they'd agree to quite decent holidays whenever invitations from other girls' parents were solicited, or, better still, forged so that she could go away alone.

She had been nineteen years old when a secretary had fetched her from a lecture on Chinese Art to meet the trustees and Marshall Stone. She stared at the famous film star, too stunned to do more than gibber as she heard the old man from the bank explain that she was now old enough to be told that she was his illegitimate daughter.

His tight embrace had been a tacit expression of mutual need. He'd visited her every Sunday. She'd waited at the window near the top of the stairs, trying to glimpse the Rolls as it turned into the gate. It seemed years before her exams came and Stone's film in Normandy finished shooting.

Like most of the other girls, she had dreamed of houses in London and Paris, and it was a favourite dormitory game to furnish them in detail. So it was paradise when Stone provided her with tiny apartments in those cities by the time she was ready to leave school.

At first they had been like sister and brother, on first-name terms and not afraid to criticize, taunt or deflate each other. Stone knew that young people used such hard words to conceal affection.

At school she'd relished his bearish hugs, because physical affection was rare where so many parents were almost strangers to their children. Later she'd learned to accept the intensity of cuddles and kisses as part of a show-biz world that she was delighted to enter. But sometimes nods and winks among their friends made her worry which of them knew their secret. Nowadays she shrank from his touch, and in public stayed a decorous distance from his fingers. She knew this hurt and puzzled him, yet she couldn't bring herself to resume their former style of embrace, and nor could she explain her disquiet to him.

Sometimes nowadays she had to steel herself to receive his predatory embraces. They were especially unwelcome at the end of a night of dancing and flirting with people of her own age. She leaned her head against the door of her apartment after closing it stealthily. By the emergency light on the landing she saw that it was three-fifteen in the morning. She heard the boy who'd brought her home accelerate, in spite of all her pleading, with enough noise to wake Stone and the whole block. She could still hear the car when it was on the far side of the Seine.

'Marshall!' she called anxiously. 'Marshall, darling!' Perhaps he hadn't arrived, or perhaps he was hiding somewhere so that he could leap at her. She hated him to do that, especially since it always seemed to end up with them rolling on the floor with their legs entwined. 'Marshall!'

When she switched on the light of the blue bedroom, where Stone had put his *Hamlet* posters and the huge baroque mirror, she found him asleep in bed.

'Darling,' he said, squinting his eyes. 'Do turn out that terrible light.' She put on the bedside light and sat down beside him. Stone said, 'Where were you, darling? Sorry I didn't wait up but I came from the airport and went straight to bed.'

'We went to Lipp and there was a party. You've never seen such a divine little garret studio, in the third. Just like Gene Kelly's place in *An American in Paris*, remember?'

'No,' said Stone.

Suzy stood up and whirled around to let the watered-silk dress catch the air. It was one of her ambitions to do this in a film. 'Of course you do, you old bear! *An American in Paris* . . . cramped little place. Gene Kelly did a dance on the grand piano. A glorious film!'

'What time is it?'

'It had a view of Notre Dame, all cleaned up and floodlit. Oh, how wonderful to be back in Paris.' She stopped twirling and sat on the bed.

'Pass me my cigarettes and lighter.'

'Marshall, darling. It's so middle-aged to want a cigarette as soon as you wake up.'

Stone smiled.

'Val's going to the demonstration on Thursday. The students say they are going to burn down the Palais de Justice. I can't think what to wear if I go.'

'Your Vanessa Redgrave outfit.'

'That's middle-aged too, Marshall, that sarcasm.'

'Perhaps it is.' He didn't care. He lit his cigarette, blew the smoke across the room and rested back on his pillow.

'Paris is divine.' She leaned over Stone and kissed him, taking his wrinkled face between her two hands and kissing it all over, as in *Camille* Garbo had kissed Robert Taylor.

When she released him, Stone smoothed his hair self-consciously. He hated the washed-out look he knew he had without darkening on his lashes, but to get up and apply some would seem foolish.

He buttoned the frogging of his silk pyjamas close up to his neck. Did Suzy still see him as the impoverished baron of *Sables with Love*, or the wounded fighter pilot of *Vector One Eight* as once she'd said she did. Or was it Edward Brummage, a middle-aged wealthy lecher, that she turned away from when his kisses became too affectionate.

From behind the bed-head she could see Stone and herself reflected in the glass of the framed poster. She crossed her hands over the brass rail and rested her chin upon her wrist. Stone began a long anecdote about a film producer being shown the adverts for his latest film. She'd heard it before but she made the appropriate reactions.

She'd learned a great deal about Stone during the three years she'd known him. The first year was one of disillusion. It had shocked her to see him switch on his charm when dealing with influential associates, and then snub lesser mortals. She had congratulated herself on her perception when the men around him failed to see how devious and insincere he could be. It was only recently that she'd discovered that Weinberger, and others close to Stone, knew him at least as well as she did and were fond of him in spite of his rudeness, cowardice and monumental ego.

She smiled. Stone smiled too as he came to the punch-line '. . , he stared at the poster and said "Good God, Mayer! You know my name was to be as large or larger than that of anyone else in connexion with this picture, certainly larger than Tolstoy's!" '

Suzy Delft laughed and moved away. 'I'll come and say good-night, Marshall darling.'

'Certainly larger than Tolstoy's,' said Stone, and reached for another cigarette.

She could still hear him chuckling as she locked the door of her silk-lined dressing-room.

She undressed slowly, looking at the glossy stills of Garbo that she had pinned around the mirrors. She'd studied old

122

Garbo films so that she could imitate the arms-akimbo stance, the open-mouthed laugh and Garbo's tilted-head smile. The more she did them all the more she looked like Vanessa Redgrave.

She put on her silk pyjamas and a cashmere dressing-gown and approved of the decorous reflection she saw. Only then did she return to Stone.

'There's some champers in the ice-box, darling.'

She smiled. She was too inebriated for it to be the dreamy ecstasy she intended.

'No, stay there, I'll get it,' he said.

Suzy kicked off her slippers, tucked her feet under her and leaned back against the brass bed-end. She had had more than enough to drink, but she made the appropriate ooos and ahhs when he brought it, and pretended with him that opening the bottle was a difficult and dangerous masculine task.

Stone got into bed and pulled the bedclothes over himself before pouring the champagne. She noticed that he'd hurriedly darkened his lashes and she was pleased that he still wanted to look his best for her.

Stone said, 'Twin Beeches is looking wonderful, isn't it?'

'Glorious, Marshall.'

'Did you see the kitchen garden? Mrs Pimm never has to buy vegetables you know.'

'You told me. The salad was delicious.'

'What I was thinking, darling . . . Looking at the new horse-boxes and now the stable has that big storage area . . . well, it could be a wonderful riding school.'

'What a gorgeous idea, darling.'

'And I was wondering if you would like to have it.'

'Have it?' She moistened her lips.

'Yes. Own it and run it as a full-time business.'

She laughed keeping her lips parted and tossing her head back. 'That would be wonderful, Marshall darling, but I'd have to have a manager and someone who knew about riding instruction. I mean . . . I have my career.'

'I don't know, Suzy.'

'Oh my God, Marshall. I thought we'd disposed of all that.' They were both silent, and when she continued her voice was soft and confidential but very very firm. 'I'm in the movies now, and I want to go on with my career. We've been all through that and I thought we weren't going to go into it again.'

'If you knew . . . Suzy . . .'

'If you knew Suzy, like I know Suzy', she sang raucously, 'Oh! Oh! Oh, what a girl . . .'

'It wouldn't hurt to listen to a word of advice. You don't know everything yet.'

'You kill me, Marshall. D'you know, when you do that heavy father schtik, you kill me.'

'I never have treated you like a child, Suzy.'

'Well, it's too late now, Father dear. I lived without you until I was grown up . . . you know?'

Stone smiled. 'You have so much energy, you're so vital.'

'Stop stroking my leg, Marshall.'

'You've got a phobia.'

'About incest? Damn right I have. How could I help it with a father like you pawing me. Stop it, Marshall, please!'

Stone's face twitched. He smiled professionally, trying to make her smile too. She leaned forward, took his hand in both of hers and kissed his fingers.

Suzy Delft knew Marshall Stone far better than he suspected. She knew the sort of anxieties that had driven him to pursue her to Paris, and she knew how competitive he felt about her young friends. She understood all those things, but that did not make them easier to endure. She sat well back on the bed and closed her eyes.

'When I did my Hamlet . . .' said Stone as he poured more drink.

She puffed herself up and said, 'When I did my Hamlet, when I did my Hamlet,' in a shrill, little-boy voice that would mock a pompous adult.

Stone smiled tolerantly.

'You mustn't be stuffy, Marshall darling. Tell me about your Hamlet.'

'It doesn't matter.'

'No! You *must*, darling. Tell me.'

'Never mind.'

'I want to hear.'

Stone was a little mollified. 'Well, when I did my Hamlet, I had those great reviews. Hardly a bad one, in fact. I was the top of the heap, Suzy. I had all manner of offers. I could have written my own ticket. I had ideas . . . you can't imagine.'

'You are such a romantic, Marshall.'

'I admit it. An actor must be . . . Did you hear on the news today, that fellow in the bank robbery? . . . when I hear of people like that, my sympathies are with them. I want to say, come here, come here, old lad, I'll hide you. I never side with authority.'

'Marshall, you are such a creep at times.'

'Very well then—'

'Now don't lose your cool, darling. Someone has to tell you. You've got such sycophants around you. But really, to talk about being against authority . . . You love authority, you . . . the man of property! My God, you own more houses, more cars and more people than anyone.'

'I have all those things but I don't need them.'

'You think it's young to say you side with the outlaw. But it's not young, darling; it's juvenile. I believe in property. I want policemen to guard me and if I found that fellow who did the bank job I'd turn him in before he could say please.'

'What I'm trying to say is . . . Well, the *Hamlet* business soured me. Soured me more than I realized at the time.'

She'd heard his *Hamlet* story before. 'You take it too seriously, darling. Personally I wouldn't have believed a word that Leo Koolman said.'

I never explain to the actors the characters they are playing. I want them to be passive.

Michelangelo Antonioni

Garrick, Sheridan, and, some say, Oliver Goldsmith, had known the cramped little dressing-rooms of the Old Royalty Theatre.

That Wilde and Barrie and the young Shaw had suffered its draughts and echoes was a matter of record. In 1929 two of the dressing-rooms had been extended at the cost of a small piece of gallery, so that the people who came to visit Marshall Stone backstage after the final curtain of his *Hamlet* could be packed in until there were sometimes twenty or more, toasting him in his own champagne, reading the telegrams that surrounded his mirror and smelling the flowers that never ceased to arrive.

The doorkeeper was accustomed to the fact that Stone was the last to leave. Often it was one o'clock in the morning before he heard the star's whispered goodnight, the bang of the stage door and the purr of his Rolls. The night that Leo Koolman, the famous film man, went backstage with flowers, champagne and a dense cloud of cigar smoke was obviously going to set new records for his final round before locking up.

The performance that Koolman saw was unusually good. The audience had been quick and responsive, and Stone had found an edge to his performance that he'd not yet learned how to create at will. Koolman was impressed and he and his assistant Sanchez remained long after all the other well-wishers had gone. Stone could see the puzzled look in his eyes as he tried to reconcile the puny actor with the towering Dane who'd dominated a stage glittering with talent.

Stone was attracted by this same paradox. The bejewelled costume drenched in sweat, the half-eaten hamburger alongside the champagne bucket, the speeches of Shakespeare and the obscenities of the cast. That a performance came out of such chaos was the magic of the stage. He looked at his reflection and saw the noble face of Hamlet surmounting a grease paint-smeared undervest.

Koolman said, 'The new script for young Franco's film is just great, Marshall, I brought you a copy.' He found a space for it among the spotlight pencils, sticks, stumps and brushes.

Stone leaned close to the mirror and pulled his eyebrows off. It hurt less when done with one fast snatch, but Stone did it very slowly.

'The gunfighter's part is down to ten days . . . star billing and five per cent of the action.'

Koolman waited but Stone was busy with his eyelashes,

taking the excess mascara off them with a tiny brush that he had to wipe on a paper handkerchief.

'And the money stays the same.'

Stone turned enough to see Leo in the mirror. 'I've told you fifty times, Leo. I'm not renewing the contract. This *Hamlet* will run six months. After that I'll do something else in the theatre. Something very modern.'

'Ten days, Marshall. We'll fly you in and out again . . . maybe eight days if we reschedule through the weekends.' Koolman drew back his lips in a grimace, an atavistic smile needed only rarely for such placation. Stone was shocked to see how the work of running the studio had changed Koolman. The bouncy man that Stone had first known was now withered and hardened, like a rubber ball left too long upon a warm stove. A chance virus infection made his voice harsh and croaky and his eyes as watery as an old man's. The heavy tweed overcoat, of a weight unknown in California, came high on his shoulders so that his hunched figure seemed to have no neck.

Stone smiled and shook his head slowly.

Koolman looked around at the sooty window, uncleaned for generations, and the paraffin stove that caused the cream walls to dribble with condensation. He thrust his hands deep into his pockets and hissed his displeasure and dismay. 'Are you crazy, Marshall?'

'This is acting, Leo. Those charades for cameramen that you supervise out there in the sun . . . that stuff has nothing to do with acting.' Stone began to unpin his hair; it was fixed skull-close to fit under his wig.

'This one needs you, Marshall.'

It wasn't Koolman, or KI, that needed him, it was the picture, as though his name had come up on a computer. Stone said, 'It's always just one more, Leo. You know that as well as I do. How many of the big names were only to do one movie?'

'Don't talk like this, Marshall. You've done some great movies for me. *Last Vaquero* is still being talked about . . . still being screened right here in your town.'

'Look, Leo, when I was in rehearsals just four weeks ago, I was the Last Vaquero – a rich Hollywood ham trying to tackle Shakespeare! This week . . . ' Stone shook his head to indicate surprise still latent. 'Well, I did it . . . now I'm Hamlet, an actor who can also be seen in some Hollywood oaters if you're so inclined, when you can't get tickets for the show. Things have changed, Leo.'

'Marshall, I'm asking you as a favour.'

'And I'm saying no, Leo, can't you understand plain English: NO.'

'If that's the way you want it,' Leo turned away, but Phil Sanchez didn't move.

'Punk,' said Sanchez. 'Cheap, no-good little punk. I remember you on your bended knee to Mr Koolman . . .' his small pink mouth opened twice, trying to find better words to express his contempt. He failed. 'Punk! Cheap punk!'

Stone turned to Sanchez. That Koolman commanded such loyalty was no surprise, but that it should be evoked from meek little Sanchez was amazing.

Koolman said, 'I'm leaving.' They were all at the end of a long day of hard work. Koolman knew he would do better to continue the discussion some other time. 'Phil, I'm leaving.'

Stone smiled at the angry Sanchez and spoke to Koolman at the same time. 'Close the door after you, Leo. There's a draught from the stair-well.'

Stone had left his hand extended in a languid gesture of dismissal and Sanchez grabbed at his finger and twisted it so that Stone must either cower or break it. Stone cowered. Sanchez released the finger and wiped the flat of his hand down his jacket as if to be rid of the contamination. Stone nursed his pain and tried to decide whether Sanchez had done it with the skill of a judo expert or the lucky wrath of a man unusued to violence.

'Leave him,' said Koolman. He said it over his shoulder, scarcely murmuring the words.

'I *won't* leave him.' Sanchez stepped closer to where Stone was seated at the mirror. 'Punk!'

The intense hatred that depleted Sanchez's vocabulary communicated itself to Stone, and it frightened him, and puzzled him too. 'I worked my contract, Phil. We had a deal and I kept to it. Where's the beef?'

'The contract! Is that all there was? Mr Koolman picked you

out of the gutter and gave you the Cinderella treatment . . . and you talk to him about contracts . . .'

'What do you want . . . four pints of blood?' Stone offered his bare arm.

'Mr Koolman has to do this movie.' Sanchez said it as if there was a more complex idea buried under its simplicity, as a man might say $E = MC^2$.

'Why?'

'He's got to. Don't ask.'

'Why?' Stone's voice was higher and more exasperated.

Koolman said, 'Leave it, Phil.'

Sanchez did not hear. 'Because if you are not in this picture for Franco, suddenly things are going to happen. Grips will fall off ladders, some star will fall under an auto. We'll have a walk-out and I'll spend three or four weeks with union guys who speak hoopla.'

Stone stared up at the reflection of Sanchez, trying to put it all together. 'These things happen,' said Sanchez. 'You don't know . . . you guys just know the bright lights and the double-page spreads.'

Stone waved down Sanchez's words and said to Koolman, 'What are we talking about, Leo? Are we talking about pro-tection . . about a crime syndicate?'

Koolman spoke very quietly, 'They are going legit these days – they have the money . . .'

Stone looked at Leo, trying to see a man who could be sub-jected to threats and blackmail, but he saw no hint of such weakness. He'd never seen Koolman troubled, not by wives, waiters, oceans or earthquakes. He couldn't imagine Koolman except in full control of his crafty world. It was this demeanour that gave Stone his deep faith in Koolman and made him uneasy when their paths diverged.

Stone said, 'I don't get you . . . hoodlums?'

'Stockholders, stupid! Stockholders!' said Sanchez.

'And little Franco is one of them?'

Koolman said, 'These guys have a cash surplus, Marshall. The industry has cash-flow problems. It's almost impossible to keep them out.'

Stone said, 'You're not telling me that hoods control enough voting shares to decide what kind of movies you make?'

Sanchez said, 'When these guys get a bright idea or a relative who wants to go into movies they don't wait until the stockholders' meeting.'

'They send a messenger with a machine gun,' said Koolman from the doorway.

'Jesus.'

'Marshall,' croaked Koolman. 'The other day, something came up about the child.'

'My child?' said Stone.

'One of the studio cops is following it up.'

'You said it wasn't possible to find her.'

'It's a lead, Marshall. It will probably come to nothing.'

'Like before,' said Stone. 'Yeah.'

'I just want to tell you,' said Koolman, 'whatever you decide about the contract, we'll still be doing our best to locate the kid, just like I promised you.'

Sanchez said, 'It shouldn't be necessary to say that,' his tone of voice admitting that to ingrates like Stone, it might be.

'We'll talk some more before I go back to New York,' said Koolman. His voice was little more than a whisper and he cleared his throat, holding a handkerchief over his face.

Stone switched on the ten bulbs around his mirror. The room was filled with an intense shadowless light; yellow tungsten that painted the miserable cell with gold leaf. The travelling-clock stood exactly at midnight. He took a paper towel and wiped it across his face. The pencilled lines, number nine stick, whitened highlights, eye shadow and the red dot so carefully placed at the corner of his eye, smeared grotesquely. 'Eight days, Leo. Not an hour more, not a minute, even.' And then the removing cream took away the last of the Prince of Denmark.

'Thanks, Marshall,' said Leo Koolman, but he didn't turn his head. The glare was too much for eyes heavy with the rheumy symptoms of virus.

The door slammed loud enough to make the champagne bottle rattle in its bucket. The draught from the stairs caused it.

Who wants to go out and see a bad movie when they can stay at home and see a bad one free on television?

Sam Goldwyn

Paris provided Stone with a respite from his fears – a time to heal. The morning was superb, the sky was clear blue, and upon it the Sacré-Coeur floated like a cloud. Stone was happy and Suzy could do no wrong. Her instant coffee, and some biscuits that had been hanging around since her last visit two months ago, he pronounced delicious. Even when the shower misfunctioned his concern was solely professional. 'The scalding water might have marked me, darling. Marked me for life. What would the production do?'

At La Quetsch a waiter knew him and gave them the best table in the place, where they could see the scramble around the counter below. Two men from Pathé recognized Stone and waved to him. He smiled back, and they pointed him out to the girls who were with them. Suzy put on her dark glasses and stared straight ahead. One of the men decided that she must be Nancy Sinatra but the other said Jane Fonda.

Stone recalled how much he had enjoyed Paris when coming here was still an adventure. There was tension in the air, a perfume that made its people quick-witted, fast-moving, hardworking and exact. Perhaps it lacked the humour of Berlin, the relaxation of London and the exuberance of Rome but for Stone, Paris was the place that fulfilled his childhood dreams of foreign travel. Paris then was wicked, Paris was dangerous, Paris was elegant, its good taste indigenous and culture unmatched. Paris attracted Stone in the same way that the brightly lit world of entertainment had always done. Once he was in its dazzling aura nothing else existed.

He returned the menu to the waiter with a flourish, and ordered lunch with the same careful diction and measured pauses that he would have devoted to a soliloquy. He stood outside himself and judged the performance and then was shocked to find himself doing it. He wondered to what extent he'd chosen from the menu dishes that provided an actor's cadences and rhythms. How awful, he reproached himself.

Yet he knew that this narcissistic necessity to reserve a piece of his mind for himself was a part of an actor's craft. He could give himself fully to no role. He must heed the other actors, note their timing, adjust his own physical action against the previous one and prepare himself for the one to come. He could give himself wholly to being no one: not even himself.

Suzy moved her head so that she could just see herself in the mirror. 'I just want you to know, darling, that there are times when I love you very much. Very much indeed.' She took off her dark glasses and smiled at him, letting her loose hair fall across her face. She put her hand halfway across the table.

'Darling Suzy,' said Stone. The cutlery trembled as he laid his fingers lightly upon her hand. An old lady at a nearby table pointed out the scene to her husband. It made her very happy to see two people so in love that they were oblivious of the whole world.

Eschewing the role of film stars, Suzy and Marshall wandered through the sunny streets hand in hand, like two young students. Why couldn't it always be like this. The only thing that marred Stone's pleasure was the number of people that Suzy knew and the enthusiasm of her greetings. She'd lived in France long enough to speak the language almost perfectly. Unreasonable though he knew it to be, he resented her feeling more at home here than he did. They sat outside the Deux Magots and watched a perfect afternoon become a perfect evening. Stone was half listening to Suzy having a silly conversation with two French boys in faded denims and sandals, and with shoulder-length hair, when he heard an American voice say, 'Marshall, can I tell you how sorry we all were that we couldn't get together on *Man From the Palace*?'

The speaker was a fifty-four-year-old American. He could have been mistaken for a senior captain from Pan American, or an Israeli Army commander, except for the expensive suit that draped in the French style of tailoring and the two-tone shoes that he wore as if he didn't know they'd ever been out of fashion. His round face was not flabby. It was bony and muscular, and an expensive Californian tan almost hid the wartime scarring. What hair remained was greying at the sides with enough distinction to persuade Stone's professional eye that it was the work of a hairdresser. The man stood at the table deferentially shuffling his feet and toying with a pouch of American tobacco and a pipe. It was the producer of *Last Vaquero*. If anyone could claim to have discovered a star in Stone, then this was that man.

'Kagan! Kagan Bookbinder!' Stone got to his feet, embraced Bookbinder, hugged him close and kissed him on the cheeks in a manner that is common only among entertainers and French generals. When he drew back from the embrace, Stone kept Bookbinder's upper arms firmly gripped and, holding him at arm's length, he looked him up and down, chuckling breathlessly.

'Yes, I was sorry about *Man From the Palace*,' said the man.

'I'm sorry too,' said Stone. He combined a wry smile with a frown as a small child might when being teased. 'But Kagan, no one told me that you were producing it.'

'It would have seemed too much like special pleading, Marshall. I asked Weinberger not to say it was me.'

'Kagan Bookbinder,' said Stone, as if still unable to believe his eyes. 'Kagan Bookbinder. It was a damned good script, Kagan.'

'The shooting script is even better. The crowd scene where Prince Felix makes the demonstrators laugh at their own foolishness is going to be just tremendous.'

'It wasn't just the money, Kagan.'

Bookbinder held up his hand protectively, 'If I had your kind of budget, Marshall, I'd pay you every last cent – and more! The kind of status and quality your performance could give that film . . .'

'The book was a big success. Who's directing?'

'Bert Hanratty.'

'Sit down, Kagan, this is like old times. Bert Hanratty, eh? Bert is very big! How can you fail.'

'I wish you were behind a desk in Wardour Street saying that.' Kagan laughed and lit his pipe. 'They did a tough deal with me, I'll tell you!'

'They are gangsters.'

'What could I do? The book was best-selling all through the option so there were others ready to pay twice my offer.'

'You could have sold your option to the other bidders.'

Bookbinder smiled. 'And I could peddle reefers outside kindergartens. But I'm a movie man, Marshall, I'm not in this business for a quick buck.'

Suzy Delft had not been listening to the conversation of the two old men. She had been watching the strollers and remembering other days. Many times she had sat penniless at this very table with a slice of cheese – no bread – and a small black coffee, waiting for a familiar face that she would wave to and talk to, and who would pick up the bill she'd pretend to overlook. She studied the girls in their bare-midriff dresses, wetlook suits, home-made caftans and see-through shifts who paraded here in St Germain with anxiety not quite hidden behind their painted eyes. She saw boys and girls she knew, but they didn't recognize her in her Pucci dress after her morning at Carita. They were close enough to touch, these denizens of yesterday's world, but they were gone for ever. Now she was part of a world they all envied: where the greatest stars in the world were casually addressed as Larry, Frank, Ralphie and Duke. It was a world where even the has-beens flew first class and stayed in suites at the Georges Cinq.

She had so much to learn and, no matter how dull it all seemed, she was determined to master the vocabulary and rituals of her new life, as once she'd mastered irregular verbs.

'This is Kagan Bookbinder, darling. You've heard me talk about him. He produced my first picture.'

'Suzy Delft. I've heard so much about you, Mr Bookbinder.'

'Kagan.'

'Marshall produced some of his own films,' said Suzy Delft proudly.

'Never again,' said Stone. He remembered the endless arguments about studio overheads and transport and all manner of trivia. Several times since, he'd insisted upon a producer's credit because it made him feel he was contributing something beyond being just a bloody stupid actor. But in future he'd leave the worries to men like Bookbinder. 'I take my money up front nowadays,' he said.

'That's the smart thing to do. But sometimes I get my hands on a story that I just have to make. No matter who gets the dough.'

'That's wonderful,' said Suzy Delft.

'And when I screen the answer-print of *Man* I'll be the happiest pauper in town, because it's going to be a fine film, an important film.' He looked at his watch. 'I'm meeting my wife for dinner. I must fly.' He knocked out his pipe on the table leg and then touched the brim of his straw hat to Suzy.

Stone looked at him with surprise. He'd been convinced that Bookbinder was going to give him the hard sell on *Man From the Palace*.

'Where are you eating?' said Stone.

'You two wouldn't be seen dead there.'

'Why?' said Suzy. For a moment she thought he was going to an orgy.

'We love the little back-street bistros. Don't we, Suzy?'

'Yes,' said Suzy.

'The Diplomate,' said Bookbinder. 'The best lobster in town.'

It didn't sound bad at all, but if Suzy was expecting an assembly of top-hatted diners in pin-stripe trousers she was disappointed. The Diplomate was a tiny bar near the rue de Vaugirard. Jammed into one room were five tables, two gas stoves and an old table where Max sliced up live *langouste*, prepared Chateaubriand steaks, chopped garlic sausage and shuffled baskets of *pommes frites*. Here also stood the large bowl of egg-and-truffle sauce that had given its name to this eating place. The ceiling was brown, cured by Max's stove, and a few dozen fly-blown postcards were baked to a curly crisp.

Max waved a cook's knife at Bookbinder's party as they came in the door. Mrs Bookbinder was sitting close to Max's work-bench, talking urgently and fluently about the price of shellfish in the market.

Suzy, in her rainbow-silk Pucci, was overdressed for a bent-wood chair with a broken seat but she did not feel so. She knew that she was the centre of attention. 'I love little places like this,' she said, wiping the chair with a napkin before sitting down. 'I love them.'

Madame took their order and put radishes and cucumber and a plate of ham on the table. Bookbinder ordered a kir for all of them, although Suzy had distinctly said an Americano. He was like that.

Stone had mixed feelings about the evening. He had an instinctive trust in the hunches and skills and experience of Bookbinder. Since *Last Vaquero* and his subsequent years in the wilderness, Bookbinder had had more than his fair share of *succès d'estime*. He'd collected a dozen awards from European festivals for very different films. One, about retarded children, got an award from the World Health Organization but went on the circuits and made money too. Another, a bizarre film about an Indian tribe in Arizona, had become a favourite of European intellectuals and resulted in long interviews with *Cahiers de Cinema* and *Sight and Sound*. If Bookbinder was going to do the very commercial *Man From the Palace* with a director as hot as Hanratty, then this could be the chance that Stone needed to consolidate himself in the modern cinema. Also, Stone liked Bookbinder's no-nonsense approach; he always had done.

'These hippy stars are no good to me, Marshall. I like to work with the greats of cinema. If wanting to work with the Marshall Stones and the Bert Hanrattys of the world is snobbery, then I am a snob.'

Stone nodded. Behind Bookbinder, Max put the point of his knife into the head of a live *langouste*. It struggled violently. Max brought the cleaver down and neatly divided it in two. Suzy gave a little whimper of sympathy but no one noticed.

'Our days are numbered,' said Stone. 'Nowadays, they tell me, the public wants unknowns.' Max put the *langouste* into a frying-pan. There was a screech that might have been the sound of butter, and smoke came from the pan. Stone fanned himself with his napkin. He realized it was an effeminate gesture and stopped doing it suddenly.

'Never,' said Bookbinder. 'The industry is changing: no

doubt about that. There'll be all kinds of movies. Some could be cheap productions with unknown actors, but always the backbone of the industry will be famous stars and famous directors.'

'Exactly,' said Stone.

'Unknown faces might be OK for run-of-the-mill pictures, but to illuminate a beautifully written story, I need fine acting. To get fine acting, I need stars. Taste those black olives, they store them in garlicky oil.'

Stone waved the olive away, but he was pleased by the reassurance that Bookbinder gave him. He poured more wine for them. They all watched the stove while Max poured brandy over the *langouste* and set fire to it with a loud 'woomp' of flame.

'Work it out for yourself,' said Bookbinder, putting the olive in his mouth and talking round it. 'By your standards, what I offered you for *Man* was peanuts. But look at it as a proportion of my budget and you'll see how much I wanted you in my movie, Marshall.'

'Who will do it now?'

'I only got your thumbs-down yesterday. I came over here to talk to a couple of French agents: Prince Felix could be a big-name French or a German actor and still come well within my money.' He signalled for another bottle of wine.

'I'd like to look at the shooting script,' said Stone. 'Just to look at it, I mean. I liked the story.'

'We'll be back in London on Tuesday evening, Marshall. I'll put one in to Weinberger's office.'

Stone touched Bookbinder's sleeve to indicate his thanks.

'I like this little dump,' said Bookbinder. 'You know why, Marshall, because it reminds me of your great little restaurant – The Flying Taco, remember?'

'Great days, Kagan.'

Bookbinder leaned across the table to Suzy Delft. He flicked a thumb at Stone. 'This man has got an instinct for success. Do you know that, Suzy? We all told him not to have anything to do with that old restaurant but he didn't give a hoot, and he turned it into the most fashionable eatery in L.A. It's an instinct.' He punched Stone on the arm playfully. 'You'll never starve, Marshall. You're a survivor. You have an instinct for success no matter what sort of advice anyone gives you.'

'Do you know something?' said Stone. He addressed the question to the three of them, looking from one to the other with a quizzical smile on his face. Suzy couldn't resist these childlike impulses to which Stone was prey. Once in a mood like this he had bought her a Lamborghini.

'What are you up to, you silly old darling?' She purred the words in a sexy whisper, and then placed her hands together in front of her face as if about to say grace.

'I think I just might do *Man From the Palace*. I think I just might do it.' He smiled.

'Goody, Marshall,' said Suzy clapping her hands. She'd been getting ready to clap her hands.

'That would be dandy, Marshall,' said Bookbinder.

'On condition,' said Stone, noting with satisfaction the hush this caused, 'that you take off that damned hat.'

Bookbinder laughed and removed the straw hat that concealed the bald crown of his head. 'There you are, Marshall: Kagan Bookbinder, in the flesh.' Bookbinder laughed. Stone envied the way that he laughed: it was so spontaneous and so infectious.

Suzy laughed too. Hers was a pretty laugh that displayed her even white teeth so that she had to use a diamond garlanded hand to conceal her open mouth.

When the *langouste* arrived at the table the aroma of hot butter, volatile brandy and juicy flesh erased the memories of its painful death.

When Suzy and Stone used Bookbinder's chauffeur-driven Lincoln to go to the airport, Stone thought carefully of the conversation that he'd had with Bookbinder. The prognosis was good. Stone prided himself upon being a clever judge of character. The political climate that had once made Bookbinder a dangerous man to be seen saying hello to had now changed drastically. Marxism – as far as Stone could understand – had become a trump card in any bid for the teenage mind.

The shops of Paris were filled with perfect fruit and vegetables, plump chickens, steaks and *charcuterie*. This plenty stilled Stone's last trace of insecurity, as did the fast-changing kaleidoscope of neon that slid across the paintwork of the luxury cars that sped alongside them.

At Orly a man from the travel agency escorted them through the formalities. A stringer from *Paris-Match* was there and anxious for a quote. There was a special urgent bustle as they moved through a straggling tour group. 'Marshall Stone!' 'Look, Marshall Stone!' A policeman ploughed a path to the VIP lounge. Twice flashbulbs popped, and again he heard his name whispered.

Stone felt good. He felt good about Paris and himself and about Suzy and about Bookbinder. He began to rehearse the short quote he would give the reporter when they got to the VIP lounge. It must be a quote that could not be separated from the title of his next film. Perhaps he could even mention *Man From the Palace*, or at least the coincidence of meeting Bookbinder who had made his first film. On the other hand, perhaps not. As Edgar had once said, perhaps in fun, publicity shared is publicity halved.

7 *You must be very careful in the use of a mirror. It teaches an actor to watch the outside rather than the inside of his soul.*

C. Stanislavsky, An Actor Prepares

There are places midway in status between antique showrooms and grimy junkshops. They sell lumpy chesterfields, china souvenirs of seaside resorts no longer smart, silver-plated trophies of unmemorable races and forgotten fights and sepia photos of embustled matrons and wedding parties. Mrs Sylvia Brummage's comfortable flat in Titcham resembled such a place. These were the mementoes and heirlooms of her husband's family and of her own. She was their final custodian, for they would not be right for a film star's home.

Both Eddie's grandfathers had been clerks: his mother's father in shipping, and his paternal grandfather in insurance. Both families had lived in Titcham for several generations. A dozen miles south of London, Titcham had then been a village complete with stream and green and pub. Now it was not even a suburb. It was just a DMZ, without the delicatessens and trattoria of central London, or the private nurseries, boutiques and garden shops of the suburbs beyond. The pub had been replaced by a supermarket, and a flyover was now spreadeagled upon the green. Pooters and Pollys had been engulfed in a tidal wave of frozen food and launderettes, cut-price grocers and used-car lots. A few survivors, kept afloat by pensions, savings or remittances, clung to their way of life.

Sylvia Brummage said, 'Home-made scones, home-made jam and real tea, not tea-bags, can't stand the things. They come out of the teapot like dead mice.' She poured from a Wedgwood teapot into matching china for the two of us.

My shorthand notes say, '. . . the voice of a barmaid imitating a duchess', but that was written while I was still smarting

140

under her mockery. She did have a carefully articulated, stagey voice, but it went with her stagey manner. What else would one expect from the mother of a famous star.

'Sit down, Mr Ashley, move those books and sit down in a more comfy chair. I hope you don't object to cat's-hair.' She was a big upholstered Marshall Stone. Her hair was screwed into a bun and her spectacles were decorated with sequins. Like her son, she used her hands to amplify her conversation. They were white freckled hands, dimpled at each knuckle. Sherlock Holmes would have guessed them to be the animated hands of a school teacher. I already knew.

'I don't mind cat's-hair.' I moved to the softer chair.

A sweet smell of detergent mingled with the sourness of old boiled cabbage. There were saucers of some sort of food placed near two elderly tabby cats who had arranged themselves to occupy a rectangle of sunlight exactly.

'I'd know you as a scribbler anywhere. We're all the same: dreamers, idealists, out of place in a practical world.'

I looked at her and nodded. I had seldom seen anyone more practical-looking than Mrs Brummage.

'Well, take that overcoat off, for goodness sake. I don't know what you need it for, on a glorious day like this. A young man like you should let the air get to his body.'

'Who wants an airy body?'

'I'll have to watch my step with you, Mr Ashley.'

'Anson.'

'A sharp tongue. No matter, I like to see spirit in a young man. I only wish my son had a sense of humour. He takes himself too seriously, that's half his trouble.'

'People in the public eye become wary, Mrs Brummage.'

'We wouldn't worry half so much what people thought about us, if we knew how seldom they did. Not original I'm afraid: Ambrose Bierce.'

'I'd like to check a couple of things.'

'Fire away.'

'The date of Eddie's birth.'

'July 20th, 1922. Born in Leeds, about ten-thirty at night, it was.'

'I thought he said London.'

'Probably. He thinks Leeds a plebeian place to be born.'

'And Eddie's father?'

'I lost my hubby in 1926. He'd been gassed in the war and he was never very strong when he came back. And yet you should have seen him when he volunteered in 1915, he would make two of Eddie. When he died I came back to live with my mother – here in this very house – of course, it wasn't apartments then. It's not good for a child to be raised in a household of women, especially a boy. I'm a strong personality, no good denying it. You get that way if you nurse a sick husband for three years. I became the breadwinner. The pensions board wouldn't give us a penny. I went to teach; Eddie went away to school. It broke my heart, Mr Ashton, and mother was upset too, but it was better for Eddie. Children need a man in the house, I don't care what you say.'

'Was Eddie unhappy at school?'

'Isn't everyone?'

'Perhaps they are.'

'Of course they are. The whole purpose of school is to teach us to put up with boredom, favouritism, discipline and lack of privacy. Parents don't understand that nowadays: children allowed to run wild will be unhappy children.'

'That sounds a bit totalitarian, Mrs Brummage.'

She leaned over and stroked a cat that had just awoken. It yawned and stretched. 'I'll tell you something, Mr Ashton. I don't give a fig what it sounds like. It just happens to be true.'

'This book,' I said, 'will be an illustrated book . . .'

'The story of Marshall Stone in Pictures. That could be a clever play on words, Mr Aston. You should think about that.'

'I'd appreciate it if you could find any photos that I could use. I would only need them for a few days and I'd look after them carefully.'

Without speaking she got up, and, using a walking-stick, she went to a decrepit bureau, adroitly avoiding four saucers of cat food. She lifted its broken front. There was a photo album inside. She gave it to me and pulled back a chintz curtain to give more light.

Its cover was battered, as if it had travelled round the world a few times. Inside, mounted with neat silver-paper corners, were a hundred or more photographs. There was Eddie aged about seven, dressed as a cat, with an elderly man in drag behind him. The beautifully written caption said, 'Eddie and his Uncle Bernard "star" in *Dick Whittington*. Brighton 1929.' There were photos of Eddie the cat in front of a painted back-cloth of Highgate Hill. There were photos of a pipe-smoking Eddie, travelling through South Africa just after the war with *This Way for Laughter*. Eddie was often on a beach, or posing near an American car, or the only unsigned face on a group photo of the whole company together on the stage. There were clippings from *The Yorkshire Evening Press* that expressed lukewarm response to *The Bridegroom Stowaway*, and men-tioned Eddie Stone – by then he'd begun to use his stage name – only as '. . . among the deckhands Peter Vincent and Edward Stone give effective support'. Here too were the shiny post-cards that actors have multiprinted for publicity. Eddie gazed up into a spotlight, while a kicker light made a halo around his hair. He twisted his head as if photographed without warning, against a background of painted clouds. There was a snapshot of Eddie in Army uniform lounging against a Humber staff car. No badges were visible in the photo because he was wearing a sheepskin flying jacket of the sort favoured by Field-Marshal Alexander. There were two stills of Eddie's gunfight sequence from *Last Vaquero*, a photocall picture of a scene from the Noël Coward play that he did in London in 1952, and a gloomy publicity portrait of him costumed for the Ibsen.

There was a cutting of that famous review of *Hamlet* in which a renowned critic said the whole stage seemed to light up when Stone entered. It was an accolade that had been repeated and quoted many times since. Less well known was the fact that Stone had arranged with the director that the stage light-ing should be increased a fraction for his entrance – *fiat lux*!

Mrs Brummage poured more tea for me and spoke about her home-made cream sponge in the manner of an essay by Brillat-Savarin. No doubt there was an element of performance there. Her eyes had the hardness that I'd seen in her son's eyes, and her talk of sponge cakes – and other invitations to think her a foolish old woman – were dangerous traps which I believe I avoided. Many people mispronounce my name. Some do it as frequently and as variously as she did, but I was not convinced that someone who had called a school register for twenty years would do so by accident. Especially not the name of her one-time daughter-in-law's husband. Perhaps it was because she had been a school teacher that she was able to convey answers without speaking them. When I mentioned sailing she told me of a boy who lived two streets away; he'd planned to sail across the Atlantic single-handed. He'd even bought the charts, she'd seen them in the house herself. Poor boy, she said, he was working in Sainsbury's and had never got farther than Brighton. From somewhere nearby I could hear the music of Byrd. For as many years as I care to remember the BBC had celebrated four PM on Wednesdays with choral evensong. I had often wondered who listened to it, and now I knew; it was a couple of million Sylvia Brummages. I turned the pages of the scrap-book. Indicating the picture of Stone and the staff car, I said, 'This is during the war?'

'When he was in the Army.'

'He said he was doing secret work.'

She passed me a letter in Marshall Stone's handwriting.

12 *Feb.* 1944

Darling Mother,

I only wish I was able to tell you the sort of decisions and plans that are being made here. I am right at the heart of planning for the day when we take the war right back to Hitler and his tribe and give them something they'll never forget. However, I need not tell you that the strictest of secrecy is now more than ever important. Continue to write to me at the same address using the rank of private and all letters will get to me OK. In the last month I have learned to drive a tank and a motor-cycle as well as to become a reasonably proficient horseman.

Discipline is fairly easy-going here since it is a Head-quarters and practically everyone is a colonel or above, apart from specialists like myself. The chap I work with – Brigadier Millington-Ash – has fiddled a sheepskin coat for me and in

144

the snapshot you will also see the Humber staff car I use now and again.

Thank you for the parcel but please don't leave yourself short as our rations are more than civilians get and we never go hungry. I will try to get leave before Easter.

All my fondest love,

EDDIE

She took the letter from me and said, 'Eddie's father was the most gentle of men, and yet in the First World War he volunteered and won the Military Medal for bravery.'

'You must be very proud.'

'But perhaps I shouldn't have shown it in front of Eddie. Do you know what I mean?'

In the back of the album there were three school reports.

Maths: C, English: B, French: C, Conduct: A. Remarks: His only other A is from his gymnastics teacher. He must try harder at class work and expend less effort in trying to make himself popular.

Master Brummage should give less attention to the school's social activities unless his academic work improves abreast of his other interests.

Number in form: 31, Position in form: 27: His low position possibly results from the time devoted to the school drama group this term and last.

'You needn't think he was a stupid boy, Mr Ashley. He was just obsessed with winning everything. Unless he could be at the top, he'd show them all he didn't want to be, by doing less well than he could.'

'I know the sort of thing,' I said. It was an attitude that could be directly compared with her own, for she was proud of her son but was most anxious not to appear so.

'The same with athletics: he'd go down to the running track and secretly time the other kiddies. Unless he was quite sure that he would win, he'd not run.'

'Why?'

'I've often wondered. Perhaps he thought his father and I

145

were failures, but happiness is success, Mr Ashley, and we were very happy, his father and I.'

'Was he an introspective child?' I hoped that I could keep her in that reflective mood, but I could not. She looked up sharply, and said, 'Are you trying to be sarcastic, Mr Ashley?'

'In no way.'

'Eddie, introspective? I'm looking forward to reading this biography if you think that a raving exhibitionist like my son – who would carve his nose off in public for a brief round of applause – might be introspective.'

'I mean, did he read a lot?'

'Didn't read at all, except to learn his lines in the school play. I went to see it one year – never again – it was frightful. Were you ever in sixth-form dramatics?'

'I wasn't even in the sixth form.'

'And got too much sense, I hope. It's never the bright ones who want to posture and strut. I found that, when I was teaching. Eddie craved attention, craved attention! I refused to encourage it. Mind you, his Uncle Bernard must take responsibility for filling the boy's head with rubbish.'

'The *Dick Whittington* photo?'

'That's him. My brother: killed in an air raid. He was a music-hall comedian. Poor as a church mouse, but at Christmas he'd usually find a job as a panto dame. There were several years when that was the only job he did find. A bunch of keys and a ha'penny, Mr Ashley. He let Eddie go on the stage in that damned cat costume one year. I date it all from that.'

'You didn't get on with your brother?'

'Everyone got on with my brother, for the simple reason that he refused to admit of the possibility that any human being didn't dote on him. He'd always arrive at meal times – gloves, spats, cane and pox-doctor suit – full of airs and graces. The neighbours thought he was a millionaire. The woman on this side, at number forty-two, just wouldn't believe he was my brother. But he'd always borrow a few bob before leaving. Oh, the theatre: what a wonderful life it was in the theatre! You should have heard the stories he told Eddie. The brotherhood of the profession, he called it. I told him to try tapping his brothers for ten bob sometime and give his sisters a rest.'

'Did you tell him in front of Eddie?'

'No point otherwise, was there? I didn't mind what Bernard did with his own life, but I didn't want him turning Eddie's head. He used to go along to Eddie's school as large as life and tell them all about his wonderful successes on the West End stage. Terrible liar he was. Eddie got it from Bernard.' She had told me too much. She straightened her cotton dress and buttoned her cardigan tighter over her bosom. She moved an unprotesting cat from the chair to her lap and stroked it as if trying to produce a genie from it. 'Eddie has been a good son, Mr Ashley. If his father had lived, Eddie would have grown up quite differently.'

'But Mrs Brummage, you must be the envy of half the mothers in the whole world. Can you imagine how many would like to have a son who is a film star as famous as your Eddie?'

She nodded and looked at me closely. 'You admire him very much, don't you, Mr Ashley?'

She was able to put me on the defensive. 'I do, Mrs Brummage. He has a great talent.'

'What did he do: "Voice of the turtle" or "A time to love and a time to die?"'

'I don't know what you mean.'

'Uncle Bernard used to do "time to love" when he'd had a few drinks. He used to make a lot of mistakes. Does Eddie still make mistakes? Perhaps you don't know it well enough.'

'Mistakes wouldn't have spoiled it for me.'

'I like "winter of our discontent" best,' she said.

'I'll ask to hear it.'

'You're stage-struck, Mr Ashley.'

'It's Anson. I'm not stage-struck, Mrs Brummage. It's simply that you are unsympathetic to everything that is Eddie's life.'

'You're stage-struck,' she said. 'You can't fool me.' She gave a wicked mocking laugh. 'I'm the mother of the famous Marshall Stone.'

I let her laugh away on her own. It wasn't the sort of laugh that made you want to join in. I said, 'You must have been lonely at times, Mrs Brummage.' She looked up sharply. Something in the tone of my voice must have warned her. 'When that girl Rainbow had the child. Did you ever think of adopting it?'

'Get out of my house.'

'You don't have to get that angry on Edgar Nicolson's behalf.'

'You shouldn't have said that, Mr Anson.'

8

*Both inhabit a fictitious, fabulous, topsy-turvy, tem-
peramental world that is peculiar to their way of life.
Their standards are not my standards. Let them be
judged by those people of decency who inhabit their
world of fantasy and fiction.*

Judge Harrison (Vidor v. Cohn *lawsuit*)

The Japanese signs and sentry boxes, and the section of a military post that had been moved here from the roof of the house
in Notting Hill, had transformed this part of the London docks
into wartime Okinawa convincingly enough for anyone who –
like the designer – had never been there. It was possible to film
so that a line of cranes and an ancient collier were in shot on
the far side of the water. As well as the collier, which had been
anchored there a month and was not expected to depart, the
unit had at their disposal – for one hundred and fifty pounds a
day – a nine-hundred-ton coaster that had been dressed with a
prop gun, Japanese name and rising-sun flag. Beyond that, there
was an eight-thousand-ton Dutch freighter. It was old enough
to be in period for the story and – grateful for the free bonus –
Preston had included it in several of his sequences. Now he was
beginning to wish he hadn't. He watched it loading and tried to
will it into delay.

Preston had decided to reform his image; the headband,
beads and fringed shirt had gone. In its place he wore a Che
Guevara beret, a field jacket decorated with military insignia
and combat boots with bright yellow laces.

It is demoralizing for any crew to stand idle. Knowing that,
Richard Preston had invented a couple of scenes to keep them
occupied. They lined up each shot carefully and completed it
without protest, but Nicolson and Preston both knew that the
crew were only humouring them.

'If that bastard is still not here by lunchtime I might just as
well wrap for the day.' Preston put his viewfinder to his eye and
framed Nicolson in it. Then he panned around the dockside.

One of the big ships was getting ready to cast off. Preston thought he might be able to use an insert of the anchor coming out of the water. He told the crew to set up the shot by the quayside. He walked back to Nicolson. The crew watched them talk together. There was no disguising the fact that both men were worried. Determined not to drink, Edgar Nicolson had got through nearly fifty cigarettes in the previous twenty-four hours, and his progress through the production could be followed by the half-smoked butts that he discarded like a trail of confetti.

'He promised without fail,' said Preston, for the umpteenth time.

'Probably went over to Paris for the *Imperial Verdict* première,' said Nicolson. 'He likes that sort of thing.'

'The boys will lynch him when he finally gets here.' Preston shook his head as if suppressing anger.

As Preston became more and more enraged, so had the spectacle of his rage seemed to calm Nicolson. He got a perverse pleasure from inflaming the boy.

'Lynch him?' said Nicolson. 'Where have you been sitting to view this little side-show? Your crew worship the ground that Marshall Stone walks on.'

'The *people* he walks on.'

'Even the people he walks on – that's the only reason they tolerate you and me. Marshall Stone knows that crew better than we will ever know them. You and I only know their names. He knows the ages of their kids and what kind of pains their wives get. He knows which ones like to have a serious word about the state of the industry and who prefers a dirty joke. No, my little friend, you've got a lot to learn about this business: when Stone finally deigns to join us here, your crew will give him three cheers and collect enough money to buy him a cut-glass decanter to celebrate the end of shooting.'

Preston thumped a Japanese warning sign and kicked the rickshaw.

'And what's more, Richard, my film-directing friend. When he comes back here you are going to join in the cheering. You'll have to treat him like a pregnant mum. Because if you don't do that, he's liable to run off again the next day and we won't have a film.'

'That maniac won't screw me around like this. If he's not here by noon, you are going to have to do something about it.'

Nicolson's car had film stickers on the windscreen, so the driver was able to drive past the dock police and collect him right at the camera position. The driver opened the door for him. Nicolson got in and brought the window down to continue speaking to Preston. 'Give him another couple of hours, Richard. You never know, he might not like it in Paris.'

If Paris was orgasmic, then London was post-coital *triste*. It was raining when Jasper collected them from the airport. Suzy sat in one corner of the rear seat, examining miscroscopic wine stains on the skirt of her Ungaro gaberdine. Stone slumped in the other corner, facing the inevitable doubts about Bookbinder, Hanratty, Belmont's script and himself.

Stone reached for Suzy. For a moment she pretended not to feel his hand upon her leg. Then she moved and Stone withdrew his hand and pretended to search for his wallet. Suzy felt that she must make conversation. 'Do you know what Richard wants me to do?' Her teddy-bear was in her travelling-bag, and as she spoke she took it out and nursed it like a child.

'What?'

'Change my hairline.'

'Why?'

'They do it with wax and electric light.'

'Electrolysis, darling.'

'It will give me a higher forehead. Would that be me?' She pulled her side hair back to show what it might look like.

'Forget it.'

'I asked Leo Koolman. He had the top make-up man at the studio try it with photos of me. Leo said it looked wonderful.'

'What does Leo know.'

'Val thought it would look great, too.'

'Oh, well, if that great international superstar thinks it will look great – go ahead.'

'Val and I are going to do a picture together.' She spoke quickly as she always did when Stone became angry. She was frightened of him. She was frightened of his absurd possessiveness. A newspaper had run a romance story about them. That was just after he'd got Edgar Nicolson to let her star in this film. That news story had trapped them in a damnable situation. And lately Stone had been behaving more like a jealous lover than a concerned father. It was certain to attract comment, and that made her uneasy. She wished he'd have another of his famous love affairs. She'd introduced him to girls without number but he'd hardly noticed them. That made her wonder whether this groping and pawing was just done to conceal his impotence. Penelope swore he was a 'latent queer' and she was the most experienced girl Suzy had ever met.

'What picture? Put that bloody bear away.'

'I am the wife of an astronaut who gets trapped in outer space or something. I've got some good scenes.' She put the bear on the floor.

'You do what Val says.' Stone's foot knocked against the bear and toppled it over.

'What are you saying it like that for? Don't kick teddy.'

'Like what?' He put the bear upright and patted it affectionately. They looked at each other. They had used the bear like this before: Stone as an object of jealousy and Suzy as a totem through which she could declare her need for uncritical affection. They used it as couples so often use their children.

'As if you know something.'

'It's obvious to a child of three. Somerset is not going to help you steal his scenes, is he?'

'Pig.'

Stone chuckled. 'Well, is he, darling?'

'He wouldn't tell me to change my hairline so that I would look ugly.'

Stone was silent, Suzy said, 'Would he?'

'When you've been in the industry as long as I have, you'll find out what people will do.'

She patted her hair and tried to catch a glimpse of herself reflected in the car window. 'You think I should keep it as it is?'

'You've done all right so far, darling.'

'Thanks to you.'

'Thanks to your own talent and looks, you mean.' Stone switched out the reading light and put a hand around her shoulder. Suzy snuggled close to him as he caressed her. When she spoke, it was in a whisper. This was the time, she told herself, this was the time. 'Leo's publicity man – Bud Short – wants to do a gimmick story about me and Val.'

'What sort of gimmick?' His hand moved; she didn't shrink away from him.

'You know – a romance. It would be good for my career, Bud says.'

'Oh yes,' said Stone. 'Better than me, far better.'

'No, darling. Darling, darling, darling, Marshall. You're wonderful for my career. Everyone knows what you've done for my publicity.'

'And this?'

'Oh, you know – two talented young stars of the New Cinema. I'd have to say that no career could be better than looking after Val, and we'd both say that we are having a battle with our contracts so that we can both film at the same locations, so as to be close to each other . . .'

'And then publicity issues the first announcement of the astronaut film.'

'That's it, Marshall,' she laughed happily. 'You're so clever no one could ever fool you for a moment.'

'How corny.' His hand stopped groping at her.

'They are going to spend a hundred thousand dollars just on this one story. They'll get a top outside photographer to do it, and the story and pictures will go to four hundred and fifty newspapers and magazines throughout the world.'

Marshall Stone moved so that he could sit well back in the soft leather seat. He exhaled a long deep breath and let it sound against his teeth. It was the unconscious mannerism of a man lost in thought. He nodded abruptly and turned his eyes to Suzy. 'Do it, darling. It's right for you.'

'Is it, darling?'

'It's right for you, beloved. It's right for your career.'

'Are you sure, teddy-bear?' She stroked Stone's face and

looked closely into his eyes to see if there was any sign of hurt there. 'I'll not do it unless you say so. There's no career so wonderful that I would sacrifice our relationship. The thing you and I have ... well, nothing can beat that ...' Her voice faltered. When she spoke again, her tone was low and she was very serious. 'Are you sure?'

Stone patted her hand. 'I wish your mother had lived. It was all my fault ... I let this bloody career of mine eat me up.'

She nodded and wanted to ask why, but she knew that he would say no more. She squeezed his hand.

'It's us first now, isn't it, darling?'

'Yes, Marshall, it is.'

'Our relationship beyond any career?'

'Sometimes I wish it wasn't, Marshall. And that's the truth.'

'Jasper! To my apartment first. Then take Miss Delft on.'

At Stone's Mayfair flat, his staff were waiting in the hall: Mr and Mrs Patterson – cook and butler – and Mrs Brooks his secretary. Jasper and Mr Patterson unloaded the baggage from the car and the cook was sent to prepare coffee. Stone brusquely dismissed Mrs Brooks and the tray of mail she was holding.

Mrs Angela Brooks had seen the look in Stone's eyes. She knew where he would go: his 'Indian style' dressing-room. It was his favourite retreat. There was Indian furniture painted in bright reds and greens, and a gold-painted statue that had been used in the temple scene of Beyond the Mountains. The carpets and the lattice screen he'd bought in a bazaar during the location shooting of that same film. Perhaps this ambience found favour with Stone partly because the film with which it was associated had been such a record success. Some of his fans had seen Beyond the Mountains a dozen or more times, and still he received letters that praised him for it.

After a shower, he adjusted the full-length swivel mirrors so that he could see himself from five different angles. He towelled himself carefully, stopping now and again to examine a spot, a mark or a bruise. He performed a few exercises: knees bend, arms stretch and fling. Dancing on his toes, he limbered up with feints and jabs to an imaginary opponent. He laughed, and holding the laugh fixed, he leaned close to examine his exposed gums and teeth in the magnifying mirror.

When he was quite dry, anointed with cologne and dusted with talc, he opened the doors of the massive wardrobe he had bought in Kashmir. There was no back to it, so he could step through into the room beyond. Here he was in a jungle of jackets, hanging gardens of trousers and an underbrush of footwear. He took his time in selecting what he would wear. From one of the clear plastic drawers he took a pink voile shirt. A Chinese medal on a gold chain emphasized his tanned chest. Bleached jeans tailored by Doug hugged his slim hips. Satisfied, he turned away from the mirror and went to his dressing-table to darken his eyelashes with a tiny brush and a tin of mascara. He peered at himself, probing and pressing his face to examine freckles and possible flaws. Only when he was quite content with his appearance did he allow his mind to consider his problem. He'd always been like this: even alone, he had to know that he was physically at his best before tackling the decisions of life, or even come to grips with its facts. He stared at the mirror. 'You stupid child,' he said. 'You stupid ungrateful girl. Val bastard lousy Somerset just wants to get you into bed!'

Mrs Angela Brooks allowed exactly one hour to pass before buzzing the house phone.

'Stone.' He was sitting behind his antique desk.

'Angela here. You are due at the location in fifteen minutes. Jasper says the traffic is quite bad.'

'I'm not going today.'

'Shall I phone them?'

'Yes, they have a phone there – in the weighbridge – the number is on the call-sheet. Ask to speak to Richard, don't send a message!'

'Shall I say you are sick?'

'Say I've been up all night with stomach pains. Say that I want to go. Say that I made a big fuss about it but that you won't allow me to, in case it's an ulcer or appendix.'

Mrs Brooks said nothing.

'Make it a bit of a conspiracy, Angela. As though you and him are keeping me in bed against my wishes.'

'I'll phone right away.'

'That's marvellous, Angela. Use your charm on him, Angela darling. If he wants to talk to me: I'm asleep. Tell him I didn't sleep at all last night.'

'I'll phone right away.'

'Wonderful,' said Stone. 'Ask Mrs Patterson to send me a bowl of that clear chicken soup from Fortnum's. And Angela, use the other line. I might want to make some calls.'

'Shall I bring the mail and messages?'

'Any scripts?'

'Three.'

'Just bring the scripts. I might take a look at them.' He felt better to know that writers, producers, studios and cranks were still sending him scripts. They would go on to the pile on his desk and make it almost two feet tall. Twenty-two scripts: he ran his fingertips up the edges of the pages, counting them for the fourth time that morning. They represented money, brains, prestige and power. Each of them meant a story purchased, months of work for a screenwriter, perhaps half a dozen modifications or rewrites. Each of those slim volumes in their shiny plastic covers represented a year of work and expense-paid high-living for a producer who could only get his production money when one last ingredient was found: a star name.

Stone flicked a nail against them, and then dialled Weinberger's private line. It was answered immediately, for it was a line used only by clients. 'Weinberger.'

'Viney?'

'Speaking.'

'Marshall. Are you busy? Can we talk?'

'Never busy, Marshall. You know that.' Weinberger waved away two secretaries and a lawyer with whom he was going through a contract, clause by clause.

'I saw Bookbinder yesterday.'

Man From the Palace.

'Right. Caught me in a public restaurant. You know what it's like. I can't tell people to get lost, it's not in my nature.' He

156

waited for Weinberger to agree but the agent was silent. 'And it's bad publicity,' Stone added.

'What exactly did you say, Marshall?' Weinberger hastily reworded the question. 'I mean, what did you say that he might have misconstrued as some sort of agreement?'

Stone laughed. 'I wasn't born yesterday, Viney. I've been in this business for nearly thirty years.'

'Was there anyone with him?'

'He's the same old Bookbinder, he comes on strong. I just think that a letter from you – it's better in writing – saying I look forward to seeing a copy of the new script. Then put a para of agent's double-talk so he won't get any ideas, right? Just to be on the safe side.'

'Who did he have with him?'

'Only his wife.'

'OK, Marshall, will do. How interested are you in *Man From the Palace*?'

'Do me a favour, Viney, I've got two, perhaps three, dozen scripts here, I haven't counted them, but what do I need Bookbinder for? If he comes up to the price, that's one thing, but . . . All I promised was to read his shooting script. He thinks I might be able to help them with ideas.'

Mrs Brooks kept Weinberger apprised of all the scripts that arrived for Stone. Thus Weinberger knew that most of them came from amateur playwrights – fans of Stone's, writing for the first time and building a story around him – hoping that he would put his influence behind the screenplay. Four of the scripts were carbons, probably from writers down on their luck, without enough money to get their work multilith-printed. Seven of them were old faithfuls, dog-eared and bent because they had been circulating for years. Four recent scripts were possibles. Weinberger had made contact with the people concerned. He said, 'OK, Marshall. Will do.'

'And let's have dinner some night, Viney. Just the two of us, talk about old times.'

'I'll look forward to it.'

'Some time very soon, Viney.'

'Good, good,' Weinberger signalled to the lawyer to place the next page of the contract on his desk.

'Next week perhaps, Viney.'

'Whenever you say, Marshall.'

'I'll be in touch, Viney. And thanks a lot for the other business. Goodbye now.'

Stone had no sooner finished speaking than Mrs Brooks buzzed him on the house phone. 'Mr Stone, I've got Richard Preston holding. He absolutely insists that he speak with you.'

'Did you tell him I was sick?'

'He was very rude, Mr Stone.'

'What did he say?'

'I'd rather not repeat it.'

'What did he say about me?'

'He doesn't believe you are sick. He insists that you go to the location right away.'

'Put him on, Angela.'

'Are you sure?'

'Put him on, Angela.'

Stone rubbed his face and looked at himself in the mirror and then fingered the tiny, silver-framed snapshot of himself and Chaplin. That man in the photo with Chaplin was not likely to be pushed around by a twenty-one-year-old director shooting his first feature.

'Marshall Stone?' Preston's voice was brusque and angry, like a sergeant's command or a warning shot from a man-of-war. Stone wondered if Preston had an audience there in the weighbridge.

'Richard. How good to hear your voice.'

For a moment the boy was caught off balance. 'Marshall, what's all this about feeling sick?'

'Just feeling a bit grim, Richard.'

'Have you seen a doctor?'

'No. I've had this same trouble before: food poisoning.'

'Don't tell me food poisoning! You've got to do better than food poisoning.'

'Yes, food poisoning, Dr Preston.'

'Don't get cute, Marshall. I'm trying to shoot a movie over here and I don't need cute actors to add to my problems.'

'What do you need, Richard?'

158

'I need you here right now, so I can strike this bloody Jap warehouse construction and be wrapped up and out of here by Saturday. On Monday this ship will sail and we'll lose continuity on all the shots that have it in frame.'

'But, Richard, Edgar should have scheduled for that possibility.'

'Edgar scheduled for professionals, not for half-arsed hypochondriacal fairies.'

'Meaning me?'

'Why didn't you see a doctor at eight o'clock this morning? Why didn't you send a message right away? Just what are you . . .'

'Let me give you a word of advice,' said Stone in a gentle persuasive voice. 'If you are going to stay in this industry – and as I'm sure you know, the labour exchange is full of geniuses who have shot one film – then you have a lot to learn. First and foremost, get it into your head that I can ankle this movie of yours. I can get sick, not when you are shooting some crappy little long-shots in a dockyard in London, but when you are scheduled for the big location scenes and you've got your whole crew in hotels. That will cost you not five thousand a day but forty thousand. And then again I can arrive on the set a few minutes later every day . . .'

'Wait a minute, Marshall.'

'What was that about Val Somerset replacing Max Georg as the American general? Val is one of my closest chums, we're practically like brothers.'

Preston grunted.

'If you hadn't rushed away on Sunday you would have met Val when he came to lunch. Jesus Christ, Dickie, if Val knew that you were trying to give me a bad time he'd come down there and kill you: that's how close we are. Val is a wonderful friend. He was worried about that Max Georg business. He asked me what you were trying to pull.'

'Marshall . . .'

'Mr Stone to you. You hear me out. Do you know how many times journalists have asked me to comment on the fact that I've had a lifetime in the industry while this is your first attempt to direct? Do you realize that I have a writer following

159

me around everywhere writing my life story? Just think about what I might say to him.'

'Marshall . . .'

'Mr Stone, I said. Just by word of mouth among my friends – stars, producers and studio heads – I could kill you and make sure you stay very dead, along with your crumby home movie. I'm sick. I'll be at the location when I feel better. Take off.'

Stone slammed the receiver down, watching himself as he did it. Observation was the great teacher.

In the weighbridge at London docks, Richard Preston replaced the receiver as though it was a stick of dynamite. For the last few days this had been the only phone available to the unit on location. The unit runner and one of the fourth assistant directors manned it and ran messages to the crew. The film-makers had given the shabby little hut a face-lift such as it had never known before. The inside had been whitewashed to give more light. Two new tables and chairs had been moved in, so had an electric kettle, an electric fire and a smart new desk-light. Hanging near the phone was a directory card with all the departments of the production typed on it. The production office was in the old house in Notting Hill. Preston looked up the producer's number and dialled it.

'Edgar?'

'Hello, Richard. Everything under control?'

'That bastard hasn't turned up.'

'Did you phone his home?'

'He says he's sick.'

'Perhaps he is.'

'Perhaps he's pregnant. Twenty-four-carat bastards like him don't get sick: they just go in for replating.'

'You don't know how to handle him.'

'With rubber gloves, you mean. How do I have to handle him? Am I supposed to kiss his arse while he screws my film?'

'Can you shoot around him?'

'Shoot around him! Shoot around him! What do you think I've been doing since Monday morning? Look, Edgar, just in case you don't know what's happening down here: I must strike the Jap warehouse tonight if I'm going to have enough space to

160

shoot the reverses tomorrow. And I must have a master shot and a couple of close-ups of Stone in front of the warehouse before we lose it. That means I need Stone today, Edgar, or we'll be reshooting all that stuff with the Dutch ship in the background.'

'I'll talk to him.'

'You're going to have to do better than that, Edgar.'

'Don't push, Richard. You've created the problem, so don't push when I'm cleaning up your shithouse.'

'Before three-thirty or we'll be on overtime.'

'Talk to the shop stewards about overtime now, Richard. And let me give you a word of advice, kid. Learn how to play it cool once in a while. A few of us old berks have picked up a hint or two in a quarter-century of movie-making.'

'Yeah. Sure, Edgar. But do you know something, Edgar. When I go home at night and switch on the box and see some of the movies you old-timers spent the last quarter of a century making, I think maybe I'd be better off taking advice from people who have spent the last twenty-five years sitting on their butt.'

Edgar Nicolson chuckled. 'That's the way it goes, Richard. Make one bad film and you're an incompetent failure. Make bad films twice a year for twenty-five years and they are writing eulogies about you in *Sight and Sound*.'

'You are full of shit, Edgar.'

'And you are full of rhetoric, Richard.'

'What's that supposed to mean?'

'You just won't take an answer for an answer. You know, Richard, I'm going to enjoy watching your career in movies. I was never in on the birth of a cinematic genius before.'

'I need him by three o'clock.'

'If you've been speaking to Stone like you've been speaking to me, and Stone decides to retaliate, this picture could have a new director by three o'clock.'

'Screw you,' said Preston and hung up.

Edgar Nicolson sighed, but did not hang up. 'Have we got a private-line number for Leo Koolman?' he said.

His secretary consulted not the Rotadex, but a small red

notebook from her handbag, where such highly classified information was stored. She read it aloud, but not so loudly that anyone in the next office might hear.

'Great,' said Edgar Nicolson.

Weinberger had described Leo Koolman's office as 'early Disneyland'. Even Koolman admitted to it being 'Hollywood modern'. The works of art and antique furniture were genuine, but they did not look genuine. This bogus appearance was exacerbated by two walls which were covered with shiny silver metal like the inside of a dented can. Even actors avoided their reflections in it, for they looked fuzzy and distorted. The desk was an antique oak table with telephone leads buried inside it. An authentic abstract painting could be opened to reveal a TV set, and a bookcase with real books opened into a small bathroom. The bathroom was a particular pleasure of Koolman's, and few visitors escaped without being shown it. It was painted matt black with a grey ceiling. The bath and sink were also grey, so that tiny spotlights, centred upon bright orange towels, reflected colour that was almost overwhelming. A pressure switch under the floor automatically illuminated anyone who stood at the sink, and between the bath and the shower there was a battery of infra-red bulbs that warmed the air in front of the wardrobe. The wardrobe puzzled almost all of the visitors, for Leo Koolman had seldom been seen in anything but the same single-breasted dark suit and silk shirt. Some said he never changed them, while others said that they were different – but identical – clothes that he changed several times a day. In February 1968 a lighting cameraman named de Wit had attempted to solve this enigma by deliberately marking Koolman's sleeve with a speck of white paint. Koolman noticed him do it and sacked him on the spot. He never again got close enough to Koolman to solve the mystery.

There were other strange and secret devices in Koolman's room. There was a Polaroid camera and a tape-recorder that could be operated from his chair, and a foot button that made a red light flash on his secretary's phone. Several times this morning he had used it. His secretary had been calling Stone's private number every ten minutes since Edgar Nicolson had spoken with Koolman. Now she was inclined to believe that Stone's telephone was off the hook. She was right.

At 12.35 Koolman said, 'Cancel my lunch. Tell my driver Marshall Stone's address. Give me thirty minutes start and then tell Weinberger that I'm going to see his sick client.'

'He'll say, "What for?"' said Minnie White. This frail-looking woman in her late forties was Koolman's secretary when he was in London. If you saw her in a bus queue you might step aside in case she collapsed. But Minnie was as tough as anyone in Wardour Street, not excepting Leo Koolman.

Koolman buttoned his jacket and straightened his tie. 'I'm taking grapes,' he rasped.

Minnie White smiled, and yet she was not a person much given to smiling.

Koolman didn't visit Stone's apartment, he invaded it. He pushed Jasper aside to enter the lounge. Stone got to his feet as if he'd been scalded. 'Leo,' he called much too loudly. 'Leo, how lovely to see you.'

He opened his arms as he'd done in *Dangerous Streets of Damascus*. The publicity boys had loved that still. Loved it so much that they'd built the whole advertising campaign around it. Stone in dark make-up and with arms stretched wide apart had been built a block wide in Times Square and painted across thirty yards of cinema frontage in Leicester Square.

Leo nodded his complete agreement.

'Stay to lunch,' said Stone. 'We don't have enough time just to sit and chat, Leo. We should see each other more often: not just for business, but for laughs.'

Leo grunted, sat down and looked around at the furnishings like a bailiff. It was Leo's opinion that his money had bought most of it. Stone wanted Leo to smile and give him a word of warmth and sympathy. He leaned over the sofa and patted Leo's shoulder.

'You're looking great, Leo. You're looking terrific.'

'And you're looking wonderful too, Marshall.'

'A One at Lloyds,' said Stone.

Koolman smiled triumphantly. 'Then why aren't you at work?'

163

'I've got these damn pains, Leo.'

'I've got a pain too,' said Koolman. 'Pain like a dagger going into my back. Ever know that kind of pain, Marshall?'

'What do you mean, Leo?'

Koolman spoke softly and slowly. 'I mean I'm paying you to do a picture. I'm paying you a lot of money. The below the line cost of that whole damn movie is going to be a hundred thousand dollars less than I'm paying you to appear in it. Your director, your producer and a hundred and five people in that crew have come to a standstill because you have pains. They are all at work, Marshall, with their pains and troubles and cars breaking down and wives screwing around and babies keeping them up all night. Those people are getting to work on trains and buses and subways and they are waiting there . . .' suddenly Koolman raised his voice to a scream, '. . . waiting there!' Stone flinched. 'Now what's this crap about your pains?'

Stone gave a shy nervous laugh, as a man would who had never before had his word disbelieved. 'For God's sake, Leo. What's got into you? No need to shout. It's just this gastric trouble I've had – it was the war.'

'Does it say gastric trouble on your contract? Does your agent say his client will be working on the film any day when he does not have his gastric trouble? Do I get a special price for actors who have gastric trouble? Did the medical you took for this production reveal gastric trouble?'

'It was the war,' said Stone. 'Nowadays I don't get it so much . . . perhaps every couple of years.'

'When did you see a doctor?'

'I know what it is, Leo.' Stone laughed. 'I know what it is. I've still got the tablets from my last attack.'

'Where did you have to go to get them, the Drugstore on St Germain?'

'Paris is nothing to do with it.' Stone twisted the signet ring on his left hand.

'Paris is everything to do with it, you schmuck!'

'I'll not be spoken to like that, I'm afraid.' Stone turned away from Koolman but Koolman grabbed his arm and pulled him back.

'You'll be spoken to any way I choose, you little gonif. Already you are in breach of contract. Just don't bug me while I'm deciding what to do with you.'

'What you are going to *do* with me?' Stone laughed.

'You flew to Paris without the written permission of your producer. Do you know what the insurance company is going to say about that? You're not only in breach with me but you're defaulting on your production insurance. If your plane had crashed, the insurance would have paid over a million dollars to reshoot with a new lead, or scrap.'

'I'm sorry, Leo.'

'Don't give me that crap, Marshall. I took a little time out to read your contract before I came here today. It's too bad you didn't do the same thing before you signed it.'

'I am sick, Leo.'

'You're sick sure enough, but this is not the place to discuss what's wrong with you, Marshall. Take my advice and you'll consult a good analyst.' His voice changed from soft advice to a harsh promise. 'But meanwhile, get this and get it the first time. My office has alerted the insurance company doctor that I might want him – no names, just I might want him. If he comes and checks you out he won't hold your hand and ask for your autograph like that old Harley Street queen you usually see. This guy is a very nasty guy, Marshall. If he finds you are still warm he will tell his company that you have capriciously declined to work today. Just as long as you are warm.' Koolman permitted himself a snort of laughter.

'What are you getting at?'

'After that no big insurance company will cover a production with you in it. Any production that has Marshall Stone in the cast is going to have to find its insurance cover privately. What's more, it will have trouble with the completion guarantee. And they are not going to like that, Marshall. Bad news travels fast in this business, and you'll be bad news. Got the scene now, Marshall?'

'I could probably work this afternoon.'

'That's right!' said Leo Koolman urgently, like a teacher pleased to find a spark of understanding in an almost hopeless pupil. 'Get across there, Marshall. Work half a day at a time. Take a break for lunch. You'll soon get used to it. Most of the world do it all year round, not just eight or ten weeks at a stretch.'

'I'll not work for you any more, after this film, Leo. You can explain that to your stockholders at next year's meeting.'

'That's right, baby,' said Koolman. 'Maybe you'll not be working for anyone by the time of my next stockholders' meeting.'

'If I collapse on the set this afternoon,' said Stone, 'then you'll sing a different song, Leo.'

'I will, Marshall. You go and collapse on the set, and the insurance pay me in full, no delays no arguments.' Koolman didn't smile.

Marshall Stone got to the London docks location at 2.27 PM. Jasper drove close to the long luxury trailer that was provided for Stone as part of the contract, together with one million dollars, four per cent of the gross and one thousand dollars a week to defray unspecified expenses. Stone's retainers were waiting for him with plumped-up cushions, the new *Variety*, small talk, cool drinks and a joke about Pharaoh's daughter and a baby Moses that 'looked great in the rushes'.

His dresser had his costume ready. The British Army battle-dress, with torn sleeve and muddied knees, was one of three which Stone would wear. Each was stained, torn and marked in exactly the same way so that he could change his clothes and still match in the filmed sequence. In the wardrobe van there was another identical uniform for the stunt man who next week would fall into the river for the second unit camera.

When Stone was dressed he went to the next trailer, which was a fully equipped make-up room. He sat back in his chair while the hairdresser pinned his long side hair up on the crown of his head so that it could be hidden by his hat. He sat patiently, closing his eyes and tensing his mouth at the request of the make-up man and his assistant. Sticks numbers five and nine, darkening for the moustache and a light powder.

Stone walked on to the set at eight minutes past three. Already the stand-ins had been lit and studied, and the light falling upon them measured in foot candles by the lighting cameraman and translated into a focal aperture setting for the operator. The focus puller had measured their distance from the camera with a tape measure kept under the front nodal point of the lens. The focus puller had set the distance and calculated the depth of field from his tables to be sure that the movement of the action would not require a change of setting. One of the assistants had drawn chalk lines around the stand-ins' feet. These were the 'marks'. An actor's skill was often measured according to his ability to stop exactly at this place where the camera was focused, without being seen to look down at the ground. The lights were keyed for this position too. A muffled or a missed line of dialogue could be faked, or inserted, after but an actor who didn't hit his marks must be reshot.

'Jesus, Marshall,' shouted Richard Preston. 'You made it, you made it. You shouldn't have come.' Stone smiled uncertainly. Preston grabbed him by the shoulders, held him at arms' length and looked into his eyes as if to discover a secret. Perhaps failing to find it, he embraced Stone. 'That's what makes a superstar. You climb out of a sick-bed in defiance of the doctors.'

'The show must go on,' piped Stone, mimicking Judy Garland.

'A four-inch pancake for Mr Stone,' called Preston. Stone had ceased to be embarrassed at his need for platforms to make him look taller when photographed against cars or doors or other actors. Now he was pleased when a director took the trouble to make him look bigger and more powerful on the screen. For the long-shots, doorways were always rebuilt smaller, and the rickshaw that was seen in this sequence had been specially constructed in a scaled-down version for him.

Preston put his arm around Stone and walked him to the first position, whispering advice, praise and affection to him all the time. The actor was dwarfed by the tall thin boy.

'First positions, everyone,' called the first assistant. 'No run through.' The stand-ins disappeared and a dozen extras took up position.

'Camera! Background action! Action!'

Stone moved furtively, stealing up to where six Japanese

soldiers were heaving boxes. 'Japanese soldiers,' shouted Preston, 'those boxes are heavy. Bloody heavy!' The Japanese soldiers moved more slowly, puffing and blowing in simulated exertion as they moved the empty cardboard boxes. The camera dolly moved along with Stone, keeping him in the centre of the picture.

They all watched Stone creeping forward. He cheated to camera as he pretended to be able to see round the corner. Then he stood up, stepped forward and froze in horror. His feet were exactly on the marks as the camera tracked in for his close-up.

'Cut. Print it,' shouted Preston. It wasn't exactly what he wanted but he too had tasted the heady elixir of melodrama. 'Bloody marvellous, Marshall,' he yelled. With a gesture he offered the star to the crew. 'A man out of his sick-bed,' he called, and began to clap. It produced an enthusiastic round of applause from all present.

Marshall Stone smiled. 'For an encore,' he said, 'I shall dis-embowel myself.'

Edgar Nicolson, and his production manager for five successive films, finished applauding and eyed each other sardonically. The production manager knew that his boss had read the riot act to Preston and had practically rehearsed the whole reconciliation.

'Good acting,' said Nicolson.

'And Stone was good too,' said the production manager.

9

*People in the East pretend to be interested in how pic-
tures are made, but if you tell them anything, they
never see the ventriloquist for the doll.*

F. Scott Fitzgerald

From the desk of
Marshall Stone

Twin Beeches
Tonbridge
Kent
Monday evening

My dear Peter,

Just had the most splendid idea and couldn't reach you on
the phone. Why not let you use my name! How much more
powerful and intimate it would be if it was an autobiography! Naturally this would mean you taking a back seat
as far as the credits were concerned, but, after all, the chaps
at your publisher's would know that you had done it and
that is the main thing, isn't it.

For a title I think we couldn't do better than *The Autobiography of Marshall Stone*, with the Karsh portrait as
cover and frontispiece. I was looking at that photograph
today and it is such a wonderful likeness. How he got such a
result from my mug I will never know! It would make a
dramatic dust cover.

It would also be possible to have someone do a really good
introduction about me. Shall I have a word with Larry or
Steve McQueen? Or perhaps Vanessa? What thinkest thou,
scribe?

Affectionately,

MARSHALL

Dear Mr Stone,

Thank you for your letter dated yesterday. There would be many disadvantages in ghosting an autobiography along the lines you suggest. For one thing, it would prevent me having chapters outside your physical presence. Also I'm not sure that it would be possible in terms of my contract with the publisher.

As to the other suggestions, these would probably be better considered at a later date. Certainly I would not want to do anything until the first draft has been seen by the publisher.

Yours truly,

PETER ANSON

From the desk of
Marshall Stone

Twin Beeches
Tonbridge
Kent
Thursday

Peter,

Have I put my foot in it?

It's just that seeing the work and trouble you are putting into it, I wanted to do everything I could to assure the very biggest sale you can get.

There being a few misguided souls who would buy anything I wrote – bless them. And a big name on the foreword might do even better than that.

Do think about this,

Love,

MARSHALL

And who was I kidding about contractual possibility. The publisher would jump at the chance of having Marshall Stone's rather than my name on the cover.

Bernie – the publicity man from *Stool Pigeon* – sent me a

clipping from an American paper. On the jungle-encrusted compliments slip he'd scribbled an explanation.

Since you are making a collection of prize flackery, allow me to donate this specimen. Please note that it originates from K I New York and is nothing to do with us. However it did syndicate into 248 publications! Best wishes,

BERNIE

SUZY IS A MOD MISS

On the millionaire-before-thirty route is nineteen-year-old Welsh thesp Suzy Delft. She's a glutton for hard work and the gayest of cherubs in the new screenstar style of the 'seventies.

'Show-biz flows in my veins. Born in a trunksville.' The 'today' jargon is what Suzy uses to tell it like it is. 'Sure, there are nasties and nowhere people here, baby. So there are anywhere, but the true pros are all heart and they are the ones I while away the hours with.'

Suzy's heart beats to another drum, a mod miss who knows her own mind, she says, 'All my money is spent on threads. Since I was a little girl in a village not far from where Richard Burton was born, I've had a talent for clothes. If I had the time I would be a haute couture fashion designer.'

Famous model Suzy has discarded her minis for knicker-bocker suits to play opposite Marshall Stone in the movie *Stool Pigeon*. Her Paris hairdresser, 'the greatest crimper in the world', she says with a smile and a carefree shrug of her pretty shoulders, has given her a streaked frizz pixie cut which makes her look fab.

Suzy is verbal about things she doesn't like ('blah things' in Suzy's language). Politics are blah and so are 'pigs' and cabbage and weekend parties where they dress for dinner. Suzy loves spaghetti, Mick Jagger and her beautiful twenty-thousand-dollar lilac-colour Lamborghini.

It ended abruptly. Some sub-editor had snipped it to fit against a furniture store advertisement. I added it to my file.

There were other letters in the same mail, including one from my stepson. Neither Mary nor Marshall Stone had been close to their son for the last few years. He'd come up to

London a couple of weeks before our marriage and we'd had a strained dinner with him and his German wife. Mary would have liked to be closer to them, but she never said so. When I first began my book it seemed a good opportunity to renew the contact with Edward John. I was wrong.

> *Northwestern Typewriters and Calculating Machines Ltd*
> *Area Manager: E. J. Brummage*

Dear Mr Anson,

Thank you for your letter. I am not in contact with my father and have not followed his career with the care that you so clearly have.

I have no memories of my father that I would care to share with you and in no circumstances would I meet with you to discuss your planned biography of him.

Furthermore, without being discourteous, I wish to point out that should your book mention me in connexion with him or his career or activities I would consider that damaging. I will not hesitate to seek redress at law should you be so ill advised as to mention me in this or any other book.

> Yours truly,
>
> E. J. BRUMMAGE.

Mary read the letter and smiled to show me that she was not as hurt as she clearly was. I suspected that she'd written other letters that had been equally rebuffed. Perhaps she knew why her son was so anxious to keep his father's world at arm's length, but if she did know she never told me.

She put the letter back into the tray on my desk, handling it carefully, as if everything concerned with my book was precious to her. I appreciated the gesture. I think the letter from Edward John helped her decide about her diaries. The next morning I found a bundle of note books and odd pages and a leatherbound diary on my desk.

1948. *September. London, Monday*

Eddie is going to be a star. I'm happy that the months of separation have finally proved worthwhile. It was in the newspapers and the phone has hardly stopped ringing all day. Eddie sent a telegram. I wish he had phoned instead.

1948. *September. London, Thursday*

Today I called the London office of Koolman International five times. Miss Samson is very sympathetic and I wouldn't like to believe that she is holding information back but do they truly not know where Eddie is? She must have heard the panic in my voice when I mentioned the bills, for she raided her own petty cash and sent twenty pounds by messenger in a cab. She has told me to send all the rest of the bills to her and they will arrange payment direct.

This diary has become more like an account book lately.

1948. *September. London, Tuesday*

If only I had known that Eddie had had an affair with the Samson girl, I'm sure I would never have been able to tell her about the bills and feeling so wretched when Eddie is away. The poor little bitch thought I knew all the time. Eddie has a lot to answer for. He is the perennial adolescent. He's sick and probably always has been. He's incapable of establishing a satisfactory relationship with anyone of either sex. People like that always want to be evangelists or reformers or actors because they get their satisfaction from exploiting other people's emotion. [*'Exploiting'* had been crossed through and *'manipulating'* inserted.]

I suppose I shouldn't have mentioned the Samson girl to Eddie on the phone. There have probably been dozens since then. He didn't seem at all concerned about me knowing. He said he only took as lovers girls he wouldn't want as friends. He thought that was some sort of compliment to me. I shall never understand the working of the masculine mind. [*'Never'* was underlined twice.] All that time hoping he would phone! Then when he phones, we argue. Perhaps he'll never phone again. I can tell it upsets him for acting. I do love him.

1948. *October. London, Monday*

Little Eddie's school is no problem. Why can't Eddie send for us. I dread to think what the answer is.

1948. *October. London, Friday*

They begin filming. I'm happy for Eddie but I would be happier with him. One letter a week is not enough. I write to him every day without fail. His letters are typewritten. Does that mean his secretary does them from dictation. I hope not.

Eddie can play the cowboy beautifully. I'd love to read the script. He has the feeling for that sort of story, and the accent won't be a problem for Eddie, he's so good at impersonations. At the office I keep telling the senior partner that I'm leaving but I don't go. One of the partners undoubtedly suspects that there is something wrong between me and Eddie. My secretary doesn't really believe that the man in the newspaper photo is my husband. Eddie's school lets him come home on Fridays now, that's so much better. Only four weeks to the start of his Christmas holidays. Thank goodness I now have enough money to make it a happy one for him.

1948. *December. London, Thursday*

What a wonderful surprise. Eddie used the occasion of Mr Koolman's birthday to persuade him to let me fly out there. And phoned from the Koolman house with the party sounds as background!

1948. *December. Malibu, California, Saturday.*

I know I'm behaving like a stage-struck schoolgirl and yet I can't help it. We live right on the beach and listen to the breakers all night. Even now in winter I can sunbathe and I'm getting a tan. But best of all, is looking round our own little house and seeing Eddie talking as an equal to the great stars. It's like a dream. It almost makes the time in London worthwhile. But it's just not fair the way they make him work! Even on Christmas Day he had a meeting that lasted late into the afternoon. And yet Eddie never complains.

1949. *January. Malibu, California, Tuesday*

I'm worried about Eddie and the little 'San Francisco' restaurant. Not just the fact that he's put money into it – that only comes to five thousand dollars – but because of the effect it's had on Eddie. The old man is a dear, although I can hardly understand a word he says, and I know that Eddie used some of his pronunciations in the film. But why is Eddie so keen to make the San Francisco a chic place to eat?

Tonight someone said 'Why is it called The Flying Taco?' and Mr Bookbinder said, 'Because it's bound to bring you down.' Eddie laughed, but he went red. I know that signal of old, don't I?

Eddie can *not* make that place a fashionable restaurant – no one can. And anyway the old man feels out of place there now. I know he would prefer it to be what it was previously: a little cheap place for his Mexican friends. Eddie is so stubborn.

What am I becoming when I write 'only $5,000'? – Last year that would have been a fortune.

1949. *April. Malibu, California, Friday*
Today I saw the film almost completed, what they call a 'rough assembly'. I like it very much. For the first time I discovered that a vaquero is a Mexican cowboy. Eddie says the film looks as if it's been put together by a man wearing boxing gloves. They are going to re-edit it. The rumour is that poor Edgar will have his part cut down. (He will end up on the cutting-room floor, as they say here). Poor Edgar, he's so sad.

Another 'Flying Taco' joke: Eddie so wanted someone to say the food is good. Gary Cooper said. 'It is good, but it takes a real man to hold it down.'

Eddie was consumed with shame. He identifies with his restaurant venture and believes that everyone who makes a joke about it is attacking him and of course that's just not true. He makes us go there almost every night. I can't face Mexican food any more and the steaks are always over-done. Tonight Eddie went into the kitchen and shouted at the cook. Everyone could hear. It's not the way to handle it. Why won't he retire gracefully from the restaurant, the money is nothing to him now. Already they are talking about Eddie getting fifty thousand dollars a film. In fact his market value is four times that but he has the seven-year contract with Koolman Studios. As Eddie says, he's one of the richest slaves in America.

Tonight after dinner we went to a gambling club with Mr Koolman and Mr Bookbinder. I almost got the idea that they wanted Eddie to fall prey to gambling and other extravagances. They are pressing him to buy a big house in Beverly Hills near the B. H. Hotel. Perhaps they think that if they can get us hooked on high-living we will be easier to handle. So many stars are in debt to the Studio. How can they bear it. I'm happy at Malibu. I can't face another move. And in a big house I'd feel more separated from Eddie.

1949. *April. Malibu, California, Monday*
Today I asked Mr Bookbinder to show me the film again. I suppose one can get used to seeing films sitting all alone like that, but I felt rather furtive. What with all the talking and notetaking in the theatre last evening I realized that today I was seeing *Last Vaquero* for the first time.

I felt ashamed. I felt ashamed that I have been living with such a man without appreciating it. Eddie's performance, as the man who becomes the marshal of the little Western town, is breathtaking. Not that the man is anything like Eddie, but that is the miracle of it. As an actor he shows a depth of understanding about people and love, and a warmth that he doesn't know about in real life. How can that be possible? When, at the end, he goes out to be shot down by the men who were once his friends, I found myself crying. I was crying for his wife. What am I doing, I thought, I *am* his wife.

Cedric Hardwicke said that as the world has become more theatrical so has the theatre become more drab. This is the paradox with Eddie (must I start to call him Marshall, as the publicity insists?) He is a brittle theatrical personality and, I fear, becoming more so every day, and yet as an actor his stature grows.

1949. *May. Malibu, California, Tuesday*
Eddie is famous. Rave reviews in almost every New York paper. A mad party started, people arriving at the house as if by magic. Eddie is just stunned with joy.

1949. *June. Beverly Hills, California, Friday*
The new house is fantastic. Why shouldn't it be for over half a million dollars? I never did feel at ease in the house at Malibu.

It was lovely being right on the beach but I was frightened of burglars, especially when Eddie was away. It would have been so easy for someone to walk along the seashore and break open the glass doors on the sun porch.

Our new house looks like an Arabian palace. There are two wonderful palms and the lawn has automatic sprinklers fixed in it like metal mushrooms. Beverly Hills is more convenient for Eddie because his new film is in the Koolman Studios in the valley. It's a gangster film. He'll do the next film there too, shot entirely inside the studio, on a covered stage. This morning I went to see Eddie being filmed. I think he was a little embarrassed by my presence. It was fascinating. Under his white shirt he has a 'squib' filled with red stain which is burst electrically by the trigger of a gun. There is a whole New York street constructed indoors and lit like daylight. There are hundreds of people there, I never realized how crowded it was. It must be awfully difficult to act in such circumstances. There is a girl whose only job it is to comb Eddie's hair before each take. Another just dabs him with face powder. I don't know how he's managed without them all these years.

The more I see of acting and films the less I understand of it. Ten times Eddie had a clean shirt after being shot. Only after the tenth take did the director say it would be good enough and yet I could see no difference.

The wonderful thing about living in Beverly Hills is that the local police are the most efficient in the world. This on account of the valuables that are housed on this small piece of real estate. Every home is passed by a BH police car at least every seven minutes. In addition most of them have – like us – electronic-eye burglar alarms, barbed wire and a security man with an Alsatian dog. For the front-drive gates Eddie has had a sign painted that says, 'Survivors will be prosecuted'. I suppose it's all in fun but like so much out here, especially in the world of show business, it has a grim undercurrent of brutality.

I went for a walk this afternoon. People driving past looked at me through their dark-tinted glass expecting to see my wrecked car somewhere ahead. Here, people only walk after an accident. Eddie says it's a wonder the police didn't stop me. They call pedestrians 'soft shell cars' and they are very rare.

Even the delivery trucks for BH have special licence plates. At night we can hear guard dogs for miles. Eddie has arranged for the whole house to have double-glazing.

Eddie is in such demand! Endless cowboy films, a costume film – Lincoln – and even a musical about a zoo! And invitations for parties – every night. Sometimes they even invite me too – but only as an afterthought.

I listen to the gardener working and the maid brings my tea while cook is preparing dinner and I wonder what I am doing here. I am a nothing, a *Doppelgänger* for Eddie. When we go out together we are described as 'the Marshall Stones', as if Eddie had arrived in duplicate.

1949. May. Beverly Hills, California, Saturday
Fred Astaire's house is just around the corner in San Ysidro Drive. How I used to adore him when I was a girl. I so wish Eddie had asked him along tonight. Almost everyone else in the industry must have looked in at least once. This was our official house-warming. Eddie wanted it to be in style and it certainly was. As well as the usual domestic staff of four we had ten people from the catering company. And the two gardeners were parking cars.

When the guests arrived they spoke with the waiters and waitresses, calling them by their first names. It was Gary Cooper who explained that they are the same staff who do everyone's parties.

I don't know how I survived this evening, particularly since the last visitors – three elderly hard drinkers from the script department – went home at 10.43 AM. I went to bed at 10.44 AM and got up for a late lunch. I feel thoroughly decadent in the true Hollywood manner. I had brunch – avocado and chicken salad – at 2.30 PM sitting at the pool-side in my swim-suit and rollers.
[*The entry had continued over the next day's space.*]

I was excited by the Hollywood magic when I first arrived but the disillusion was only made worse by that. Last night there were all the great names of the cinema here in my house. These were the faces that had inhabited my youth and yet it had the nightmare distortion of a Mad Hatter's tea party. I saw an elderly actor – who is reputed to be a gangster – put his hand up a very young girl's skirt and get a wink of approval from his teenage daughter. There was a bright-eyed old queer, who I thought one of the most masculine men I'd ever seen in cowboy films, who spent the entire evening sitting in the kitchen trying to fix a dinner date with a bottle-blond waiter. There were actresses whose faces had been lifted so many times that their skin was stretched and shiny like candle wax. This California sun seems to do terrible things to the skin. Everyone is wrinkled, and they all tell me how lucky I was to have grown up in English weather!

These aged midgets were only parodies of the people I remember on the cinema screen. I knew last night that I won't be able to stay in this atmosphere indefinitely. I said this to Weinberger and he said that if I could put up with it for three or four years then I would learn to love it. That's another reason for not staying three or four years. I only pray that Eddie comes to this conclusion too. I must be careful not to let him think I am influencing him about his career, he gets terribly upset about that.

I suppose my misery must have been evident last night, for the famous Mr Leo Koolman – he now runs the whole studio – came over to me and said, 'Your husband is going to be big, Mrs Stone, very very big.'

I nodded. He said, 'It won't be easy.' I felt like telling him that it hadn't been a pushover in the past, but I just smiled.

He said, 'If there's anything I can do, just say the word.'

I think he expected me to ask for a screen test. Eddie says lots of wives ask for screen tests. I said, 'Can I have a job in your legal department, please?'

He didn't answer for a long time, he'd suddenly become very interested in the party. He watched Edgar Nicolson dancing with Jane Wyman, who had just won the Oscar for *Johnny Belinda*. Koolman said, 'Can you mambo, Mrs Stone?'

I said, 'No.'

He said. 'You'll have to learn. We have an instructor at the studio. He does a class once a week – Thursday afternoons, I think – Eddie has only to ask for a ticket for you.'

What a funny man he is. I just smiled and said, 'I'll remember that, Mr Koolman.'

He said, 'I know you have a British Bar exam, but that's no good in the state of California, honey.'

I said, 'That's why I need a job while I study for the local qualification.' He jiggled up and down in time with the music. He said, 'I go along some Thursdays.' He was still looking at Edgar. I suppose he was trying to decide if I would be more likely to foul up his investment in Eddie from inside or outside his legal department. 'OK, Mrs Stone. I'll call you tomorrow.' Which, I suppose, means that I have got a job in the Koolman International Pictures Inc, Legal Department.

1949. July. Beverly Hills, California, Sunday

I've been so busy with my law books that I have missed almost two weeks of entries in my diary. I haven't been guilty of such a lapse since I was twelve. Is it a sign of growing old? I mustn't complain, I have seldom been so happy, even if Eddie does think that my only motive was to spy on him.

I thought the legal department would give me an insight into the rationale of Hollywood but there is more lunacy to be observed here than on the set. Looking at the accounts for *Last Vaquero* I found a bill for five hundred plaster cactus plants shipped air freight to New Mexico. The location was full of cactus, so they were not needed, but since they had already filmed some of the plaster ones, they sprayed all the real plants a brighter shade of green to match them. Total cost, sixty-seven thousand dollars, plus two days' delay.

There is a contagious disease that flourishes in legal departments: lawyers become independent producers. Three have succumbed since I arrived eight weeks ago.

1949. July. Beverly Hills, California, Tuesday

It still fascinates me to walk through the back lot. There are acres of permanent sets. It's a nightmare world: a harbour without water, a galleon bared to reveal its gundecks, a waterfall with a camera-crane behind it, cliffs, ponds and villages of straw huts. There's a New England courthouse that became a Greek temple last week, a Wild West saloon that's been crated to go to a location. There are nondescript alleys and narrow streets that become Hollywood's idea of Paris, Moscow or Vienna at the hands of the set dressers who garnish them with posters, signs, letters-boxes and kiosks. Behind the building that houses accounts and the legal department there is a three-acre space where they store fireplaces, doorways and walls by the hundred. Inevitably we are described as working on Wall Street. Some of the walls are surfaced with foam rubber for heads to be beaten on – very useful here in Hollywood! I often feel the need for one.

1949. *December. Beverley Hills, California, Friday*

Leo Koolman phones me every Friday morning – in person, not his secretary – to ask if I am happy in the legal department. It's amusing how puzzled he seems to be that I want to work there, when he is paying Eddie a fortune. Twice he's taken me to lunch at the commissary and once to a French bistro in Beverly Hills. Each time he spends his entire lunch telling me what are the ingredients of a successful film: colour, conflict and confrontation. Plus all manner of afterthoughts lumped together as 'production values'. Koolman is by no means the ogre that he likes to be thought. He clearly despises the people who kowtow, and since that includes almost everyone working for him – except Phil Sanchez, and sometimes Weinberger and Eddie – he feels isolated. He fishes for compliments like a little boy.

Eddie says 'Bless you' to everyone who compliments him, does him a favour or even passes the time of day. It's not the blasphemy that I find offensive but the obvious insincerity with which he says it. He got it from one of the TV quiz masters, who says it instead of 'goodnight'. I wish I could tell Eddie how terrible it sounds without prompting a row. Although I must confess a lot of people seem to love it. If only he would forget about that restaurant. He drives me silly talking about it and today Leo was pumping me about it too. What am I supposed to say? Eddie has tried to get Koolman there without success. 'Would I like the food?' Leo said. He would hate the food and the atmosphere and the service. I said, 'It's very simple.'

I shall never get used to calling Eddie Marshall.

[*The entries become perfunctory except for detailed lists of her law books, dates of her exams and her marks. It's only long after she is fully qualified and they return to Blade, New Mexico, where* Last Vaquero *had been shot, that the diary takes a more personal turn.*]

1953. *June. Blade, New Mexico, Saturday*
Marshall is thirty-one today. He was twenty-six when he was here to make *Last Vaquero*. It's so strange to be back at the same place after so much has happened. We are treated so differently now. The Hollywood rot has set in: I fear I now expect to be pampered! There is a helicopter to take us from our hotel in Albuquerque to the desert location. Most days Marshall goes alone. Four o'clock in the morning is too early for me, and even in Marshall's air-conditioned trailer I am drinking ice water all day to keep cool. Was I once so in love that I didn't notice this heat and dust, or the cockroaches, gnats, snakes and scorpions?

1953. *June. Blade, New Mexico, Monday*
By the most amazing coincidence Kagan Bookbinder is here, also doing a Western. He hasn't changed much. He's still full of talk. I now see him quite differently to the way I used to see him. At first I shared Marshall's great respect for the man who'd given him the big chance. But when I found out that he'd been carrying *Last Vaquero* round for two years trying to get the money, and that it was Marshall's screen test shown to Leo Koolman that got him his deal, then I started to think again.

And the lies that Kagan told about Marshall! He told Koolman that he was one of Britain's top Shakespearean actors, that he was so popular and famous in Europe that he'd recoup the film's cost at the British box office alone. Koolman's London chief was sacked about that time and there are those who say that Kagan paid him fifteen thousand dollars to keep quiet about Marshall being virtually unknown in London.

I remembered Marshall telling me how Kagan introduced him to the great Koolman. Kagan Bookbinder took Marshall aside and said, 'Now I've laid my head on the block for you,

Eddie kid. I've told my partner – Mr Koolman – that you and me are very old friends.' Note the 'my partner Mr Koolman' and the way that Marshall was made a party to the deceit from the very beginning. He couldn't very well admit that he'd only just met Bookbinder after being introduced as an old old friend. This was typical of Kagan Bookbinder's style. He always claims that he knows every actor, writer, director – and for all I know lawyer – that anyone mentions. The friend of the stars: Kagan Bookbinder. My God, what a confidence man, and it paid off for him, for a time.

1953. *June. Blade, New Mexico, Tuesday*
I'm sorry that yesterday I wrote what I did about Kagan. Lo, how the mighty have fallen. His present production is a terrible little quickie, crewed – Marshall says – by the worst dead-beats in the industry. The lighting cameraman is a notorious drunk and one of our crew says that half of Kagan's boys are not even in the union.

We are filming around a beautifully designed ranch that our crews have built, way out in the desert. But Kagan is working on the same old street that was originally built for *Last Vaquero*. It's been enlarged since then, they've put a livery stable on one end of the street and a church at the other. Now that the owners of this ranch have discovered how much money can be made by letting tourists in, the whole place has become ghastly. All the time Kagan Bookbinder is shooting, his set is crowded with tourists, roped out of frame but still getting in the way. One side of the street has been turned into shops. The saloon where Marshall had his gunfight with the train robbers has now become a Pizza Parlour and the other shops are selling plastic souvenirs, popcorn and ice-cream. The ground is littered with Kodak cartons. They even stage a fake gunfight for the home-movie enthusiasts.

Of course none of the big companies use that place any more: it's mostly for B pictures and TV serials. And they have much better places: Apacheland and Old Tucson. Marshall was so upset. It's never good to go back, I told Marshall that before we came here.

Tonight Kagan shared our helicopter and we had a meal

together in Albuquerque. He was talking about his film. Of course it's going to be wonderful and it's going to win an Oscar, no less. In a six-week schedule! The same old Bookbinder. The proposition he put to Marshall was so fantastic that we both laughed. We thought he was joking. *The Masked Rider*: it would take only one day of Marshall's time, he said. The secret plan was to film Marshall putting a mask on for the beginning of the film and film him taking it off at the end. The rest of the movie would be someone doubling for Marshall and wearing the mask all the while. Marshall would be billed as the star and get thirty-five per cent of the profits but nothing up front.

Kagan had obviously banked everything on getting Marshall to agree, 'for old time's sake.' Marshall said he would think about it and after a little more champagne (Marshall is drinking too much and getting fat), he even softened to a point where he said he will do it if there are no conflicting contract obligations. Kagan Bookbinder almost cried. I felt very embarrassed. Marshall will never do it. He told me so, but he just can't tell Kagan because Marshall Stone must always be loved by everyone. I suppose poor old Weinberger will be the scapegoat.

Today Marshall bought a new car: an Edsel. He is so keen to be the first person to have one among our friends.

1958. *April. Brighton, England, Sunday*
Could a trip to England have been more miserable. The first error was trying to do an outdoor film so early in the year. Eleven days standing idle upset Marshall to a point where we scarcely spoke for a whole week. It's still raining, no wonder the photo that the agents sent us showed the garden to be a mass of flowers. I've had a coal fire, and all the electric fires, going every day and still the bedclothes are damp – and Marshall gets so angry. But he's too young to be so worried about rheumatism, or is that just an excuse for scolding me. The truth is that Marshall should never have agreed to do this script – no matter what Leo threatened, I'm sure I could have handled him – Dickens is not right for him but I dare not hint such advice. I pay the price of him making a fool of himself and then bear the brunt of his bad temper. I feel so sorry for myself.

Just eight more days filming and then we can have a holiday before the recording begins.

1958. *May. Brighton, England, Tuesday*

Had we taken the holiday the weather would probably have stayed wet. As it is, the sun has been glorious every day. I sit in the garden listening to the BBC and I quite forget that California ever became part of my life.

Marshall is away again. He said he had to go to Pinewood for looping and stay there until it was complete. This afternoon the editor phoned and asked for him. I couldn't say he was recording, the editor would know if there was still looping being done. I said Marshall was in London for a meeting. Judging by how quickly the poor man said goodbye, his guess about Marshall's whereabouts was rather along the same lines as mine.

Mr Weinberger always addresses the letters to Mr and Mrs Brummage, I believe that it's his way of telling me that he is not a party to Marshall's philandering. How long can I go on being humiliated. In the letter he enclosed a clipping about that film that Kagan Bookbinder was making in New Mexico when we were there about five years back. I don't remember hearing any more about it and yet apparently it won prizes at four European festivals including Cannes and Venice. It's not like an Oscar, but Marshall will be so surprised. He was certain it was going to be a flop and he would so love to win a festival prize.

1958. *May. Brighton, England, Friday*

Today I told Marshall that I wanted a divorce. His mind works only one way: he immediately began to guess which of our friends I might have been to bed with. As if I would want to have anything to do with any of the people he named! He called me unfaithful. I said, 'What is being unfaithful? Is it me telling you I can't put up with you any longer? Or is it you keeping our house constantly full of spongers, publicity people, con men and film hangers-on, all of them knowing more of your life, your plans, your ambitions and of your activities than I do?' I didn't mention anything about the women, what's the use?

185

1958. *May. Brighton, England, Saturday*
Flowers everywhere, love letters, a diamond brooch. Oh Marshall! I don't want to keep Marshall captive. Especially not in this little cottage. But even he admits that it's nice to sit in front of the fire and know that the phone doesn't work properly. Edward John is growing up and I so love to see him with his father, but Marshall is a stranger to him and he mustn't get so angry that the child isn't fully at ease with him. He loves his father but Marshall just doesn't spend enough time with the boy for him to become really close. I hate it when he runs to me, I know it hurts Marshall but I can't reject the child when he's frightened.

He's not old enough for a pony. Marshall holds him but Edward John is nervous of heights, and shouting at him won't make things better. What does it matter how much the damned pony cost. Marshall can be so stupid at times.

A divorce would hurt his career, I know that. But for him to talk about wanting to have Edward John is madness. The first time he wet the bed – well, I dread to think what Eddie would do. How I've kept it from him all this time I don't know. Dare I believe we can make a new start and be happy together.

[*And then four misplaced entries from 1952. The pages had been screwed up as if they had been thrown away and later put back.*]

1952. *July. Dorchester Hotel, London, Thursday*
It's now arranged that Marshall will do the Italian film *Storm Clouds* with an Italian director that everyone says is a genius. I wonder if Marshall doesn't want me to go to Italy. He said it was Leo Koolman that didn't want me to go, but when I mentioned it to Leo on the phone he laughed and said he'd fix it. Will Marshall think I went over his head and be angry?

I'd love to be in Italy again. That holiday there with Marshall just after the war – it was a disaster in some ways but we were so in love. If only it was possible to turn the clock back. I am never truly happy nowadays and I crave just a little happiness. Leo is arranging for me to go by boat. By the time I rejoin Marshall I might have a lovely tan.

1952. *September. The motor yacht* Spool, *Italy, Saturday*
We missed Marshall by only one day. He was in Porto Sepino
yesterday when we were anchored there overnight! This morning we arrived at the location and phoned to his hotel but he'd
gone without leaving a forwarding address. It's my own fault
for arranging to surprise him. They don't need Marshall for
another week, he could be anywhere. Now I don't know
whether to return to Monte Carlo on Leo's yacht or stay here
and wait for Marshall. The local hotel is very dirty and it would
mean one of the crew moving to even worse accommodation.

1952. *October. Hotel de Paris, Monte Carlo, Thursday*
Marshall is missing for twelve days. Weinberger has booked a
call from Rome for five o'clock and this might mean news. It's a
person-to-person for Leo so I can't phone back to find out.

I daren't use the hotel entrance, there are at least two dozen
reporters and photographers waiting outside. Luckily there is
an underground passage that they use when the motor race is
on. So I am able to get out that way. Even so, yesterday I was
recognized. It's difficult to know what attitude to adopt. If I
wear bright colours they will think I don't care, if I wear black
they'll print that I am in mourning. Luckily half the residents of
Monte Carlo wear dark glasses and wide-brimmed hats so my
disguise isn't as conspicuous here as it might be elsewhere. If
only he would phone.

1952. *November. Hotel de Paris, Monte Carlo, Wednesday*
The sudden explosion is better than long-drawn-out misery.
Was it my fault? Do I truly want a divorce? I'm not sure that I
understand all the ramifications of Marshall's residence and
domicile qualifications but I shall just let Koolman's specialists
work it all out. The main thing is that I get custody of Edward
John. I can make enough money for us. I hate the way they talk
about money for me: I don't want to be bargained over. I'm not
going back to California. I couldn't bear to see that house
again, it holds too many memories. I can't believe that Marshall will really cite Leo. It's stupid and unfair, and I'm sure Leo
will never forgive Marshall. We were only on our way to see

him, and he knows it. Whatever can be Marshall's motive.

[And then, in the neat lawyer's handwriting that I had learned to recognize:]

1959. *Hampstead. London, New Year's Day*

Dare I believe that this is going to be a wonderful year? Today I went to see Mr Brooks at Brooks and Gerber. Most of the City still think of them as a stuffy little investment house, but since their links with Rome and Paris last year and this new one with New York, they have suddenly become a force to be reckoned with.

They are interested in the entertainment industry but only on their terms. Brooks says, rightly, that they have no one expert enough to talk to record companies and film and theatre people. In fact they have no one, with any authority, under fifty-five years of age, so offering me a senior position there is rather a revolution. I explained that in spite of my California licence and my experience at K I, I was far from expert. I know my way around talent contracts and production. But the New York lawyers do the distribution and exhibition side of Koolman's business.

I will be spending six months with the Rome affiliate and then six months in New York. Brooks plans to retire in 1965 by which time he will be seventy. Gerber has a son who is not qualified and only comes to the office when he feels like it. Who wouldn't be excited at such a prospect.

1959. *February. Hampstead, London, Tuesday*

Officially separated from Marshall at last and everyone good friends – or are we. The flat is tiny, but I close the door and it's all mine. Goodbye, Marshall. No longer am I competing with every sexy young starlet you meet. Goodbye low-calorie salads, and hello lobster mayonnaise and steamed puddings. Now I can listen to Bartok and Bruckner instead of Herb Alpert, and wear my spectacles and not have to have my hair done because we are meeting important people. Goodbye film wives and premières and small talk and movies, movies, movies. I'll never go to the cinema again.

I turned to my notebook and read the notes I had made. I had tried to write about Marshall Stone's first wife and not about my present one.

Mary Singleton always used her maiden name for her professional work. Query: did she suspect that one day she would separate from Stone. Was this the basis of her anxiety to get the California exam.

She is slim, dark and about five feet two inches tall. She's very attractive and it is not easy to decide her age. A penetrating sense of humour, although used sparingly, is devastating when aimed in your direction. She has abundant energy and when she talks on two phones at once the callers seldom guess it: a complete reversal of the Hollywood technique, which is to speak on one line as if you were on two.

Her office is a jumble of books and documents, as is her study at home. There are maritime law books mixed up with Kine Yearbooks and Police Journals stacked with copies of *Elle*. She has a high-pitched voice that has an unusual cadence. She begins a thought in a rush and then leaves it incomplete in order to develop some new idea from it. On the phone, a room away, her voice can sound like some new South American dance rhythm. In contrast with all this, her appearance is neat and well considered: Chanel suit, short dark hair, almost imperceptible eye make-up, a gold brooch that Marshall Stone gave her and the simplest of clip-on earrings that she snatches off each time she answers the phone, manipulating them between her fingers if the phone call poses problems.

I'd noted some of her comments about Stone.

'The craft of the actor requires the same amount of stamina as does that of a gymnast. The difference between an actor delivering a *Hamlet* soliloquy while rather tired, and doing the same acting performance with great reserves of energy just below the surface, can be the difference between mediocrity and stardom.

'Actors — and, for all I know, actresses too — obtain this energy from what they call love but what the rest of the world calls praise and admiration. The effect of even insincere praise must not be underrated. A poor performance praised can become better, a poor performance criticized honestly can go to pieces. This makes the job of the director very difficult, it makes the role of wife virtually impossible.

'Eddie liked to have a dozen or more people to dinner every night and he preferred to eat in restaurants rather than at home. Usually he ordered something complicated. A chicken stew but made only with white meat. Or he'd want veal with fresh basil, and the waiter must bring him some basil to show him that it's fresh – not dried.

'Such fastidiousness means that everyone present can discuss Eddie Stone's digestive tract, opinions, palate, health and beauty. By the time that the carefully prepared dish arrives at the table, it's outlived its usefulness. Eddie will shunt it round his plate and abandon it.

'This is very typical of his attitude to the whole world. If someone can be useful to him, he will give them all his charm, attention and energy. The moment they cease to be useful, he switches off. You don't exist – as far as Eddie is concerned – except through him.'

PETER: 'This sort of singlemindedness is not uncommon among geniuses.'

MARY: 'Peter, it's not uncommon among door-to-door sales-men. I'm afraid that nature follows art in this respect. Many people in our society have learned how to use the devices of show business for their own ends. Politicians have become masters of the soft word, the conditioned tear-duct, the mis-pronunciations of the common man. They have learned about cosmetics and lighting and how to tell which lens is on the camera. I've said to you how I rejoice when I see or hear of a politician saying something extremist, foolish or ill timed, be-cause I know that show business has not yet taken over the whole world.'

10 *The reason so many people showed up at Louis B. Mayer's funeral was because they wanted to be sure he was dead.*

Sam Goldwyn

The same world to which Stone had sacrificed his sense of humour had taught him the artistry of the raconteur. This change from spontaneity to skill had remained imperceptible to all but his most intimate acquaintances.

'I'll tell you a story, Viney.' Stone got to his feet. He felt gagged and inadequate unless he could move and use his hands. If a story was worth telling, it was worth telling with all the skill and enthusiasm he could employ. When Stone was too tired to talk with this sort of intensity, he didn't speak at all. Often, he would arrive at dinner parties and be the life and soul of the evening for an hour or more. Suddenly he would feel exhausted, excuse himself and depart abruptly. Hosts who did not understand actors sometimes felt rebuffed or insulted by such exits.

'Two goats in the Mojave desert. Have you heard it, Viney?' Weinberger shook his head.

'They find a tin of film. One of them nuzzles it until the lid comes off. The film leader loosens around the spool and the goat eats a few frames. The second goat eats some too, and they pull all the film off the reel until they have eaten the whole of it. There is nothing left except the can and the spool. The first goat says, "Wasn't that great?" and the second goat says, "The book was better." '

Stone laughed heartily and Weinberger joined in although he'd heard it before. Agents always heard things first. They were the only people who regularly visited all the film company offices. Weinberger went to TV and record companies too, and publishers and the serial departments of magazines and newspapers. Often he knew who was hired and fired even before the men involved. More than one top executive had discovered Weinberger in his subordinate's office before being officially told that the subordinate was to be his successor.

Stone touched his moustache self-consciously, as if it was held on his lip with spirit gum and the laugh might have dislodged it. He held a copy of *Man From the Palace* in the air before placing it upon the shooting script that he'd received from Kagan Bookbinder. 'Better than the book!'

'Who wrote it?'

'Looking for writers, Viney?' Stone smiled and waved an admonitory finger. 'It's by the author of the book.'

'Probably the first script he's done,' said Weinberger. 'Kagan probably got him cheap. Young writers will do that sometimes, rather than let someone else mess up their masterpiece.' Weinberger smiled. 'The pros take their money and deliver their darling to the executioner.'

'I'm so glad I'm not a cynic like you, Viney. I love this business. I really love it. How can you work in the industry when you never have a good word to say for it?'

'I work in it, Marshall, because there are great actors, fine writers and directors and other creative people who love their work as you do. That makes them unsuitable to negotiate deals, draw up contracts or handle day-to-day business that is very dull but very important in keeping the industry working.'

'You're right, Viney. Creative people are idiots at business.'

'How's Suzy? I have to talk to her about tax but she keeps putting it off.'

'I think she's going to be a really great actress, Viney. She's fresh, attractive and full of enthusiasm. I see in her the sort of drive I had twenty years ago.'

'The *Stool Pigeon* film is going to be good for her.'

'You think Leo is still mad at the way we screwed Suzy's whereabouts from him?'

'Correction, Marshall. We exchanged Suzy's address for a considerable number of concessions and a lot of percentages.'

'That contract got up Leo's nose, Viney. He told a lot of people how we screwed him on it.'

'Leo is always happy to concede a moral victory when he gets the best of a deal. Just as you are happy to concede profits providing your ego stays intact.'

'That's bloody rude, Viney.'

'Well, it wasn't meant to be, Marshall. I just want you to see these deals with the same jaundiced eye that I do.'

'Suzy was worth it.'

'Sure she was, Marshall. Once you made up your mind about locating her again we had no option but to give Leo what he wanted. I'm not blaming you, but some of those odd bits and pieces have added up to a lot of money in the last few years. Anyway, it will all work out . . . a couple of pictures from now and Suzy will be getting a good price for herself.'

'About Suzy . . . I've been trying to arrange for a publicity story – a romance – between Suzy and Val. Koolman's publicity boys jumped at the chance. They're thinking of tying it into their first announcement of the astronaut film.'

'Val Somerset?'

'You think I don't like him, Viney, but you're wrong. He's a nice kid. I'd go to a lot of trouble for him – and I think he has a secret regard for me.'

'Sure, Marshall, sure.'

Stone replaced *Man From the Palace* on the shelf that contained only record-breaking best-sellers. He'd read them because he felt it was part of his job to know what was the public taste: *Valley of the Dolls*, *Mary Queen of Scots*, *The Carpetbaggers*, *The French Lieutenant's Woman* and *Love Story*. The bottom shelf held the few books he'd read for pleasure: Ellery Queen, Rex Stout and Ed McBain. There were no paperbacks. Stone disliked paperback books: they were lower-class, untidy little things that became even worse if read. And Stone hated muddle, mess and disorder. He fingered a book that had become a little scuffed and, after a moment's hesitation, took it from the shelf and tossed it into the waste-basket that was a hand-painted replica of a Scots Guards drum. He turned away from the bookcase. 'Did you speak to Kagan?'

'I sent a letter. That's what you wanted, isn't it?'

Stone pursed his lips and hushed away the idea that he would argue about it. 'You know best, Viney.'

'You like the shooting script?'

'Shall I tell you something, Viney: it might be a masterpiece.'

'You've read it quickly.'

'Well, obviously I've only read my own part.' He opened the script. 'Someone in Bookbinder's office indicated my lines in red pencil. And Kagan enclosed such a nice note. He's screened six of my movies again last week. He says he'd be "honoured", that's the word he used, to have me in the picture. He says I've always interpreted my roles with a creative and scholarly analysis of which few actors are capable. He said my Hamlet was ten years ahead of its time. Quote: Done now, it would put all of these tricky Edwardian, Victorian and rehearsal-clothes Shakespeares into perspective, unquote. It's a lovely note, Viney; "honoured" was the word he used.' Stone laughed to release the tension he had built. 'Sounds like a good working relationship with a producer, eh?'

'Did he have someone in his office underline "honoured" in red pencil?'

'Now wait a minute, Viney. This business doesn't just consist of hard-nosed cynics like you. There are one or two people who think a lot of that Hamlet I did.'

'But just one of them is asking you to sign a contract, so him I have my eye on.'

'Well, I'm not working for Leo again, Viney. I told you that.'

'Yes, you did,' said Weinberger.

'He's a barbarian ... and in my own house too! I feel like taking a page in Variety to tell everyone in the industry what sort of a man he is.'

'Check with me first, Marshall, or we might find you paying Leo half a million in damages. Anyway, the industry knows what Leo is like, they would just wonder why it took you so long to find out.'

'I'd write only what's true and I'd say why I was publishing it.'

'The greater the truth, the greater the libel, Marshall, you know what the lawyers say. You add malice to it and you'll be in the hole for a million plus.'

'Don't lecture me.'

'Well, don't take any chances, Marshall. Leo's got some bright kids working for him, no one's in a better position to know that than I am after thrashing out your *Stool Pigeon* contract.'

'It's all agreed?'

'Yes. It will make a nice change to get a contract signed before the movie is released.'

'That Leo is a bastard. I saw right through him today. I told you what he said about me collapsing on the set.'

'He was joking, Marshall.'

'He was not joking, Viney. I can tell when people are making jokes. Besides, Leo never makes jokes. What did he say when you saw him tonight? He didn't apologize?'

'He was still pretty angry, Marshall.'

'I'm not frightened of the bastard.'

'We'll patch it up.'

Stone shook his head. 'Look what he did to Peter, and look at poor Freddy; they both disappeared without trace. Peter went from half a million a picture to one hundred thousand inside eighteen months. Now he's only getting jobs on German productions. No American or British company will touch him: they all stick together.'

'That couldn't happen to you, Marshall. You have enough money to hold out until something you like comes along.'

'How much time?' Stone went to the mirror, bared his teeth, and when he spoke it was to his reflection. 'I'm no Duke Wayne, Viney. I'm no Jimmy Stewart. They have faces like certain sorts of airline baggage: the more battered they get, the better they look. My face is patchy, my gums are going and I'm losing my hair, no matter what André does. He's tried infrared, ultra-violet and this new Swedish treatment, but every morning my comb gets hairier and my head gets balder.'

Weinberger laughed. 'Jesus, Marshall, that's the first time I ever heard you make a joke about yourself.'

'It's no joke, Viney. Look at this gut I'm carrying. I've cut down on food until I'm practically not eating, but I can't shed this damned rubber tyre.'

'You look fine, Marshall.'

'Roger – at the gym – says I should have extra time there. He can't understand why I'm slipping back.'

'How much does Roger charge per hour?'

'For God's sake stop it, Viney.'

'Last week when we saw *Silent Paradise*. Everyone there said you had never looked better.'

'I'm talking about four or five years' time, Viney.' Weinberger noticed that Stone's hands were shaking as he nervously twisted the signet ring round and round on his finger. He walked across to the drinks cabinet and noisily moved the bottles. 'Another drink?'

'OK.'

'And I'll have one too. Screw the diet.' He poured the drinks and sat on the sofa next to Weinberger. From as close as this Weinberger could see the tiny muscles flickering under his client's eyes, and he watched as Stone clenched his hands together in an effort to still them. 'The scripts they send me . . .'

'What about them?'

'The roles they offer me. Half of them are character parts.'

'Not one.'

'Yes, Viney. I don't mean that they are small parts. Some of them are big ones because they want my name on the marquee, but the roles are for old men. Take the story about the atomic physicist: he's a crazy nut, Viney. It's the reporter who will appeal to the audience. Take the one about the hippy village. Can you imagine me playing the school teacher?'

'That's not a bad script, the best in some ways. And I know that company, they are going places.'

'But the school teacher, Viney. Can you imagine what the kids would think of me?'

'You are worrying too much about details, Marshall. Both of those stories are men facing a crisis in their lives. The school teacher has to choose between his daughter and the people he respects and lives with. No one is going to think you are anti-hippy if you play that role.'

'Wrong again, Viney. In fact they will think I am a school teacher. You've seen people come up to me and talk to me as if I am the Executioner.'

'Cranks.'

'Not just cranks: well-dressed, sensible people too. Look, Viney, there is a youth revolution going on. We are not harnessing the energy of that upheaval.'

'What are you talking about?'

'I'm talking about declaring myself a supporter of the kids in their fight against authority. I want those kids on my side, Viney.'

'It sounds as if they would have you on their side.'

'Val Somerset was called a superstar of the youth cult in his review last week.'

'He's twenty years younger than you are, Marshall.'

'He was an unknown until that business with the pot at London airport. And the reason my *Executioner* series has been so successful is because he's a symbol of anarchy, a law unto himself.'

'For whatever reason, those films *are* a big success. I'm always telling you that. I don't know why you are so upset.'

'You think I should do it on TV for Leo, don't you?'

'Perhaps. We'll think about it.'

'Yesterday you were getting all steamed up because I wouldn't agree: today it's just perhaps. If I *should* do it, let's phone Leo now and settle it once and for all.' Stone looked at his watch. 'He's probably in his preview theatre.'

'Hold it, Marshall. We can't simply phone him like that.'

'Because he's mad at me?'

'Marshall, I heard he's offered the TV end of *Executioner* to some kid from the Royal Shakespeare. It might not be true, but I don't want Leo confirming it to you if it is true. Let me keep my foot in the door. I have to see him before the weekend about Suzy's tax.'

'You think he might come back to us?'

'I don't make predictions, Marshall. Who knows what any of us will do, given the right circumstances.' He almost added that by tomorrow Stone might have changed his mind back again, but he did not say so.

Stone went to the mirror and looked at himself briefly before speaking. 'In *Snap, Crackle, Pop* I had a line: "Hate and love are ourselves. When we look in a mirror and see a foolish child full of energy, hope and purpose, we declare ourselves in love. If we see an old man with failure in his eyes we call it hatred." '

'That's what was wrong with that bloody film, we should have asked for script approval.'

'I'm frightened, Viney.' The admission and Stone's tone of voice alarmed Weinberger. He turned in his seat. Stone was shiny with perspiration.

'Marshall. You've got everything a man could ask for: you are rich, famous, successful, a superb actor. What else do you want?'

'I'm frightened.' It was the voice of a tiny child, squeaky and silly, a voice that in other circumstances would have been comic. 'The skids are under me. I feel it as never before.'

'Bloody nonsense.'

'It's true, Viney. A sort of vertigo.' He wrung his hands. 'You don't have vertigo when you are climbing up. But now . . .'

'What, Marshall?'

'You'll laugh.' Stone shivered. He got up and switched on the fire. He continued to crouch at the fire while he spoke. Even racked by anxiety, Stone used an actor's device in order to speak over his shoulder. If it had been the movies, the camera would have been in the fireplace recording the facial tic in enormous close-up. 'I'm afraid of losing my looks. I'm beginning to look old, Viney, and the world hates old people.'

'I don't hate old people.'

'Well, I hate them. They remind me of what's happpening to me every day.'

'Look at Bogart.'

'Look at Bogart, look at Bogart. Everyone is looking at Bogart as they dodder to the grave. Bogart was for us, but that doesn't mean that today's kids would like Bogart. These pink-faced brats want to see themselves. They want violence, rape, destruction. They hate with a terrible rancour. They hate everyone in the world, especially the aged. I'm almost fifty, Viney. To those kids that's like being a hundred and fifty. They hate us all, and kids are the cinema audience, you can't deny it.'

'You're depressed, Marshall. This Preston boy may not be the right director for you. My fault, I never should have allowed it. We'll get another picture with a good script and a better director and you'll be your old self again.'

'I don't think so, Viney. I've glimpsed the end of the tunnel, but there's no daylight shining there, no train expected and the tracks are overgrown with weeds.'

'*The Knight and the Lady*, reel three.'

Stone smiled briefly. It wasn't any the less true because it was a quote. 'I've thought of retiring, Viney, but I'm not sure I could handle it. I'd go crazy doing nothing all day.'

After a long silence Weinberger said, 'You could go into independent production.'

'That's what the Press releases say when the axe has fallen. "Whatever happened to old so-and-so?"' Stone imitated Koolman's voice. '"A wonderful guy. Right! He's been wanting to go into independent production for a long time. We're going to do a deal with him ourselves, if our schedule permits."'

'You could certainly get a production deal. If you find a script you really care about and we talk about the casting . . .'

'After what you've said about my ability to choose scripts?'

'I'm just trying to crack this irrational fit of depression, Marshall. I'm trying to show you that you are still a young man with twenty years of star roles ahead of you.'

'Don't baby me up, Viney. I may be just a stupid actor but I know a thing or two about the film game. My face is collapsing. Look!' He emphasized the lines of his cheek muscles by drawing his fingers down them. 'Do you realize what's happening to the muscles and bones there? I've seen Harley Street men. When I was in Zurich I saw the Swiss doctor who did such wonderful things for poor old Joan. I even went to New York specially to the clinic. There's nothing they can do about it. It's just age, they tell me. They don't realize that middle age to them is a funeral to me.'

'Take it easy, Marshall.'

'Oh Jesus, Viney.'

Better than many a psychologist, Weinberger knew the sort of physical activity that presages hysteria. He watched in alarm as Stone's fidgeting escalated from movements of his hands to anxious striding across the room. He watched him as he almost dropped his cigarettes and had trouble in lighting one. This displacement activity enabled him to steady himself enough to give a bitter smile.

'Now, stop it, Marshall.'

Stone puffed at his cigarette. 'What am I supposed to do now, Viney? Phone central casting and tell them I'm available? Can't you see what a trap I'm in? If only I'd known how it all ends up. Now I can no longer walk on the street, get on a bus, check into a hotel or buy a packet of cigarettes without putting on a performance for someone. Don't your clients ever tell you what a prison it all is, Viney? I'd give all my money just to be able to get a job with the Birmingham Rep again, or just once more carry a spear for the Royal Shakespeare. But I'm a leper. That's what being a star does to a man: it marks him with a pox so that he can never again be judged on his merit. From this day on I will always be the ex-famous ex-star: Marshall Stone.' He laughed. 'It's not even my real bloody name.' He threw the cigarette away.

'What's this Preston kid doing to you?'

'It's nothing to do with Preston, Viney. He's just another thirty-day wonder. I can handle Preston.' He shrugged bravely. 'I'm sorry, Viney.' Under wobbling pebble-lenses of tears, his blue eyes were huge and soft. When he moved his head the surface tension gave way and rivulets of water deluged his cheeks. He sniffled as he felt the tears on his nose and wiped his face angrily with the back of his hand. 'I'm making such a scene, Viney, and you have so much to worry about already, without my stupid hypochondriacal ravings.' Stone found a handkerchief in his pocket and dabbed his face with it.

Weinberger's voice was gentle.

'It's not hypochondria, Marshall, because that's a fear of something that doesn't exist. What you fear is ageing, and that does exist. You must come to terms with growing older . . .'

'Just don't say, "It happens to everybody".' He sniffed to

swallow his tears and his speech was blurred. 'If one more person says that, I'll have hysterics.'

'No one is exempt, Marshall. No one can talk or buy their way out of it. Some don't even want to. There's a rhyme – "You know you're growing old, at least that's how I find it, When you not only are, but also do not mind it".'

Stone gave a perfunctory smile. He knew that Weinberger was trying to cheer him up, but he seemed almost wilfully incapable of understanding the problem. 'It's my work . . .'

'No, Marshall, it's not. I seldom contradict you, but this time I must. I've got to know a lot of actors both before and since that little talk we had in that hospital room in Rome. Lots of actors have this problem. Nearly all of them rationalize it by saying it's their work, but there is just as much work for old actors as for young actors, more, in fact. Better work, more challenging roles. What actor hasn't dreamed of Macbeth. Or Lear. Perhaps the greatest role an actor can play, but has any young actor ever mastered it?'

'What about Romeo . . . what about Hamlet?'

'Romeo is a dummy, and you've played Hamlet. Your Hamlet was a milestone. Even so, are you going to tell me your Hamlet couldn't be improved by you today, with an extra ten years' experience under your belt? What I'm telling you, Marshall, is that your fears are nothing to do with your work. You are frightened of growing old, as a person. As a person, Marshall. It's a fear of a loss of virility, of not being attractive to young girls. It's nonsense, Marshall. Who was more worshipped by youngsters than Bertrand Russell, who is more attractive to a young girl than Fred Astaire or Cary Grant? Shake off these fears, Marshall, for your own sake.'

'I don't want to be has-been, Viney. You know the way they talk about poor bastards who have slipped. Take Peter, for instance.'

'You'll never be like him. He's a drinker. He didn't lose work because of his age. It was the bottle.'

'Huh,' grunted Stone. 'Why do you think he started to hit the bottle?'

Weinberger said nothing; Stone was right.

'Let's do a deal on *Man From the Palace*. Hanratty directing, a good script. Bookbinder's got a good track record. It could turn out to be a fine picture.'

'I think you are right about the picture, Marshall.'

'But?'

'The company putting up the money is shaky.'

'Who?'

'They're financed by a firm called Continuum. In the City the story is Continuum has to find eight million dollars by October.'

'Could that affect the picture?'

'Probably not. Bookbinder says he'll be in rough-cut by then. He has a stop-date on Hanratty who is going to do the astronaut film for Leo.'

'Kagan says they want the daylight too. After September they will be working a short day if they are outside.'

Weinberger nodded. 'So let's say they will be in rough-cut by October. Even if Hanratty is cutting and in pre-production for Leo at the same time, he's a hard worker, so the film need not suffer because of that.'

Weinberger decided he would sip some of his drink. He chased the olive with his fingers, and when he caught it, ate it with relish. 'The trouble is: Continuum. Suppose they tighten up on Kagan. Suppose they are really in a spot, they might even decide to sell *Man From the Palace*. If the rough assembly looked good and they were in a spot they could sell world-wide rights as part of their loan repayment.'

'So?'

'If we had part of your money as a deferment – and let's face the truth, we're not going to get it all up front – we could find ourselves trying to collect from some little company we've never heard of. For instance, some smart bastard could buy and resell the movie while retaining all the commitments. Then he bankrupts that little one-hundred-dollar limited liability company and pays you off at a dime to a dollar.'

'Jesus, Viney. Your mind is a cesspool.'

'My mind is a cesspool. If I do the autobiography you keep urging me to do, that could be the title.'

'But really, Viney. You are so complicated. Look, this might be a truly great movie. Let's just do it, for what they can afford, plus a piece of the action. OK, Viney?'

'OK, Marshall.'

'You think that's a good idea? Really a good idea?'

'No. But I'm worried about you, Marshall. I want to get you out of this mood. If *Man From the Palace* will do it for you, I'd even agree to us paying them!'

Stone smiled. Not a sardonic smile that reflected his anxiety, but a real film-star smile that guaranteed anyone within range a charge of fire and enthusiasm. 'Don't let's go quite that far, Viney.' He gave his agent a playful punch on the arm.

Weinberger smiled, put away his papers, and for the first time in many years drained his second martini glass.

'Another?' Stone asked. Weinberger shook his head. 'Stay to dinner,' said Stone. 'Or, better still, we'll go somewhere.'

'Take Suzy to dinner, Marshall. I must go home, I promised to have that writer over.'

'Writer?'

'Anson.'

'He's come a long way from that flyblown writer's block: fifty bucks a week and all the pencils you can take home.'

'He works at it, I'll give him that.'

'What did Mary see in him, Viney?'

'Those two are loners, Marshall. Mary was never a part of your world.'

'Does he make any money, do you think?'

'They have a couple of nice kids, a comfortable house. Between them they do all right. People like that don't want the things you like.'

Clearly those unnamed things were not anything that Weinberger wanted, either. Stone said, 'I hear him talk about the Cinema with a capital C, and I wonder what business I've been in all these years, Viney.'

They both laughed. Weinberger looked at his client, trying to see if the spell was broken. It was hard to decide. Stone shook his head. 'It'll be OK now, Viney, I feel fine.' Already his voice was reassuming the reedy strength that his fans would recognize.

Weinberger patted Stone's shoulder in the diffident way of a man not given to physical contact with other men. 'Don't worry Marshall. You'll do the *Palace* and it will be a great movie.'

Stone saw him to the door and hoped that he would say something about a rapprochement with Koolman, but he didn't. Stone tried to imagine what Weinberger's life was like. He worked hard all day arguing with executives and placating angry clients. Each night he drove out to the big house near Blackheath with a case full of documents to work on. He kissed his wife and they worried about whether his eldest would get into university or his youngest get pregnant. He cut his own lawn, watched TV, ate frozen food and sorted his stamp collection. The people he had there for dinner were likely to be local grocers and stockbroker neighbours, anxious to hear an anecdote about the glamorous world in which Weinberger spent his working day. Perhaps it wasn't exactly like that, but a life even remotely like that was Stone's idea of lingering death.

There was no need for Stone to put away the bottles of vodka and vermouth, stack the mixing jar and glasses in the tiny sink behind the bar, or empty the ashtray, but he did all those things without realizing that he was performing chores that he'd not done for a decade or more. His Rolls was in the garage and Jasper within call, but there was nowhere he wanted to go. His boat was ready to sail and his pilot on four-hour alert, but there was no one waiting for him. Generous hostesses, ambitious starlets, eager head waiters would have put their all at his disposal, but they had nothing that he required. The room contained many books, but the idea of reading them did not occur to him. He undressed slowly and went to bed.

In a world where superlatives were commonplace, tears were the ultimate superlative. Stone used the word frequently; he was often 'moved to tears', and, less often, he 'laughed until tears came'. Sometimes he'd confess that he'd been unable to suppress a tear, as a way of expressing his gratitude for a gift or generous praise.

In his childhood Eddie Brummage had learned to produce tears to curtail a scolding or evade a beating. He had never cried when alone. He did nothing alone, which is why he dreaded that condition. But now, almost fifty years old, he cried. He sobbed into his pillow and left there a spidery pattern of mascara from the movement of his lashes before he went to sleep.

11 *The more McCarthy yells the better I like him. He's doing a job to get rid of the termites eating away at our democracy.*

Louis B. Mayer

'Leo Koolman, only twenty months ago you joined this organization as a parcels clerk in dispatch. You took over that department before becoming assistant to the personnel manager. In less than one year you had been promoted to a senior position in publicity and two months later we made you a vice-president. You are the youngest executive in charge of production that any of us can remember. Today you become president of this company. It's a success story that can only happen in the dynamic free society that America has produced. What do you say, Leo?'

'Thanks, Uncle Max.'

A mixture of cynicism and admiration, that joke summarized Hollywood's attitude to the Koolmans and everything they did. The relationship between the old man and his nephew was the basis of endless show-biz jokes. Any vituperative exchange, liberally sprinkled with cuss words and blasphemy, was accredited to the two Koolmans and quoted by name-droppers.

In fact, few other capable men would have taken the tongue-lashings that Leo Koolman took from his uncle with relatively mild rebukes. Fewer still would have sieved the abuse to discover the good advice and experience that was almost hidden in it.

'A Tribute to Mister Hollywood', said the sign outside the Beverly Hills Hotel, where the industry gathered to celebrate the thirty-sixth anniversary of the Koolman Pictures Corporation.

Others had laid claim to that title, but none were granted it more willingly than the old man who celebrated the occasion by becoming chairman of the board so that his nephew could get into the president's seat. The stockholders remained unconvinced, but there was no hint of the proxy fights that were to come a decade later. In 1947 anything that old Max wanted was as good as done.

The photographs show a grinning little gnome in his bright neckerchief, baggy white suit and Stetson. The cinema histories have recorded some of old Max's more absurd utterances from the time he was regarded as a doyen of Hollywood's right wing. But the young rowdy, who first came to Hollywood in 1909 when it was a sunny rural backwater, was a fugitive. He'd made a dozen one-reelers in a New York loft, but his crews had been beaten up more and more regularly and his last two films had been locked up by a court injunction from 'the trust'. Max was down to his last eight dollars.

The trust was the Motion Picture Patents Company, a pool of patent-holders who were the only people able to buy raw film. They made movies, and cinema owners paid a dime a foot for them whatever the length, the story or the stars. And cinema owners could lease the patented movie projectors only if they agreed to show trust films exclusively. To break this total monopoly Max had to get a movie camera from Europe, buy raw film on the black market and then find a place to make films where trust agents, process servers, sheriffs or strong-arm men couldn't find him. New York had proved not to be that place.

Hollywood attracted Max for a number of reasons. It had sun almost every day of the year, and in those days films were lit by sunlight. The 'interiors' were half-rooms, built outdoors and swivelled to follow the orbit of the sun. Most of his films were Westerns, and there was a convenient settlement of Red Indians living in shacks at the Santa Monica end of what is now Sunset Boulevard. There was nearby Griffith Park with lakes, forests and canyons. But the greatest attraction for Max was that when the trust agents were prowling around, or a gang of goons were in town breaking up pirate equipment, he could load his two cameras into the back of his Ford and drive like hell for the Mexican border. Perhaps they'd not admit it nowadays, but many other Hollywood pioneers who followed old

Max to Hollywood frequently raced with him to the Mexican border.

Europe's film industry was far ahead of America's until the beginning of the First World War. In America the trust prevented the showing of any film longer than one reel, but France had produced a four-reel film starring Sarah Bernhardt as Queen Elizabeth, and the Italians did *Quo Vadis* in eight. Hollywood might have remained just another American village had not the First World War diverted Europe's cellulose to the manufacture of explosives. Thus Europe's supply of films came to an abrupt end, and the cinema owners had to buy American productions. When, in 1917, America came into the war, the East Coast movie industry was wiped out in the same way as Europe's had been. There was a shortage of manpower, electricity and raw materials. Thus Hollywood became the world's movie centre by a process of elimination. Asked the secret of his success in 1935, Max said, 'Stay as far away from any war as you can get,' but he threatened to sue a paper that quoted that in 1942.

Max led the movie world with new ideas, especially forbidden ones. When long films were forbidden by the trust, he made a six-reel *Barnaby Rudge*. When it was banned in trust cinemas, he rented a Chicago theatre and screened it there. The trust insisted that actors be anonymous, lest they demanded more than the ten-dollar-a-day contract that was so common. Max lured them away with fees of five hundred dollars a day plus big screen credits not only for producers but for stars and directors too. And it was Max who demanded to see his costly stars in big big close-ups at a time when most cameramen were determined to include the actors' feet in every shot, lest the audience think they were watching people who'd been cut in half.

Max realized that films from the classics could attract the middle class into cinemas which until then had relied upon a working-class audience. To help make cinemas respectable, he furnished his with fitted carpets, chandeliers and soft lights to replace the nickelodeon's board floors and spittoons.

But life was still dangerous for Max. Like de Mille, he wore a six-gun when he was at work. Even so, attacks on his employees continued, but they were becoming rarer. His enemies realized that Max was here to stay. Driving along Santa Monica Boulevard now, it's difficult to believe that every day, even into the late 'twenties, old Max rode from here to the studio on horseback. When it was no longer practical to do that, Max sold his house and five-acre lot for close on a million dollars and bought a house in Cahuenga Pass. Each morning he could breakfast on his balcony – frequently with an unidentified young female companion – criticizing his crews as they shot Westerns at the bottom of his garden.

Old Max's real-estate dealings alone had made him a multi-millionaire by the 'thirties. His bright-red custom-built Mercedes-Benz – even bigger than Valentino's cream-coloured one – could be seen outside the Garden of Allah, the Brown Derby and the dozens of little night-spots that catered to the film colony. He used the car to commute between his town house and his vast ranch in the San Fernando valley.

None of Max's money went into any bank. He started a chain of cinemas with his own capital, and sank every penny he could find into sound-recording equipment at a time when most of the industry predicted doom for the new gimmick. After he sold his ranch in the valley to his own company, it became the elaborately equipped Koolman International Studios, bigger and more valuable than Universal City nearby.

During the 'thirties Koolman Studios had the keenly contested reputation of being the meanest employers in Hollywood. Writers had less say in the movies than did the waitresses in the executive dining-room, and they clocked in considerably earlier. Actors and directors did half a dozen films a year on the notorious seven-year contracts by which they could be suspended without pay, and the lost time added to the other end of their contract. Thus a 'difficult' actor could stay under contract for life. Old Max enjoyed the rows and the tears and the champagne reconciliations. He managed his stars like a madam in a whorehouse, which in several other ways the studio resembled.

'Jesus Christ, tell those stupid college bastards to give me some pictures where the good guys get the dough and the broads once in a while, will you. Goddamn! I'm sick to the stomach with slumps and Okies turning into hoodlums.' Old Max's remark was transcribed into a written memo by Phil Sanchez. It created the pattern for Koolman films in the 'thirties. The memo said, 'Above all, gentlemen, *American* films. Ones that entertain while showing the youth of our great nation that the values of God, truth and loyalty, hard work and talent, result in success and happiness.' It was a philosophy that Koolman employees found difficult to reconcile with their day-to-day experience, but 'American films, gentlemen' signs were tacked up in the studio.

It was tough to be on a Koolman production. Accountants scrutinized every budget, and a producer who went over by even a few dollars had a lot of explaining to do before he got another deal. Leo Koolman was just a child during the 'thirties, but he spent most of his spare time in the studios with his Uncle Max. By the time the Second World War began, young Koolman had become an unofficial assistant and courier for old Max, who was now over sixty and still had a peasant's mistrust of the Santa Fe railroad and the newfangled aeroplanes that hopped to New York in easy stages.

The nineteen-forties brought the draft and shift work. Wives, girlfriends, mothers and lonely soldiers had money in their pockets and no one to stay at home with. It was a bonanza for the industry. Every year brought the Koolman Pictures Corporation bigger profits. Peace, the returning soldiers, the housing shortage and Europe's cinemas meant even more money for movie-makers. Perhaps the effortless way in which every picture made money lulled the industry into a false sense of security. There was no reason to believe that young Koolman was inheriting anything but a mint. But old Max, with a cunning that never deserted him, had chosen exactly the right moment to step down.

Fiscal 1947 showed that the war boom and its subsequent echo was now not even a whimper. Stockholders hoping that their previous $3.6 million might be bettered heard that the Koolman Pictures Corporation profit was $493,928.

Purring stockholders could become wild animals, and moguls like Mayer, Schary, Schenk and Zanuck sometimes got mauled. No longer did Leo envy mighty MGM, with its great

Loew's chain of movie theatres, for the Supreme Court had invoked the Sherman Anti-Trust Act and ordered all movie companies to sever connexion with cinemas. No longer would Koolman Pictures make films on a production line and feed them to their own cinema chains. Selling the cinemas was young Koolman's primary and most complex task.

The 'fifties saw the closing of a quarter of all US cinemas, while TV sets increased tenfold to fifty million. Milton Berle on Texaco Star Theatre kept cinemas empty every Tuesday evening, and other performers were hell-bent on doing the same every other night of the week.

Hollywood's embargo on the new medium was broken when Columbia sold their old movies to the networks. Koolman immediately did the same with two hundred old Koolman feature films. As part of the deal, he made two million dollars' worth of fifty-minute TV films. He financed his new TV subsidiary by selling a recording company in Manhattan and some downtown real estate. He adjusted the earnings from his TV deal to bolster KPC quarter returns, which might otherwise have been in the red. He fought off an attempt to sell pieces of the big studios in the valley by persuading the stockholders that the land was worth more in one piece and agreeing to look at the situation again in 1955. By that time he'd renamed the company Koolman International Pictures, pulled the profits back up to two million and found both profit and prestige in films starring Marshall Stone.

Old Max died in 1956 after a tiring cross-continent train journey. He was sitting in a New York hotel suite holding the hand of his wife and swearing at Leo for calling a doctor.

'You stupid little bastard. Is that what I taught you. Don't you know what that will do to Koolman stock when the news gets out.'

'Shut up,' said Leo. 'Everyone knows I run the company.'

When he spoke again Max Koolman's voice was so weak that Leo Koolman had to bend low to hear him. Thus Max's wife did not hear the obscene word that was her husband's last.

Even by 1947 Max had grown weary of the journey between Los Angeles and New York. Distrustful of aeroplanes, Max found four days on the Superchief to be almost beyond endurance. But the scheduled air services were opening California to new faces and new thoughts. Until that time Hollywood designers and writers fed upon previous Hollywood examples of their craft. Now, many cinema-goers had seen what Europe and the Far East looked like, and they wanted realism. European film-makers – lacking money enough for sets, lighting or costume – made startling use of real locations. Unless Hollywood was prepared to make films solely for its domestic market – as the British industry had always done – it had to beat European film-makers at their own game.

When in 1947 the House of Representatives Committee of Un-American Activities – HUAC – renewed its probing into Hollywood, old Max dismissed them as 'a bunch of anti-Semitic nuts', and congratulated himself upon keeping his name unchanged, for an anglicized name was enough evidence on which to bring a charge of subversion against many of his friends. But the Committee had chosen well. Not only was their new victim guilt-racked and histrionic, it was also recriminatory to a point of hysteria. As an added bonus, the members of the Committee had only to whisper a famous Hollywood name to get headlines and TV coverage around the world. It would have been a temptation to even the most retiring of politicians.

At first, no one took it seriously. Dorothy Parker said, 'The only ism that Hollywood believes in is plagiarism.' But then came a reaction from the banks. They told Max that the film colony was going to come under great pressure, and no one in the US Government had the power and the inclination to save them. Once convinced, Max became a virulent anti-red, arranging that Leo play the part of the young liberal conscience.

Thus, while Leo placated the progressives, Max went before the Committee and shamelessly apologized for a couple of films that had portrayed the Russians as shaved and laundered. It would never happen again, he vowed, and it never did. Old Max was at the famous meetings at the Waldorf Astoria after which the 'Waldorf Declaration' announced that the ten men who had defied the Committee would not again be employed.

'What's all this pleading the First Amendment: either a man is an American or he's a gonif. Send these reds back to Russia,' said Max Koolman, who had been born in Odessa.

212

So well did Max do his job that Leo was not called to the hearings, and when in 1951 HUAC renewed their hearings, Kagan Bookbinder was the only Koolman employee blacklisted.

Not that there was any blacklist! Max and Leo would put their hands on the place where their hearts were reputed to be, and swear to that. There was no blacklist, for a list is a piece of paper. The agreements that they made were little more than nods and winks. The previous attentions of HUAC had shown the industry that there were advantages in being unified. Unified not against the Committee but against directors, writers, producers and stars. Leo pointed out that it was to their mutual advantage to be rid of fellows suspected of communism. For with them could go fellows suspected of sarcasm, 'arty ideas' and sleeping with the wrong wives.

In all those respects Bookbinder was a candidate for the mythical blacklist, but the guard at the main gate had only his instructions and a drawerful of Bookbinder's personal effects. An hour of talking failed to get him past the gate and his phone call didn't even get past the switchboard.

But that was in 1951. When Leo Koolman first took control of the company the situation was quite different. In that first year of his reign the new president needed a project that could be widely publicized in a way that would influence stockholders as much as the audience. The company had grown rich on Westerns and their singing, whistling, roping stars, but now other companies had surpassed them in this genre. Koolman liked Westerns and so did Uncle Max, and so did two of the most important, and more troublesome stockholders.

Bookbinder entered Leo's office with a story idea that had been turned down by every major studio, including old Max. But now it had an added ingredient that caught Leo's imagination: Edward Stone, a famous Shakespearean actor from Britain – and a personal friend of Bookbinder – had agreed to play the lead for a nominal fee.

Leo gave Bookbinder an office, a typist, a studio pass, a writer and a parking space. Koolman Studios project number 130 (A42) 1948 was assigned a production file and an accounts record. Leo had reason to hope that a rough-cut of this production shown at the stockholders' meeting could arouse hopes of history repeating itself. Such a dream could give Leo another twelve months of power, and he assigned the studio publicity machine to the task of building this Englishman into a star.

Koolman's determination to succeed was to some extent motivated by the stock option he'd been given along with his $200,000 salary. The option was for five years at 1947 market price. If Koolman stock continued to rise, the option could make him a multi-millionaire. If the industry's problems depressed the market, it could erase his salary and break him: the clause had been designed to make Leo perform.

Don't give her [Rita Hayworth] too much dialogue . . . Give me ten to twelve reels of film, a couple of dance numbers, some conflict between her and Glenn Ford, and some exotic backgrounds. If you do that, I'll give you a deal for another picture.

Harry Cohn

'Happy birthday, Leo.'

'Happy birthday, Leo.'

The moon passed close to earth that night, and the mulberry colour of the sky reminded you that Hollywood shared its latitude with Rabat, Baghdad and the Khyber Pass. Koolman was young, and as lively as a puppy, shaking hands, smiling and waving aside congratulations that showered over him like Confederate nickels.

'Happy birthday, Leo. Great party.'

A columnist calculated that nine hundred guests attended Leo Koolman's party that night. At ten o'clock, when the orchids were scattered over the girl swimmers, and the orchestra played 'Happy Birthday, dear Leo' to an accompaniment of popping imported champagne, there were at least four hundred. They were in the house, on the lawns, sitting by the pool and even playing tennis. When a producer and a potential leading lady were found in the changing-rooms next morning asleep naked on the floor, Leo Koolman blacklisted both. 'They didn't even have racquets.'

Koolman moved through the crowds, smiling at his guests, greeting his colleagues and nodding to the private detectives who were guarding the valuables. The film colony admired and envied this conspicuous spending at a time when so many people were saying that the old days were gone for ever. Old Max was there, watching his protégé anxiously, for they both knew that within a year nepotism might be proved the dangerous expedient that their enemies declared it was. But Max knew that to offer his nephew any glimmer of sympathy would be a cruel betrayal.

Thus young Koolman was alone with his fears. Even the protestations that his young wife Rochelle made, when she discovered that the studio was not going to pick up the bill for the party, drew from Leo only confident smiles.

The oriental garden had been rigged with lanterns, and with stalls from which Chinese waiters served food. A smell of warm soy and scorching pork drifted through the dwarf palms to the wishing well where Koolman stood talking to Stone.

Koolman was wearing a nipped-waist white jacket with a white bow-tie and black silk shirt. His wife told him that the shirt made him look like Al Capone, but Koolman did not change it.

After Koolman and his star had posed for the Press cameras, Koolman prised him away from Bookbinder and Weinberger, and engaged him in an earnest conversation that only a foolhardy man would have dared interrupt.

Koolman said, 'We have an either/or situation here. I'm just putting it to you: the final decision has to be yours.'

'You're right, it has to be,' said Stone.

'You're in love with this girl Rainbow. OK, I understand that, she's a sweet kid.' Koolman turned slightly so that he could see the garden. The formation swimmers were climbing out of the pool, their leader pulling off her swimming cap. Her hair fell down over her shoulders. Spotlights came to rest upon her and there was a round of applause before the orchestra played

'Stardust' and couples began to dance. 'But has she got any right to ask you to sacrifice your career?'

'She's asked for nothing.'

'Because she knows what it would be like to spend her life with someone who has given up a career. Can you imagine the first time you had a row – can you imagine what you are likely to say to her? Did you think about that, Marshall?'

'I love her,' said Stone, 'and there will be the boy.'

'Suppose it's a girl. Suppose you stop loving her. Suppose that after a few years another cute broad comes along.'

'This is for ever,' said Stone.

'Isn't that what you told your wife, Marshall, when you married her six years back?'

Stone didn't answer.

'Well, is it?'

'I suppose so.'

'Maybe you had forgotten that.'

'I hadn't forgotten it.' Stone knew that the creation of guilt had to be a skill of a man who'd spent half his life dealing with broken contracts and the anxieties of actors. A Japanese servant offered them fried octopus; Koolman waved him away.

'It's not what you think,' said Stone. 'We're in love. I was going to speak to a lawyer about a divorce.'

'You don't speak to no lawyer about divorce, sweetheart,' said Koolman. 'You speak to me. I've got stars – stars! – who've been waiting years for my OK on a divorce for them. I run a clean, honest respectable corporation.'

'It's not like that,' said Stone. 'Honestly.'

'They speak to me,' said Koolman again, in an aggrieved voice. 'Why d'you think we put a morality clause in the contracts.'

'I'm sorry.' Stone noticed a tall slim man of about forty-five standing near the pool. He was looking all round him, but his eyes lingered on Koolman. The stranger wore a pink suit and a voile shirt, his cuffs – at which he tugged – were fastened with large jewelled links. He moved towards Koolman, crabwise. The angle of his approach enabled him to grasp Koolman's right hand and elbow simultaneously. 'Leo, Jesus, you're looking fit!'

'I'm OK,' said Koolman.

'I've just come back from Palm Springs.'

The stranger waited for Koolman to speak but when no answer came he said, 'Bernard Cavendish: you remember: I did *Lady Luck and the Moon* for you.'

'Sure,' said Koolman. 'This is the guy who produced *Lady Luck*,' said Koolman to no one in particular. Cavendish stared at Koolman and held a smile. He shook his head in a gesture of good-natured disbelief. 'Great to see you, Leo. Directed, as a matter of fact: directed *Lady Luck*.'

'Sure,' said Koolman still watching the swimmers as they got into position on the high board. 'Fall of forty-five. Came in two days over.'

Stone said, 'Good to know, you, Bernard,' but he didn't offer his hand. Cavendish looked at Stone and smiled, but failing to recognize the actor, he turned his whole attention back to Koolman.

'Leo, kick me. No, I mean it, Leo, kick me.'

'What's this?'

The man hurried into an explanation, talking so fast that Stone had difficulty understanding him. 'You've probably forgotten. You've got so many things on your mind: *Duel of Kings*, Leo. I said it couldn't be done. I argued with you, but you were right. I got writers working on it and we licked it into shape.' The man looked up to see if he was making progress, but Koolman was looking over his shoulder at the party. He waved to someone.

'Greg Peck,' explained Leo.

'Hi Greg, hi Greg,' said the man, but he didn't turn far enough to see him. '*Duel of Kings*,' said the man. 'Sure, I said, it's a great idea, but can it be done, I said. You said it was possible. I wasn't so sure—'

'Have you tried those pork dumplings – *Pao tze* – just great. It's a guy down near Sunset. Best Chinese food anyplace on the Coast.'

'Wonderful,' said the man. 'The whole set-up here is wonderful, just like the old days. Just like with your Uncle Max.' He smiled. 'Better, in fact; I'd say better. And so I thought to myself, I'm going to give Leo's idea a try, I said. Leo knows a

217

thing or two about stories.' He smiled the briefest possible smile to celebrate his audacity at doubting it. 'Shall we say lunch Tuesday?'

'Sounds dandy. But talk to Phil Sanchez's secretary. Christmas is only a few weeks away . . .' Koolman brought his hand up to show the rising level of an engulfing tide.

'I'll surprise you, now, Leo: this may not be your kind of movie. This might be for Twentieth or UA, but I want to be able to say you saw it first.'

Koolman nodded.

Cavendish's voice was a semitone higher when he continued. 'This is a vehicle for Davis or Crawford.' He released the grip on Koolman's elbow, but only in order to pat his shoulder. 'Weepie? Yes. But weepie with a difference. *Lost Weekend*, but with a dame playing the Milland role, get it?'

'We're just . . .'

The man held his finger up in front of Koolman's lips. 'You've got business to talk. I can see that. I'm going, but don't let this one get away, Leo, it could be dynamite.'

There was no reply.

'Who let that creep in here,' said Koolman when the man had moved away.

The conversation unnerved Stone. At first he'd found the man's anxiety rather comic. He'd noted the pitch of his voice and the way his hands tugged at Koolman's sleeve. He saw the way his shoulders slumped as he came to terms with yet another snub. There were lots here like him; men who could no longer bluff their way past the secretaries of the production chiefs. Some of those men were actors.

Koolman let Stone cook for a few minutes while they both watched the party. Hoagy Carmichael was playing the piano – 'Sleepytime Girl' – and the guests were gathered around him. All the Hal Wallis stars seemed to be there. Earlier that evening Bogart and Dick Powell had arrived on motor-cycles and driven them right up to the buffet table. There was still gas rationing and motor-cycles were popular. Stone had decided to get one for himself. Now his conversation with Koolman had driven such matters from his mind.

'No one's going to admire you for it,' said Koolman.

'It's not that . . .'

'An actor has a duty.' Koolman paused. The orchestra was playing, and no scenic painter would have dared to make the moon so large. 'A duty to the people who taught him what he knows. A duty to his parents. A duty to himself and to his art.' Koolman nodded to himself as if to confirm the accuracy of an off-the-cuff remark, but actually it was one of Max's old speeches.

'But what will happen to her?'

Koolman knew that providing he made no false move, Stone had made his decision. He was not going to give up his career because of an infatuation for a pregnant girl. Probably he had never intended to, in his subconscious mind. All this nonsense was just to appease his conscience. It was just to persuade himself, and anyone who would listen, that Stone was not the callous creature of ambition that he so clearly was. Koolman paused before answering. In previous cases like this he'd always said that the Studio knew how to deal with such girls, but Stone required more sophisticated reassurance than that.

'We'll need your advice about that, Marshall. Our only concern would be to spare no expense so that the mother and child would have everything that my own family could expect: the finest medical care, scrutinized foster-parents and a trust fund to send the kid to college—'

'She'll keep the child,' said Stone. 'We've talked about that. Whatever else happened she would keep the child, bring it up and give it real love. Any child deserves that, Leo.'

'That can be arranged,' said Koolman. Again he watched his guests having fun while Stone came to terms with his inevitable decision. Ava Gardner waved at Koolman, and he waved back.

'I can't desert Ingrid,' said Stone.

'What's the alternative. You are out of work and trying to scrape together the cost of a divorce while looking after two wives and two kids. Can you imagine the sort of squalor you will commit all those people to? Can you imagine living in one of those shacks at the bottom of Santa Monica?'

'I could put up with it.'

'Sure you could, Marshall, and so could I, but I wouldn't ask my bride or my kid to put up with it.'

'You're right,' whispered Stone. 'You've made me see it.'

'Take my advice, sweetheart, bring your wife out here. It's better. I'm getting you out to New Mexico. You've got a picture to make, and it's going to be hard work.'

Bookbinder was talking to Weinberger near the entrance to the rose garden. They must have been expecting a gesture from Koolman, for he'd hardly moved a finger before they hurried across to where he and Stone were talking. There was an exchange of greetings, and then Koolman said, 'Marshall and I have sorted everything out. He will be going back with you tomorrow evening, Kagan.'

'That's just great,' said Bookbinder.

Koolman turned to Weinberger. 'You will have to stay here a few days to work out the details. Marshall will be talking to his wife tonight. He'll tell her that he'd like her with him at the location just as soon as she can make it. Right, Marshall?'

'I guess so.'

Koolman continued. 'When Mrs Stone arrives here, Marshall will fly back from the location so that over Christmas they can be seen together in a couple of night-spots. I'll want that covered by some columnist that we control – talk to my head of publicity about that.'

'Will do,' said Weinberger.

'From now on, the stories are going to soft-pedal the sex-appeal bit for a couple of months.' Koolman looked at his watch. 'Time for my speech,' he said. He put on his dark glasses. There was a loud crackle and a splutter of carbons as a searchlight beam moved across the dark sky until it found the small airship. It was in position exactly on time. For this night the cigarette advertisements on the blimp's sides had been covered with newly painted signs that read, 'Happy Birthday, Leo, from Everyone.'

'Happy birthday, Leo,' said Stone. Koolman patted his back before stepping forward into the coloured lights. The girls on the board prepared to dive, and a fifty-voice choir began to sing the greeting in a solemn arrangement that would not have been inappropriate for a memorial service in Westminster Abbey.

The blimp came even lower, and the guests joined in the second chorus as a girl in a swimsuit climbed out from the cupola of the blimp and released twenty-eight white birds. One for every year of Leo Koolman's life.

12

Any film which tells a story is putting itself at the disposal of the ruling class.

Jean-Luc Godard

The Merchant of Venice at His Majesty's Theatre: the first night. Stone's taxi was in a traffic jam, with only five minutes to go before curtain. Yet he needed at least an hour and a half to get into the complex costume, wig and elaborate make-up. In his mind he went through each step of the preparation, inventing and rejecting short-cuts and omissions. Desperately, he wondered if he dare go on stage with a cloak over his street clothes and no make-up at all. What would the critics think, and what in the name of God would they write of him: a superstar. Shakespeare and a first night.

Now only three minutes to curtain. He touched the wrinkles in his face; perhaps he was aged enough without make-up. He remembered something the Swiss specialist had said about the dryness of his skin. Mary pedalled past his cab on a bicycle. She smiled and waved as he had done when he saw her on the yacht, but again she didn't hear him.

It didn't require any feat of imagination to guess that Mary was going to the *Merchant*. She'd be there when the slow hand-clapping protested his non-appearance. Mary had planned it like this. He had the alarm clock in his hands trying to see what time it was, and so he slowly came awake. Three A M.

Dreams may not be warnings of future events, but they often reveal the intentions of our subconscious. In this one he recognized the self-tormenting tendencies that had always guided his decisions. The tablets helped him to achieve a dopiness in which to endure the remainder of the night. At eight o'clock he rang for breakfast in bed: grapefruit, diet bread and black coffee.

Stool Pigeon was on a five-day schedule, and there was no *Silent Paradise* looping this weekend. He opened the *Variety* that was on his tray. *Tigertrap* takings had improved marginally, but not enough to predict a profit. *Imperial Verdict* – Val Somerset's film – was showing in New York, breaking box-office records. Stone grunted: each new film had a chance to break records because the prices of admission kept rising. It would be more accurate, thought Stone, if they gave the number of admissions instead of total takings. He read the reviews and checked the list of movie people due to arrive in London that week. There was no one he wanted to see, certainly not in his present mood. Koolman was listed as flying to Los Angeles. At nine-thirty the phone rang. It was Weinberger.

'Marshall?'

'Hello, Viney.'

'How are you feeling this morning? It's beautifully sunny.'

'Fine, fine.'

'Feel like a business lunch?'

'With you?'

'Kagan and Hanratty. They phoned me here at home ten minutes ago. Did you give them this number?'

'Not me,' said Stone.

'They're hot for you, Marshall. I think Kagan might give a personal guarantee for your money.'

'How much?'

'Ah well, that has yet to be discussed. They want to soften you up by having you hear Hanratty's plans for the movie.'

'OK.'

'And Kagan says he'd like me along so we can go through the finance side of it. They seem pretty straight.'

'Well, well!' said Stone. 'They *really* must have got to you.'

'Lunch today, then?'

'Would they come out here to Twin Beeches?'

'They would rendezvous in orbit.'

'Twelve-thirty for one, then. I'll tell cook.' Already he felt a little better. Perhaps the best way to get out of his present mood was to know that someone he admired and respected needed him in a movie: a good movie.

'And a word of warning, Marshall. I was with that fellow

Anson last evening. I think he knows about the Rainbow business.'

'But Leo arranged that Edgar would say—'

'Edgar said it. And then you said it too. These sort of guys can be almost psychic.'

'Leo wouldn't . . .'

'I'm sure it's nothing to do with Leo.'

'Does Mary know?'

'I'm sure she doesn't.'

'The hell with it. What does it all matter? These days the public know that these things happen. For Bergman . . .'

'You don't want it all dug out again, Marshall. And there is Suzy to consider, too.'

'Let's see what happens.'

'Exactly,' said Weinberger. 'There's nothing to worry about, but don't let him pump you.'

'Screw Cannes and Venice, and even the Academy. Let's just try to make a movie the way we think it should be done.' Bookbinder smiled. He was a mandarin, thought Stone, or at least he looked like one. His golden skin fitted tightly over his globular head to make his eyes into slits and stretch his mouth into a derisive smile. He wasn't bald, but even as a young man his hair had been wispy enough to be unnoticeable from across the room. And like a toy mandarin he nodded gently to show that he was listening, pausing only long enough to inhale from the expensive Havana cigar which he brandished like some symbol of office. Nor were his hands the pudgy instruments that so many Hollywood producers used to carve dreams from tobacco smoke. Bookbinder's hands were mandarin's: slim and bony. His fingernails were lighter than the skin and the gold identity bracelet, which still bore his Army number and blood group, was almost the same colour.

Bookbinder carefully took off the cotton cord jacket that had once been the native costume of Madison Avenue. He placed it over the back of a chair, but a servant took it away immediately and brushed it perfunctorily before hanging it up. 'I wanted to bring the writer – a wonderful guy – but he couldn't make it.'

'Great writing,' said Hanratty. 'If I could write like that . . .'

That's how these sort of meetings always start, thought Stone. Someone always says great writing. Certain names – Greene, Chandler, Dostoevski – will be incanted, as if their literary magic could be transmuted into cinema. He looked at the famous Bert Hanratty. He was a tall Irishman.

From Scott Fitzgerald to Joe Kennedy, such Irishmen had brought blarney and enchantment to stir into the schmaltz and the chutzpa that Hollywood already had in abundance.

Hanratty looked like a gardener or a roadmender, and this was endorsed by a shabby suit and unpolished brown shoes. He was a heavy muscular man and yet, because of his height, slim. His hair was short and inexpertly trimmed, with tufts at the crown and patches of neck-hair that his barber had missed. His face was bony and skull-like, the high cheekbones, stubborn chin and button nose ruddy and chafed. There are many such physiques, not only in Ireland but in France and Belgium too. Peasants, with soil under their nails and straw in their hair: tough men, taciturn and single-minded.

At a loss for words, Hanratty smiled. A dentist in Spain had persuaded him to have his ravaged teeth repaired with gold, and it glinted in the light from the window. 'Great writing,' he said.

Some directors devoted a great deal of time and energy to getting publicity, and since directors had more to say to the unit publicist than the stars did, they often got a big proportion of it. Bert Hanratty was not such a director. He'd made twenty-five films, not counting a few travel shorts and some Crown Film Unit instructional films during the war. Some of them were outstanding, but not until his last film – *Naked Summer*, an all-location film, devoid of stars but lavish in production and made for a penny-pinching two million and some dollars – did he find fame. For it looked as if it might gross sixty. Some said it was going to gross eighty and thus out-gross *Love Story* or *The Sound of Music*, the champion money-makers of all time.

'Before Bert talks about the picture,' said Weinberger, 'how would you like to fill me in on Continuum?'

'That's my boy.' Stone laughed, but he was embarrassed that Weinberger had stated his pecuniary interest so early and so bluntly.

'He's right,' said Bookbinder. He watched Stone with more care than he'd admit to. Particularly he watched what he drank. He was an unpredictable bastard. There had been that film in Italy – *The Storm Clouds* in the autumn of 1952 – during which Stone had gone off on a desperate and terrible drinking spree. All alone and halfway through the production he'd got permission for a weekend by the sea, and been found three weeks later in a hospital in Rome. It was the sort of thing he was liable to do without motive or warning. Bookbinder would have to be sure of Stone's sobriety before he actually signed. 'None of us are in this for our health.' Bookbinder removed his Ben Franklin spectacles and polished the half-lenses, breathing upon them and holding them up to the light until he was sure they were spotless.

'Except Bert,' said Stone. He wanted to get a smile from the Irishman.

'Especially not Bert,' said Bookbinder. 'He turned down eight per cent of *Naked Summer* to get an extra three thousand up front.'

'Jesus,' said Stone.

'Let's see,' said Weinberger, for whom such figures were an irresistible challenge. 'You made it for two point one, right?' Hanratty nodded. Weinberger continued. 'They'll charge you two point five of that – say break even at five point two – if it does sixty million – which according to *Variety* looks likely – then you'd have got eight per cent of fifty-four plus . . . Well, even after they had screwed you and rewritten the accounts a couple of times you still might have got hold of four million dollars.'

'I took twenty-five thousand straight.'

There was a solemn silence until Bookbinder said, 'Never mind, Bert. This will be the one.' Then Bookbinder blew his nose on a gigantic linen handkerchief and Jasper brought a tray of drinks. It took a few minutes to sort the Negronis from the Americanos, and then they were back to business again. 'Four million is a lot of scratch,' said Bookbinder, 'but the industry is changing and the people who guess what's going to happen in the next few years are going to make four million sound like pin money.'

'For instance?' said Stone.

'Cassettes, for instance. Only one person in four goes to a movie theatre more often than once a year. But a cassette that plugs right into your TV set. Can you imagine what that could bring in royalties.'

'Blue movies,' said Stone. 'Imagine what kind of business blue movies at home would do.'

Bookbinder said, 'Sure, it will start with porn. So Continuum have bought the rights on this new Swedish skin-flick *Attis and his Lover*. But then it will move on: education films, classics and good family entertainment too. And they aren't totally rejecting movie houses, they've just bought seven more so that they have twenty-one cinemas across the US.'

'That's a lot of cinemas,' said Stone.

'This is a solid company,' said Bookbinder. 'People say they are shaky but they have a hell of a lot of collateral.'

'And the cassettes?' asked Weinberger.

'Mail order; like a book club.'

'Can't miss,' said Stone.

'Three young guys from the Harvard Graduate School of Business. This is history repeating itself. This is Mary Pickford and Doug Fairbanks putting the United Artists empire together.' Bookbinder sipped his drink and looked at Weinberger, inviting him to reply.

Weinberger said, 'It's been said so many times before . . . and there are rumours that Continuum are heading into trouble.'

'They are,' said Bookbinder. 'They'll need eight million before October, to pay back what they owe.'

'And you're not worried?'

'They've expanded too fast. But look what they have: twenty-one cinemas – big-city real estate, right? They have a team of very bright guys planning their cassette project . . .'

'Employees are no collateral,' said Weinberger.

'But they have the Anglo-American rights on three films. The two German films are so-so, but the Swedish one – *Attis and his Lover* – is the rawest piece of porn I've ever seen. It's done

227

incredible business in Germany and Scandinavia. Those US rights could be worth ten million. That's what I call collateral!'

'But if they were pressed?'

'So the cinemas pass to the debtor. A man who gets a company like Continuum isn't going to close it down, is he.'

Weinberger made a sucking noise to indicate doubt.

'Look, they'll have that eight by October and another five for expansion.'

'How will they get it?'

'The stock market.' He leaned back in his chair. 'I've been advising them about the expansion. They have the site and the drawings for a factory to make the cassettes. But I'm sworn to secrecy, so not a word.'

Stone said, 'They're depressing the price of their own stock to buy it?'

'A risky business,' said Weinberger disapprovingly, but he couldn't fault the cunning of it.

'I've got a chunk of their stock and I'd advise you both to think about doing the same.'

'Why not let it sink even lower?' said Stone.

'The way I figure it, Marshall, if I've been able to work it out, then any time at all the price will start climbing.'

'You're right.'

'Same with the movie. They have given me a very tough deal because these guys are no philanthropists, believe me, but I'm quite happy to take a piece of the action on this one rather than have too much up front.'

'You can't have too much up front,' said Weinberger drily.

'That's agent talk. That's what Bert's agent told him on *Naked Summer*.'

'Touché,' said Weinberger.

'It's true,' said Bookbinder. He laughed.

'We'll work something out,' said Weinberger. 'You show me your Continuum deal on paper, and we'll work it out.'

'That's what I call good sense. Bert, tell them about the movie.'

'All location,' said Hanratty. 'Great crew, people I've had with me ten years.'

228

'Who's doing the wardrobe?' asked Stone.

'Billy Speed, the uniforms, but you'd wear your own suits for most scenes: dark suits.'

'Rent them to you,' offered Weinberger.

'Done,' said Bookbinder. They laughed.

'So, Billy on the wardrobe, Swanny on the sets, with Jimmy the Bird as set dresser.'

'I know them all, top notchers,' said Stone.

'You can get almost anyone at present,' said Hanratty. 'A lot of the boys haven't worked for months.'

'It's grim,' said Stone. He shivered. Jasper came in to say that lunch was ready.

The table was set in the small dining-room. It opened on to the rose garden, and was one of Stone's favourite places in the house, especially on a fine summer's day like this one. The meal was simple by Twin Beeches standards: cold spinach soup, lamb chops and salad, cheese, raspberries and cream.

Stone poured the chilled rosé wine into Waterford glasses. Weinberger watched Stone closely. He was acting well before this audience but Weinberger knew that all was not right with him.

'Tell Marshall about your lighting, Bert,' prompted Bookbinder.

Hanratty looked to Stone. He had no doubts about what Stone's name would mean to the film. Quite apart from any box-office advantage, Stone's participation would persuade the Continuum board to let him have the money for the battle scenes in Italy. Without Stone, he'd be trying to improvise his war within commuting distance of London, so that he didn't have to put his crew into hotels. 'You saw *Naked Summer?*'

'Of course. I saw it twice. I thought, I've just got to go back again and see if it's really this good.'

'All bounce-light and aluminized umbrella lights like Wexler used on *Medium Cool*. I'll punch it up here and there, but only with 750 watts, maybe less. Beautiful light, Marshall! It will make you look really good. It's glamour lighting: no hard shadows on the eyes or the nose and so no fillers to get rid of them. That means no brutes or gennys to make a noise or make the recording difficult. So we'll have little or no dubbing.'

Bookbinder said, 'It will make it an actor's film, Marshall: your film.'

'We'll still have marks?' Stone asked.

Hanratty said, 'Not for the lights, just for the focus puller. And no worries about casting shadows as you move.'

'Kagan said you'll be using two cameras. I don't know if I like that. I like to play to a camera. I like to know which lens is on. After all, a twitch of an eyelid on the two hundred needs a wave of the arm on the wide angle.'

Bookbinder looked anxiously towards Hanratty, who said, 'It will give you a freedom you've never known, Marshall. You will think you've been reborn. Trust me.'

'I'll take a lot of convincing, Bert.'

Bookbinder said, 'He did 520 camera set-ups on *Naked Summer*: thirteen a day.'

Hanratty said, 'Easy now, Kagan, actors get worried at the idea of working that fast.'

'Thirteen set-ups a day,' said Stone. 'I can't remember ever doing more than eight. Preston can only get two or three done on some days. He's going to fifteen takes on some of them.'

'And you improve your performance on each take?' asked Hanratty.

'No,' said Stone. 'After about the sixth time I start to lose it.'

'Because you hold back at the beginning.'

'I'm afraid I do, he never gets it the first shot. It's Preston's first feature,' said Stone. It would be good to work with real professionals again. That Preston boy worried him. 'He spends more time with the crew than with the actors. Sometimes I think he's directing them instead of me.'

'Kids always surround themselves with more equipment than they can control. And they like to go to a dozen takes. It makes them feel more like a film director. I did the same on my first film.'

'But thirteen set-ups a day,' said Stone. 'That's too many for me, Bert.'

'No, it's not,' said Hanratty. He was gentle but firm. He knew that the relationship between director and actor was already forming. It was better to lose Stone altogether than get off on the wrong foot. 'I will want you to put everything into the first take! Everything, Marshall! We'll try and do the whole film with just one take at each set-up.'

'It's difficult to deliver a line cold, Bert. I doubt if I could get it right the first time.'

'Not cold, Marshall. We'll rehearse each shot very carefully until you are ready. Then I shoot.'

'It's worth a try.'

'You wait till you do the pre-production walk-through with him, and Bookbinder. 'He's more meticulous than anyone I've ever seen on the floor.'

'That's the time to iron out problems,' said Hanratty. 'I do a set-ups plan in pre-production too.'

'Using models of each location,' Bookbinder added proudly.

'You two should get married,' said Stone.

For a moment Bookbinder was put out. 'Bert's the best, Marshall. I mean it: the best.'

Stone smiled.

'You'll see, Marshall. This will be the finest thing you've ever done. The scene in the attic: that's pure Dostoevski.'

Stone thought, there we go. Now we'll be lucky to escape Nietzsche. 'And I'll be rich, too.'

'He's a sarcastic bugger,' Hanratty said to Bookbinder.

'We really want you to do this film, Marshall,' said Bookbinder.

'How could I resist?' said Stone. He pushed the button to tell the kitchen that they were ready for the coffee, the brandy and the cigars.

'Could you do the fall from the roof?' asked Hanratty. 'I'd like to do it with one of the cameras giving me a close-up.'

'Just schedule it at the end of the shooting,' joked Stone.

'Suppose we need a retake,' said Hanratty glumly.

The others laughed but Stone scarcely noticed. 'Let's talk about the uniforms I'll wear,' he said.

When Bookbinder and Hanratty had gone, Weinberger sat down for a quiet drink with Stone. Weinberger had brought a voucher copy of *Monday – the Magazine of Sport and Enter-tainment*. There was a coloured photo of Stone on the cover. It wasn't flattering. Stone was standing on his head in a yoga pose, so that his cheeks were puffed and his eyes narrowed with the strain of it. Inside, the same photo had been printed, face only, right way up. When only Stone's face was visible, and it wasn't evident that he was standing on his head, his strained face looked ridiculous. The enigmatic photo caption, 'No round of bills or spiritual trough', was a quote from the text of the article.

EXISTING THROUGH NATURE. 'Showgirl' visits Marshall Stone.

Yoga, Eastern mysticism and meditation make up much of the world of Marshall Stone. If a hiker or a cyclist in the midst of rural Kent hears a Hindu call to prayer, the lilting tones of the sitar or the even more ancient vina, he may not be going crazy. 'My mornings begin with the call to prayer,' says Marshall Stone, with a twinkle in his eye, as he switches on his eight-hundred-pound tape-recorder. The stereo re-cording of strange Eastern music makes yours truly start up with surprise. 'I began to practise yoga and meditation while filming *Tigertrap*,' says the youthful Marshall Stone. 'Now I spend two hours of each day in solitude and contemplation, live on a macrobiotic diet and read a great deal of Indian philosophy. The East has a lot to teach us about ourselves. Our lives here in the Western world can easily become a round of bills, publicity, salaries, traffic jams, arguments and unhappiness. Ancient Eastern philosophers can teach us to know ourselves and find true and lasting happiness. It's a matter of becoming a part of the universe and existing only through nature.'

Marshall was dressed in a psychedelic gown – orange, reds, pinks and yellow – and a bright saffron headband. He leaned back upon the multi-coloured cushions and rush mats that covered the floor. There were vases of coloured flowers everywhere and uncountable hundreds of beads draped around the room. He put his arm around Suzy Delft, the well-known young model who he has starring with him in his next film, *Stool Pigeon*. 'I want to dig everything,' said Marshall. 'Life is too short for me to conform to the spiritual trough of bourgeois formality. Suzy and I know and understand that. Through the wisdom we have discovered in the East we have expanded our consciousness. We have discovered true spiritual happiness. That's something that many old people will never find out, but that young people know instinctively. There is a youth revolution in progress,' said Marshall. 'Youth will smash the establishment and prove that love and self-knowledge can rule the world. But first violence and destruction will wipe the slate clean in order that we can begin afresh'

At one time actors – even Marshall himself – were reluctant to discuss controversial topics. Now all that is changed. Marshall and Suzy talked to me about everything that is important to them: communes, freaking, bum trips, black activism, geodesic domes, revolution and Zen. They also talked of Yin and Yang, the two opposite components of life according to the oriental prophets. Yin and Yang are incidentally Suzy and Marshall's pet names for each other. Now that the secret is out I know that many of my readers will adopt those names for their nearest and dearest beau.

In the tiny silken room, the floating and spiritual world that is Marshall's favourite place for meditation, I am able to understand a little of what he explained. I ask him, 'Have you tried LSD and the hallucinogenic drugs to achieve expansion of consciousness?'

Marshall smiles. He thinks for a moment before answering. 'I'd rather not answer that one,' he says, 'except to say that drugs are very unhip. My friends in show business have been able to achieve a lot by group contemplation. On *Tigertrap* I persuaded the producer and the crew to share my morning prayers. I explained to them all that these were prayers of goodwill that in no way contradicted the Christian faith.'

As I left Marshall's three-hundred-thousand-pound home in the heart of Kent, I looked back to see Marshall and Suzy standing together in the doorway. 'Come again,' called Marshall, 'and next time we'll pray together.'

The happiness on both of their faces was a wonderful advertisement for yoga and meditation. Or was it just old-fashioned love?

(*Next week: 'Showgirl' visits David Frost at home*)

'Bloody marvellous,' said Stone. 'She's just invented it!'

'There's no "she", Marshall. It's put together from other cuttings. I talked to George. He says it's not actionable.'

'It's bits of the interview that George wrote for the *Tigertrap* première and some doctored quotes from that piece that the French magazine did on me and Preston talking together. But most of it is pure invention. Jesus, the nerve of these bastards. They live on us like lice, sucking our blood to stay alive.' He read it again. 'Yin and Yang. Did you ever hear me or Suzy call each other Yin and Yang?'

'Don't be too upset.'

'It's this stuff with Suzy. I'm going to look a right fool, Viney. Why didn't they check it first?'

'Why don't any of them check anything first. In case we objected to their stupidities in time to stop them.'

'It's a disaster,' said Stone. '*Life* may not run their article if they see this one. As for this Suzy stuff, I'm going to look a right berk when Leo's boys start to run their Val and Suzy stuff next week.'

Weinberger nodded.

Stone said, 'Perhaps we'd better ask the Koolman publicity department to hold that story for three or four weeks.'

'I did ask, Marshall.'

'And they refused? Those little bastards refused! I'll talk to Leo.'

'Leo won't help, Marshall. See this from their point of view. This story helps them. It will be a Suzy-Delft-loves-Marshall-Stone, Suzy-Delft-is-not-so-sure and then a Suzy-Delft-loves-Val-Somerset story.'

'And-this-time-it's-for-keeps story.'

'And-this-time-it's-for-keeps story,' nodded Weinberger. 'Sure. That will give them ten times the mileage they could get otherwise.'

'It's bad news,' said Stone. He was hoping desperately that

Weinberger would contradict him. When Weinberger remained silent, Stone added, 'And that stuff about violent revolution will screw up my chances of a K for years.'

Stone's pursuit of a knighthood was a joke they shared, except that for Stone it was less of a joke than it was for Weinberger. A knighthood was what separated the men from the boys nowadays. Stone especially coveted it because of the prestige it would give him in America. It was something American actors couldn't aspire to, and that made it doubly desirable.

'What did the wonderful George say?'

'Wonderful George says keep stumm, it could be worse. And he's right, Marshall. They could have dreamed up some stuff about you and Suzy living together. And with Anson sniffing out that Rainbow story . . .'

'Peter Anson isn't going to shit on his own doorstep. He's got Mary to worry about.'

'I think you're right, but, as George says, don't talk to the Press. And don't be tempted into denying that crap or they'll twist it into fresh statements and keep it going for as long as they can.'

'You mean, quote: I hate Suzy Delft and screw Indians and standing on your head makes you impotent, unquote.'

'So don't talk to them.'

'And for this I pay my Press agent two thousand a year?'

'George is all right,' said Weinberger. 'You just take a look at that sentence about the Eastern prayers in no way contradicting Christian faith. That was George. It took him an hour on the phone and a big lunch at the White Elephant to fix that. And without him softening that one a bit, we might have been in a lot of trouble in the Catholic countries. The nationals get hold of a thing like that and they could make it sound as if you are doing the black-magic bit.'

'Who is this "Showgirl"?'

'I told you, Marshall. George says it's a dozen kids. Don't know their arse from a hole in the ground. All set to win a Pulitzer Prize – you know.'

'I know all right.'

*　　*　　*

Marshall Stone was relieved when Weinberger departed. He wanted to be alone. He found himself remembering childhood incidents that had gone from his mind for many decades: Uncle Bernard putting on greasepaint. His mother being so surprised that he could learn all the lines of a play, almost overnight. *Cavalcade*: two pounds a week and supplying his own costume. My God, what an innocent he'd been in those days.

Bookbinder and Hanratty had cheered him for an hour or two, but he was pleased to see them go. They didn't really understand him or his work. They could never understand any actor. They were obsessed with cameras and film and how to focus. They'd hardly mentioned the story or the character he'd play. It made him laugh when people called it a director's medium. Any film consisted only of actors. When all was said and done, what did the rest of them do, except photograph the actors' performance.

He felt sorry for actors: they were all condemned to a lonely rootless life; so much of it spent in planes, trains and cars, living out of a suitcase in some Godforsaken location. He'd tried to explain it to his mother once, but she couldn't really understand. She understood the loneliness, all right: what could be lonelier than her life, in that grimy old house, amid the junk that his grandparents had unloaded upon her. But her loneliness was not his loneliness. It was wealth that made him lonely.

He sat at his desk. In one of the trays there was a pile of household accounts and miscellaneous bills that awaited his signature. The sight of that depressed him even more. He knew that buried within their indecipherable figures were all manner of deceits and frauds. He accepted cheating as he accepted dentistry, income tax and reviews, as one of the inescapable penalties of his life, but he resented it. He'd been indignant when he first encountered the sort of dishonesty that is levied upon the wealthy like an unofficial tax. But soon he had learned that rich film stars are fair game for otherwise scrupulous tradesmen. Not even his closest friends offered sympathy for his grievances; only grins of amusement. Now he nodded, and did not kick when he detected the surcharges, padding and fictitious costs that were an inevitable part of every account.

Weinberger had once estimated that in a five-year period Stone lost close to three million dollars to the crooked manipulations of Koolman's accountants. So the fact that the housekeeper at Twin Beeches regularly larded her books with non-existent bills was not worth losing any sleep about. Only Angela his secretary, Jasper his valet and Weinberger were above suspicion in their financial decorum, and this mutual trust bound them to him more firmly and profoundly than any love he'd ever had for his ex-wife or even his mother.

He'd been cheated in other ways. He seemed to attract the most heartless and predatory villains in the world. There was a butler – two before Jasper, so it was many years ago – who gave a stupid interview on a Los Angeles TV programme. There was a housekeeper at Grasse who wrote a libellous fiction about his life with Mary and sold it to the worst of the French magazines. Not only had the old bitch made a fortune, but she'd stayed just within the law, and excerpts had been syndicated throughout the world, sometimes in august publications that should have shown more responsibility. Nowadays his private correspondence was locked away, and there were no extension phones that a servant could use to eavesdrop without fear of discovery. It had taken him twenty years to learn how to be a film star, and now that he'd learned, he was almost too old to make use of the knowledge. Perhaps all men's lives were like that. It was at times like this that Stone ached to know the father that he could not remember. In him he might have found the man that was missing.

In spite of all his introspection, he knew so little about himself. Sometimes he felt that Marshall Stone was less real than the parts he played. He wondered if he was just a mask that those fictional men put on. He'd spent his life searching for his true character. Often a script had persuaded him that he'd found it, but when the production ended he'd been relieved to return to his own faceless world. So far he'd searched only among the parts available for heroes, but now he was old enough to suspect that he'd never been a hero and that, too, troubled him.

Not even Weinberger knew how many nights he'd spent worrying about the next day's shooting. No one had guessed why he'd refused to continue the beach location shots in *Tiger-trap*. Weinberger still believed that he'd feared pneumonia. In fact, Stone had decided that the oilskin coat he was wearing in that scene was wrong for him. He was moving like a robot, and without a view of his legs as he climbed the ladder to the loft, where the girl was hidden, he looked jerky, like a puppet. By feigning a chill, he'd persuaded them to postpone it and do it as a cover shot. In the studio he'd got rid of the oilskin and done it in torn jersey and rolled-up trousers. His naked feet were right, and the studio lighting did so much more for him. To say nothing of the fact that in the studio the ladder didn't creak, and thus make the girl want to grin when he put his arm round her. She didn't realize that just keeping the lips taut didn't hide a grin: she'd threatened the atmosphere of that whole sequence.

That had cost him a week of sleepless nights, and yet no one would ever know. When they'd seen the rushes they'd all said it was good, but they'd not admitted how much better it was than the shots at the location. In fact at the time the director had complained bitterly about having to abandon the beach because the hotel accommodation had been paid and he'd rented an extra Mitchell camera. That was how their minds worked: always concerned with cameras or contracts or transport or money.

Glibly, they spoke of actors being exhibitionists, carefully ignoring the discipline that skilled acting needed. They thought that acting was embellishing the written part, and yet it was exactly the opposite: it was a process of distilling the written part to its irreducible minimum until just the essence of a man remained. Patronizingly, they 'knew' that actors were 'gregarious', but they didn't know the loneliness of studying a part for weeks, or even months. Nor did they know how solitary a man felt reading his Press cuttings, how isolated was the idol facing his adorers, or how outcast was the actor turned down for a part. Nor would they ever move among that ultimate assembly of lonely souls: an audition.

Stone picked up the script and, without opening it, put it down again. No more reading of the script could help him with his decision. The time of thinking was past, the awful time of decision was here. No one could help him, either now or later. None of them would be blamed if the film was a disaster. Only Marshall Stone would have the critics spitting in his eye as though he'd tried to pass a counterfeit bill and been caught in the act. For such was the denunciatory attitude they adopted to all who failed to meet their high standards. His critics seemed to believe that it was better to do nothing than to try and not excel. How would Weinberger like to have someone tell him how he rated as an agent. '. . . Willie Morris goes to number one for the lovely pay-or-play deal they squeezed out of Fox, with Weinberger sliding to eighth place for fouling up the cross-collateralizing clause in Marshall Stone's epic. Surprise of the charts this month is a new agent who really handles a contract in a way I like. Operating out of a slum in Toronto comes . . .' How would his bank manager like to be reviewed by some ex-bank clerk, or by a lady customer who didn't know an audit from a hole in the books. How would his dentist, or his analyst, like to be reviewed. How would that bloody astrologer like it. *Tigertrap* was entirely his fault. Stone hoped he was more accurate about *Man From the Palace*.

Often Stone had given wonderful performances in bad films. Once or twice he'd given poor performances in quite good films. What he dearly wanted was to give just one superlative performance in a really fine film. It was all any actor wanted. Again he picked up the script. He had put *Man From the Palace* into the Gucci cover, and it already made him feel that he was a part of the production.

He read a few of his lines. Silently, and then aloud, to get the speed and the rhythm of them. The performance might well be very different, but a first reading aloud gave an idea of their basic merit or their irremediable faults. Stone often claimed that a performance was something like a symphony: an andante beginning with a clearly stated theme, variation, recapitulation, scherzo and a restated simple end. Stone had used that for the basis of all his performances. Then he prepared a high point and snatched away the force of the performance at the very time the audience – or a director – was certain there was more to come. That was what acting was all about and only people who had done it knew one's triumphs and one's disasters.

These idiots talked about *Last Vaquero*, but didn't realize how much of it was tricks. He'd had no idea of that role at the time he'd done it. What they all liked was the pace of his performance, some sly bits of upstaging and a grin that he whittled down until it was as slow and as subtle as he dared.

Only now, a quarter of a century later, was he really equipped to do justice to that role. And yet the critics had raved at his gimmicky performance.

He remembered the dinner party on the sun deck of the Malibu beach house. No one was able to eat, and every time the phone rang he felt a pain and his heart stopped, literally stopped. It was almost midnight when Weinberger came through from New York: almost every review was a rave. Bookbinder grabbed a bottle of champagne and poured it over Stone. He was drenched in it. Mary said, 'If you must do that, use the domestic champagne.'

Bookbinder passed the phone to him. It was a bad line, and Weinberger was almost incoherent at the other end. 'Let me speak to the kid,' Stone heard him say.

'Eddie here.'

'Marshall! Not Eddie, Marshall! From now on forget Eddie. Marshall, it's a boff.'

'A boff?'

'A click, a hit. Marshall, you are going places, just like I told you. You'll have a lot of calls. I want you to stay away from the phone and give no interviews until I get back there tomorrow night. The publicity I'm lining up here will be terrific, and we don't want it pre-empted by local Press and trades.'

Stone tried to say all right, but the excitement had affected his vocal cords. He'd read of such things, but had never taken it literally until then. He just couldn't speak.

'Are you there, Marshall? This goddamned phone . . . Marshall, are you still there?'

Stone passed the phone to Bookbinder. 'A click': he still had the front page framed behind the bar at Twin Beeches, 'Brit ~e Clicks in Hoss Opry.'

They looked everywhere for the director, to tell him the wonderful news, and found him shivering in the ocean with a young Mexican actor. Then it was half an hour before they found their clothes. Funny how Mary had not realized about the director until then, but she always was an innocent in some things. Bookbinder grabbed the bedroom phone and began to call everyone he knew. It was Stone's first experience of the showbiz instant party. His first experience of instant fame, too. People who'd looked through him the previous day were all over him that night. And not only girls, but executives too.

Gary Cooper was there. Stone knew he'd seen *Last Vaquero* in rough-cut. He asked him if he'd liked it. Cooper said. 'Get rid of that pony, son. He's wearing suspenders.' Coop knew, as Stone did, that the film was not outstanding: just another 'oater', one of the boys said. Coop noticed that Stone had not mastered the walk that came from a lifetime of wearing heavy leather chaps and low-slung six-guns. Stone had insisted upon wearing real guns: they were too heavy and, far from improving his walk, they hampered him.

He'd learned a lot since then. He'd learned that just to reproduce physical circumstances was not always a help to an actor. In the planning stage it was useful to wear the right clothes and bear the right weights, but afterwards it was better to act it than suffer it. After the sequel, *Return of the Vaquero*, Coop came over to Stone's table at Dominic's in Hollywood. He said nothing. He just patted Stone's arm and smiled. It was the finest accolade that Stone could remember.

Stone got to his feet to try out some of the *Man From the Palace* scenes. There was a waiter in Rome who had some of the mannerisms that Prince Felix would need. He'd have to take another look at the old boy. He had a curious jerk of the head and a hesitation as he handed out the menus. Too, there was the way his hair was done: parted high with a wavy quiff. He'd need a hairpiece at the top and a perm for his side hair. Stone looked in the mirror and moved his hair to see how it would look. Already he was beginning to put together the physical and the mental parts of the character. Prince Felix was younger than Stone, and he would have grown up in a sheltered environment, mixing with aristocrats and soldiers whose bearing would be that of a century ago. All of this Stone would have to show to the audience in the first five minutes of screen time. For if this was not clear to them by the time of his argument with the prime minister on page seven, then they would not understand his indignation at such a small rudeness.

There was one line he liked very much. He thumbed through the script to page fifty-three. Already he'd decided how this would be delivered. He'd be in a dark-blue nineteenth-century cavalry uniform, medals on the breast and gold-frogging everywhere. Under his arm he'd hold a polished helmet. He'd hold it tight, and his chin would be high and his eyes narrowed.

130   INT. LONG-SHOT. CONFERENCE ROOM OF
     PALACE.   NIGHT.

PRIME MINISTER: Join your regiment? That would be quite out of the question, Your Highness.

PRINCE FELIX: I'm a good soldier, Billy, and we'll need good soldiers. There are no more decisions to be made here.

PRIME MINISTER: And what would the Cabinet do to me, if something happened to their Prince?

PRINCE FELIX: What would they say if their Prince went to California and opened a chain of hamburger stands?

131   INT. MEDIUM-SHOT. CONFERENCE ROOM OF
     PALACE.   NIGHT.

The PRIME MINISTER starts forward to pick up his document-case into which he has put the treaty and the other documents. He is bewildered.

PRIME MINISTER: Your Majesty . . .

PRINCE FELIX: King-size 'burgers, Billy.

PRIME MINISTER: Are you . . . threatening me, Majesty?

PRINCE FELIX: I must get some sleep now, Billy. If anyone wants me tomorrow, say I've gone to war.

132   EXT. LONG-SHOT. HILLS BEYOND THE CITY.
     DAY.

A TROOP OF CAVALRY are patrolling. We hear the sound of the horses and the jingle of harness before we see them.

133   EXT. MEDIUM-SHOT. A BUGLER. DAY.

A MOUNTED BUGLER *ascends a rise until he is silhouetted on the skyline and then sounds a call.*

Stone had already decided that he would break up the words 'California' and 'hamburger' into separate syllables, as if they were unfamiliar to him. The final word – 'war' – he'd flatten to a sound like 'whirr'. This would catch the attention of the audience and give the line the emphasis it must have if the action was to halt for a moment. Then the bugle call must come early to accompany his close-up. He'd not want that as a medium-shot to be shared with some character actor playing the prime minister. Perhaps a medium-shot zooming to Stone's CU. And there must not be a cut to the cavalry. There was too much cutting nowadays. He'd fight tooth and nail for a slow dissolve – a very slow one – with sounds held down except for the muted bugle call. It was a key scene and it was only fair that he gave it as much as he could.

He turned again to the end of the script. He'd like to delete the last three pages. The film should end with Prince Felix dead inside the blockhouse. That's what he would argue for, at first. Only after convincing them that he'd settle for nothing less than deletion would he announce his compromise: the last three pages must be filmed in nothing closer than mid-shot. He certainly would never agree to the girl getting a final close-up with tears running down her face. Good God, it would be delivering the whole film over to her. What else would the audience remember as they left the cinema.

There were other things, too, but Stone was too tired to worry about them now. It had been a trying day after a restless night. He put the script aside and rang for Jasper.

'Yes, sir.'

'Would you like to run a movie for me, Jasper?'

'Indeed I would, sir. Which one?'

'I haven't seen *Last Vaquero* for ages, have I?'

'Not since the party at Christmas, sir.'

'We'll look at that, Jasper.'

Stone pushed the accounts back into their pigeonhole and then closed the front of the desk and turned the key. He ran his fingers over the antique lock, appreciating the perfection with which it had been fitted to the inlaid frame. Then he poured himself a cup of strong black coffee from the silver pot on the tray which Jasper had set beside him. It was stupid to drink strong coffee so late at night, but he had his pills.

He took his coffee and followed Jasper into the most prestigious of sanctums: his private cinema. As modern as any in the world, it was provided with rock-and-roll projectors, stereo sound and soft leather armchairs. In its air-conditioned comfort Stone found solace and strength, just as predecessors had found when this was a private chapel. Two angels – a part of the carved ceiling – had been hinged at the wingtips to permit the screen to descend down to the altar rail, upon which it locked with a satisfying click. Jasper opened sections of the parclose screen that concealed the loudspeakers. Stone settled back and put his hand-made brogues on the footstool. There was a flash of light as Jasper checked the projectors, and a buzz as he adjusted the amplifier. The acoustics were perfect in here: as the architect had prophesied.

The lights dimmed. There was a fanfare and a roll of kettle-drums. On the screen came the distributor's trademark; a Greek vase with the letter K on it. The Koolman Pictures Corporation proudly presented Marshall Stone in *Last Vaquero*. The fiery letters moved off the top of the screen. As the roller revealed the names of the men and women who had worked on the film, a banjo and harmonica struck up the sort of music that Hollywood allocated to the Wild West.

Stone read all the credits carefully, he always did. As a child, the credits had seemed an unnecessary bore to him. Nowadays they were more interesting than the films that followed them, for they provided a chronicle of his friends and his enemies, their progress, their skills, their luck or their misjudgement.

As the director's name faded, there was an insert of a yellow map with burned edges. Crudely lettered upon it were divisions labelled 'Cherokee Nation', 'Creek Nation', 'Choctaw Nation'. A slow dissolve became a long-shot of a horse and rider. A mid-shot showed the horseman to be Marshall Stone and, following it, an insert was a horse's head as it drank at a river bank. A long-shot: placed symbolically upon the skyline there was a prop tree, its solitary bent branch enough to tell any Western fan that it would eventually be used for a necktie party. Stone remembered how it broke when used. The villain had fallen to the studio floor in a shower of plaster. My God, how they had laughed!

A shot rang out. There was the briefest of cuts to a distance shot of the whole canyon. Then, in mid-shot, a stuntman, doubling for Stone, tumbled off the horse into the river. Another insert of the horse as it looked up in alarm and then a close-up of Marshall Stone, eyes closed, water breaking over his face. The camera tracked in until the face was in big close-up. It was a studio shot, beautifully lit, as only studio takes could be. The theme music – 'Shall We Gather at the River' – could just be heard under the sound of the water.

This was the warm comfortable world of Marshall Stone. It was dark and nostalgic. It was peopled by faces he knew and lit by men he trusted. Villains had descending chords, mortal injuries, black hats, shared dressing-rooms, were under-lit and fell off roots. Heroes had theme music, slight flesh wounds, key lights, kickers, close-ups, white horses, Oscars, doubles and a million dollars a picture. Who said there was no justice.

13 *The writers want to be directors. The producers want to be writers. The actors want to be producers. The wives want to be painters. Nobody is satisfied.*

Gottfried Reinhardt

For Marshall Stone, his life was not made of the stuff of which biographies are written. He remembered his life only in terms of the houses in which he'd lived, the custom-built cars he'd owned, the boats, aeroplanes and appreciative notices that he had treasured and the people who had loved him. There were no tragedies in this sort of life; farewells soon become hellos, tears had smiles showing through them, and disease and death were the tasteful asides and painless exits that screenplays have always claimed they were.

Only the famous had a speaking role in Marshall Stone's remembered life, and they were only permitted upon his stage long enough to deliver a word of praise or a message of congratulation. He had shown me scrapbooks crammed with laudatory telegrams and eulogies from his fellow actors. For, like professional bodies of lawyers, doctors and surgeons, show business denied its ranks the luxury of mutual criticism.

The drawers of his desk were loaded with the inscribed mementoes that were exchanged at the end of each production. As well as the trinkets that were distributed to the whole crew, there were more valuable ones that stars, producer and director exchanged: onyx cuff-links, a silver letter-opener and a jade paperweight. Each engraved name reminded Stone of someone he loved and respected, and inevitably he would recall evidence of their admiration and affection too.

Marshall Stone saw no reason why his biography could not be like this. He envisaged a literary version of 'This Is Your Life', or one of those old Technicolor films in which a man creates a new sound, proves that he can fly, or demonstrates a different way of painting a chapel ceiling. Such heroes didn't experiment, discover or conclude: they knew exactly what they wanted from infancy.

It was no accident that Hollywood portrayed success in this way. There, dedicated youngsters, obsessed with ambitions to be stars or directors, or coveting the riches of production, did know exactly what they wanted. The 'big break' wasn't the result of exhaustive research, contemplation or years of hard work; it was meeting the right man in the right place at the right moment. Because of the instantaneous result such human mixtures showed, the film world referred to it as chemistry.

So it was difficult to convince Marshall Stone that I didn't have his story plotted and ready to write. I asked him what secret he had nursed that *Last Vaquero* could make him into a star. He gave me only modest smiles and shakes of the head. Stars didn't provide story lines: writers did.

In fact, Marshall Stone provided me with more stories than he cared to admit, as one morning's mail showed.

A piece of office notepaper had Peter Quarrel's inimitable scrawl in every direction, the postscripts going vertically up the margin and down the other side.

Yes, yes, yes, indeed, Eddie Brummage, private soldier soon to become corporal, acting unpaid, was with the mighty Milly-Ash. He was Milly-Ash's batman – and a good one too by all accounts – until he got permission to join a concert party. Hie, hie to the gypsies away: monologues. recitations and impressions of Cagney, complete with police siren and machine gun, and all done with the mouth alone! Naturally this led on to corps dramatic company and finally to Browning in *Barretts of Wimpole Street*.

Love and kisses

P.Q.

PS Still looking for a title? *Per Ardua ad Astra* any good?

PPS Ever wondered about E.B.'s horsemanship? Or perhaps you thought that *Last Vaquero* was all done by mirrors. No! He used to groom Milly-Ash's horse – (oops! charger, I mean, I've learned the lingo in the last few days). He taught himself to ride! That must have taken guts.

The second letter had rows of Italian stamps and was typed on pale-blue airmail paper with that sort of typewriter designed to produce the effect of handwriting.

Pastor Location Services
Rome London Hollywood Madrid

Dear Peter,

Flattered to hear from you in connexion with your new opus. I regret that on *Last Vaquero* I was so hurried that I had far less time to spend with you than I usually spend with the writers of my scripts. I'm not sure that I can do justice to your charming compliments. By the way, Peter, if the decision had been mine, you would have got a script credit on *Last Vaquero*, but you know how it goes.

I did fourteen movies altogether; all for Hollywood majors. Before that I worked in editing for about sixty films, half of them B pictures. My last film was *The Battling O'Briens Return* which I did immediately after *Vaquero*.

I didn't get along very well with Stone. I thought he came on too pushy for an unknown, in spite of his mock-humble way of talking to me. I was betting that he'd sink without trace, but that shows how wrong I can be. The only anecdote that I recall is the time that Edgar Nicolson brought news of the final cut to Stone and me.

I probably don't need to remind you that at Koolman Studios in those days directors weren't welcome in the cutting-rooms and I had already been moved on to the next picture. I was sitting with Stone and that fellow Weinberger (who became Stone's agent), pushing a Caesar salad around my plate and trying to eat it without looking at it, when Nicolson came in looking rather sweaty. He'd come straight from seeing the rough-cut. He'd sneaked into the theatre without permission and was all atremble. You remember what a terrible old woman Nicolson was. He slumped down at the table and put his head in his hands. When he had our attention, he heaved a deep sigh. Marshall responded – what's wrong Edgar, you look terrible etc, etc. When they had both sucked the situation dry, Edgar Nicolson told us about the final cut.

He said, 'You were wonderful, Eddie, wonderful. Apart from that scene in the jail where they have used the long-shot instead of cutting to the profile close-up, you dominate the whole film. That editor says you look better in the long-shot, it's great, the low camera and the wide-angle lens makes you look very tall. All through the film you are great! But Jesus, Marshall, they have cut my part down to nothing. Nothing, Marshall, really to nothing. I've got two lines, apart from the gunfight, when all my lines are off camera anyway. They've cut me out of the saloon entirely and they have cut my campfire sequence: that's become just a slow dissolve to you riding on alone the next morning. You thought my campfire scene was good, didn't you, Marshall?' He turned to me. 'You shot it, Lawrence. I was good, wasn't I, and it was right. It was right! You said so. Everyone was talking about it. Jesus, Marshall, what am I going to tell people? My family will be going to see that film, expecting my big break-through. I wrote them all about it. What can I do, Marshall?'

Marshall rubbed his face and turned to me. He said, 'You hear that, Lawrence? They've cut my close-up in the jail scene. That's the sort of bastards I've got to deal with.'

That story just sums up actors for me. Three years ago I sat at the next table to him here in Rome but he was so concerned about himself that he had eyes for no one.

I can't give you any of the answers to the questions about the selection of Stone. Certainly I gave his test a nod, but we didn't have the kind of say in casting that directors get nowadays. We were all on contracts. Actors, producers and directors – and I guess writers, too – did as they were told or got themselves fired, am I right, Peter?

That is a feeble answer to your letter, I'm afraid, but I've been out of the production side of the industry for well over twenty years now. I enclose brochures of my equipment rental company. We also opened a small recording studio in Madrid two years ago and this has proved a popular facility.

There are two completely self-contained location sound units. We use Mercedes trucks built especially to our standards. Generators are built in, thus making our teams completely mobile and totally independent of mains supply for location shooting anywhere.

Should you mention me in your biography of Marshall Stone, I would appreciate if you could mention my company and as many of its facilities as you are able. I enclose an addressed envelope in the hope that you will send me the address of Mr Edgar Nicolson who, I note from your letter, is now producing. I would like to contact him again.

Yours sincerely,

LAWRENCE CLARK PASTOR

There was also a packet with a 'Kagan Bookbinder Productions' label. It contained a red-covered script and a hard-cover edition of the book. There was a note attached. Whatever kind of economy Bookbinder was exercising, it didn't extend to his stationery. The paper was heavyweight and of the clearest white. The letterhead design was an elegant exercise by the sort of typographer that calls himself a graphic artist. A lightweight grot type linked a formalized computer to a coat of arms that was blind-embossed. Bookbinder's name was small and discreet and the letter was perfectly typed on an electric machine.

Dear Peter,

Marshall was telling me about the biography. His next commitment is to play Prince Felix in my production of *Man From the Palace*. Bert Hanratty (whose *Naked Summer* is one of the greatest successes in film history) is under contract to direct, and in case you haven't yet got around to the magnificent best-selling novel I am enclosing a copy. I am particularly honoured that the author has himself prepared the superb screenplay.

It's wonderful to hear that you are doing Marshall's biography – who better? If I can help in any way with answers about *Man*, or anything else, don't hesitate to call me on my private number.

250

All my warmest best wishes,

KAGAN BOOKBINDER

He had signed it in a shade of red ballpoint that exactly matched the letterhead. In the margin he'd noted his private line.

Man From the Palace was an interesting book. On the face of it, the story of a contemporary prince who, in the first chapter, succeeds to the throne of a mythical European country: Rurimania. To discover an answer to student riots, violent crime, strikes, traffic congestion and many other problems of Western urban life, he buys a computer. The sardonic humour of the book emerged as the computer gave logical, rational answers which revealed most of the Cabinet's decisions as the dogmatic, self-interested, vote-catching nonsense that so much political debate is. The computer was not programmed to allow for personal or national pride, and the solutions it proposed did not take into account Rurimania's history or its mistaken belief that it remained one of the big three nations of the present-day world.

The ending shows the whole country split by the machine. Lined up against it are the TUC, the Protestant Church, an organization of student revolutionaries and the Navy. An attempt to destroy the computer is foiled by a last-minute alliance of the Army and the Communist Party under the command of Prince Felix. The final battle scenes are shared between Prince Felix on his charger and a Glaswegian riveter – his communist C-in-C – working out his battle tactics with the aid of the machine.

The book had been a huge success in America and Germany, but was bitterly received in Britain and France. There, Rurimania was seen as a warped version of those countries, and intellectuals refused to accept the computer as either comic, critic or hero. The reviewer's trenchant asides, about the book probably having been written by a computer, firmly placed such machines back into their rightful role of villain.

Bookbinder's film script said Britain was Rurimania in everything except name. Although the battle scenes were to be shot in Italy, the opening sequence was to be Prince Felix driving down the Mall with Buckingham Palace in the background. A horse-drawn carriage 'like a state coach' linked a couple of scenes and, in case any doubt remained, there was a midnight crisis introduced by an establishing shot of Big Ben.

I wondered to what extent all this would prejudice the chances of the film. Much of the book's humour came from its deadpan style. Some of the descriptive matter had been transcribed to screen dialogue, but the film was clearly intended to be a more direct attack upon British cant, hypocrisy and corruption than the book had been. Like the book, it hit out at all classes and political opinions. It certainly didn't spare the rod on any aspect of the 'youth revolution'. Personally, I hadn't noticed that youth had any great yearning for criticism. And they made up the bulk of the cinema's audience – or declined to do so.

I'd read *Man From the Palace* when it was on the best-seller list the previous year. One of the boys at the paper sold his review copies for half the marked price, and even Mary had read halfway before abandoning it, which was one of the greatest tributes to readability an author can get. I phoned Bookbinder just before lunch and fixed a three o'clock appointment.

His production offices were on the eighth floor of one of those ugly office blocks near Holborn. It was a weird place for a film company to live, but it had all the trimmings: rubber plants, IBM machines and Italian sofas. Later I was told that this was a floor of an advertising agency that had been contracted to handle the film advertising. It was a departure from the usual procedure in which the distribution company farmed it out.

'Financially, I'm walking a tightrope, but that is nothing new to me,' said Bookbinder. 'Distribution companies have screwed me in every possible position, and now I'm applying those lessons.' He picked up some notepaper and labels. 'I get a percentage on all the print we buy, directly and indirectly, posters, car stickers: everything. Then there are the film ends, they can be used to film inserts and second unit sequences. Music: usually renters take your music track for their own company without so much as a thank you. This time the production will get any profit from records or music.' Bookbinder gave a cunning smile as if I was the only person he'd told.

In 1970, *Sight and Sound* had given Bookbinder six pages.

> FROM CRISIS TO CRISIS.
> KAGAN BOOKBINDER, HOLLYWOOD'S
>   NON-CONFORMIST.
> Hollywood is not renowned for film-makers *engagé*. In
> finding his way through the maze of commercial interests
> to a subjective, anti-realist cinema, Kagan Bookbinder has
> often strayed into the superficial and the half-truth.
> *Sandcastle* was overloaded with fashionable attitudes and
> gratuitous sociology. Yet, in spite of that, his essential
> content remains the pursuit of the American dream.
> Thankfully often, he achieves a lyrical expressionism by
> an economy of means that the underground cinema with
> its exasperating *longeurs* might well envy . . .

The photos that accompanied the *Sight and Sound* article
showed a much younger man with a remarkable variety of
headgear. In person he proved to be bald, except for grey hair
that he encouraged back over his ears. This, together with the
half-spectacles worn low on his nose, made him look very
owlish. If the vogue for nineteen-thirties tailoring hadn't
caught on, no blame could be placed upon Kagan Bookbinder's
heavily padded shoulders. And yet he did not appear to be a
careful dresser. His tie knot was a tangle and his face was
stubbly where his razor had missed places at the corners of
mouth and nose. The white bristle might lead a hasty observer
to believe that here was an alcoholic, for he had exactly that
kind of disarray, and yet I knew him to be temperate to the
point of asceticism.

'I wish I knew how to write,' he said, motioning me to a chair
and throwing an expensive cigar at me. He said it sorrowfully,
as a man might regret that he did not ride a bicycle or had
never tried to ski. 'It would save so many fruitless arguments.'

'Would it.'

'Irony is fine,' he paused. 'In a book. But in a film, irony is
wrong. It's dangerous. It puts too much responsibility on the
actor.'

'It's an actor's job to understand the motives of the
writer.'

'Jesus, Peter, don't talk like some dumb hack. The actor has got enough trouble without helping the writer do his job. Irony is dangerous: it can leave half your audience thinking exactly the reverse of what you are trying to say. What I want is plain old-fashioned pro and con argument. You can't beat it. You know that.'

'I thought the script was good.'

'The author did a great job on the first draft, but here and there it needs tidying up.' He chopped the end off his cigar and passed me the cutter. 'I'm talking to a couple of radio writers this afternoon. That's the wonderful thing about working in Britain, there's an endless supply of talent trained by the BBC. Not only writers but actors, and from the TV side, directors too. Sometimes I think that without the BBC you'd have a film industry like New York and as many live theatres as Los Angeles.'

'I'd like to have your optimism.'

'Then look at American TV, the great writerless desert of talk shows, quizzes and cardboard Westerns. Those gay little secret agents and silent spades ... Jesus, if the kids really wanted to put a firecracker up the arse of the system ... it's not the cops that keep the silent majority hypnotized night after night.'

'The audiences have grown to like the pap they are fed. Censorship is out of date, commercial TV has conditioned the audiences so that in the US they'll switch off anything that is complex or thought-provoking.'

'And crap is cheap.'

'Not only cheap. An audience watching crap is relaxed and receptive to the commercials. People watching something important become impatient and antagonistic when their train of thought is broken by commercials.'

'Do you know one of the problems I faced getting the money to do this picture. The networks said unless the script was toned down, they'd not buy it for TV. They wanted me to end up with the kids in control and the prince saying he'd been wrong about the computer all along.'

'And?'

'So far, no TV sale. But if we are a really big hit they will run after me. You know that. If we're not a big hit then maybe only the BBC will buy.'

'Who are you kidding. The BBC are chasing the ratings. By the time you are ready for TV they will be screening the same rubbish . . . Gresham's Law, you know.'

'Is that the new private-eye series?'

'Something like that.'

He grunted and got up. He went to the window and opened it to see the jammed traffic below him. It was an actor's gesture, and like an edited effects track, the sound of the street came into the room. For a moment he held his position, hands upon the window catches, head bent. Then he closed the sound out and turned back to me, his lips compressed as if he was trying to remember what we were talking about. The baggy sleeves of his Fair Isle sweater made him look like an owl. He picked up his cigar and puffed on it.

I said, 'I had a letter from Lawrence Pastor this morning.'

'Lawrence Clark Pastor?'

'He runs a rental company in Rome.'

'Now tell me something I don't know! I get a brochure from the bastard every week. He's had a tough time in the last couple of years. He invested too much in equipment, now he's facing the music.'

'Poor old bugger.'

'In more ways than one. I was railroaded for embracing communism, Pastor for embracing a second assistant who talked. We had our timing wrong: nowadays we'd be what Koolman calls pioneers of the youth trend.'

'Colour, conflict and confrontation.'

'I had the colour, you had the conflict and Pastor had the confrontation. This business has changed since you were in it, Peter: more surprises, more risks, more people chasing fewer jobs.' My cigar had gone out and he leaned across the desk with a lighted match. I nodded my thanks. He said. 'Jump-cuts, lens flare, strobing, echo on the track: all those things we worried about. Now they give you awards for having them.'

'It's always been a technician's art.'

'The operator manipulates the camera, the director manipulates the operator and the producer manipulates the director.'

'And who manipulates the actors?'

'Jesus, Peter, we all do: actors seem to like it.'

'That's what the hunters say about the fox.'

'An actor is an innocent – an absolute innocent – but he's also an egomaniac.'

'Are we talking about Marshall Stone?'

'I'd carried that idea with me for three years before Koolman gave me my *Last Vaquero* deal. I'd used up a lot of my own dough on it, I knew what I wanted and I was determined to get it, in spite of Stone, in spite of Pastor . . .'

'And in spite of me?'

'You were trying to write social realism into the script, Pastor was screwing that Mexican fruit and Stone was telling me that I had to shoot him in chronological sequence.'

'Why not?'

'Jesus, Peter. You remember little Eddie Stone. When I brought him along to that first script meeting he didn't know the Scarlet Pimpernel from Scarlett O'Hara. He wasn't ready to be let loose on any of the key scenes. And especially not with Pastor directing him. I decided to head-up the schedule with links and long-shots. In that way he could feel his way into the role and modify his interpretation even after we were two weeks in.'

'It sounds like an expensive way to rehearse.'

He sighed and nodded. 'Koolman still thought Westerns could be shot in Topanga Canyon or the Corrigan Ranch where old Max had made his first million. He couldn't understand why I'd want to waste his money shipping the whole shebang out to New Mexico. So, I'm telling you, Peter, Koolman and his side-kicks were looking at every foot of it as it came in. On Stone's really bad days I cheated on our paperwork and maybe just sent the second unit results pretending it was our main unit footage.'

'Did he have many days as bad as that?'

'For two whole days we didn't even turn over. I invented some story about the colour of the cactus plants and how they had to be sprayed. That first day, when Stone looked at himself with full make-up and costume, he realized that the work he'd done on the role was not compatible with his appearance. He broke down and sobbed his heart out.'

'So?'

'What could I do? We went for a run in the pick-up so that he could see some wranglers roping and working. I knew that would help him. About lunchtime we found some cowboys in a little hospital corral doctoring some sick cattle. They were bored, cooking up a mountain of beef and beans, just like in the movies, eh?' Bookbinder laughed. 'Funny thing was, in their Sunday Stetsons, Gene Autry shirts and wristwatches and stuff you'd have thought they were the dudes and Marshall was the foreman. He was wearing beat-up old jeans and the battered Stetson that the wardrobe gave him for the role. I'm telling you, mister, he had those cowpunchers going. And Marshall could make a cigarette with one hand – he'd learned it from an old Duke Wayne picture – and they watched him bug-eyed. I had a crate of scotch, so we took chow with the boys, and the foreman says to Marshall what outfit is he with and Marshall is giving them whole chunks of dialogue. It was working and Marshall knew it was working. Those cowpokes talked to him like he was one of their own, 'I'm telling you.' Bookbinder leaned back in his chair and blew a perfect smoke ring. 'Next day we started shooting. Marshall was . . . well, you know how he was.'

'Don't tell me you didn't prime those cowboys.'

'Anybody says I didn't prime them, and I sue,' threatened Bookbinder, and gave a booming laugh. It was all manipulation, the whole damn business was that.

14 *Hollywood is like being nowhere and talking to nobody about nothing.*

Michelangelo Antonioni

Christmas Day 1948, Bookbinder remembered it only too clearly. He wondered why Edgar Nicolson pretended it had happened in that notorious hot-pillow motel on the far side of San Jorge. God knows, Stone had never been fastidious about where he'd taken his girls for a quickie, but the Sunnyside was not Stone's scene. His hunting grounds were more stylish than that. One of the first things he'd demanded after getting the role was membership of all the clubs.

Even on Christmas Day Stone had invented some excuse to leave Mary, and dragged Bookbinder off to The Planter's Club for lunch. Between 11.30 AM and sitting down at lunch, Stone had chatted up a nineteen-year-old blonde from Denver and shared thirty memorable minutes with her in one of the club's private conference rooms.

The Planter's Club was described as a meeting place for producers, directors and stars, but the management was smart enough to let kids in if their shape was right. They wrote actress on their applications, but you'd see those same faces on The Strip, serving sodas and movie tickets. They came here to be discovered.

The Planter's Club was crowded on Christmas Day. Even the gym and the steam-room were full. The restaurant had put on a special lunch for which the waiters had worn red cloaks and white beards. Now they had discarded the costume and were picking their way through the tanned bodies bearing trays full of drinks. Some of the drinks were more like vases of flowers, stuck with garnishes of cucumber and cress, pineapple slices and cherries. Each time a waiter came through the swing doors there were a few bars of 'Nature Boy' or 'Too Darn Hot', played on an electric organ. Sometimes the music was 'Silent Night', but that was the only reminder that this was Christmas Day.

The sunbathers took their task seriously. Seldom speaking, the girls writhed this way and that, shielding an arm or a nose and oiling themselves systematically. Their swimsuits were tiny and their desire to be tanned all over provided a reason for their lewdly spread thighs and unfastened bras. Provocatively, they met male eyes with a blank face as they stroked their breasts with oil and caressed their legs in performances that on film would not have survived the censor.

Bookbinder put *The Hollywood Reporter* upon Kinsey and Jo Palooka, using his highball to prevent the pages flapping in the breeze. He looked around and for a few moments listened to the Pacific Ocean taking a grip upon the shingle and heaving itself up on to the shore like an expiring swimmer. A gust of wind brought a few giggles and a smell of baked crab from a party having a late lunch right at the water's edge.

Bookbinder knew the men: his publicist Weinberger, two of Koolman's distribution people and Edgar Nicholson. He heard Stone stir and heard him gently slap the girl beside him. She wriggled sleepily. 'Who are you looking at, Kagan?' said Stone.

'So you are awake?'

'I never go to sleep in the sun. Sunburn can wrinkle your skin in a way from which it never recovers, a doctor told me that. Who are they?'

'Weinberger and your limey pal, Edgar Nicolson, who I tested for your part.'

'Was he any good?' Stone examined a mark on his forearm. He studied it with the same dispassionate care that a doctor would offer a rich patient.

'He'd be OK for a butler or a duke or something. I thought maybe the thief could be a Britisher.'

Stone was a deep bronze colour: he'd need no make-up to pass as a half-Mexican cowhand. The ancient bleached shorts, ragged and torn around the leg, were in keeping with the hard muscular physique. He affected battered sneakers, too, so that a casual glance persuaded many members that he was a beach-comber or hired help from the club's kitchen.

Lazily he said, 'Hold on, old son. I have a couple of tricky scenes to do with the thief.'

'It's just an idea.' Bookbinder turned to look at the ocean. The subject was closed. The North Pacific current brought large man-eating waves, deceptively gentle in colour and as quiet as an ambush. They were not like the waves that had destroyed Stone's sandcastles on English beaches. These were giant waves. Everything here was big: not only the sea but the rain-storms, train wrecks, droughts and disasters. The fees and the fame were gigantic too, and the humiliation crippling and the obscurity profound.

Stone stirred his drink so that the ice clattered. He liked the sound. Only last year he'd been an unemployed actor tramping around London in the rain because he couldn't afford a cab. He turned over and dug his shoulders into the sand. Above him the blue sky was latticed with palm fronds like a cutaway shot in some corny movie. It was wonderful to feel that sun. Better this pampered luxury life under California sky than the poverty-stricken unheated austerity of London. Better the plastic smiles and bogus halloos of Hollywood than the bitchy faint praise the English offered in the name of sincerity, and the envious jibes they called wit.

'I'm here to stay, Kagan.'

'You'll roast. And if you get much darker you'll have problems with the doorman.'

Stone gave a nervous laugh. 'You know what I mean. Whatever happens to this one, I'll do another picture and hundreds more after that. I'm staying, and I'm going to the top.'

Bookbinder laughed, not scornfully, but with genuine full-bellied amusement. Stone laughed too: it had sounded like something from an old Joan Crawford film.

'That's called the Hollywood bug, Eddie.' Only a few weeks ago, Stone had been lecturing him on the superiority of European films and the supremacy of the stage.

Stone picked up a handful of warm sand. Long before they began shooting, the producer had established his right to patronize his discovery, but Stone did not resent this. The Hollywood bug. Stone smiled. The producer's time at the war had provided him with the experience of hardship, but he couldn't understand how different was the permanently under-privileged life from which Stone had emerged. 'I don't care what it's called,' said Stone, 'Hollywood is a sort of Pandora's box . . . you'll never understand what it's like for an actor like me . . .' Stone pulled a face. His face-pulling and sudden laughs were what marked him as a nervous hopeful rather than the cool sophisticated young star that he so much wanted to be.

'Pandora's box!' said Bookbinder. 'From that came all the ills the flesh is heir to.'

'You know what I mean,' said Stone.

'Yes, I know,' said Bookbinder.

Stone squinted into the sunlight. 'Is that Koolman coming out of the restaurant – the one in the gold-coloured beach robe – he's looking this way.'

Bookbinder sat upright, pushing his hands deep into the sand in order to see over the bodies. 'I heard he flew in this morning – Christmas morning, can you beat it. That's Leo Koolman, and that's his Uncle Max behind him on the porch.'

' "The Koolmans are coming, hurrah, hurrah. The Koolmans are coming, hurrah, hurrah," ' sang Stone softly, in his carefully practised accent. It was almost perfect.

Just behind Koolman junior was a fellow from NY Publicity and, stepping with caution, Phil Sanchez, who had now become young Koolman's senior executive assistant.

Phil Sanchez was twice Leo's age. Until a few months before he had been old Max's hatchet-man and helper. He'd taken Koolman junior to his first ball-game. Now he was an important factor in the continuity of the Koolman empire. 'Your uncle would never do business with him;' or, 'Your uncle checked those sort of returns with the local bank: I've got the names and phone numbers.' Sanchez had been in the fur trade with old Max, and one chronicler of the Hollywood scene called him 'the court jester to Sultan Max'; others, more cruel, called him court dwarf. The truth was even more anachronistic: he was a story teller. He read books selected as possible epics and recounted them to old Max on journeys, between meetings or strolling around the studios. Sanchez was close behind young Koolman. All four men wore dark glasses and plain beach robes, and they achieved a curious uniformity as they marched in step across the sand. Stone's murmured song made them both silly and sinister at the same time.

Bookbinder drank some of his highball, and Stone ran a comb through his hair. The bodies around them did not move: they were stiffly posed like shop-window dummies, each placed upon its coloured rectangle of cloth and inside its exact plot of sand.

'They are going for a swim,' said Stone.

'Into the ocean,' noted Bookbinder with surprise. The pool was crowded, but it was not considered smart to swim in the sea. 'Let's go,' said Bookbinder.

'Where?'

'Into the ocean with Koolman.'

'Why?'

'Don't be dumb, Eddie. He wants to talk with us.'

'What about?'

'Jesus only knows.'

'How can you tell that's what he wants?'

'I don't know how I can tell, Eddie: it's something to do with being around this town too long, but believe me, that's what they want.'

Leo Koolman was not then the thick-necked, bald tycoon that Ben Shahn painted for a 1955 cover of *Time* Magazine, or the pop-eyed groveller that a mistimed flashbulb had captured bowing to the Queen at the Royal Command film a couple of years later. He moved across the beach with the spring and poise of a middleweight contender. Nor was his voice the harsh croak with which he was later to feign perpetual anger. This Leo Koolman could still laugh, and if his syntax had been copied from the Cohns and Schenks and Mayers, at least there was an element of mockery to be heard in it. That this irony soon disappeared from Leo Koolman's demeanour must be blamed upon the men around him who were so determined not to detect it.

But on Christmas Day 1948 Leo Koolman was young. He enjoyed parodying Harry Cohn's strut while holding a finger aloft in a mannerism he had invented for himself. He stared straight ahead, talking out of the side of his mouth, as he explained in exact detail how his subordinates were to splash about in the ocean and how they were to smile as they did it.

Koolman and his two aides gave their robes to the lifeguard and stepped into the sea. His aides found excuses to linger in order not to get too far ahead. Phil Sanchez held a clasped fist high against his throat in a stagey gesture of apprehension.

Bookbinder followed Stone as he picked his way through the girls like a master *rôtisseur* checking a chilled meat wharf. The lotions and imported perfumes hung in the air until they reached the salty putrefactive smell of the sea. Stone entered the water cautiously. He was concerned about the special tanning lotion that the make-up department had compounded for him, and about the lacquer that held his hair in place, and the trace of mascara that darkened his lashes. Stone hated all oceans. His face was contorted, and he closed his eyes as its coldness struck his body. It was a surprisingly childish gesture for a young fit man, Bookbinder thought.

'Are there sharks?' said Stone.

'If there are, they won't come near Koolman,' said Bookbinder.

When they were only a few yards away, the great man dipped under the water and came out spluttering. Now that his hair was plastered to his skull, Bookbinder noticed a bald patch on his crown. He'd go bald before he was thirty-five, just as his uncle had done.

Bookbinder tried to anticipate what they would say. All three were up to their chests in the water. The breakers hit Koolman first, lifting him a fraction of a moment before the other two, so that they were like parts of a mechanical toy that shared the same mechanism.

'Enjoying Hollywood?' Koolman called softly to Stone, as soon as they were in earshot. It wasn't a question to which Koolman needed an answer. 'Yeah, yeah,' he continued, 'of course you are, of course you are.'

'It's wonderful,' said Stone.

'Bookbinder treating you OK: car, dressing-room, a chance to see the town once in a while?' Again Koolman answered himself. 'Sure he is, that's fine. That's terrific. You're looking good, Kagan. Swell, I saw some of your rushes. It's good, maybe it's a smash: too early to tell yet, but . . .' He turned to look at

263

his grim-faced aides. They had come closer to hear what he said, for he did not raise his voice. 'Didn't I tell you guys to splash around and have fun. Didn't I tell you I didn't want to attract attention – just have a little conversation with Mr Stone here – all it needs in a place like this is some dummy with Louella Parsons' phone number and suddenly I'm in the middle of . . .' He turned back to Stone. 'Places like this . . .' he shook his head in despair, '. . . full of dead-beats trying to make a buck in the movies.' Behind Koolman the two executives again began jumping up and down in the waves, laughing and chuckling and throwing water at each other. None of it splashed on to Koolman. When he spoke again his voice was sad and plaintive. 'What are you trying to do to me, Eddie?'

'What?' said Stone.

'I thought we had this whole thing straightened out. At my party when we fixed for your wife to fly out here. You promised to stay away from this girl. Why do you do this to me, Eddie?'

'I've only seen her twice.'

'And phone calls.' Stone nodded a confession. Koolman said, 'Hurt me, you hurt the movie. Hurt the movie, you hurt yourself. Can't you see that, Eddie?'

'Two visits and three calls,' said Stone. 'That's all, honestly.'

'Suppose the super at her place recognized you, or some cabbie had carried you before? Do you know what kind of muck-opera the papers would make out of this?'

'You're right,' said Stone.

'OK,' said Koolman. He turned awkwardly as a wave knocked him askew. Under the arm of the publicity man there was a towel, and now he took this and unwrapped an envelope from it. He passed it to Stone.

Eddie Darling,
    They will have told you about it. I'm going away. They've given me a lot of money so I'm going away, I signed all the papers like your friends said. It wouldn't have been any good with us because I was married three years ago to a guy from New York. He left me. He was no good. I wouldn't have been

right for you Eddie. It's better that we split like this specially with the money and all. Don't try to find me, it's better. I thought about it for both of us. And there is your wife. And it wouldn't have been no good. Not with it spoiling it all for you and the movie like you said. There's nothing for me to stay here for. I'll be seeing you in your movies, Eddie. And I know you'll be thinking of me sometimes and wondering if I'm looking at you on the screen. Your wife is a lucky woman Eddie but I suppose she knows that already. It wouldn't have been any good and I shouldn't have told you wrong about being married and all that but it was only because I loved you.

INGRID

The note was written on lined paper torn from a school exercise book. As he read it, Stone noticed tiny drops of seawater that splashed on to the words and made the ink run down the sheet in rivulets of light blue.

'Where is she?'

'Give me that,' said Koolman. He took the letter from Stone and read it carefully. 'Someone left it with the cop on Gate Four, just after midnight last night. That's all I know.'

'And you just brought it along to me?' said Stone. Nothing seemed more unlikely. If the girl had really run away, Koolman would be demanding information about her whereabouts. But perhaps it was better like this, easier on his conscience to believe that the girl went away of her own accord. Stone was sweating. He dabbed a hand in the sea and rubbed it over his face. He could taste the salt.

'Oh, I guessed it was from the girl,' admitted Koolman. 'Phil talked with her last week, but she promised not to write notes or any of that.' Koolman passed the note to Sanchez. 'That piece of paper could cost me your whole publicity campaign. That's the gratitude I get: I pleaded with her not to write.'

'Poor Ingrid.'

'She's got five thousand dollars,' said Koolman.

'More than that,' said Stone.

'You're right – more than that. You've got through ten grand in as many weeks and not a nickel has gone into your bank.'

Stone didn't answer.

'So you had better start talking,' said Koolman. 'She's putting the bite on you.'

'I gave her a used Chevvy and some money for clothes. I want to take care of her.' He smiled bitterly. 'The bite on me! Ingrid's not like that.'

'I want your mind on your work,' said Koolman. 'You owe that to your director and to Bookbinder here. He's really gone out on a limb for you, kid. Isn't it time you started giving him a little trust and affection in return.'

'Someone's got to take care of her,' said Stone.

'I was taking care of her. I will take care of everything if that's what you want,' said Koolman. 'But stop meddling.'

'Yes, you take care of her.' Stone sighed with relief. 'I leave it to you.'

'Don't snow me, honey,' said Koolman.

'No,' said Stone. 'You take care of her.'

Koolman had grown up on a generous diet of gratitude. He'd not leave Stone without a helping of it. 'Your wife . . . how can you do these things to us all?'

It was only with effort that Stone kept his voice level and without rancour. He spoke slowly. 'You take care of her, Mr Koolman.'

'A wonderful wife you have in Mary. You should be ashamed . . . you promise me you'll go back to Mary right away: ask her forgiveness and promise to cherish her always. You'll do that for me?'

Perhaps Koolman was the only person present who didn't expect Stone to become angry. There was silence until a red Ferrari came down the ramp of the San Jorge turnpike. The driver gunned the motor so that it throbbed with a visceral note. It pushed up to a hundred on the straight past the club entrance. Many people turned to watch it go. Something about it: its colour, its newness, or perhaps the way it was handled, made them sure that there was a famous star at the wheel. The sound of its motor continued through the hum of the holiday traffic even when it was far past Sandy Point. Stone said, 'I'll do as you say, Mr Koolman.'

Koolman looked away from the sound of the car. 'There are

266

pile-ups on that stretch every day. Nearly every fatality makes a production problem somewhere.' He beckoned his men and they moved closer. Phil Sanchez still kept one hand unnaturally high and close to his chest. To the men Koolman said, 'We're not out of trouble yet.' He turned to Stone. 'It's better the girl and the kid disappear. No more letters, no visits, no nothing.'

'Yes, Mr Koolman.'

'An official adoption through a recognized society.'

'Can that be done without . . .'

'Sure, sure. The studio donates fifty grand a year to one of the adoption societies: I'm on the committee there. I'll just need your signature on some papers, right?'

'Yes, Mr Koolman.'

'And this British actor . . .'

'Nicolson,' supplied Bookbinder. 'Edgar Nicolson.'

'Edgar Nicolson, right. Will be the father. His blood group is compatible. He'll sign the paternity and we'll have it all kosher for you. The witnesses have been taken care of: and anyway, one Britisher looks like another to people round here.' He took Stone's tanned arm. 'But this time, sweetheart, it's finito. This time you'd better know that I'm taking no more chances. Right?' He raised his index finger.

Stone looked at him closely and gave an almost imperceptible nod. The other men all said, 'Right.'

'Are we sure that Nicolson will play ball?' said Bookbinder.

'Yes,' said Koolman as his mind moved on to his next problem. Only a man with custody of fame and fortune in such large amounts could predict men's actions with such certainty. 'Maybe he would be good in that part of the horseman who rides on . . .'

'We tested him for that part already.'

'And how was he?'

'Perfect, Leo.'

Koolman smiled. He stepped between Bookbinder and Stone and, taking them both by the arm, moved back towards the shore. The waves tried to wrench the three men apart, but Koolman clung too tightly to allow it. 'Give this Nicolson a few extra lines, Kagan. I'll send you a couple of writers. If you don't like the way it looks, you can always lose that footage in the final cut. Got me, Kagan?'

'I've got you, Leo.' Even Bookbinder was sweating by now. Beads of perspiration formed on his temples and along his upper lip. Perhaps it was due to the heat reflecting off the ocean. All the men were sweating, except Koolman. He said, 'The Studio is a mother and a father, Eddie. You remember that in future. The first sign of trouble, you come and see me, any time of day or night. That's the way it works in this industry: at least, in my outfit it does.'

Stone nodded. Bookbinder said, 'We're grateful, Leo, and that's a fact.'

'Yes,' said Stone. 'Thanks a lot, Leo. I appreciate the way you came and talked to me personally. Especially it being Christmas Day and everything.' Bookbinder nodded to Stone as if he'd just mastered a complex phrase in conversational Sanskrit.

Koolman scarcely heard Stone. He was tired, and now, his task fulfilled, he allowed fatigue to show on his face and in his voice. 'And get him back to his wife, Kagan. Full of whores and dead-beats, places like this.' He didn't wait for Bookbinder's assent, he waved to his Uncle Max. Perhaps there was something in the gesture that told the old man that everything would be all right, for he turned and went back to his car.

The lifeguard was waiting with Koolman's beach robe. Koolman made a little signal that caused Phil Sanchez to open his raised fist and smooth flat a warm crumpled dollar bill, which he handed to the lifeguard.

Koolman marched off across the beach weaving between the sunbathers. His aides waved goodbye with haste enough to keep only a pace behind the master.

15

MGM is like a medieval monarchy, palace revolutions all the time.

Gottfried Reinhardt

Man From the Palace has a place in the history of films. Even before it was on the floor, and despite what happened afterwards, it was still a milestone. A new style of film finance company was putting up enough money to make a large scale feature film. The split of the cassette profits were already agreed, and there were people who thought they would be worth ten times the money that the film earned in cinemas. Such benefits had persuaded a superstar to take all his money in deferments and percentages, and that example set the style for a budget that was confined only to expenses that would be seen by the camera. Taken in conjunction with the reputation of the three men involved, this added up to a new departure for an industry that seemed to be going nowhere. Those journalists who'd predicted a movie revolution every year for the last decade were predicting it again.

Of course, one had to allow for the hyperbole of both journalism and movie-makers. The money had come from a new sort of company, but Continuum's twenty-one cinemas could never liquidate the investment, so some time in the future they would have to do an old-fashioned distribution deal. The cassette business might become bigger than the circuits, but how long would it be before enough customers owned machines to screen them. The pessimists said that the interest charges on *Man From the Palace* would make it impossible to recoup its cost. Stone had agreed to take no money up front, but they were doling him out a thousand pounds a week in unquestioned expenses, and that can be very nice if you are in Stone's tax bracket. What's more, the production was still footing the bill for superbly furnished dressing-rooms, luxury trailers and limousines with drivers on duty twenty-four hours a day. None of that would be seen by the camera, and nor would the lunch that I was having that day with Stone, but Bookbinder's publicity department had already offered to pick up the bill.

Stone said the TV people would be finished well before lunchtime, but I knew better. His vast house was a challenge to any documentary camera crew, and they trailed cables through every room and littered the hall with lights to shoot Stone looking down from the carved *galleria* and have the painted Venetian ceiling in shot beyond him.

The TV interviewer was an elegant teenager of about fifty. His coal-black eyes and a fierce scowl were known in every home in Britain. He wore a lounge suit of conservative cut, but made from brocaded tapestry. It was said to be the first one. His hair was long enough to cover his ears and touch the deep collar of his shirt. His handkerchief was being refolded for the fifth time. This time it was exactly right. 'You can put the mirror down now,' he told his director, who had been peering over it to talk.

'Poor little rich boy,' said the director, resting his chin upon the top of the mirror.

'Empire without an heir,' explained the interviewer. 'Track in on that. It's just a thirty-second clip for the summing up. Big close-up: frightened eyes for the end. Your interiors for the beginning.'

'Suppose Stone digs all this bread, though? Suppose he's an unfrightened happy little rich boy?'

'The script's been approved now,' said the interviewer, 'it's too late for changes like that.' The director gave me a secret wink and raised his eyebrows in anguish.

Their filming began with Stone reading a tooled leather edition of 'any great-looking book, the title won't read with the wide-angle on', as he sat at the fireplace of his Louis XIV library. 'Gas poker or something, Harold. Any flame out of focus behind him, we'll flicker a red gel on him for firelight. And for Christ's sake draw the curtains, or we'll get the sun on the river.'

The camera and its crew tracked with him to the library door, then they moved their equipment and continued the filming upstairs in the Japanese dining-room – 'So who the hell's going to know it's a different part of the house?' – and finally the breakfast-room that led to the garden.

'During the tracking shot I'll be spouting some crap like, "but not all students of drama end up with less than five hundred pounds a year. Marshall Stone is one of the highest-paid actors in the world. It was at his country house in Kent that he answered the same question." Hey, that's not bad. Did you get that down in shorthand, Agatha? Great, great, great.' He liked to add his own creative touch to the script. That's why he wouldn't allow the *TV Times* to describe him as a TV personality. That's just for jokeless comics who wished they could sing and dance. He was a creative man, a specialist on the arts. Just as he'd been TV specialist on cars, America and ballroom dancing at other stages of his career. He smoothed his greying hair before applying a holding spray to the sides.

To me the great house, and its extraordinary and varied décor, had always looked like the dressed sets of a studio where a dozen epics were waiting to go. The presence of the TV technicians and their equipment made it even more so. I wondered if they were going to play it like that in 'The Business of Acting – a TV Inquiry into the Arts Today'. But if they intended to roast an actor for their feast, they were too artful to give him a hint of it.

'What do you think?' said Stone.

'Be careful,' I said.

'What of?'

'I don't know.' Stone thought it was an instance of media battling for him. He smiled knowingly and walked over to the interviewer.

Stone was pleased that the TV people were so affable. The interviewer admired his antiques and his horses and exchanged with Stone his considerable knowledge of both. The interviewer strolled across the lawn to where his Bentley was being used as a dressing-room and wardrobe. To Stone he said, 'At my place in Dorset I'm having to put in more stabling. So far

I've done no racing but there's one filly that I bought two years ago for a song . . .' He crossed his fingers.

'It's a damned expensive hobby,' said Stone.

The interviewer nodded gravely, as any rich owner would. He touched the huge knot of his tie and closed his eyes as the make-up girl applied a touch of colouring to his lips. She moved away and he looked around to be sure that the two chairs had been placed so that the oriental garden would be seen in the background of the two-shot.

'You've got the tea pavilion and the hump-backed bridge.'

'Out of focus,' said the camera operator, his voice muffled as his face pressed against the viewfinder. The interviewer leaned close and Stone smelled an expensive cologne that was advertised as being made from rum and tobacco. 'These talking heads are not very boxy, Marshall, old chap. Keep your face as animated as possible.'

The boy on the Nagra nodded to show that he'd used that to adjust his recording level. 'Let's go,' said the director.

The interviewer's screen voice was rich and responsible, like a High Court judge in a treason trial. The voice he used to the camera crew might have been instruction for a jury, but interviewees were men accused. 'For you, Marshall Stone, superstar extraordinary, the rewards have been bountiful and the privileges many. Cars, jet planes, yachts and palaces are at your command. At your instance film companies have paid vast sums to bring great playwrights and eminent writers to your service, and yet you have remained essentially a commercial actor.'

Stone blinked. He wasn't sure whether he was being invited to comment. The interviewer nodded to him. 'I'm not sure what a commercial actor is,' he said. 'Surely the only people who are not commercial are those who live on charity.'

The interviewer gave no sign of having heard Stone's reply. He leaned close to his script and read the next question. 'Nowadays you employ agents, secretaries, accountants, business managers, lawyers, PR men and Press agents. You command an army of domestic servants in your many houses. You have a yacht crew and a private pilot for your jet. Tell me,

Marshall Stone, have you time left for the simple art of acting?'

Stone fielded. 'I don't know about simple.' He touched his eyebrow with a fingertip. It was nicely spontaneous. 'You talk of time: all these things are ways to buy time. Time is a sacred element in an artist's life: time to study, time to think ...' another pause, '... and the root of all drama: time to observe life.'

'The root perhaps of all art,' affirmed the interviewer, with godlike impartiality. 'But there's a Parkinson's Law for business. And, whether you like it or not, Marshall Stone is a business. You employ as many people as, and gross much more than, many small factories. Can an actor run a business?'

Stone smiled into camera. 'I've had no complaints so far. I think I'm a pretty good businessman.'

'Given the astronomical fees that your name commands, would a good businessman spend so much on non-productive personal comfort? Would he devote so much time to observing, thinking and studying? Surely a good businessman would be tempted to take the money and run?'

'You can't expect me to discuss the possible temptations of hypothetical businessmen, still less their possible fall,' said Stone. The interviewer waited for him to continue. 'My plane means that on location I can get home overnight instead of staying in a local hotel. My house in Beverly Hills is there because a lot of my work is still done in California. My yacht provides my only absolute and uninterrupted relaxation, and my technical advisers are a necessary evil in a system that levies invidious taxes upon successful men.'

The interviewer smiled. 'All of which, Mr Stone, leads me to ask why. To whom are you hurrying home in your jet plane? For whom are you working so hard that you need a yacht to relax? To whom will you be leaving the empire you have built, aided by armies of tax advisers and managers?'

Stone wore a fixed smile. The TV man continued, 'You've a reputation for being a loner, Mr Stone. It is a long time since your name was linked to anyone's in any meaningful way.' Again he paused, and this time it was clear that he wanted to strain Stone's smile to the utmost. 'You have mastered the business of acting better than anyone, but in doing so you have built an empire without an heir.'

It was a fade-out line if ever I heard one, and the camera operator must have thought the same, for he began a slow zoom that would end as a big close-up of Stone's frightened eyes. I think they were hoping for a 'yes'.

'Cut,' said the director.

Stone leaned towards the interviewer and said, 'When I saw that piece of cabbage stuck to your tooth, I thought, oh my God, he's lost a cap, but then during your last question you swallowed it.' Stone smiled.

'I see,' said the interviewer, and he smiled carefully, without opening his lips.

Stone waved a perfunctory farewell to them as he took the bend on the drive a trifle too fast. A shower of gravel sprayed over the whole crew. The interviewer was sitting alone on the lawn doing his noddies. He was saying, '. . . doesn't this luxury sometimes cause you to lose sight of the simple art of acting?' into the lens, and then doing a few smiles and nods so that they could cut back to him while Stone was talking. As the gravel hit them he frowned, and the cameraman stopped work until he could do his hair again.

'Wouldn't you know he used to be on BBC2,' said Stone. 'The questions are longer than the answers.'

'And more carefully rehearsed,' I said.

Stone gave a short chuckle; the joke was on him, and he didn't hide the fact that he knew it.

'A Roman Holiday,' he said. 'Yes, film stars are always a good target for bastards like that. I hate television. Do you know that, I really hate television and all those pompous bastards in it.'

'Yes,' I said. 'I liked the cabbage on his tooth moody.'

'I should have listened to you,' said Stone. 'I'm too trusting, that's my trouble.'

'As a matter of fact, Marshall, I agree.' We were doing ninety, so he only shot me the briefest of glances. At that moment I was as close to him as I ever got. The grimace that he gave me instead of his bright smile was the nearest he came to lowering the armour glass behind which he cowered.

He concentrated on his driving for ten miles or more. 'Did you see the camera?' he asked.

'Yes,' I said, 'Sixteen millimetre.'

'An Eclair with an Angenieux twelve to one-twenty zoom, and you know what that means.'

'What?'

'It means that last shot was just my eyeballs. Those snide bastards. Do they think I'm queer or something. Is that what he was getting at?'

'Christ knows,' I said. We drove in silence. I wondered whether he'd remember to have my MG brought up to town as he'd promised to when suddenly remembering that we must eat lunch in town.

Stone handled his Rolls well. He dedicated himself to controlling it, doing all sorts of fancy hand signals, and giving neat stabs of the accelerator that made heads turn. It interested me that he should be so particular about the car, even to the point of closing the door after me and wiping the handle clean of my prints.

We couldn't speak in the car, the windows were open, and the clock and the wind and the roar of the engine prevented it. I wondered why Stone had been so keen that I should ride in his car instead of following him in my own. Perhaps he just wanted company, but watching him at close quarters made me believe that for him it was just as important that I saw him as that I listened to him. He had, after all, made his fortune by his use of other men's words, not by his own.

'I made a twit of myself, didn't I?'

'No, certainly not.'

'I know I did, Peter. Sometimes I can't find the words. It's all right for you writers, you can always take care of yourselves. Did you ever notice how every book about movies tells you the actors are creeps, the producers are bastards and the writers long-suffering geniuses? Every book!'

'They write in pretty good parts for themselves,' I admitted.

'Just a quick lunch. I've got to see these people,' he said sadly. 'A star is only as good as his last publicity.' He glanced at me. 'That's a joke. I read it in *Reader's Digest*.'

We drove in silence for a long while, except that a couple of times he said, 'Queer, is that what the bastard was getting at?'

The traffic slowed us to walking pace at Marble Arch. Stone said, 'What do you think of that, then?' There were two young girls on the pavement ahead of us. His remark was out of keeping with our previous style of conversation.

'I don't fancy yours,' I said.

Stone smiled and sounded the car horn imperiously, and then slowed the car alongside them. 'Jump in, girls,' he called.

The girls turned round and giggled. Several people were watching the exchange with varying degrees of amusement and disapproval. Had Stone wanted to prove to me his total ineptitude with women, he could not have arranged it better.

'They *want* to get in the car,' he assured me. 'They've recognized me all right.' I tried to smile and make a joke of it. I wasn't sure how much I liked it as a biographer, but as a bystander it was monumentally embarrassing.

The two girls took another look at him before hurrying into a shop.

'The hell with them,' Stone shouted. 'There are millions more. All the girls want to know what it's like, doing it with a film star, Peter.' He laughed. 'And I'm always happy to show them. On the back seat, sometimes!'

'I envy you, Marshall.'

'Never short of crumpet. That's one thing about this job.' He wove neatly around a bread lorry and a taxi which hooted angrily.

'We're eating at Jamie's.'

'Good.'

'You may not have heard of it. It's an expensive private club near St James's Palace. The food is great. They know me there.'

'You talked me into it,' I said.

He looked at me in surprise, and then laughed.

We got past the doorman all right. In fact he took the car to park it. The reception clerk recognized Stone, and said how nice it was to see him again. It was a waiter in the hall beyond who told Stone that it was a members-only club. Had Stone said he was a member, instead of, 'Never you mind about that,' that probably would have been the end of it. As it was, he got into an argument with the waiter that only the manager was able to quell. The manager was a small man with a happy mouth and patent-leather hair.

'Delighted to see you again, Mr Stone,' said the manager. 'The boy didn't recognize you.' The manager smiled and tugged his cuffs. He clearly hoped that Stone would smile too, and that it would be a joke they could share on many future visits, but he needed only a few seconds to decide that Stone wanted more than that.

'Imbecile!' the manager called softly at the waiter's back. Even as he said it he was smiling in case he was seen by customers across the room. 'Imbecile! Get your cards! You get your cards! You take a week's pay and you get out of my place! I don't want your sort here! Imbecile.'

'I wouldn't have minded,' said Stone graciously, 'but he grabbed my arm. I can't stand people grabbing my arm.' He amended it. 'I can't stand waiters grabbing my arm.'

'It's all right, Mr Stone,' said the manager. Again he threw an arm in the air to show the waiter that he was fired. 'Come this way, sir. Patrick! Mr Stone has Bloody Mary. A nice Bloody Mary for Mr Stone, Right away, Patrick. No matter about anything else. Is that right Mr Stone, a nice Bloody Mary?' The manager never ceased talking as he ushered us into his restaurant. His words were a salve upon Marshall Stone, as the manager knew they would be. I decided that Marshall Stone was better in the manager's hands than mine. To be a witness to an angry scene can make a barrier between two men that takes years to erode.

The toilet at Jamie's was like the reception hall of a Florentine palace. Far across the marble floor I heard a man say, 'It's going to be a fine day.' It was a pronouncement, as if Leo Koolman had it all planned and paid for. He caught sight of me in the tinted mirrors. 'Hold it, kid,' he called to me. He pressed the lions-head taps and rinsed his hands under the water. A notice said it was specially softened water gently heated to 68 degrees Fahrenheit. Koolman used it as if he'd never known another kind. He screwed up his eyes to see me more clearly. 'Anson. Peter Anson. Right?'

'That's it, Mr Koolman.'

'Came in with Marshall Stone.'

'I'm doing a story on him.'

'Tomorrow they start shooting that movie,' he said. He worked on the principle that only his own films should get free word-of-mouth publicity by having their titles mentioned. 'What's the budget?'

'I don't know.' It was true, but only Leo Koolman would have asked. Just about the only rule the industry clung to was the secrecy of the budget.

'One point seven,' Koolman guessed aloud. He threw water on his face. 'At the most,' he added, and then said, 'dollars.' Since I was no longer one of his employees, Koolman feared that I might not fully understand him.

'Could be,' I said.

'They need six million to do that one properly. It will look like nothing for less than three.'

'Hanratty's a good man.'

'He can only shoot what the production gives him. What's that coronation sequence going to look like on a shoestring budget?'

'I think they might have cut that.'

'They are nuts,' said Koolman. The white-coated attendant put a warm towel into his hand. The notice said they were sanitized and treated under infra-red and ultra-violet light for Koolman's protection and convenience, but I suppose anyone would get the same kind of towel. Koolman finished drying his face and put his spectacles on so that he could look at me closely. 'Best chapter in the book, the coronation. It's got confrontation and colour and conflict. You know why I turned it down?'

It was one of those questions. If I said no, then Koolman is a fool; if I said yes, he'd ask me to tell him. 'Well . . .'

'I turned it down because there are only three directors in the world who can handle big scenes like that. All of them are tied up for the next three years.'

I nodded, although I didn't believe Koolman. He was just preparing a cover story for his stockholders in case *Man From the Palace* was a smash hit. Anyway, Koolman liked to believe that everything came to him first.

'You think it will be a success, Mr Koolman?'

'Married to Stone's first wife, are you?'

'That's it. You think the film will be a success?'

'Call me Leo, Peter,' he said, thus giving himself time to think. Perhaps he was surprised to face a direct question of the sort he was so expert in delivering. He came close to me and lowered his voice. 'You know this business, Peter. They are going to meet problems they don't even know the name of. OK, they get a couple of million bucks from a merchant bank or some other sucker, but all they wind up with is a can of film. They've got to get that movie into theatres. That means selling the trade on the idea that it might be a hit. Publicity and distribution costs me three million a year. How are those amateurs going to compete?'

'A big success, and the trade will come to them.'

'You mean, release it in Europe and hope for a miracle? But can you bet a couple of million bucks on a thousand-to-one chance?'

'Personally, no, but there must be organizations that can.'

Koolman stabbed himself cruelly with his thumb. 'My organization can, Peter, and we turned it down. Remember?' He reached into his pocket, and from his wallet he produced a dozen Xeroxes of a trade Press cutting. He handed it to me and said, 'You want a biography of a kid who's going to be really big, you should be talking to Val Somerset.'

L. A. Spotty; 'Imp' Wow 75G 2d
'Tiger' Tame 75G in 6 Sites
'Tornado' Calm $16,000 3d

Los Angeles

Imperial Verdict showcasting at Chinese hits 150 plus in first two weeks. Equals *Tigertrap* in six locations drive-ins and nabes. *The Long Tornado* is a calm $16,000 in third Crest lap.

'A record-breaking success. You keep it,' Koolman said,

waving the cutting away. He flicked his shoes with the wet towel, and the end of it went black. 'I'm going to be interested to see what your little movie does.' He threw the towel into the basket provided. I had the feeling that anyone even remotely connected with *Man From the Palace* was going to be regarded as Koolman's personal enemy.

'Yes, we'll see,' I said.

He patted my back very gently. 'Don't put any money in there, Peter.' He threw a fifty-pence coin into the saucer under the notices.

'I promise.' Perhaps he meant he was paying for my towel.

'Give my best wishes to your lovely wife.'

As I came from the toilet I passed the manager and the waiter who had incurred Stone's wrath. 'Of course you are not fired', said the manager, 'but keep out of the bastard's way in the future. These people come in here because we are the only people in the world who *do* recognize them!' He looked quickly around the restaurant to be sure that it was all working smoothly. He held his calm confident obsequious smile as he walked quickly but unhurriedly back to his desk at the door. That's show business.

16 *People sometimes say the star system is dead, but this is just not true. Film stars are being paid more now, and have more influence, than ever in their lives. If the movie star is dead, I'd like to be dead that way.*

John Frankenheimer

Cherrington is a public school by definition, simply because it is represented at the Headmasters' Conference, but apart from that, and the facts that it was founded two hundred years before Stowe, and is isolated in 187 acres of fine Shropshire farmland, there is little to be said in its favour. Its scholars write 'public school' when applying for jobs that Etonians, Harrovians and Wykehamists get.

It was at Cherrington that Edward Stone first became aware of the advantages that his cherubic face, short stature and nervous smile could provide for him. He evoked a protective instinct from grown-ups who helped him with his prep, protected him from bullying and turned a blind eye to his misdeeds. The grown-ups were often like Mr Greenwood, the English master — soft-skinned men with gentle voices, damp hands and a look in their eyes that he learned to recognize.

The lessons of Cherrington continued to prove useful. He coexisted with the homosexuals that were attracted to him, accepting their favours without joining their ranks. He kept his virtue, walked with queens nor lost the common touch. Although loving friends did not hurt him, he did not always keep his head.

Lawrence Pastor, director of *Last Vaquero*, caused Stone to lose his head. A chance remark one evening in the viewing theatre, a grasp at his arm and an off-guard look in the director's eyes were enough to launch Stone into a feverish succession of love affairs. Starlets, a script girl and a dozen quickies at The Planter's Club seemed necessary to keep Pastor at his distance.

Stone still found it necessary to reassure new acquaintances with confessions of heterosexual lechery. Just as he'd never been able to keep any of his secret affairs completely secret, for part of the therapy came from telling of them.

But in fact his sexual drive had never matured beyond those years at Cherrington, when his angel face had granted him disproportionate favours. Perhaps the two things were inextricably related: he'd never wanted to mature and face the harsh unforgiving world of adults. For example, his charm never worked in the Army.

It required little effort for a fit young ex-public-school soldier to be sent to an officers' selection board, but it needed more than that to get through. The most successful candidates on Edward Brummage's entry were rough-spoken provincials who proved their aptitude for making bridges from old doors, finding a loose distributor lead in a dud engine and 'appreciating ground'. The British Army was, at that time, disregarding a potential officer's table manners, speech patterns and sophistication. At least, they were in the sort of regiments within Edward Brummage's feasible ambition.

'A public school lad like you, Brummage! Shouldn't have to be told not to dodge round the water obstacle, should we?'

'I'm awfully sorry.'

'No, Sergeant-major, you horrible little man!'

'No, Sergeant-major.'

When the twins from Walsall did it, the bloody sergeant-major grinned and looked the other way. Nor did his school go down well with the other candidates, or the officer instructors.

'Cherrington?'

'Shropshire. Founded two hundred years before Stowe.'

'Stowe, is that another public school? I didn't realize there were so many.'

If only he hadn't said so much to his mother. Uncle Bernard was no problem, but how was he to tell his mother? He knew what was going to happen when he saw his name on the orders.

'I'm awfully sorry, Brummage, I really am. Usually the major would have told you himself but he's up at Div until this afternoon. Look here, stand at ease. It doesn't mean you can't have another crack at a commission later on . . .'

'Where will I go from here?'

'Holding Unit just outside Bristol is where chaps usually go. Cigarette? Public-school chap, aren't you?'

'Cherrington, sir.'

'Yes, I remember.'

'Shropshire.'

'I saw it on your record. Shropshire, is it? Yes, I wondered where it could be. Drama school too, I notice. When you get to a unit, I'd try and follow that up. We had a cook on my last unit. He got on to a concert party as a conjurer. Made an awfully good thing of it too, I remember.'

'It's telling the mater, sir.'

'Ah, yes, that's often the worst bit. Some of the chaps say they've been selected for special duties and have gone off somewhere . . .'

'Spying?'

'Special operations, commandos, anything of that kind. Well, as I say, I'm awfully sorry your marks were too low, but being an officer isn't everything. We need first-class chaps in the ranks too, you know.'

'Yes, sir.'

'By the way, Brummage. The ordnance Brigadier at Division has been screaming for a batman . . .'

'Well . . .'

'It's a devil of a good job for the right chap, Brummage. I'm not allowed to assign a soldier to that job but . . . well, you'd be right there with the top brass. Right where the decisions are made. You'd know more about the progress of the war than I'll ever learn. Or the Major, either. Think it over.'

That same afternoon Private Brummage packed his kit, wrote a difficult letter to his mother and an easy one to his uncle – 'Dear Bernard, You were dead right, and they can stuff their pips where the monkeys put their nuts, all the best, Eddie' – and was on his way to be the personal servant to Brigadier Millington-Ash.

Edward Brummage was bouncing along the by-pass in a 30-cwt rations lorry by the time the Major returned to his office.

'Did you fix old Milly-Ash's bloody batman, John?'

'The actor.'

'Jolly good. You said he'd do it.' The major picked up the telephone and said, 'Get me Brigadier Millington-Ash at Div. Soon as you can.'

'I gave him the "nerve centre of command" speech.'

'Jolly good, John. Old Milly would never have got a batman through usual channels. Even the General has had trouble. He's got a pioneer fellow who scarcely speaks English and keeps serving him his tea in a glass. Hello, sir. Major Hamble here. I think I might have got a rather good chap for you.'

The Major twisted Private Brummage's records around so that he could read them. 'My clerk has just gone to check it now, he won't be a jiffy. A young public-school chap. Yes, public school.' The Major read the name of the public school and then pushed the card away. 'I'm afraid I don't know which public school but, by jove, rather stylish, what? I say, while I'm waiting for my clerk, can I have another word in your ear about these blankets and Sten gun ammo. The . . . yes, I know everyone wants the same thing . . . It's OK? This afternoon? . . . Ah, splendid! There's my clerk now. It's all laid on, apparently: Brummage, Private Edward Brummage.'

THE BIOGRAPHY OF MARSHALL STONE
CHAPTER SIX. FIRST DRAFT

As far as the mountains that looked like purple cardboard, the land was desert. Not undulating dunes of white sand, but rock and scrub and cactus, with hills and mountains high enough to provide homes for bear and mountain lion. There was no road across it, but the best trail for a stage coach was marked by a line of drunken posts between which telegraph wire sagged low enough in places to decapitate a horseman. That was the route the stage took and halfway along it was the ramshackle township where it stopped to change horses.

Even in winter the dusty streets of the town were hot

enough to discourage running, but people did run. The stores and saloons were thronged with restless men. There were a dozen outside the sutler's, and more crowded around the telegraph office. The El Paso stage was having its horses changed in record time and two men were bribing a clerk to sell them a seat on it.

Mrs Grant, the farrier's wife, and her grown-up daughter, Ellen, carefully raised their skirts to ankle height before stepping over the gutter outside the haberdasher's shop. Everyone was responding to the same news; Sioux war parties had been spotted south of the river.

The people all moved with an obsessive silence. The footfalls on the boardwalks were scarcely audible. Horsemen everywhere used all their skill to quiet their mounts, and the stage coach and the wagon had been greased and oiled to eliminate every last squeak. Most bizarre of all was the way in which the call for action caused them to mouth words without uttering a sound. It was all dumb-show.

There was no mistaking the walk of the man who crossed the road as the camera panned gently to hold him in frame centre. He tipped his broad-brimmed hat to the ladies and waved to a soldier who galloped past. It was all there in Stone's walk: the Mexican background, the years of desperate fighting, the calm confidence of the skilled gunfighter. Stone had not given the marshal the slumped-shouldered gait of the cowboy or just the walk of the horseman. He threw his head back and kept his chin high, lifting his boots like a man walking among trip wires. And yet there was a measure of neurosis mixed into this careful portrayal. This man fidgeted with his hat brim too long before tipping it, and too long after, too. His hand went too often to his belt buckle and it seemed sometimes to tremble.

'Cut,' shouted the director.

Behind him an assistant yelled in a fiercer voice, 'First positions, and let's hurry it. And keep the noise down.'

The camera-crane that had slowly brought the purring instrument, and the operator who crouched over it, down from the tower of the fort, stopped. The technicians huddled around it and began their anxious talk. Beyond them, almost hidden in the grey dust, cables were woven into a wide path that led back to the throbbing generator trucks. Jamming the street there were prop trees, dummy cactus plants, signs and notices, some chairs and ten horse-boxes, including a red one that transported special horses that the stunt riders used. Parked on the other side of the make-believe town were sleek trailers housing the make-up studios, changing-rooms, offices and stores. 'Special effects: the gun-fight next. I want to go in five minutes while the marshal is still keyed up.'

Kagan Bookbinder was a muscular man with close-cropped grey hair. He clapped one of the soldiers on the back. 'That was great, Spike, but look up when you speak. The sound guy is having troubles.' The producer watched while a make-up man put more grey powder into the sides of Stone's hair. 'That will do. Go and fix that woman's hair will you, Billy.' He pointed to the farrier's wife. The make-up man waited long enough to remind Bookbinder that he was employed solely to do the hair of the stars – not the feature players – and then he went. Kagan Bookbinder smiled. He had come back from the war a hero. A pursuit pilot with USAAF, he was credited with shooting down three Japanese bombers. He'd brought a lot of technical expertise to this film. Bookbinder knew what really happened when a bullet hit a man. It came with the impact of a sledgehammer: it could knock him over and halfway down the street. For the gunfight sequence the young English actor Edgar Nicolson was being attached to two wires. One of them to take his weight and the other to drag him over backwards as Stone's gun fired.

There were other devices too. Bookbinder rejected the compressed-air pellet-gun that the special effects man used – at close range but out of frame – to knock pieces of plaster out of the wall behind which Stone was sheltering. Book-binder had had small explosive charges placed in the wall to give the effect of high-velocity bullets striking deep into the brickwork. Already there had been small accidents. Twice fragments of brick had broken an actor's skin.

Kagan Bookbinder reached towards his star and twisted

his head in his hands as a vet might inspect the face of a frothy-mouthed dog. 'You'll do, marshal,' he said. The grim-faced actor nodded. He never relaxed enough to become his normal self. So afraid was he of losing the feel of the character he was playing that he acted like him even in the hotel at dinner. The previous night Bookbinder had warned him about spitting on the floor. Everyone was calling him the marshal. It was a good sign, thought Bookbinder.

The first assistant had the amplifier in use again. 'Absolute silence everywhere. I want to hear a pin drop.' He'd said it a thousand times. He would say it at least a thousand more. It wasn't a joke or verbal flamboyance but his standard instruction. 'A pin drop.' His voice echoed against the flimsy wooden sets, some of them only flats. It carried as far as the Indian reservations and across the desert to where the coyotes, the sidewinders and the scorpions waited patiently for the human invaders to finish their work and leave.

The special effects man finished strapping Edgar Nicolson into his harness and placing the blood capsules under his shirt. Nicolson looked back along the street into which the cable would hurl him. Unless he fell expertly there was a good chance of getting hurt. The script called for a stunt man, but he had insisted upon doing it himself and the lens on the second camera had been changed accordingly.

The special effects men straightened from their tasks and waited while the sound crew recorded a couple of minutes of silence. Silences have their own characteristics just as do sounds. When the time came to edit the sound track they might need to intercut a matching moment of silence. This would be it. Two hundred and fifty actors, actresses and technicians remained silent and motionless, as if commemorating those fallen in battle. Even the beat of the generators had stopped, the mighty arc lamps had spluttered and died, as had the air conditioners in the offices, dining-room and commissary.

'OK. That will do. Thank you, everybody. First positions, please.'

Stone moved his hand back alongside his thigh with a smooth movement that drew the heavy Colt Peacemaker out of its resin-softened holster and let it spin on the trigger before it came up, hammer back, in his gloved hand. Again and again he did it, concentrating all the time upon not allowing the exertion to affect his expression. Only by doing the fast draw as a purely instinctive action could he use his brain entirely to act.

The unit publicist watched the gunplay with great satisfaction. Still in his early thirties, Jake Weinberger was an engaging young man with a gruff voice and an Austrian accent that had granted him a short wartime career playing U-boat commanders, Gestapo agents and sentries who inevitably mistook invasions for cats. He'd given this gunfight sequence as an exclusive to a stills photographer from *Look* Magazine. At first the pictures editor had not been keen on it, but after forty-five minutes on the phone to New York, Weinberger had persuaded him that this film would give birth to a star. Weinberger nodded to the stills man. Now he believed it too. This young English actor had the glint of ambition shining in his eyes. He had the look that his friends would soon be referring to as 'star quality'. His enemies would call it 'the killer instinct', but both groups would know that they were talking of the same thing.

'Edgar Nicolson and Edward Stone,' said the stills man, writing the names in his caption note to go with the pictures.

'Make that Marshall Stone,' said Weinberger on an impulse.

'One L?'

'No, two.'

'As in Marshall Plan?'

'Sounds the kind of thing,' agreed Weinberger.

'Ready when you are, marshal,' called the director. Already the actor had learned to identify the lenses. This 50mm used at this distance would give him a medium close-up, taking in his gun hand but also the slightest of changes of expression. He was adjusting his performance accordingly.

'This here was a decent town before you yankee soldiers came here brawlin', cussin' and filmin' our wimminfolk,' said Stone in the voice that he'd evolved for the part. It was a harsh Mexican-accented voice, pitted with hatred and sibilant with spittle. It took the crew a hushed moment to recognize the joke.

Stone read the chapter twice. It didn't seem exactly right, but it was near enough to enable him to recall that day when he got his new name. Just after shooting that gunfight scene they'd had camera trouble: the loader had tried to clean the pressure plate and had bent something so that the film wasn't held flat. Stone went back to the trailer and poured himself a beer. He turned the fan so that it was just a few inches from his face and then he picked up the Los Angeles paper that came each day after lunch. He read the war news from China and noted that his choice of horses had been wrong again. He would have been asleep before the bottom of page ten if it hadn't been for a single column item on a page of local news.

> **ACTRESS DIES IN TURNPIKE PILE-UP**
> Ingrid Rainbow, 25-year-old actress under contract to Koolman Studios, died in the early hours of yesterday morning when her 1948 Chevrolet convertible hit a stanchion of the San Jorge turnpike at the Ocean Plaza exit. Rainbow had been seen in ingénue parts for director Lawrence Pastor, and a studio spokesman said that only recently she had been chosen for an important part in a new Koolman Studios musical. 'She had everything to live for,' said the Studio today.

Finito. Stone read it a second time but had to put the newspaper flat upon the table in order to hold it still enough.

17

All the trouble in the world has been caused by Jews and Irishmen.

Harry Cohn

A film is born on the day that the man in charge of the money nods. It can be weeks later that a letter is written or a Heads of Agreement signed. The film business prides itself on word-of-mouth deals, but most producers take the precaution of having their agent witness the nod just the same.

Soon after that, an extra desk is put into the producer's office, and an associate producer goes over the budget for the fourth time. To give another opinion, a production manager is hired to provide the actual names and figures, the salaries and prices and estimates of the script, page by page for the break-down. The director must be at these meetings to decide where the budget ends and the film begins. 'We don't have to fly the whole crew to Italy, Bert, we can do the sequence by back projection.' A locations manager begins to scout for a likely 'alley in Central European capital', convenient 'hills beyond the city' and possible palaces. And then to haggle with owners and residents about taking down the TV aerials. An art director is crowded into the same office, brandishing large sketches of how his sets might look if built. A costume designer is also there, buried under layout pads and paste papers of delicate colours. Most of these men have chauffeur-driven cars and a secretary to handle their paperwork. So suddenly there are production offices, printed notepaper and a dozen girls hammering typewriters. A unit accountant is hired to pay them, arrange their tax and make everyone economize. He needs three secretaries.

So it went with *Man From the Palace*. Marshall Stone had been given producer's status in return for his investment, ie, taking his fee after the film had been made and exhibited. At first he'd declined this honour that Weinberger had demanded for him. Finally he'd been flattered enough to say yes, although he would in no circumstances accept a producer's credit on the titles and publicity. Bookbinder agreed. But Stone was an actor, and they both knew that when the film was complete Stone would fight tooth and nail for that producer's credit and any other credit he could get, as he had before in such circumstances.

Within two weeks *Man From the Palace* took the giant leap from plan to reality. The offices in Holborn were busy until late evening. Desks were littered with uneaten sandwiches and paper cups that smelled of whisky. There were a dozen phones that seldom ceased to ring, and the GPO worked overtime to install the PBX. Thus began the hectic weeks of pre-production, a time when everyone was needed except the actors.

As *Stool Pigeon* dragged to a close, Marshall Stone changed as he always changed. When the end of a film schedule came near he always resolved that he would go away for a long holiday to somewhere sunny and quiet where his face was unknown. But as the day of his release got nearer, anxiety began to burn in him. He worried about the next offer. Financially there was no need for him to back-to-back his films, and Weinberger was always advising him to arrange more time for rest and preparation, but still the need of a new contract gnawed at him. Even when a script and contract was agreed, he was not calm again. He'd worry whether he'd committed himself to a poor script or a silly director. He'd worry whether the schedule overworked him, or about spending too much time idle. If it was a location picture, he'd worry about the places he would be staying. Was the hotel luxurious enough, and would other stars have been given better accommodation. How good was the air conditioning and what was the food like. Sometimes he'd persuaded film companies to engage a special chef for him. There was the weather, too: what sort of climate was there at this time of year. Stone believed that extremes of temperature played havoc with his complexion.

These baseless fears grew worse every year. The astrologer had been right about that, perhaps because so many of the astrologer's other clients were actors. It was stage fright. Stone remembered watching one of the grand old men of the theatre vomiting into a fire bucket three minutes before an entrance. That was *Heartbreak House*, in Glasgow, when Stone was nursing one line and getting the tea and selling programmes. It had amazed him that stage fright could so afflict an old trouper while Stone strode on to the stage without a qualm: but now he knew more about this 'industrial hazard' of actors. Men who work in tanneries get more and more liable to anthrax, miners gradually succumb to silicosis and old actors finally become paralysed with fright.

Anxiously, Stone waited for the filming to begin, knowing that when it did he would feel much better, just as on the stage a cold tranquillity possessed him and he became an acting machine. And, like a machine, his memory and skill functioned so that each line came automatically and he could use his wits upon his craft, watching the audience in order to judge his timing and his movements, and even to corpse his fellow actors. Just one flick of the eyebrow could do it: he'd made one of the actor knights laugh in the middle of a speech once, but the great man had converted it to a cough before it emerged.

On the first day of filming, Kagan Bookbinder arranged a small celebration. There was a dinner party for the actors and a few of the higher echelon of technicians. Gold cuff-links and telegrams were exchanged, and there were hugs and kisses for all. In Stone's trailer, the mirror was almost hidden under laurels of telegrams from all over the world. Bookbinder bought half a page in *Variety* to say:

> Kagan Bookbinder in partnership with Continuum
> Industries Inc is proud to announce that filming of
> MAN FROM THE PALACE
> will commence in London on September 3rd
> Starring Marshall Stone
> Directed by Bert Hanratty
> A Kagan Bookbinder Production
> based upon the best-seller

Of course he put the cost of it on to his publicity budget along with the gifts and congratulatory telegrams. The typography of the advert was striking. The names of Stone, Bookbinder and Hanratty were the largest elements. Continuum had its logo – the tree of knowledge in which sat a peacock – built into the advert. The name of the man who had written both book and script was not there at all. On the other hand, he was the only person concerned who had already been paid.

This advert brought a warm and spontaneous response from all quarters. Telegrams came from almost everyone with whom the makers of *Man* had ever done business, and not a few who hoped they would do in the near future. Weeks after shooting began, greetings were still coming in. Stone opened a newly arrived one during a sandwich lunch in his trailer.

'Schmuck,' he said. He passed the telegram to Bookbinder.

WISHING YOU AND YOURS ALL THE MOST WONDERFUL GOOD LUCK STOP THINKING OF YOU ALL AND LOOKING FORWARD TO GREATER AND GREATER THINGS FROM A GREAT TEAM

EDGAR NICOLSON

Stone said, 'He's in New York trying to get a deal on that haunted farmhouse script.'

'What's his title?' asked Hanratty.

'Who knows what the title is,' Stone replied. 'He changes it every week.'

Bookbinder said, 'Back in the 'fifties Edgar did some great little movies.'

Hanratty answered, 'No one wants a guy who made some great little movies. Especially if he made them in the 'fifties. What everyone wants is guys who made bloody awful twenty-million-dollar movies. If Edgar had made a twenty-million-dollar flop, he'd be in business.'

Bookbinder said, 'It's the magic of the numbers. There's more drama in a guy who squandered twenty million than in a guy who made ten grand profit.'

It was warm inside the trailer, but the portable gas fire made the air heavy and Stone feared he might get one of his tension headaches. He leaned back and slid the tiny window open.

Lunch was just beginning. The drivers and the hangers-on were always first in the line at the catering bus. He watched his stand-in and his driver take their trays and walk to the trestle tables that had been erected in the garage. Beyond them the forecourt of the 'palace' was crowded with transport: buses, cars, generators, arc lamps, pantechnicons loaded with extra furniture and a gilded coach. A taxi driver who had delivered two dozen enormous bunches of flowers for the reception scene tooted impatiently at the men unloading the furniture before driving across the lawn to escape.

Plasterers were taking moulds of the front doors to reproduce replicas for the location shots in Italy. The house and grounds were crowded with busy workers, and cables and wires went into the house through every window and door, as if the ancient mansion was undergoing some bizarre emergency surgery that it might not survive.

'What happened to the Arctic film you did with him?' Hanratty asked Stone.

'Koolman is crazy for it,' said Stone. 'Everyone says it's certain for an Oscar. Leo says I'll get a nomination, at the very least.'

Hanratty nodded. 'Koolman likes Nicolson, I've noticed that. Every time Nicolson is in trouble, Koolman arrives like a fairy godmother and waves the wand. You ever notice that?'

'No, I can't say I've noticed that,' said Stone. He put a mint in his mouth. He had a constant fear that his breath would offend someone.

Bookbinder smiled. It was the first time he'd smiled since Continuum started pestering them to cut back on their budget. This lunchtime chat was to decide if the battle scenes and the whole Italian location could be deleted. But so much construction work had already been done, and so many contracts signed, that the resulting saving of cash would have done little to reduce Continuum's anxieties. The filming in Italy would stand. Hanratty looked at his watch. 'Time to go.'

Stone said, 'How soon will you need me?' He put aside the newspaper on which he'd carefully marked the horses he favoured.

'I've got the long-shots to do, then I can get rid of the

extras.' Hanratty crouched down in front of Stone and spoke to him earnestly. 'Your first shot this afternoon,' said Hanratty. 'The prince coming up through the entrance hall . . .'

'Yes?'

'This is not Richard and Liz entering Sardi's. The prince doesn't pause or look around to see who's there. This prince is a guy who has never known obscurity. Don't look where you're going, Marshall. He knows that no one, and nothing, will ever be in his way. Talk to your aide and look only at him as you speak. That will be camera side, go right on through the door until I yell: I probably won't cut on the aide's line.'

'I'm still having trouble with those bloody high boots.'

'Leave them off for this shot. We won't see you below the waist. But keep the sword on.'

Stone said, 'Have you worked out how I open the window without the girl seeing me?'

Hanratty smiled. 'Don't worry, Marshall: the magic of cinema.'

'Good,' said Stone and went back to the racing page. Hanratty had worked out a way to do a tricky piece of business that they were both keen to do as one continuous shot. Stone had grown dependent upon the surly Irishman. There was never a question about plot, character, lighting, movement, set or make-up for which Hanratty didn't have an answer. They were good answers, too. Hanratty stood up.

'Can you get rid of the lights today, Bert?' asked Bookbinder.

'The two brutes? I'm sorry I had to use them, but I couldn't fix the bounce-lights without marking the ceiling, and only the brutes would have the throw we needed. They'll go back today.'

'Great,' said Bookbinder. He brought out his pigskin cigarcase and offered it to Stone, who declined with a shake of the head.

'The production will soon be cutting back on the producer's cigars,' said Stone.

Bookbinder looked up. It wasn't the first time that he'd suspected Stone of sarcasm. 'That's about it, Marshall.'

'If you get into real trouble you can always use the guest suite at Twin Beeches.'

'I might take you up on that, the way it's going.'

'Union trouble?' said Stone.

'Depends what you mean by trouble. Is it trouble when they force me to pay first-class air fares for the whole crew, from clapper boys to wardrobe assistant, when tourist tickets would give me an extra week of shooting? Is it trouble when they make me hire cars to collect them from their homes because it's not good enough to pick them up in a mini-bus?'

Stone shrugged. 'It's the same for every film.'

'But that doesn't make it a good idea, Marshall. Already Continuum are asking me why I didn't make it an Italian-based production, and I'm having trouble in giving them convincing answers.'

'But the problems are money problems?'

'It's that filthy stuff, Marshall.'

'Continuum has got to understand that no movie keeps to its budget to the exact penny, Kagan. Haven't they got anyone there who knows the movie business? I'll talk to them. Kagan. Perhaps they'll listen to me.'

'That's nice of you, Marshall, but it's not like that.' Bookbinder looked at his unlit cigar for a moment, and then thought better of it and brought out his pipe and tobacco. He filled his pipe slowly, as he thought out what he was going to say. 'We are going to be four hundred thousand dollars over, Marshall.'

'No wonder Continuum are squealing.'

Bookbinder smiled grimly. 'They don't even know that part yet. I did the completion guarantee myself.'

'The bank let you do that?'

'I guaranteed the money personally.'

Stone whistled. 'That's a lot of scratch, Kagan.'

'They've got my house, my Continuum stock – a whole heap of stuff.'

'You must get Continuum to give you a signature for it!'

'That was my idea, but they've just been turned down by the money people. The fact is, Marshall, we're nearly at an end of all the money I can raise.'

'But you said the money was going to be OK. You said they were pleased with the rough assembly you screened for them last week. After all, with you, me and Bert taking nothing up front, this film has to be a bargain.' Stone chuckled to balance the boast. 'Let Continuum give the money men a mortgage on some of their cinemas, or something, until this film starts earning. Hell, I'm no businessman, but even I can see it. Those boys from the bank must be crazy.'

'They're not boys, Marshall.'

'Old twits, probably. Guys who go to the movies once in a decade and fall asleep even then. What do they know . . .'

'It's not boys, Marshall. It's a woman who made the decision.'

Stone looked at Bookbinder, unable, for a moment, to see what he was getting at. Then he laughed. 'You're not telling me that Brooks and Gerber are doing the Continuum deal?'

'And your wife is handling it.'

'Ex-wife,' said Stone.

'She turned them down,' said Bookbinder. 'She wouldn't look at our rough assembly. The trouble is that a couple of the Continuum directors think she only did it . . .' Bookbinder made a movement with his pipe and then inspected the burning tobacco.

'To spite me?'

'It's crap, I know,' said Bookbinder. 'In that position she'd be more careful than ever to do exactly what was right. And anyway, Mary wouldn't do that.'

'Wives can be funny creatures,' admitted Stone. 'Remember that movie I did for Koolman back in 1956? The wife was behind all the attempts to kill her husband. It rang true that movie. I've often thought it rang true, Kagan.'

'I was thinking of sounding out that husband of hers, the writer, what's his name: Anson.'

'Forget it!' said Stone. 'Mary's not the kind of person who discusses business with her husband.'

'Well, you should know,' said Bookbinder. 'Maybe you could make contact with her. Could you persuade her to look at what we've done so far? Even with the music running wild, it has a lot of what we're trying to do. What do you think, Marshall?'

'Confidentially, Kagan, Mary is still a little in love with me. This might just be her way of drawing attention to herself. She always felt a little outshone by me, you know?'

'You'd better get ready for your set-up, Marshall. I'll send your wardrobe guy over, shall I?'

'Great,' said Stone, 'and stop worrying, for pete's sake. I'll talk Mary round, she'll do anything for me. I'll put up the money myself if no one else will do it.'

'Thanks, Marshall, and mum's the word. You and me and Bert are the only people who know we have a problem. Even the unit accountant doesn't know. A thing like this . . .' he shrugged. 'The first thing you know, we could have trouble getting credit or something.'

There was a knock at the door, and Stone's hairdresser came in and began to work. Bookbinder waved goodbye and stepped down from the trailer. He closed the door very quietly, as he was always telling everyone they must. Three times they'd reshot because of the sound of slammed doors.

'I'll see Mary,' Stone promised himself aloud.

18 *The role is a cinch. The role doesn't bother me. I've been doing the role for years. I've worn that trench coat of mine in half the pictures I've been in.*

Humphrey Bogart

In 1952 the tourists guessed wrongly: September was entirely gentle sunshine and soft winds. The storms of August had not lasted, and now the stone of the quay had once more absorbed the heat of an Italian summer sun. The mooring rings were too hot to touch and yet all but one of the yachts had slipped their lines and departed.

At first the small dinghies had gone, then the swallows and the dragons. Most of the bigger boats had gone at the first break in the bad weather of late August, so that now only one – *Spool – Monte Carlo* – remained. It was a white staysail ketch with deep cream sails. Stone eyed the boat enviously. Soon he would be able to own a boat like that one, except that he would have a schooner. Not because he preferred the rig. He knew nothing of rigs but what he'd learned from the script of *Alone on the Atlantic*, which had been shelved just before shooting was due to start. But a schooner sounded more raffish, more suited to a star than a ketch could be.

Spool was being readied for a voyage. Deckhands were folding chairs and coiling ropes, and a steward threw enough croissants from the stern to make the gulls thrash and wheel like the turbulent wake of a paddle steamer.

The tables of the waterside restaurants were almost empty. The waiters had not bothered with their starched jackets, for only a few expatriates were taking coffee and they would pay winter prices.

Marshall Stone strolled past the fashionable seafood trattoria without seeing anyone he would care to greet. Even the cheap end of the waterfront was devoid of tourists. The candy-floss stall was closed and the gas jets under the waffle fryer had been extinguished. The smell of the warm oil hung there – yesterday's joys – a depressing odour, sour and ancient.

Anyone who had known him in England might have passed without recognition the Marshall Stone that four years of Hollywood had produced. His linen slacks were cut to fit close to his hips, without the girth that side pockets add. His custom-made shirt had his new initials embroidered on the pocket, and his shoes were soft and unique to him. His hair was razor-cut with such skill that even this sea breeze didn't disarrange it, and his hands were soft and white, with perfect nails unbitten for years.

He passed an English couple sitting over cold coffee at the cheapest place on the front. The girl's shoulders were badly sunburned and she was pouring iodine into a large bottle of oil because they could not afford Ambre Solaire. The man wore clumsy hand-knitted socks, and sandals. His shorts were baggy, and the pens and sun-glasses in the pocket of his Aertex shirt made it sag on one side. He was reading a dog-eared *New Statesman* and frowning at some social injustice. It could have been Eddie and Mary a few years back.

Ugo's still had linen tablecloths flapping, and glassware that caught the sun. It was the most expensive eating place, a trattoria in name only. On the tables there were plump pink prawns, black olives and huge radishes. There was a certain style, noted Stone, in laying it all out when so few visitors remained.

The waiter recognized him in spite of the mirror-lens glasses. He flicked a napkin across the chair, pressed it as Stone sat down, and smiled while bowing.

'A fresh orange juice and a large espresso.' The waiter smiled as if Stone had complimented him. It was three years since *Last Vaquero*, and yet in this part of Italy it was being distributed for the first time. The waiter had seen it the previous week. He'd told Stone how much he'd enjoyed it with all the Neapolitan enthusiasm of hands, arms, eyes and voice. 'Is-a fantastic! This fellow is fanstastic, ehhh! Bang, bang, bang. Ehh!' Stone noted each gesture and sound for future reference.

It was good to be away. He was never able to relax near a film location, and this Italian director was working him very hard. There was no script. At first Stone had found it exciting that a scribble on the back of an envelope could be the only written plan for a day's shooting, but now the strain of it was beginning to bear upon him. He liked to plan and prepare: he was not a spontaneous actor, and made no claim to be. He'd be glad to be home again, and was surprised to find himself thinking of his house in Beverly Hills. He sighed.

He was glad that an impulse had brought him here for his three days' break in the shooting. He'd been here with Mary just after the restrictions were lifted after the war. They were happy then, and looking around him he was able to remember the tiny things that had granted them so much pleasure.

The rest of the crew of *Storm Clouds* were struggling with a difficult sequence in the bay a few miles along the coast. He wouldn't be surprised if he had a telegram telling him he'd not be needed for another week. He moved the umbrella lest the sun tan him darker and spoil the continuity of his earlier sequences.

The crew had refused to believe that he wasn't shacking up with some starlet here. He'd gained a reputation in the last couple of years – it was difficult to avoid it, the way his publicity was slanted – and now he'd begun to relish the sly jokes that greeted him if he came on the set looking tired. But this weekend was strictly for resting. He looked around the tables. And anyway, there was no crumpet here.

The waiter brought his orange juice and the strong black coffee. He swung the little bag of sugar backwards and forwards before tearing the corner off. The English girl saw the movement and looked at him. Stone smiled and tipped the sugar into his coffee. She looked away. Stone knew she'd recognized him, and that gave him a warm comfortable feeling.

Stone sipped his coffee and watched the ketch riding on the water. His boat would be very like that one: he'd call her *Nobody*. Long ago, in New York, he'd wangled tickets for a première and taken Ingrid Rainbow with him. He'd spent his last few dollars on hiring a white Lincoln with a Negro chauffeur, so that as they arrived at the marquee the crowd emitted a sigh of expectation. A dozen Press photographers charged at the car. The first opened the door and levelled the camera at them in one smooth movement. Stone had smiled at the lens and gripped Ingrid's arm. 'It's nobody,' said the photographer, and they turned away to the next car. He remembered how his arm had trembled with the shame of it and Ingrid had folded a hand over his to tell him that it didn't matter. To her it didn't matter, but a fine ocean-going schooner named *Nobody* could erase such memories. Perhaps it would even enable him to talk about it, and possibly even transform it into a joke.

The Italian courtesy flag was lowered. The sailors were unusually smart and efficient for a private boat, with scrubbed uniforms and white caps. The captain disdained the diesels and artfully put to sea in silence. The sails stretched tight against the blue sky with a soft clap and there was a drubbing sound of the water pounding against the hull.

It was impossible not to daydream about her. As yet Stone's services were still earning the relatively small fees that his seven-year contract had demanded as part of the deal. But one day he'd be negotiating payments based upon his box-office value. Then a yacht like that one might represent less than one-third of his annual earnings: less than a quarter if the US tax on foreign location films remained law.

A man could sail the Atlantic in a boat like that. Many times he'd dreamed of earning a headline on his own account instead of performing antics prescribed by some screenwriter he'd never met. He'd walk the deck as that fellow there did, watching his crew and supervising his captain. Or better still he'd sail alone across the sea; Stone clasped that dream tight and never let it go.

'Leo. Leo Koolman,' Stone got to his feet and yelled into the breeze, but his voice could not compete with the gulls that followed *Spool*'s wake. It was undoubtedly Koolman whom he glimpsed through the blurred wings and cruel beaks. Koolman moved rapidly along the deck giving orders and watching how they were performed. He shouted to someone out of sight beyond the wheelhouse.

The drumming of the water upon the hull quickened as the boat gathered speed in the morning wind. The second figure stood close to Koolman, but not so close that it was meaningful. She was dressed in a dark woollen dress with a fashionable square of silk tied against her chin. Framed by the brightly coloured scarf, her face seemed long and thin, like a Modigliani portrait. Sun-glasses concealed her features, but there was something in her posture that enabled Stone to recognize her. It was the stance of a beautiful woman who distrusted all the world.

'Mary,' said Stone. He went back to his table and, still looking at the boat, bit into a piece of celery. The mainsail of the ketch flashed in the light as the helmsman gybed to bring the wind upon her starboard quarter. Over Stone's shoulder the waiter peered to see his empty coffee cup. 'Another espresso, Signor Stone?'

'No,' said Stone, 'nothing.' There must have been rocks in their path, for *Spool* changed direction again. Now she was running free, and more sail was hoisted: a large ballooning jib exploded with a soft crack of new canvas, so that the sound carried even against the wind. Her course was directly away from him now, so the white sails did not move across the horizon, they just became smaller and smaller.

'No, make that a brandy and soda,' said Stone. 'Or, better, a double brandy and soda.'

It says much about the thraldom in which Leo Koolman held Hollywood that it was so much later before Stone considered the possibility that Koolman had not planned that incident.

Twelve days later Stone awoke in a sunny cell-like room. The walls were an uncertain shade of cream, and a freshly painted crucifix was the only decoration. The lowered sunblind was too bright to stare at, and through it came sounds of battle: bugle calls, armour, kettle drums, whistles and shouting. Soon he was able to recognize this as a Roman morning, and he distinguished nearer noises too: jangling trolleys, whispered orders and tiptoeing feet. There was a smell of carbolic and cheap floor-polish and, more distinctively, the trace of ether that somehow reaches to the most distant rooms of even the largest hospital.

'When I woke up, I thought, Mama mia: I died!' Stone

laughed and Weinberger joined in. The door opened and a nun stared at them reprovingly. 'See what I mean?' said Stone.

'We were worried about you,' said Weinberger.

'You mean Koolman Inc got nervous about its investment and sent the Marshall Stone expert to check my woodwork for worms.'

'Is that what I am?'

'Well, aren't you? Listen, Viney, you may be the greatest publicity guy the studio's got, but did you ever wonder why you are assigned to every movie I make for them.'

'I suppose.'

'Next week I'll be back filming like nothing happened. You tell them that. I've never felt better.'

'Koolman is in Monte Carlo.'

'You don't have to tell me where Koolman is. Sure, he's on his boat – *Spool,* cruising in the Med. Oh, sure! You want to know the crew list?'

'Mary?'

'Want to go on to the next question or take the thirty-two bucks?'

'There's nothing in that, Marshall. I mean ... I'll tell you there's nothing in it ... but: oh boy.'

'Oh, boy, what?'

'Nothing, Oh, boy, nothing.'

'What?'

'Don't tell me you don't see this as a way of breaking your contract, Marshall.'

'Breaking it?'

'C'mon now. The Studio has had three nice years. They'd cut their losses. Leo on the yacht with Mary! C'mon now.'

'Did Leo think I disappeared to break the contract?'

'He thought you might send him an ultimatum from Shangri-la: a new contract or he is landed with the front half of an Italian movie!'

Stone was silent. Echoing in the narrow street outside there was the deep rumble of a heavy truck and a bray of horns as a couple of motor-scooters skirted it and thundered off up the hill.

'I never even thought of it.'

'I'll never work again if Leo suspects you got the idea from me, Marshall.' Then he laughed at his own fear. His teeth were large and uneven: appropriately wolfish, thought Stone.

'How would you like to be an agent?'

'Your agent?'

'I can't sign you to represent Spencer Tracy.'

'I know nothing about flesh-peddling, Marshall.'

'You know enough. You know what a seven-year exclusive-services contract is like. After this caper they could suspend me for six months – a year even. I wouldn't get one cent during that time. Mustn't even get a job as an usher or a gas-station attendant. And the six months goes on to the other end of my contract. It's slavery. You help me break that contract and you've got a client for life, Viney.'

'You don't need me to break the contract.'

'No? Can you imagine those boys who represent me doing a job like that on Koolman. Never, they have too much to lose. One Studio puts them on the shit-list and they've lost maybe one-tenth of their total business. No, Viney, agents represent employers, not actors. They'd sooner lose a dozen Marshall Stones than give Leo one headache.'

Another nun came in and checked the saline level and smoothed the already perfect sheets. 'And in addition to their commission my agent gives Bookbinder ten per cent of my contract.'

'Ten per cent?'

'It was a condition. Nicolson's agent went up to fifteen but Bookbinder said he'd rather have me and ten.'

'What a wonderful guy.'

'You don't believe it?'

'Never mind what I believe, Marshall. Giving Bookbinder ten per cent of your gross for seven years is like alimony without the fun of the adultery.'

'So what should I do?'

'Stop paying. The revolution will come before Bookbinder makes another picture in Hollywood. McCarthy chewed him into hamburger: they say he was a member of the party. You want them to say you're putting that dough of yours into some kind of commie slush fund?'

'Jesus, Viney. I need you. Think it over.'

The nurse had been fidgeting with a jar of disinfectant, now she took a thermometer from it and thrust it into Stone's mouth.

Weinberger smiled. 'I don't have to think over the prospect of ten per cent of your gross, Marshall.'

'But?' said Stone around the thermometer. The nurse gave him a disapproving glare and lifted his hand to take his pulse.

'But could I compare with an international outfit: smart lawyers and telex machines and guys with million-dollar accents who give Studio chiefs a vacation on a yacht?'

There was a long silence until the nun removed the thermometer from Stone's mouth. 'Use my lawyer, use my accountant . . .'

'. . . and next year use your yacht. OK, Marshall, if you still feel the same way when you come out of your delirium, we'll take a look at the expiry date on your present agency contract.'

'It's up for renewal.'

'You've not signed?'

'You'll break my contract with Leo? Tackle him head-on?'

'Within sixty days, you'll either have a new contract with Koolman Incorporated or I'll be back to playing Gestapo chiefs.'

The nun wrote Stone's thermometer reading, pulse and breathing on the board at the end of the bed. She must have sensed that something important had been decided for she looked up to see the two smiling men and she smiled too.

'Mazel tov,' said Weinberger.

19

When you tell people you have made a picture, they do not ask, 'Is it a good picture?' They ask, 'How many days?'

Gottfried Reinhardt

The countryside grew dark more slowly than the town. The twin beech trees that had given the house its name were clearly drawn upon a luminous blue sky, like the picture on a cathode tube. Wood pigeons chanted their monotonous rhythm and shifted nervously as the headlights disturbed them. When Mary Anson's driver closed the car door, one pigeon climbed away into the sky with a slow thudding of its wings. It circled the house warily before returning home.

'Is Mr Stone expecting you, madam?' Jasper's voice was doleful, but nicely intimidating. This technique of address had helped to make English butlers show-biz status symbols that outranked the Rolls with California plates.

'He is.'

'Whom shall I say?' He gave her a sniffy appraisal. The little woman with a woollen overcoat from Harrods cut no ice with a man who opened doors to minks, vicunas and genuine leopards. He looked over her shoulder to see the uniformed man at the wheel of last year's Rover. It might even have been hired for the evening.

'Mrs Anson,' said the woman. She only came up to Jasper's shoulder, but a few years of board meetings had made her more than his match at a game like this. She walked into him, or would have done had he not backed hurriedly away from her.

'Wait here, madam, I will see if . . .'

'Or say Mrs Eddie Brummage,' said the woman, and smiled. Mary Anson was still smiling as Jasper turned on his heel and stalked away. She opened her coat and pulled it aside to see the length of her skirt reflected in the antique mirror. It was still not right. She only went to that shop because it was owned by a girl who used to be her secretary. They would have to alter the waist again. The shoes were a success, though: gold shoes. She touched the gold brooch at her throat; Eddie had given it to her. She turned away from the mirror and examined the tiny Renoir, the dull Sisley and the superb Pissarro with its train puffing through a landscape exploding with colour. She sighed. Eddie had bought them just as investments, he'd admitted that they gave him little or no personal pleasure. 'I'm not an art person, Mary, you know that.'

Nervously, she opened a small gold evening bag and searched for a cigarette. She'd forgotten the gold case that she was always hoping for a chance to use. From a packet she took a tipped cigarette and lit it from a candle on the hall stand.

'Mr Stone will be down immediately, madam.'

She nodded and thrust her coat into Jasper's arms. The first round was entirely Mary's.

'Mary, Mary, my darling, Mary.'

'I thought you were going to say "Quite contrary" for a moment, Eddie.'

He smiled without hearing her. He was dressed in an evening suit with a red velvet jacket and frilly shirt. His shoes were black velvet, with his initials embroidered, like large buckles, across the front of each one. His velvet tie was knotted in a large loose bow. He put his arms round her and they kissed as a brother and sister might. Only when he was as close as this could he detect her perfume: it was a light flowery smell, more suited to a ladies' lunch than to a romantic tête-à-tête. He saw the choice of perfume as gauche rather than considered. It was just one more sign of the boring life she led. Suddenly, he wanted to show her the things he'd seen, the things he'd learned during the years they had been apart. He kept his arms round her. Mary was small, and her smallness reassured him. Some of the new actresses were abnormally tall. Even with Suzy he was using a three-inch pancake for the close-ups. Mary's body was tense, and he felt the flesh of her arm rough with goose pimples as his fingers touched her. She wriggled away from his embrace and smoothed her skirt in a nervous gesture that she'd not used for ten years. Eddie had always been able to make her feel stupid and defensive. She had dreaded this meeting, and yet she was too feminine to deprive herself of it. An evening out with Marshall Stone: it sounded like the first prize in a bumper competition to discover the world's most beautiful shopgirl. It was a cruel thought, and she pressed it back into the dark crevices of her mind, along with other memories of her marriage. She forced a broad smile.

'Wonderful,' said Stone. 'Great. Super.'

'You're looking well, Eddie. That tie is rather unusual.'

'You like it? I had it made.'

'It looks as though a vampire bat has got you by the throat, Eddie.'

Stone laughed. It was a fine laugh: brief and manly, with a low tone and a resonance that made an echo in the tiny hall. He'd created that laugh in his first weeks at drama school. Soon after Mary met him she'd confessed to her room-mate that it was one of Eddie's most attractive features. Not so long afterwards Eddie had persuaded the room-mate to tell him that.

'You haven't changed, Mary. You still look the way you did the day we met.' He held out his arms. He could see them both in the mirror. He could see the grey in Mary's hair. He guessed she tinted it herself rather than admit to a hairdresser that she wanted to look younger. That was always her hang-up; she would never admit to needing help.

'Younger, if anything,' said Stone.

She knew he used the words he most needed to hear. 'You too, Eddie,' she said. 'Young,' she added belatedly, and the word hung in space between them: an intimate falsehood. Two strangers meeting at a party might have been drawn together by such concessions, but for these two middle-aged ex-lovers they served only to measure Eddie's need and Mary's indifference.

'Eddie,' said Stone thoughtfully. He repeated his real name with unease and curiosity. For this evening he would be Eddie. It was a role he did not relish or fully understand, but he felt confident that he would do it justice.

'Are we going out? Your secretary didn't say.'

That was a mistake, thought Stone; he should have phoned personally. A woman like Mary would hate having such a message from his secretary.

'I was at the location,' he said.

'Your girl explained.'

'She's not . . .'

Mary smiled. 'Do you have an ashtray?'

He reached for one, and took her arm with his free hand. 'Come into the bar. Cook is fixing a meal for us – simple food, you're probably on a diet.'

'Do you ever remember me on a diet, Eddie? No, I can eat for two.'

'You don't mean . . .?'

'Eddie!' she laughed.

It was a coarse sound that reminded Stone of their endless arguments. He walked across to the bar. 'Gin and ton?'

'Yes, thank you. Gin and ton.' The way she said it left Stone in no doubt that her friends and colleagues didn't call tonic 'ton'.

He measured gin into two frosted glasses from the freezer, and opened two bottles of tonic water that Jasper had put into the ice bucket. Beside them on the counter top there was a small teak board, a stainless-steel knife and a perfect lemon.

'It's going to be one of those sort of evenings, is it?' said Stone. He mixed the drinks, brought them to the coffee table and took a seat beside her on the silk-covered sofa. Already he'd decided that she'd say she didn't know what he was talking about, but to his surprise she said, 'I'm sorry, Eddie.'

Stone grasped her arm and released it and then he changed the subject. 'How is my son?'

'You'd never recognize him, Eddie. He's so tall. And there's a good chance he'll get the London area manager's job next year. There's a retirement.'

'He's what . . . twenty-two next birthday?'

'Twenty-five.' Stone caught her eye, and they stared at each other for a moment, both remembering the times that Stone had preserved his own youth by changing their son's birth-date by a year or two. Mary stubbed out her cigarette carefully and then looked up at him again, determined to be bright-eyed and laughing. 'What are we having for dinner?'

Stone tried to remember what cook had promised him. She'd asked what his ex-wife liked to eat, and, rather than say he didn't know, Stone had invented a couple of favourites. But now he had forgotten. 'I'll ring for cook.'

'No, Eddie. It will be a surprise: better that way.'

'So you still believe that surprises will be good news?'

'Stupid, isn't it?'

'Not another cigarette.'

'Stop trying to reform me, Eddie.'

'Sorry.' He smiled. 'I like the dress, Mary.'

'I couldn't think what to wear. It was so hot today in the office.'

'Hottest September day for eleven years. I heard that on the news.'

'September is always warm. We always used to take our holidays then. Remember?'

They smiled and were at a loss for words. Neither was able to recollect the sort of things they talked about in those days.

'Yes, September is good,' said Stone.

He'd often thought of making a new life with Mary, at least putting together what was left of their old life. There had been no other girl who had understood him in the way that she did still. Even her cruel jokes showed an insight into his problems and his nature, and that was better than the silliness of the narcissistic starlets that he'd had by the score. They thought only of their own problems and their 'careers'. He remembered one girl sitting where Mary was now sitting, telling him of the admiring comments her body had brought from a string of famous lovers. And then there was the red-haired acrobat who told him obscene jokes while keeping a delicate smile on her face to appease her deaf husband. And the blonde who would only do it in ways that would not disarrange her hairdo.

'Did you ever fall in love again, Mary? At first sight, I mean, as we did?'

'We can't turn the clock back, Eddie,' she said quickly, as if she'd prepared the answer. He was sure now that there had been no other person in her life but him.

'Why not?'

They both knew what he wanted to hear, but she could at least deny him that. 'I have a new life now: the children are wonderful, I love Peter, I enjoy my work. I'm happy, really happy.'

'That's wonderful, Mary!' He chuckled, and she remembered how like a little boy he could be and how attractive she'd found it. Until, too often, he'd use the same technique when confessing his endless infidelities. 'You're young and full of energy. You'll always be the same little girl that I fell in love with. There's never been anyone else in my life.' He smiled, and she smiled too. Eddie had not changed. She had a weird feeling that they were repeating some conversation that they'd had before the divorce. He meant now, as he'd meant then, that because casual affairs meant so little to him, they must be disregarded by everyone. Including the unfortunate girls.

Her smile encouraged him to move closer to her, and he reached along the back of the sofa and touched her hair. He felt her shoulder stiffen as his arm went round her. She shivered ever so slightly as she felt his hand grasp her. Only Eddie had ever held her like that, and her memories of him – happy memories of their destitute youth – flooded into her mind so fast that she could not separate the images. Eddie trouserless, triumphant with applause, sitting on the stairs weeping, enraged to the point of striking her, locked out by an angry landlady. All these Eddies paraded before her as she closed her eyes and allowed him to turn her body to him and kiss her.

He felt the tension within her and was surprised at the total relaxation of her mouth. Her arms hugged him and yet her body did not yield. The kiss ended by common consent, and she stood up and touched her hair. Her lipstick had smudged and she went to the mirror and rubbed her mouth with paper tissues. Stone had forgotten that women wore lipstick. None of those who dated Stone arrived wearing any.

Mary did not want the evening to be like this, and yet neither did she want to reject him in any way that would hurt. She said, 'The divorce: there was nothing left after that, was there.'

'The lawyers destroyed us. That's how they make their money, by stirring up trouble.'

She smiled.

Stone said, 'Oh, I didn't mean you.'

'That's all right, Eddie. I no longer think of myself as a lawyer.'

'We were younger then: more easily hurt and wanting to strike back.'

'Would you really have cited poor Leo? You knew that there was nothing . . . the yacht was just to surprise you.'

'We all behaved badly, Mary.'

'Leo was frightened, he really was. But you came out of it all right. You came out of it with a new agent, a new contract from the Studio, a new life.'

'But Leo has never forgiven me. Even after all these years . . .' He took a drink. 'One of the things I liked about this present film is that I've escaped from Leo and his gang.'

'It's going well?'

'*Man From the Palace?*'

She nodded and came back to the sofa.

'It's going to be a wonderful film, Mary. It's easily my best performance. Kagan – you remember Kagan – says it's one of the best performances he's ever seen on the screen. Hanratty – he did *Naked Summer* – said I'm shattering. That's what he said: "shattering".' Stone smiled. 'Of course. I don't know. An actor can't judge his own rushes, I always say that. Kagan had a job persuading me along to see them, but he's so proud of this film.'

'That's wonderful.' She was alerted now both to Stone and herself. Whether it was the remnants of their love or just nostalgia for it, she was still vulnerable to his charm. She stayed at her end of the sofa.

'Kagan has let me bring their cutting copy of *Man* back home: that's quite an honour, Mary. They guard that rough assembly like . . .' He shrugged; he couldn't find a comparison. 'I've got a private cinema here now – double-head equipment –

it couldn't be shown in an ordinary cinema. That's why I wanted you to come here.'

She smiled. 'I don't know, Eddie. I shouldn't see the film.'

'Why not?' His voice was a little louder and slightly more shrill than he'd intended.

'Because I might like it very much, Eddie.'

'Well?'

'It will just confuse the issue. My report to my company has nothing to do with how much I like the film.'

'But what about its commercial potential?'

'I wouldn't attempt to judge that.'

'Then why did Brooks and Gerber send you to talk to Continuum?'

'I'm qualified. I'm a partner. I often make decisions like that: bigger decisions, sometimes.'

'Yes, but why this particular job. Why Continuum?'

'They think I know everything about the film industry. I keep telling them that I don't, but in fact – by their standards – I do.'

'Have you ever been in production, darling? Oh yes, you know the paperwork but you've never seen a film come to life. You need an instinct for that.'

'Perhaps production is instinct and an emotional response, but financial analysis is an exact science. We look at basic ratios, return on assets, price earnings multiple, margin on sales. . . .'

'Really!' He almost choked on his indignation.

'It has to be done like that. I couldn't become an expert on every technical process for which cash is needed. Last week I promised six million to an experimental electric car company. I couldn't understand a word they were talking about.'

'Then why?'

She smiled artfully. 'They have a ten-mile test run: two hundred and eighty acres of land in an area due for re-development and zoned for industry. That land is collateral.'

'It's beyond me.'

'Don't be silly, Eddie. Land can always be sold. It's like the collateral of a company that has a thousand tons of sand compared to a factory with sophisticated electronic machinery.'

'You mean the sand is better?'

'It's so easy to sell.'

'Collateral.' Stone nodded sadly.

'That's it, Eddie.' She picked up a snuff-box and examined its pattern. Then she put it back on the table.

'And films have no collateral?'

'They can be sliced up for banjo picks.'

'Thanks.'

'I'm sorry. That was a stupid thing to say.'

'But Continuum have collateral, Mary.' There was a warning glint in her eyes. 'I'm not trying to teach you your job or anything, but they *have*.'

'For instance?'

'They have the British and American rights on this Swedish film *Attis and his Lover*. That might recoup you your ten million dollars, for a start.'

'We can't invest money because we don't have any. We just underwrite a stock issue.'

'You haven't answered my question.'

'We underwrite stock. Our biggest buyers of stock are banks. Banks are very choosy and they just won't want to buy stock in a company that is making pornographic films.'

Stone smiled. 'Continuum didn't make *Attis and his Lover*, they just bought the American and British rights.'

'It will have the Continuum name on it. Most of the audience will think they did make it.'

'Perhaps it's not a porno film.'

'Come along, Eddie. A lot of people read the classics. They know that Cybele forced Attis to castrate himself when he married another woman.'

'Did you know that?'

'No, Eddie, I looked it up. I said a lot of people will know. Especially people in banks.'

'It's not a real porno film.'

'It will be sold and advertised as if it is. You know that as well as I do. It's the same thing.'

'Ridiculous.'

315

'It is. But we are stuck with it. The cinema industry is not a favourite investment, Eddie. *Time* Magazine said that the gross earnings fell by twenty-eight per cent in the last twelve months.'

'That's not so. Even if it was true, there is still enough money in the industry to justify investment.'

'I think it is true. And anyway, the people who buy stock will believe *Time* Magazine.'

'This is all self-justification for what you previously decided.'

'Eddie, most of the money that Continuum have to repay is owed to an investment company. That means that the money our stock issue raises to get Continuum out of trouble will go to that investment company. How will that look to the average investor? How will it look to Wall Street and the City?'

'What do you mean?'

'Don't be naïve, Eddie. It will look as though the big investment companies are sticking together. It will look as if we are prepared to soak the public in order to help each other recoup money.'

'Jesus, you've got a mind like Weinberger's.'

'A lot of people have, Eddie. That's why we have to be so careful.'

'But Continuum have cinemas and real estate. They own land, like your test tracks. What can be safer as an investment than real estate?'

'Nothing could be safer. But most of those cinemas are in run-down slum neighbourhoods. If they owned drive-ins which could be sold as suburban developments or supermarkets, it might be different, but these are ordinary urban cinemas.'

'Hard tops.'

'Yes, hard tops. In ten years they might become valuable sites. Might! But in ten years the same money could multiply many times faster in growing industries.'

'Like what?'

'We are doing a deal now with a company making pollution control equipment.'

'Pollution control equipment,' said Stone disgustedly.

'People want investments that they can move into and out of quickly. They don't want broken-down real estate. Continuum will never get their money from the stock market. That's not just my opinion, it's a fact. They will have to break up all those bits and pieces: sell what they can, borrow on what they can't. Otherwise they won't survive.'

Stone hesitated before betraying a confidence, but this was a matter of life and death – for the company and for the film. He got to his feet and walked across to the fireplace as if to see if the fire needed another log. Then he turned to Mary. 'Suppose I told you that you might be on the verge of making an awful fool of yourself, Mary? Suppose I told you, in confidence, that Kagan has been working on a plan to expand to the tune of ten million after the debt is repaid?'

'It's gone beyond all that nonsense,' said Mary. 'You're talking about models of their cassette factory, architects' drawings, surveys and all that pezazz they were putting on a couple of months ago to drum up a bit of confidence. It did no good. It just makes the market suspicious, that sort of show-business.'

'I've promised Kagan to keep them going with my own money,' said Stone.

Mary Anson lit her cigarette with exaggerated care. Stone did not offer to light it for her. She said, 'Why, Eddie?' Without waiting for him to answer she took off her beautiful gold shoes and put them up on the sofa beside her. They were magnificent, but they pinched. If she had them stretched the gold might crack.

Stone watched her caress the shoes. She was more concerned with them than with Stone's problems. Why, Eddie? She treated him like a stupid child. She'd always done that.

'Kagan has a thirty-seventy split. I'll buy a piece of that.'

'Of the profit. Act your age, Eddie, there will be no profit. Continuum will make sure of that. Anyway, he's sold that share to keep going.'

'Sold his shares to keep turning over – the wonderful lunatic. That's Russian roulette.'

'More like the charge of the Light Brigade. Only a fool would provide his own completion guarantee. Now he's broke. The

317

best he can hope for is that one of the majors will pick up the pieces so that he can avoid the bankruptcy court. If that picture ever gets a release Kagan won't see a penny and it probably won't even have his name on it.'

'Well, I'll tell you this, Mary. When the chips are down I'll be lining up with the Kagan Bookbinders, not with the investment companies and their dime-a-dozen specialists.'

'Somebody called?' She laughed. She hadn't meant to be unkind, and yet as soon as she laughed she knew that Stone saw the laugh as a taunt, as a terrible gloat over Stone and Bookbinder and everyone who was worried in the whole troubled industry.

'Yes, you're one of them,' said Stone. 'But these guys at Continuum are as bright as you are, Mary. Youngsters, but as sharp as knives. Two of them are from the Harvard Business School.'

'Well, this isn't the Harvard Business School, Eddie. This isn't the movies, either. This is what we call real life.'

'I don't know what that is,' said Stone with heavy irony.

'A sort of documentary.'

'You stupid bitch!'

The muddle of contradictory feelings that she'd known since arriving, ended. Eddie's affection was just a mask that had now slipped askew. What had once been ingenuous charm had long since become an act; an act for which he was far too old. Her voice was steady and kind, but there was no longer the same tenderness in it. 'Let's not quarrel, Eddie. I've explained my reasons for turning Continuum down. I've said too much, in fact. My directors all agreed with my report. So will any other company they go to. Anyway, Eddie, do you really think I liked turning it down? Do you think I wouldn't sooner have you fawning over me in gratitude than spitting with disappointment?'

'Screw you, you bitch.'

'Doubtless that was the idea, but I've been inoculated against show-biz charm.'

'Yes, you were always disloyal to me. That showed what a clever, fully liberated woman you were.'

'Is "loyalty" still your favourite word of praise, Eddie? I

know what you mean now. Loyalty means holding your hand at any time of night or day. It means sympathy about a blackhead on your bum while my foot is bleeding in a beartrap. It's thanking you lavishly for any gift or compliment and forgetting all the slights and arguments and humiliations. I don't remember you showing any loyalty to me.'

'Perhaps you've got a bad memory.'

'And perhaps it's not half as bad as I'd like it to be.'

'You are so proud of yourself.'

'I am, Eddie, but not sinfully so. I don't gobble praise from sycophants, or employ people to garland me with compliments. I've won a place for myself in a man's world, and it's not been easy. I'm proud of all that, Eddie. Yes, I am.'

'Making a bit of money has turned your head.'

'I've made no money, in your terms, Eddie. I have the same as my partners take: a chauffeur-driven Rover and a small London house with a broken-down cottage in Spain that Peter and I see once a year. If money has changed me, it's not my earnings that have done it. I've seen a world I never knew about. I've been close to men and watched them become millionaires within a week or two, when we've helped them go public. I've seen some of them corrupted by money, others aged and demoralized when they realize they have exchanged it for control of their companies. I've learned what money is. I don't worship it.'

'Well, I do. I told Kagan that I'd keep the movie going and I'll do it in spite of you.'

She exhaled the smoke from her cigarette in a rather theatrical way. 'Are you serious, Eddie?'

'You're damn right I am, sweetheart.'

'Not just trying to impress me? I'll fix that if it's what you want.' She smiled.

'You fix it.'

She reached for the telephone and dialled a number. She stared insolently at Stone as she waited for the telephone to be answered. There was a voice at the other end. 'Hello, Florian. Mary Anson here. I'm with Mr Stone now, and we've been talking about the film – your film – *Man From the Palace.*' She listened for a while. Florian Backhouse, chairman of

Continuum, made a joke and Mary laughed briefly. She continued. 'Marshall Stone has already arranged to find you the end money you were worried about.' She reached for an ashtray and Stone moved it nearer to her. She flicked ash into it and nodded her thanks. 'I thought it would remove one of your problems.' Again she listened. 'Certainly, tell Mr Bookbinder. Tell any of your people, but I imagine Mr Stone will want to arrange the Press release through his Press agent, so tell your end to keep it to themselves.' She laughed again, 'He's right here with me so you can tell him yourself. Here he is.'

He put his hand over the microphone. 'You clever little cow.'

She smiled: round two went to Mary.

For a full minute Stone stood looking at his hand. 'Hello, Mr Backhouse, Marshall Stone here. I thought you'd like to know. It's going to be a great film, you see, a really great film. I'm not doing this as a charity, I'll make a killing out of it. If you listen to my advice you won't let any of it go.'

Backhouse said, 'About that Press release, Mr Stone. This is an awfully delicate . . .'

'That's just Mary's fun, Mr Backhouse.'

'Oh, I see.'

Stone listened while Backhouse repeated his thanks and the complimentary things about Mary and then hurried on to the farewells.

He replaced the phone with great care, as if he was trying to avoid the small tinkle it made as it disconnected.

'Thanks.' Stone was angry. He was even more angry when she picked up one of her gold shoes to look at it. She was seeking a reason not to look into his eyes, but Stone didn't know her well enough to recognize the guilt she felt. He snatched the shoe away from her and tore it in half across the instep. At first she could hardly believe what he had done, and then she saw the violence within him and was frightened by it. The torn shoe in his hand made her feel sullied and despoiled.

'You are a disgusting man, Eddie.'

He allowed her to take the shoe from him. She looked at it for a moment or two and then she took the other shoe from the sofa. Her first inclination was to throw them both into the waste-basket but she did not want to leave them anywhere where Stone might handle them again.

She did not wait for her coat – he could send it on. Had she suspected that the evening would end like this when she'd told her driver to wait? She slammed the door hurriedly so that the courtesy light would switch off. She wanted the darkness. 'Home,' she said. There was no catch in her voice, and only when the driver was occupied with the evening traffic did she blow her nose. In that respect, at least, round three was Mary's too.

'Don't cry, Mary! Mary, please don't cry.' He called twice, but he didn't expect her to return. He heard the car start up, and saw the headlights flash on the curtains as it turned. They did that as a lighting effect in the Army production of *Murder for Love* in 1945.

Stone walked around the sitting-room. There was a moon, and he drew back the curtains to look at it. He could think of so many good lines about the moon. If Mary was still here he could tell her the things he had prepared. He grieved that they could never spend more than five minutes together without such scenes. It wasn't his need that made him sorrowful. Nor was it hers, although that was more nearly it. He was sad at the division between them when once they'd been so close: the waste of so many years. It didn't need much to make him ache with melancholy, and sometimes he admitted that such feelings produced a shiver of excitement. He gazed at the moon for a long time. 'Don't cry,' he said.

Weinberger had finished supper and was sitting with Lucy listening to a jazz record. Weinberger had nearly seven hundred jazz records. He removed the pick-up arm from the record before answering the phone. Here in his study the phone was a private line. When it rang it was inevitably a client.

'Hello,' said Weinberger.

'Don't mention names,' said Stone.

'Very well,' said Weinberger. It was not an uncommon request.

'You know who it is?'

'Of course.'

'How much money have I got?'

Even Weinberger was surprised by that question. He reached into his pocket and found a silk handkerchief to wipe his face. He finally said, 'You should ask your business manager that one.'

'I don't want to talk to him,' said Stone. 'He preached at me like a bloody shop steward last time.'

'That was April: the money you lost at the tables in Vegas. He's going to have trouble persuading the Inland Revenue that that wasn't a put-up job. It was dollars, too; that may not be legal.'

'He was angry about the shares.'

'Well, you are not good at playing the market. I'd hate to think what your hunches cost you last year.'

'The tin shares were a good tip, it was the market that went wrong.'

'That's like Oscar Wilde saying his play was a success, but the audience was a failure.'

'I don't pay you for witty quotations,' said Stone.

'But you pay your business manager to help you hang on to a bit of money. So why not listen to him.'

'Just answer the question. How much can I lay my hands on?'

'Depends what you mean, lay your hands on. In cash we couldn't throw together more than fifty grand without a loan.' Hurriedly he added. 'A loan is easy to arrange. I have guys at the office every day ... any of them would loan you cash.'

'I'm talking about my money.'

'The house at Beverly Hills and the house in Grasse. The staff ... and the upkeep is enormous. Sell both those places later on – say, in spring – and we might do something very nice.'

'Selling the Beverly Hills place would really start the tongues wagging. People would be saying the skids were under me, Viney. And Grasse ... well, I was there last year.'

'For a long weekend. Shall I tell you what that works out at per hour?'

'I don't want to hear.'

There was a muffled sigh and Stone could imagine Weinberger rubbing his face in a characteristic gesture of melancholy. 'We're just getting into a tax battle ...' Again Weinberger paused as his mind went through years and years of accounts and ten thousand extravagant cheques ... the car for the girl ... lots of clothes and trips for her. '... Did you think about selling some of the horses?'

'This is not the right time, and anyway there's nothing there that's going to win the Derby.'

'That's not the way I heard it when you were buying them.'

'What about that bloody aeroplane, and that ratfink who calls himself a pilot?'

'Now don't let's start all that again. I explained about the financing: it's the same as the Fifth Avenue duplex you never use. It's never a good idea to share these kind of things. You want the plane; they want it! They want to buy a new motor; you want to refurbish the old one! It never works. Anyway, we can't get out of that deal for at least two more years. That damned pilot's contract is for five years, and you know how I opposed that.'

'He seemed like a really good egg, at the time. You know, I get so fed up with these sort of discussions. Sometimes I feel I don't make any decisions at all. I just conform to a lot of laws about tax and real estate and companies and domicile and all that crap. I mean, it makes me wonder if it's worth earning the stuff.'

'You haven't mentioned the boat. Everyone would vote for that going. Did you see the last bill? The accountant asked them if they'd fitted Polaris.'

'Very funny,' said Stone. 'Very, very funny.'

'No one's laughing. Your accountant was just trying to protect your money. That refit cost nearly half of what the boat cost. Look, why don't we get everyone concerned to the office for a real session about this. A sort of policy ...'

'No,' said Stone. The mere thought of such a meeting filled him with dread. It would be like doctors trying to guess what he'd die of. 'All I want is a simple answer.'

'Immediately: fifty grand, another forty in stocks, another fifty of odds and sods that we could borrow on. After that

323

you've got the houses, and the boat. Sell that lot in a hurry and we'd be lucky to get out with a million dollars which might – just might – be what the US Internal Revenue will settle for. And, incidentally, you'd have nowhere to live.'

'Thanks a lot!'

Weinberger paused long enough to be certain that there was no trace of anger in his voice. 'Your earning power has never been better, but you must listen to reason. Do a couple of productions in some location where gambling is illegal and the phone so bad you're not tempted, and you'd have a lot of cash under your belt. Did you ever think of that?'

'And do you know, if I went to the location in a Mini every day I'd save the price of three gallons of gas.'

'Now you're being silly.'

'Yes, I'm being silly.' Stone hung up. Everyone treated actors like children, and that angered him. If he'd made his money in any other business from surgery to extortion they would have respected his opinions. 'Silly!'

20

I want to be taken seriously.
                    Errol Flynn

This whole episode was as artificial as a bad film. Real people
were involved, but the words they spoke were the words of
other men in other places. As always, Stone was miscast. He
smiled to himself and wiped his brow. The heat always made
him irritable, but today he must not show it.

He stumbled against a chair that was heavy enough to
bruise him. It did not topple. He cursed automatically. There
was a good view from the window. In one direction there were
rolling hills that became bleached scrub, and then, in the hazy
distance, grey cliff chewed breakers from a light blue sea. The
other way a dirt road meandered through rock-strewn land,
descending through groves of stunted olive trees until it got to
the village of Santa Sovora. The track was a little better after
that. Eight miles on, it joined the super highway that connects
Reggio to Naples.

He looked at his watch and waited. Exactly as planned, the
explosions sounded, like beats on a bass drum. Two columns of
oily smoke climbed into the sky. The breeze bent them like
dandelion stalks and blew their heads into grey puffs. It had not
been difficult to persuade the owners of the olive plantation to
let them fight their way through the groves, for the olives were
puny, mottled fruit whose flesh only thinly covered their large
stones.

Each side of the dirt road was marked by broken crates and
metal drums, scaffolding poles and cross-pieces. Three lorries
were unloading before going back to Cinecittà for more bits
and pieces of the summer palace. Now that they had completed
the pre-war shots of the prince walking through the un-

damaged olive groves there would be nothing for him to do for a few days. He debated whether to go back to London or to keep an appointment he'd made with an Italian actress who might get the part of the teleprinter operator. It was only half a dozen lines, but she would do anything to get a part in an Anglo-American production. She had said exactly that. Her apartment overlooked the Tiber and there was a roof garden where she sunbathed nude. It sounded better than London.

Two black limousines came into sight from behind the ridge. The drivers cautiously picked their way between the rocks and the pot-holes. They moved at walking pace, but the breeze from the sea picked up the disturbed surface of the track and drew long clouds of red dust after the cars as if they were going at breakneck speed. Like slow motion, thought Stone, and was reminded of a nightmare. He turned away from the window and glanced in a fly-specked mirror. He touched the new refrigerator which had been connected to a generator so that he could have ice when he wanted it. The thermostat cut in and the refrigerator began to throb. It was a sound that preyed upon his nerves, for it always began when he least expected it. They had intended to have an air-conditioned trailer brought up here for the visit by Florian Backhouse and his merry men, but Bookbinder decided that it would be regarded as a foolish extravagance. Stone smiled to himself; Leo Koolman would never criticize money spent to show homage, but these people were different. Again he looked out of the window: the cars seemed very little nearer.

There was another peasant cottage some fifty yards away. Sitting outside in the full heat of the sun was his stand-in and one of the men who fetched and carried for him. All of his film deals included their wages and expenses as well as those of his driver, use of his car and the wages of six of his London staff in lieu of hotel costs. The two men were playing cards. It was incredible that they could tolerate the intense heat.

When the cars arrived Stone still did not emerge. He stood in the doorway and smiled. The drivers, and some sort of attendant seated beside each driver, jumped out of the car and held the doors for the passengers. Bookbinder and Hanratty were dressed in sweat-shirts, straw hats and chinos, but the other men were in black suits and hats of a sort that a wardrobe department would reserve for undertakers or bankers or mafiosi.

Stone shook hands with each of the men and asked them what they thought of the preparations for the battle scenes of *Man From the Palace*. They nodded. Bookbinder had arranged for the special effects boys to blow up a tin shed that would have been in shot. 'Black powder!' said Hanratty. 'You always get that sort of bang and the oily smoke: it's the lack of compression; but we have to use it because of the safety restrictions. Of course, we can put a better bang on the soundtrack, but we're stuck with the black smoke.'

'It looked good,' said Bookbinder. 'The dirt on the second one was really effective-looking. You'll see.' Stone added his comments, but the six dark-suited men watched them with amused tolerance and expressed only perfunctory interest in what they had seen.

'Campari, Punt e Mes, gin and ton?' said Stone, but only the film-makers accepted alcohol. The businessmen took chilled tonic water. Soon the relationship between the men became more clearly defined. The attendants were of a lower status than the other four, and now they arranged the chairs around the table as if expecting a meal to be served.

The cottage was unchanged through several generations of farmers. Some of the interiors would be shot inside the cottage. For that reason the chairs, polished table, its lace runner, the religious pictures, the candles, mirror, crucifix and rush mats had been purchased from the owner. They would be shipped back to London for use in the studio interiors. Stone had already laid claim to the lace runner.

Hanratty was looking at the light. It would be difficult to reproduce exactly, for the noon sun made yellow patches on the flagstones and filled the air with a golden radiance in which one could almost swim. The walls dribbled with reflected light and the polished table shone like glass, so that when Florian Backhouse sat down at the head of the table, his reflection was almost perfect. He indicated that Stone should sit on his right and one of the attendants put the seat in position for him. The other men chose seats in an established order.

'What's this, a conference—?' said Stone. He was going to add, 'or a wake'. For a more receptive audience it would have been a witty observation. The six mournful men were unlikely to find it amusing. The skin around the eyes of Florian Backhouse tightened as though a bright light had been shone upon him: it was a smile.

Stone's question was answered by the document-cases that were placed upon the table and the files and papers that came from them.

'How do we stand now, Enzo?' said Backhouse. He said it while looking at Stone.

'One point eight eight oh.'

'To the nearest thousand,' agreed Backhouse. He nodded.

The man said, 'Transportation: I'm allowing one hundred and fifty thousand dollars but I'm prepared for it coming to a little more.'

'Your airline,' Bookbinder reminded them.

'No,' said Backhouse.

Backhouse had a curious voice. He articulated each and every syllable with a needless attention to its ending. It would be a very good voice for using over a defective radio-phone on a thundery day when under artillery fire. He added, 'We sold our interest last month.'

Bookbinder said. 'Well, don't tell me you didn't include our transportation contract as an asset.'

Backhouse gave his perfunctory smile. He said, 'Let me tell you something concerning your end of the business.' He paused long enough to establish that the airline was not Bookbinder's end of the business. 'Without the generosity of Mr Stone and his guarantee of end money, I would have made you cut this Italian location. You'd be inside a studio now. We've said it before, but I'd like our thanks to Mr Stone to be on record.'

It was only then that Stone noticed the man taking shorthand notes. Bookbinder had opened his mouth to speak when he noticed him too. He changed his mind.

Backhouse said, 'Enzo has been looking at the figures and his projection disconcerts me: I admit it. You fellows have spent your life in this industry, and I respect your opinion, but I'll be relieved to get out of it with my investment intact. Incidentally,

Kagan, this visit will not be charged against you, we had business to do in Rome.' He wet his lips. 'Fair is fair.'

Stone looked up. 'Fair is fair' spoken like that would be perfect for Prince Felix; but then fear overcame his professionalism.

Bookbinder said, 'I've just about come to an end of my money. I was on the phone to the bank today ...'

'I am informed of that,' said Backhouse. There was a silence while one of his men passed him some accounts. He looked at the totals on each page, closed his eyes while he did some mental arithmetic, and then slid the papers back across the polished table. 'That's why we need Mr Stone's bank to take over the cash flow. A simple guarantee will be the quickest way. We have to hurry, you'll need the salaries and living allowances at the end of the week. The hotels and the construction bills can wait, but the unions will blow the whistle if we are late paying the crew. Am I right, Kagan?'

'That's about it,' said Bookbinder.

'For this reason, Enzo, my senior accountant, has talked to Mr Stone's bank in order that a special authority, acceptable to them, can be drawn up right away.' Backhouse reached for a cigarette-case and selected a Turkish cigarette. Stone noticed his slim white manicured hands. Backhouse placed the cigarette carefully between his lips. One of his men lit it.

'What sort of money are we talking about?' said Stone.

'This week: one hundred and eighty thousand dollars. But this ridiculous situation with Mr Bookbinder must be regularized. The production must reassume responsibility for the nine hundred thousand that he has signed for.'

Backhouse shuffled some papers and continued. 'But we are talking pocket-money. When Mr Stone contracted to play Prince Felix the budget was doubled. I can give you the exact figures if you like, but there will be little or no small change from five million dollars. And there are distribution investments ...'

Stone swallowed and began to sweat, as he always did under emotional stress.

Backhouse said, 'Mr Koolman of Koolman International was negotiating for the production until last week. We came quite close to an agreement, but then he withdrew. Last night I phoned him at home to see how he would feel about reopening talks.'

Stone nodded but didn't trust himself to ask the verdict.

'And?' said Bookbinder.

Backhouse turned very slowly until he faced Stone and looked him straight in the eye. A very thin smile appeared. 'Whatever did you do to Mr Koolman that he becomes so enraged?'

'If someone was to take over the production,' said Stone, pausing in the way that Backhouse paused, 'it had best be a company equipped to handle the technicalities.'

Backhouse said, 'It's not a lack of technicalities, Mr Stone.' he smiled the deep-frozen smile, 'it's a lack of money.'

'It would be just as well if you spoke with Koolman again,' said Stone.

'You,' said Backhouse, 'have agreed to find the money. If you wish to resell the production, or a part of it, I will provide all the existing paper work, but I cannot start a whole new series of negotiations. In any case, I have already committed the money you have promised to bridge a sea salvage operation – Lloyd's open form – that's three weeks late.'

Stone put both hands on the table like a conjuror who wished to prove that there was nothing up his sleeve. He wanted to tell them about his conversation with Weinberger, and that reminded him of the wrath he would now face, not only from Weinberger but from his other advisers, too. He looked round the table. These men husbanded every penny they laid hands on, and parlayed it into a pound. The fact that he earned a million dollars a picture was all they needed to believe that he was a billionaire. They did not understand the rate that cash flowed through his hands; the houses, his tax, the servants, the percentages, his bad luck at the tables and his disappointments with the horses that he owned and the ones he merely lost money on. 'You're holding me to that phone call?'

'Are you saying it was a hoax?'

'Not . . .'

He had been going to say not exactly but Backhouse interrupted him. 'Your ex-wife confirmed your offer at a meeting the next day.' He turned to the man on his left. 'Do we have the minutes of that meeting? It's the one in which we discussed the audit costs ...'

'No matter,' said Stone. One of the two attendants was sitting just inside the door, taking no interest in the conversation. The plump one stood near the refrigerator, looking out of the window toward the olive groves that would soon become a battlefield. There was a sudden screech and the matronly attendant turned from the window to the sound with an unexpected agility. Stone noticed that the man's plumpness seemed to be only on one hip.

'Sorry,' said Hanratty. It was his chair that had made the noise. 'Must get back to work: the palace must be ready by noon tomorrow.'

Bookbinder left at the same time, walking down the hill to where the construction gangs were building only the steps and one side of the summer palace.

'Don't blame your wife,' said Backhouse kindly. 'She didn't want it to go on the minutes, but there was no way she could do it without being open to some serious trouble. Lawyers, you know, are circumscribed in that way.'

'The only problem we face,' said Stone, 'is the way my money is tied up. I don't have the sort of fluidity that you people talk about.'

'We realize that,' said Backhouse and for a moment Stone thought he was saved. 'Mario has drawn up an agreement so that one of our companies lends it to you. That will be quite good enough while we transfer legal title. After all, Mr Stone, you are a man of substance.'

Other papers passed across the table. 'Three signatures,' said the man he called Enzo.

'Yes,' said Backhouse, 'just three signatures and Enzo will do the rest of it.'

'I must put this through my people in London,' said Stone searching for another excuse for not signing. 'It's formality, but that's the way I always work.'

Backhouse allowed him a minute of euphoria, then said, 'No. It must be settled before we return.'

Stone said, 'You're like Sam Goldwyn, eh? A verbal agreement is not worth the paper it's written on.' Stone laughed and looked round the table, inviting them all to join in the fun.

If Backhouse realized it was a joke, he gave no sign of doing so. 'A verbal agreement,' he explained as if to a child, 'has all the validity of a written one. That is the law.'

Now that Bookbinder and Hanratty had gone, Stone seemed to detect a note of malice in Backhouse. Perhaps he was too fanciful, but he found menace in the three other black-suited men and their two attendants. There was something cinematic in the way they were placed in the room: raven-black figures against the sunwashed stucco, their pallid faces ensuring that no touch of colour marred the monochromatic power of the composition. Suddenly the refrigerator began to throb.

'Suppose I say to hell with the law? Suppose I say to hell with you, too? What are you going to do then: take me to court?' In spite of anticipating it, he could not prevent his voice going a little shrill, so that now its sound vibrated on the warm air. He got to his feet. His head almost touched the worm-eaten beams that supported the cracked plaster ceiling. Through the window he could see the old man who ran his messages finishing the game of cards with his stand-in. Even they had admitted defeat to the noon sun. They had rigged a shade, and the stand-in was stripped to the waist in an attempt to keep cool. The old man had won the game and was collecting his dirty screwed-up Italian notes. He flattened each one of them and placed them in his wallet. Lucky bastards, thought Stone, and to think that they envied him!

Stone turned to Backhouse who said, 'Take you to court? Of course not, but that situation could never arise.' The others were looking at Stone as if measuring his height and girth. Stone pitched his voice low. 'Are you threatening me, Mr Backhouse?'

No one answered. The two accountants began to put their documents back into their cases. Backhouse had not moved a muscle. Beyond him Stone could see the parched landscape, with its shrivelled trees and dusty cactus plants. Life was a struggle against the hot sun when water was in short supply. The air was hot enough to dry the back of a man's throat as he breathed, and the dust formed a crust around the nostrils. One of the attendants picked up the lead that fed electricity to the refrigerator. He pulled it sharply and the beat of the motor ceased. Now the sounds of the countryside could be heard: the buzz of flies and burr of insects.

'You could have saved yourself the journey from Rome, gentlemen,' said Stone. He paused, for by now he had adopted Backhouse's timing. 'You need only have asked the people who know me. They would have told you that I would never let a production die.'

He reached for the three documents and signed them contemptuously. 'I will need four days – five at most – I'll get the London plane this evening. By Friday my people will take over the production.'

Stone found himself leaning slightly forward, preparing for the smiles and handshakes, perhaps a warm embrace, for the kindest and unkindest cuts of show business were eased with such balm. But Backhouse stood up only to give a formal bow. 'Can I offer you transport?'

'My car is due,' said Stone. The men stood when Backhouse did. The two attendants hurried out and signalled to the drivers so that the doors of the limousines would be ready to open and the air conditioning fully working.

'Ask the production office to get me a seat on the London plane,' said Stone. 'In case of difficulty they should call . . .'

'There will be no difficulty,' said Backhouse.

The cars went down the hill even more slowly than they had come up it, and looking even more like a funeral. Stone felt the perspiration cold and clammy on his backbone. It wasn't the fear of physical violence that had affected him, but the tedious, time-wasting business of worrying about it. He no longer had the energy to be cautious of dark hotel rooms, or to send his strong-arm man Arthur out of the stage door first to be sure the alley was safe, or to walk on the inside of the kerb in case a car swerved unexpectedly. Just as he no longer had the stamina for protracted lawsuits, or the sort of vendetta that a certain news magazine and a London daily paper had waged against him not so many years ago.

He looked around the tiny room; perhaps it was better to

live like this. A bird flew past the window chirruping noisily. Another followed to argue. For a moment Stone could persuade himself that his six visitors had been only a dream, but then he saw the half-smoked Turkish cigarette in a flower pot. He went to the window and stayed there until fleeting glimpses of his pale blue Cadillac came into sight through the olive trees. Only then did he sit down.

When life began to return to a brain numbed by anxiety, Stone experienced an almost orgasmic relief. Now the problem was defined; he knew what had to be done. The three days since he'd spoken with Backhouse on the phone had been far worse than this. He'd known all along that something bad would come out of this film. His friends had warned him, and so it was his own fault in a way. He should have listened to dear, dear Weinberger, and he should never have quarrelled with Leo. It was clearly his own fault.

It was no good taking this problem to any of the other companies with which he'd worked: Fox, Columbia, Paramount, UA. No, Koolman had made millions out of him and Koolman would always owe him a favour. Even Leo admitted that such a debt was due, although he would never define it.

Stone knew himself to be a more astute businessman than any of his associates would give him credit for. After all, it was Stone who lived in high style, saying, doing, going, screwing – who, how or what he pleased. It wasn't the Backhouses or the Weinbergers or even the Koolmans who had the freedom that success brings. But sometimes there was a price to pay for such freedom and luxury. He would have to concede to Koolman's wishes in the matter of the TV series. Perhaps he'd even have to apologize. It would be a matter of business expediency, and so nothing that would mar his real dignity or pride.

The guilt that wealth evokes from puritans had been a hazard of the movie industry ever since its birth. Some men assuaged it by joining the Communist Party, others by donating huge sums to charity, but by far the greatest number found solace in repentance. For such men the Koolmans of the world provided a productive form of atonement that was, to say the least, mutually profitable.

But these were not the thoughts of Marshall Stone. He was already deciding the details of his penitence. If he could discover the amount of money that Koolman had offered for this production, then Stone need only offer him a margin of money to sweeten it. Stone smiled, glancing in the spotty mirror as he did so. Difficult, perhaps, but not impossible. Not for one moment did Stone consider that *Man From the Palace* might be an investment that would return his money plus a big profit. There was something within him that knew that a few thousand yards of celluloid was worthless. It was trickery that enabled him and this bizarre industry to live by such things.

Not yet did Stone think of conceding to Koolman changes in the plot or a different ending to the film. But one part of his brain was preparing this for rationalization should he prove unable to save himself in any other way.

Stone put his case on the table and opened it. He selected some documents and arranged them on the table: last week's call-sheets and a script change. His eyes scanned the complex planning and he wondered how he had become a part of this crazy world. Not in an analytical way, as he had watched Backhouse in order to borrow some of his mannerisms. He did it idly, as a commuter read the advertisements when a train was overdue. None of his craft had come easily to him: learning his lines, facing an audience or a camera had been mastered, as had his other problems – fear of horses and a fear of flying – out of necessity. He'd got no help from his mother or from his wife. Only Uncle Bernard had encouraged him: and that old drunk was no advertisement for the profession or demonstration of its rewards.

The Cadillac turned off the grove track and on to the uphill one. It slowed to get round a props lorry. Stone decided that he'd never know the answer to his question, but he didn't care very much. And in his indifference lay the secret of his great talent. Stone had little or no curiosity about his own motivation, and still less about that of the fictitious men he portrayed. He was an empty canvas. He borrowed voices, faces and physical habits from all around him, using them to prop up bad bits of dialogue, leap illogicalities of plot, garnish thin characterizations and rescue unlikely finales. That was the craft of the actor, and not even Shakespeare could manage without it.

He heard the car outside. He uncapped his fountain-pen and leaned over the papers.

'Ahem,' Jasper coughed just like a stage butler.

'Jasper! Already?' Stone looked at his watch and put his pen away. 'Time has just flown this morning.' He gathered the papers together and put them into his case. He smiled at Jasper before snapping the locks closed. Jasper picked up the case and then went to open the car door. Inside, Stone was surprised to see his Gucci bags, a freshly pressed suit and change of linen.

Jasper said, 'Mr Backhouse said you might need it. I had the hotel put it into one of the production cars.'

Stone knew the hotel was one hundred and eight miles away. He had to know the mileage exactly in order to charge the production for his car. Stone looked quizzically at Jasper, who explained. 'Mr Backhouse told me this morning at the airport, as soon as he arrived.'

FROM: STONE
TO: WEINBERGER
TELEGRAPHIC ADDRESS: ESCARGOT, LONDON,
    TELEX.

ARRIVING THIS EVENING STOP SET UP KOOLMAN MEETING WITHIN TWENTYFOUR HOURS FOR REVIEW ALL CONTENTIOUS POINTS INCLUDING TV STOP MEET ME LAP WITH ON FLY TICKETS YOU AND ME IF HIS WHEREABOUTS NECESSITATE STOP BEST WISHES MARSH

21

To get an Oscar, what's required is a certain amount of wheeling and dealing, public relations, advertising, solicitation, phone calls, telegrams, threats, bribes.
George C. Scott *(winner of Best Actor award, Academy Oscar of 1970)*

Show-business trade papers reflect the heady optimism of the people who read them. So Leo Koolman's news was a two-column headline in thirty-point bold type, high on page one.

> KOOLMAN INKS STONE: $5-MIL PACKAGE
>
> Stone has script yea or nay on triple package with Koolman International. First pic to roll is *Copkiller* with Frisco locations on Jan 20th.
>
> Stone (tipped for Oscar nomination) replaces young actor Somerset after budget took a transfusion of four million dollars plus. Stone plays cop-killing revolutionary with Suzy Delft signed for distaff role of anarchist student.
>
> Producer will be Edgar Nicolson who worked with Stone on *Silent Paradise* slated for London bow Nov 1st and tipped for best picture Academy nomination. *Copkiller* director is yet unnamed. Stone's deal will include ten TV films written around *Executioner* role.

The office of the president of Koolman International Pictures Inc (who was also chairman of Koolman International Pictures (Gt Britain) Ltd, and a dozen subsidiaries not mentioned on the plaque outside the building) was an exquisite example of what interior decoration can achieve on an open-ended budget. His desk was a seventeenth-century oak trestle table. A Dutch marquetry escritoire held two hundred scripts. The president used a Finnish swivel chair, and his guests sat upon the classic Barcelona seat, specially upholstered in bright blue leather to match the Koolman trademark. They could admire the Adam fireplace, or look at the Larry Rivers above it. Under their feet there was a Scandinavian carpet with the Koolman monogram woven into an abstract pattern that reached almost from wall to wall. Pencil-thin spotlights cased in stainless steel lit a Siamese Buddha, New England Redware and a Florentine triptych.

Only one unsightly element marred the room's perfection: Leo Koolman, who sat behind the desk. He signalled me to a chair, spilling cigar ash over the carpet as he did so. Then he reached into the pocket of his white shirt and found a small silver box from which he fed himself a pill, while cradling the phone in his other hand. 'New York,' he explained. 'The closing price.'

Before I was seated he was talking again. 'Down three-eighths, eh? So what does Benny say?' He listened attentively and then replaced the receiver. No one in the film business ever said goodbye on the telephone. Perhaps it was a superstition, like mentioning *Macbeth* in a dressing-room.

'Movie-making is a business,' said Koolman. 'A business like any other kind of business. If the Government wants me to make movies that improve public taste, they've only to give me the money I lose doing it. Until then my stockholders expect me to make a profit.'

A pasty-faced boy came into the room brandishing a toy pistol. 'My boy,' explained Koolman. 'He's at Eton.' The child expected to find his father alone, and as he caught sight of me his eyes widened. To cover his acute shyness he turned slowly, firing his cap pistol at the artefacts. 'Would you guess he was my boy?' said Koolman proudly.

'No question of it,' I said. Nothing could better embody my feelings about Koolman than an Eton schoolboy firing a plastic gun at an art collection.

'You tell Jimmy to start,' Koolman told the boy.

'Aren't you coming too?'

'I've seen it before,' said Koolman. 'After, ask Jimmy to show you the new Marshall Stone movie: *Silent Paradise*; you're going to love it.'

'OK,' said the child. He levelled his gun carefully at his father's head and pulled the trigger.

338

'Stop pointing that gun at people,' said Koolman. 'And say hello to Mr Anson. He's a famous writer.'

'Hello, Mr Anson,' said the boy, and when I smiled he shot me too.

'Run along,' said Koolman.

He turned to me when the child had gone. 'I like kids, always have done. They're our audience today and tomorrow's audience too.' Koolman liked to have his cake and eat it.

'There is a rumour to that effect.'

'Kids today have very fixed ideas about morality. They're more prudish and intolerant than the Victorians in some things. In the nineteenth century you could have any kind of hero, now you've got to be careful. For instance, I dare not have a movie where the hero is a cop or a soldier or a business-man or a scientist, or even a white Southerner.' He laughed ironically. 'If I let a script talk about Negroes the way half my pictures talk about cops and soldiers I'd be picketed from here to Alaska.'

'Give the audience what they want, eh?'

'And if you think otherwise, you better talk to the exhibitors.' He moved his cigar from the place where it was beginning to scorch the desk. 'That kid . . . pointing that gun like that. I don't like it . . .' He looked up at me. 'He brings his buddies over to see horror films once a week. They won't let them see them in the movie theatres, they're too young.'

He chuckled again. I've never seen him in such a happy mood as he was that day. Or perhaps Koolman and his child and his office were not like that. Perhaps I was already distorting reality into something I wanted to remember. I said, 'But some good films make money.'

It sounded pathetic. He nodded sympathetically. 'Sure, some good ones make money. Some bad ones make money, but mostly the ones that make money are neither very good nor very bad. In the sense that you are using the word good,' he added. He fixed me with steely eyes. 'I'd appreciate it, Peter, if you didn't quote that out of context. Quote the whole thing or nothing, right?'

'This is background,' I told him. I pushed my notebook and pencil away from me to reinforce the statement, but Koolman was an old hand at talking to the Press. He knew that that was one of the oldest tricks in the reporter's repertoire to trap someone into being indiscreet. Phil Sanchez – Koolman's ever-present official witness – was sitting in the far corner. He looked up and smiled at me. We all knew that whatever Koolman said, one against two equals no quote they didn't like.

'So what is good. Is good the pictures that get four stars on the back page of *Sight and Sound*? Is good the picture that you approve of, or that Miss Stewart approves of? Or maybe you believe good films are the ones that win Oscars. Maybe you'd like to see the wheeling and dealing and promises and pressures that are going on for those nominations. Not for prestige, for money. A film with a nomination or an Oscar will get a reissue and double – maybe quadruple – its take.'

'Are you wheeling and dealing for a nomination for *Silent Paradise?*'

'You're damn right I am. The whole membership vote for "best picture" directors, writers and editors ... And I'll ask every damn one of them by a personal signed letter to see *Silent Paradise*. For Marshall's nomination only the actors get to ballot, so I'll be giving them special attention.'

'Special attention?'

'Screenings in my private theatre – in my home – every night during the last week of January and into February too. There will be food and drink there, and girls from the studio will be around to answer questions.'

'And I bet I know the questions.'

He picked up a fancy programme fixed with red ribbon and embossed with the KI logo. Inside it there were not only stills from the film, but also candids and portraits and biographies of the stars and personality stories about the making of *Silent Paradise*.

Koolman gave me a few moments to look at it. 'And lots of other work, too. Big ads in the trades. Paragraphs for the columns. Disc jockeys, journalists ... a lot of work selling Marshall to the voters.' He went behind his desk and sorted through the trays, but he didn't cease to talk. 'We had a little sixteen-millimetre film made of that production in progress.

The BBC are going to show it next week in prime time, and I'm talking to CBS about networking it in the States. I've had the theme music rewritten and I'll be talking to Barbra and Johnny Cash about albums. Hopefully, the title "I'd Love to Get You to a Silent Paradise" would be the title of the album. That gets us into the record stores with our movie title. A very well-known writer is working from the screenplay to put together a book of the film that we will paperback at the time of the première.' He looked at me as if he'd suddenly remembered something. 'There's one for you to do if ever you have time and want to put your hands on ten grand.'

'Ten thousand dollars.'

'Plus a share of the royalties. It can be real money.'

'I'm sure.'

Koolman made a signal to Phil Sanchez. 'Phil, open that bottle of Dom.' He turned back to me, 'Champagne's the only thing I can stomach in the morning. Any kind of drink goes acid on me.'

'Don't apologize.' I said.

He nodded, as though making a note of my advice, and no more was said until Sanchez came back with the drink and glasses. He poured a glass for us. I said, 'You are using Marshall Stone in *Copkiller* now?'

'It's great chemistry.'

'What happened to Val Somerset?'

'Val is wonderful, but can Val hold down a ten-million-dollar film? Something tells me he's not ready for that yet. Next year, maybe.'

'And Marshall is doing your TV series?'

Koolman was ever so slightly defensive. 'I wish you wouldn't say TV series, Peter. It's a package of films, specials. Maybe they'll go for a prime-time screening if there's an offer big enough. Maybe not. But they'll be expensive packages, with name casts and good crews. Anyway, it's in my interest to get it into the theatres: the TV price is always bigger then.'

'And your deal with Stone was to give him Somerset's role in *Copkiller* in exchange for the series?'

He held up his glass of champagne to me, smiled and swallowed a mouthful of it. 'That's the reporter in you. You musn't invent news, Peter.'

'And was it a part of the deal that Val Somerset is put on the shelf for a year or two?'

'We've got great plans for Val,' said Koolman, quite unruffled.

'What are they?'

'We are not ready to announce them yet.' He waited to see my reaction. 'Probably he'll do the astronaut story – *Moonprobe* – with Bert Hanratty directing and Suzy Delft in the part of the wife. We are still negotiating.'

'I see.' I reached for my notebook again.

Koolman said, 'I've got a big investment in that boy Val Somerset. I'm not likely to sell him short, believe me.'

'What sort of investment?'

'What sort of investment?' said Koolman. 'Why, I've spent almost ten thousand dollars on that boy's mouth. When we tested him, his teeth were a mess. Most of them were recapped in Switzerland at the Studio's expense. Then he had riding lessons for that second film he did, and out of that we didn't earn a nickel.'

'No doubt the price of a few teeth and a couple of riding lessons can be lost somewhere in the million you got for the TV replay of *The Executioner*.'

'A big successful movie like that will give the network a record audience that night: it's worth every penny.'

'And when you've put *Man From the Palace* together, will that get you a million for a replay?'

'You've seen their assembly. Maybe you know more about it than I do.'

'That seems very unlikely,' I said.

He smiled to acknowledge how true that was. A phone murmured twice. He leaned away from it and shouted 'No calls' into a device I could not see.

He said, 'It's very self-indulgent: arty! They call it a "fine cut": I call it a "first assembly". But I'll spend money on it, reshoot a couple of little scenes that don't play right and add a big coronation . . .'

'A coronation?'

'The set will be eighteen square yards bigger than Westminster Abbey. That alone will cost two million dollars.'

'What are you going to do with it afterwards, give it to the nation or tow it to California?'

'And our rewrite changes the ending so that the kids wind up in command.'

'That will ruin it.'

'For you, maybe. But having the kids looking stupid would ruin me. I can't afford message films. If you have a message, send for Western Union, you know the old saying.'

'I can't imagine Hanratty going for that idea.'

'Hanratty is a very happy man,' said Koolman. 'I've offered him a four-picture deal that will put more money into his pocket than he's earned in his entire life before. And I'm going to get hold of a book he wants to do and give him the budget it needs. He's got plenty to be thankful for. Especially after that last fiasco.'

'And Bookbinder?'

'And Bookbinder! Kagan is a grateful man today. He would have been wiped out financially. He sees that now.'

'He that films and runs away . . .'

'. . . Lives to film another day. Ha, ha, ha. Right. And say, did you see Marshall last night on the box?'

' "The Business of Acting". Yes, I was at Twin Beeches when they filmed the part of it that ended on the floor.' There had been a drastic policy change since then. The sardonic exchange I had seen being filmed was gone. In the version they put on, Marshall Stone, dressed *Last Vaquero* style, galloped behind the titles with a soundtrack that sounded like a buffalo stampede. He then had a deferential interview and was seen in clips from his best films as well as a short sequence from *Silent Paradise*, described by the interviewer as a masterpiece. 'Who blew the whistle?' I asked.

'TV companies get a lot of free programming from our clips, and from interviews that our publicity department sets up. No big renter need tolerate exposé tactics.'

Koolman said it meaningfully and let me digest that truth.

'It was damned good publicity for Marshall.'

'Actors are like children, Peter. They need protection. They need love and care and attention. And that's what you've got to remember when you get down to this biography. Give your readers the Marshall Stone they want to believe in. Your readers are his fans. His name on the cover will sell it, your name won't move one copy. This is not going to appeal to those people who like biography: they want to read about statesmen and kings and history.'

'I see.'

'Sure. Stone's fans are your readers, and they don't want to be told they are all wrong. No one likes to hear that they are not a good judge of character: that's a universal conceit, like driving and sex.'

I smiled, and that encouraged Koolman to continue. 'On the other hand, Peter, a good swinging show-biz style biography could fit into our plans very well. I'd use them as gifts at the screenings of *Silent Paradise*. That would mean five thousand copies. As well as that, I would use it as the official K I Christmas present: that means another ten thousand. With a guaranteed sale of fifteen thousand you've got a best-seller on your hands before it's written.' He drank his champagne. I drank too. Koolman was almost a caricature of himself. He sat there ticking off the profits of my non-existent book on his stubby fingers. In my book I would use him just like that.

I finished my glass of champagne and said, 'Well, I'm not sure if I'm going to write that sort of book. What I want to say about him can only be said as fiction.'

He was indignant. 'Sure, write fiction,' he said. 'Write about the effect of a neurotic childhood on a sodomite liberal, living in New Jersey. Sure, you write literature, but don't have your agent coming in here trying to sell me the film rights.'

'All I'm saying,' I explained patiently, 'is that a book of fiction can get nearer to the truth than a biography.'

'Never,' pronounced Koolman, and then a new thought occurred to him. 'What you mean is, you are going to dig up some kind of dirt about him and then say it's fiction.' The idea did not seem to distress him. 'What will you call this guy?'

'I don't know.'

'Starr.'

'A bit obvious; perhaps Stone.'

'Marshall Stone,' he offered.

I said. 'Perhaps.'

'So that's your hero. Who'll be your villain? Me, perhaps.' He said it as if it was the most unlikely possibility he could think of.

'Well, it has worked out well for you. You got *Man From the Palace* at what I hear is a bargain price, and you are free to change it as you like. You've got a new contract with Stone, and you've set the cassette business back a few years.'

'How did I set it back?'

'After Continuum's experience there's not likely to be a rush of money into the cassette market.'

'Now, come on, Peter. You know that was nothing to do with me. Continuum was a failure of management. Your wife will tell you the same thing.' He smiled slyly and added, 'Or do you think Mary and me are in some kind of conspiracy together?'

I didn't answer him.

'It's years since I last saw Mary,' said Koolman.

'I know.'

'Well, then . . .'

'Mary explained the Continuum deal to me.'

Sanchez poured some champagne for me, as if that might loosen my tongue.

'I'm glad,' said Koolman and gave a loud sigh of mock relief. 'Anyway, a Jewish villain . . . you'd never get away with it.'

'He'll be a bit like you, my villain. But his company will have the same name he's got: Koolman. It's less complicated like that.'

'Take it easy on the guy. Say, that's not a bad name for me – Koolman: cool man, yes, I like it. Take it easy on him. He's got his problems with this jerk . . .'

'Marshall Stone.'

He gave a genuine smile of pleasure when he heard the name he'd invented. 'Yeah, Marshall Stone. Him and his agent are probably a couple of greedy gonifs who spend more time trying to find a way of cheating on a contract than on working it.'

'The way I'll write *Close-up*, Koolman will be more than a match for this Marshall Stone character. He'll undermine his confidence, stick-and-carrot every contract. In the last resort

345

he'll even make it a part of a deal that he has this actor softened-up by heavies on an Italian location and delivered to him on a plate.'

'Now you are talking like an original!' said Koolman happily. 'Now you are talking like something I should buy the screen rights of.' He looked me in the eyes and smiled.

'OK,' I hedged. 'Perhaps no softening-up. Or perhaps I'll write it so that the Italian business could have been only in his mind.'

'And what else is just going to be in his mind? A traffic pile-up on the throughway is going to be in his mind, a murder?'

I must have looked surprised.

He laughed. 'Sure. I know this kind of book. We get them fired into our story department all the time.' He leaned across his desk and sighted his letter-opener at me. 'Well, you take this one home and feed it ants' eggs, Peter Anson. Maybe there was no crash. Maybe this guy Cool Man, or whoever he's going to be, invented a traffic accident and filed it to a newsdesk with a fifty-dollar bill. But did he make some orphan kid into a daughter that never existed? You'll need to know that, before deciding which chapters get the italics.'

'Is this your next gimmick. Does Marshall get to marry Suzy if he's a good boy?'

'That's bitter, Peter. No, no, no.' He looked at Sanchez, 'But we might grant him a measure of incest now and again.'

Sanchez grinned. Koolman said, 'Open another bottle of Dom, Phil. This one is dead.' Sanchez had already put another bottle into the ice bucket. He brought it out and wrapped a cloth around it like a loving mother taking a tiny baby out of a bath. Still nursing it he got a grip upon its neck and used his powerful thumbs against the cork. It succumbed with a whimper and a gasp.

'Beautiful,' said Koolman. 'He's done it a million times, Peter.'

'And not only with bottles,' I said.

Sanchez smiled.

'That kid . . .' said Koolman. 'I don't like to see guns pointed at people's heads.'

Sanchez noted it as an instruction, but to me it sounded like a new aspect of Koolman.

346

'Close-up,' said Koolman. 'I'd never buy a title like that. It'll mean nothing on a marquee in Omaha. What's your fade-out?'

I smiled and drank and let him think it was a secret, but in fact I didn't have an ending. All I had was this beginning.

CLOSE-UP

CHAPTER ONE

The heavy blue notepaper crackled as the man signed his name. The signature was an actor's: a dashing autograph, bigger by far than any of the text. It began well, rushing forward boldly before halting suddenly enough to split the supply of ink. Then it retreated to strangle itself in loops. The surname began gently but then that too became a complex of arcades so that the whole name was all but deleted by well-considered decorative scrolls. The signature was a diagram of the man.

If you have enjoyed this PAN Book, you may like to choose your next book from the titles listed on the following pages.

James Leasor

FOLLOW THE DRUM   50p

'A whirlwind of passion, hate, fear and
courage' – SUNDAY TIMES

India, 1857 – when the lives of millions
changed forever . . .

A sweeping panorama of terror, excitement
and bloody incident mirrors the lives of very
human men and women, both real and imaginary, overtaken by the cataclysm of heroism
and tragedy that was the Mutiny.

Trapped in those dangerous days are the hot-
blooded daughter of a regular officer and an
idealistic nineteen-year-old who began that
summer as a boy and ended it a man . . .

'No author in years has produced a novel dealing with the period that is any way comparable
with this tremendous story. FOLLOW THE
DRUM is a minor masterpiece.' – BOOKS AND
BOOKMEN

Wilbur Smith

THE SUNBIRD   50p

'A screaming nightmare of blood and flame and smoke, a horror of shining black faces and sweat-polished bodies . . .'

Another magnificently entertaining and imaginatively portrayed novel of high adventure by the author of WHEN THE LION FEEDS.

From the drama and excitement of modern Africa – big game hunts, terrorists, intrigue and merciless bushmen – the chief characters are projected into the battles, romance and tragedy of their Carthaginian past.

'A bonanza of excitement' – NEW YORK TIMES

Also available in PAN:

WHEN THE LION FEEDS	40p
THE SOUND OF THUNDER	40p
SHOUT AT THE DEVIL	40p
GOLD MINE	35p
(shortly to be filmed starring Roger Moore)	
THE DIAMOND HUNTERS	35p
THE DARK OF THE SUN	35p
(already filmed as *The Mercenaries*)	

'A natural storyteller – THE SCOTSMAN

David Morrell

FIRST BLOOD   40p

'A terrific thriller – both terrifying and terrifically good' – SATURDAY REVIEW

'A vortex of suspense and violence' – CHICAGO SUN-TIMES

Bare-bottomed naked, Rambo roared out of Madison on a stolen motor-cycle – leaving a trigger-happy cop spilling his guts on the cell floor . . .

Be-medalled Green Beret, Rambo had survived captivity and torture in Vietnam. He was an expert in death.

If Police Chief Teasle kept on pushing, Rambo would give him a fight to remember. Sonofabitch . . .

'The most chilling story of a man-hunt I have ever read . . . ends in massive violence.' – DAILY EXPRESS

'A thriller of real power' – THE FINANCIAL TIMES

'Brutal, bloody, violent, profane and absolutely superb' – OVER 21

'First-rate excitement' – NEW YORK TIMES

Gerald A. Browne

11 HARROWHOUSE STREET 40p

Wonderfully entertaining – a wild sit-up-all-night-to-finish clincher.

A hero in the Bogart mould, a heroine who is every man's fantasy, and the biggest diamond robbery in history, combine to make a vivid, suspenseful caper adroitly blended with a dazzling eroticism . . .

'Perfect escape reading . . . the plot glints and sparkles' – LOS ANGELES TIMES

'Fantastic dreamy thriller' – OBSERVER

'Double-triple-quadruple-cross, complete with chase, gunplay and Nemesis . . . the action is breathless' – NEW YORK TIMES

'A winner' – COSMOPOLITAN